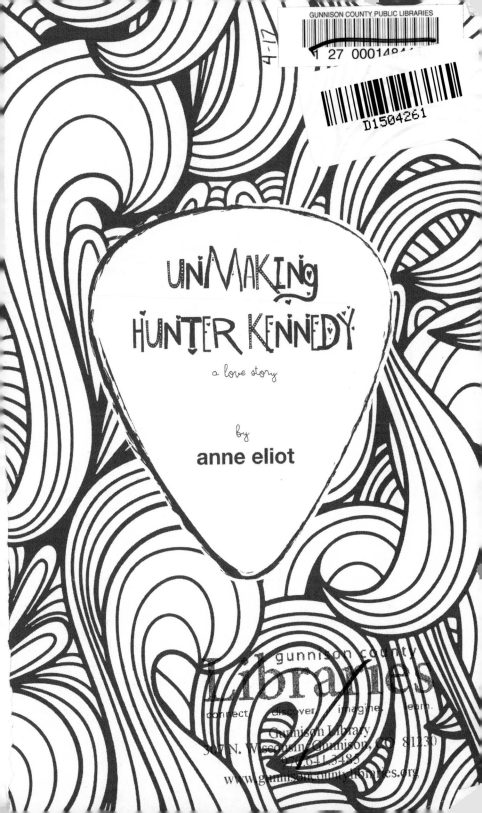

unMaking
HUNTER KENNEDY

a love story

by
anne eliot

Copyright © Anne MacFarlane 2012 writing as Anne Eliot

1 3 5 7 9 10 8 6 4 2

ISBN 978-1-937815-03-5 (Print Version/Reg. Bowker)
Butterfly Books, LLC. First Ed. 2012,
Cataloging Information: Eliot, Anne
Unmaking Hunter Kennedy / Anne Eliot
(Note: eBOOK-ISBN: 978-1-937815-02-8 - Reg. Bowker)

Summary: *Sweet Teen Romance, first love. Suitable for younger teens — After an accident and a suicide attempt, a teen pop star, recovering from depression is forced to move to Colorado and live in disguise so he can rest, but falls in love with the girl next door.*

1. Young Adult Romance & Teen Romance (Children's Love and Romance) — Juvenile fiction. 2. Social Issues — Fiction. 3. Teen Depression — Fiction. 4. Social Anxiety (Social Issues) (Social Situations) Emotions and Feelings — 5. Pop Culture 6. Contemporary Romance 7. Teen Literature

Book design concept and book design by Peter Freedman & Chiara MacFarlane. PeterFreedman.com Cover Images, Brand X Pictures, Philip & Karen Smith, Print Ed. Header/Cover Fonts from SicCapital by Andrew Hart Printed/Created in the United States of America.

Dedication:

For Tom,

I know. I will rescue you.

We can run away to the woods by the sea with my dusty old books and your guitars. We will search for cool rocks every day. Okay?

In the meantime: Rock that Gypsy Jazz, *Minor Swing* song for me one more time!

I love you. Thanks for loving me back.

Forever, I'm yours...
XO XO XO

What Readers Say:

"Hunter's my new favorite fictional boyfriend - so tortured, so talented, so ready to fall in love. You'll devour him and his story in no time."
-Judith T., I Love YA Fiction 'IloveYAfiction.com'-

"Anne Eliot held me captive this entire novel. I would recommend this book to anyone who ADORES poetically written first kisses and loves a true romantic novel." -Tabby V., Blog: 'Insightful Minds Reviews'-

"When Vere & Charlie first meet Hunter - I was laughing my head off. I found myself doing just that all through this book. Hunter has officially been added to my fictional boyfriends list. -Kayla, Blog: 'The Ramblings of a Toddler's Mom'-

PART ONE:
THE UNMAKING

1: shiny black casket

HUNTER

1:50 A.M.

"Damn. She's early." Hunter Kennedy swallowed a lump of dread as he watched his mom's limo snake along the outer grounds. He shoved his iPhone into his pocket and covered his unease with a forced smile to Barry, his therapist. "She's never early."

"This is good." Barry smiled back. "Shows responsibility."

"Shows she doesn't want to miss the fun of dumping me off again. Plus if the woman came late, she'd have to take me home, right?"

Barry didn't answer. He was also the owner of this fancy, fenced teen hospital. They both knew *home* was not an option. Instead, Hunter was heading for phase-two of his mom's latest crap-Hollywood-parenting plan: kid misbehaves, pay for therapy, ignore him, then convince others to handle the dirty laundry.

Handle him.

As if six weeks locked up in this place hadn't been enough.

His whole spine lit with goose bumps. He pulled on the hideous, white-and-silver hoodie she'd sent ahead for him to wear, making sure the sleeves were long enough to cover his wrists.

No need to remind Mom what got me here. Time to play along like I said I would. It's not like there's anywhere to run.

The limo had stopped at the ornate first gate. The gate that 'kept up appearances' because it featured no razor wire or guards with guns. The other two gates would take longer thanks to the vehicle search, ID checks, metal-x rays—all that *resident safety* junk this place featured so proudly.

♥ 1 ♥

It would be awhile.

As the gate swung open, a loud, mechanical buzzing increased, sucking up all of the air around him. It echoed off the wide flight of marble steps where they waited.

"Dude. That thing is dying." Hunter winced, realizing the noise wasn't just in his head. Its source was a bronze, sculpted sign above the portico that was supposed to read *Falconer Hope Residential Solutions.* Now, because of burned out bulbs, only part of the first word was lit.

It flashed: *l-oner, l-oner, l-oner...*

So. Appropriate.

"Guess I waited too long to call someone to fix it." Barry, as though happy to have something to do, hopped up into some terraced planters to take a look.

Hunter slouched against a marble pillar, annoyed that his whole outfit blinded him. When he'd pulled the all-white costume out of the bag, his skin had crawled at the thought of putting it on.

But the outfit had also come with a note written in his mom's large scrawl: *Hunter. Make sure you wear everything in this bag. Everything. Please.*

So, because he was trying to prove he was a *good boy*, and because his mom rarely said *please*, Hunter had dutifully zipped himself into the too-tight white jeans, tapered in—as usual—from his calves to his ankles.

He'd layered on the silvery graphic-tee and added the humiliating long chain that boasted a dangling, fist-sized medieval sword. It hung down past the matching chainmail belt. The sword acted like a weighted, sharp-tipped pendulum. His mom had probably picked the thing on purpose because it punched his junk every time he moved. Hunter had even pulled out the top edge of the lame silver boxers to prove he'd worn everything.

Everything. As commanded by her.

Cherry on the wardrobe-hell-pie? White sneakers that rated worse than the boxers. Because they had girly, *glitter* soles! His band's name, *GuardeRobe*, had been stitched into the heel and over the toes with silver thread. Not to be outdone by the amazing laces that featured his tiny initials painted top to bottom: *HK, HK, HK, HK.*

All in more shiny, sparkle *shit.*

So messed up. What had the designers been thinking?

Being dressed like an epic ass was nothing new for Hunter. Wardrobe choices were never his department. But wardrobe choices worn without a fight always kept the mom happy.

And today, that was Hunter's goal.

Besides, the nightmare-suit gave Hunter a small shred of hope. Why else would he be dressed for work? The outfit was a good sign that his mom might have changed her mind.

Please. Please. Please.

Hunter sucked in a big breath. The cool night air shocked his lungs.

He'd forgotten to breathe again. If he'd learned anything good in this place, it was that he had to remember, no matter what, to simply *breathe.*

Barry slammed his hand into an electronic box behind the sign, succeeding in quieting the buzzing. As he climbed out of the planters he said, "That thing is going to cost a mint to fix."

Barry looked tired. Hunter was sure the poor guy wasn't used to being awake all hours like he was.

"I guess this is *it*, huh?" Hunter said, trying to distract both of them from the stress of waiting. "It's been—interesting."

Barry smiled. "I'm sorry we had to release you in the dark like this. It is not our normal procedure. But your mother said—"

"She's right." Hunter flicked another glance at the limo,

watching the guards at gate two search the trunk. "The paparazzi would have been all over this place. I'm surprised none of your staff leaked I was here."

"We've built our reputation on discretion. They are all screened and paid very well *not* to have seen you. It's why parents all over the world choose us to help their kids. I wish you could have taken part in some of the group sessions. I know you would have liked them."

"Yeah. Too, bad." Hunter nodded as though he totally agreed. There was no point in hurting Barry's feelings at this late date. Barry's *cry-and-hug* sessions were not on Hunter's wish list. "Maybe next time," he added, shooting Barry a wry glance.

Barry gave him a look. "Let's hope not. I'm going to miss you, Hunter. I really am. But I never want to see you again—if you know what I mean."

Hunter smiled. "Yeah. Back at you, dude. And thanks for curing me."

Barry gave him a small bro-hug that Hunter returned. "I've never said you were *cured*. Depression does not have an *on-off* switch. Don't make me lecture you all over again here, because I will."

"Work in progress. I know the speech." Hunter pushed a hand through the mop of hair that hit his forehead now that it hadn't been cut for so long. "Are you billing me for this extra therapy hour?"

"Of course I'm billing you. Double for after-hour charges if you're keeping track."

"I like that you never pretend things aren't about the money." Hunter yawned.

Barry frowned, placing a gentle hand on Hunter's arm. "I get paid well because I'm good at what I do. Just like you get paid well to sing and play the guitar. Not everyone wants to use you, son. You need to change your views on that."

Hunter shrugged. "If I come across real evidence of your theory, I'll reconsider my ideas. But from where I sit, it's the view I've been tracking forever."

"That view is what your mom is trying to change by sending you to Colorado. Your reality is skewed. You need to get it back on track. This time is going to give you the chance to analyze your real feelings. Try to make honest friends. The kind with no strings attached."

"Please. An impossible idea." Hunter kicked his shoe against the steps. "Back on track, my ass! She wants me locked down. You should satellite-map the town of *Monument*. It's in the middle of a bunch of trees. I bet everyone who lives there has a blade of grass stuck in their teeth. And it's probably the kind of grass you can't even smoke!"

Hunter paced the length of the portico. Barry followed.

"Living off the Hollywood grid is the only way you'll be able to figure out what being normal feels like. You've never known anything different."

"Forget normal! Everything could be over when I get back. *Hell.* No one seems to care about what I want. How could I ever be normal after the life I've lived? The life I *plan to keep living* as soon as I get Mom to stop being pissed off at me."

"From what I can tell, you weren't living much of any life. Just working."

"I love to work. So what? It's my solace." Hunter shook his head. "And besides, I haven't been to my Aunt Nan's since I was eight. I think she must be like...*seventy* now? Does she even remember me—want me in her house?"

Barry nodded. "Seventy-two. She's excited to have you for the school year. Your mom told me."

"You've talked to her about this?" Hunter whispered as he felt his throat closing up. "When and *why* does she talk to you, but never to me?"

"She told me it's too soon. She's not ready."

"And you *bought* that?" Hunter exploded. "You think Mom's silent treatment is about the dumbass prank I pulled at home six weeks ago?"

"I thought we'd stopped referring to it as a *prank*."

"Yeah, yeah." Hunter glowered, changing the subject. "That woman hasn't spoken to me about anything real since my bottom-feeder step-dad ran to Florida two years ago with the intern—or—*personal assistant*. Whatever she was."

"You mentioned that. I know it causes you pain."

"Well, not how you think." Hunter blinked. "Mom got really pissed when she discovered the intern had also been *personally assisting* me in every way." Hunter smiled at the look on Barry's face.

"No."

"Yep." Hunter nodded. "Like twice a week in our hot tub and all over the house. Mom stopped talking to me when I told her I missed the girl more than I missed having that guy around pretending to be my dad. Because I still miss her—or what she could do with her mouth, anyhow."

"Holy shit." Barry, who hardly ever looked shocked or surprised, now looked shocked and surprised. "Why didn't you tell me about all this?"

Hunter shrugged. "I thought I'd keep my first girl to myself. I told you about the masses of girls *after*. How will one more twisted story about my sex life make my 'mental-health-file' any better? At least you get now that I can never be normal. Never make normal friends."

"Yes, you can." Barry threw his arms wide. "That girl should be in prison. The stuff was done to you, Hunter. Done *to* you. You were a kid two years ago. Hell, you're still just seventeen."

Hunter shrugged again and met Barry's gaze. "I was old enough to willingly participate. Not gonna lie. I loved it. Thought I loved her," he scoffed. "She was only seventeen herself. Wicked-step-daddy was smart enough to wait until she became legal before taking off with her. Totally bummed me out when she left like that, though. I had no idea."

"Wow. I'm so sorry you went through that."

Hunter grimaced. "She tried to keep things going with me. I turned her down. Back then I hated sharing my toys."

"And so you share now?" Barry asked, ramping back to his calm-doctor voice, but the guy couldn't hide his bugged-out eyes or horrified expression.

"No. I still hate sharing. I've simply stopped playing with dangerous toys. Mom paid them both tons to never contact me again. The assistant dumped the loser the day after the check cleared. Take some notes if you need to," Hunter offered.

Barry shook his head. "You and your mom have been through so much. I know she's also seeing her own therapist. She'll speak to you when she gets herself straightened out, but probably not before."

"Whatever." Hunter glared at the limo, still holding at gate two. "If I'm forced to go to Colorado today, I'm done with her. And I'm not going to be sitting by the phone waiting for *Mommy* to call. I learned long ago not to believe that woman's promises. My agent swears he's going to get me out of the judge's contract in a few weeks."

"Luckily, your mom made sure the agreement is rock solid. Report to Colorado after we release you, or report to the nearest juvenile detention center. It's for the whole school year whether your agent likes it or not."

Hunter crossed his arms. "Martin is a strong force to be reckoned with. He'll win for me. You'll see."

"Son, you need to rest. It's critical." Barry trapped his gaze. "I'd think twice about Martin's intentions. Can't you see he's obviously in it for the money?"

Hunter sighed. "I know." He flicked a glare at the limo. "But at least he keeps his promises. He'll come through. And like I said, isn't everyone in it for the money?" Hunter fronted, hiding his true panic about the situation. If Martin couldn't convince his mom to change her mind soon, Hunter was stuck.

Stuck in Colorado.

His own mom had slapped huge vandalism charges on him. Between his totaled car, and the damage Hunter had done to the house, he'd wrecked about a million dollars worth of stuff.

$240K came from his pimped out Porsche 911 alone.

But it had been his Porsche!

His house!

His front door, his silk carpets, his stupid antique, Italian fountain. All paid for with money he'd earned! All things he'd offered to replace.

Sadly, none of that had mattered to the judge.

Every item Hunter had trashed was in his mom's name. They'd screwed him to the wall with that one fact. The judge had also bought his mom's sob story that her son might *recover better* while on a forced rest out of the public eye. And in another state!

Barry let out a long breath as they watched the third gate admit the limo into the inner driveway. "Well I'm happy you have no choice. For *your sake*, Hunter. Not for the money."

Hunter didn't respond. They both knew Barry had been paid $865 an hour to hang out with him all this time.

Her limo finally parked. It reminded Hunter of a wheeled, shiny, black casket.

For my funeral.

"You going to be okay?" Barry asked, as though he sensed Hunter's heart couldn't decide if it should slow down or stop beating all together.

"Wish I knew."

Barry broke eye contact with Hunter and ran his hand through his sparse salt and pepper hair. His expression slipped to nervous. Hunter couldn't blame the guy. His mom terrified the shit out of everyone.

"Take it one day at a time, son. One hour." Barry was babbling now. "Call me if you need to talk. You need time. Time."

"Yeah. Time to get my own set of lawyers."

2: stupid dumb crush

VERE

"Seriously? This form makes me feel like a drug addict."
Vere Roth scrawled her full name across the signature line at
the bottom of the *Palmer Divide High—Zero Tolerance—Drug
and Alcohol Contract.* "I took headache medicine at my locker
before coming in here. According to number seven, I think I
should report myself to the police. Or...is it the principal?"

Vere glanced at her best friend, Jenna, before frowning
back at the form. "Actually, now that I've told YOU about
this 'drug ingestion' *you* must report it or face your own
suspension!"

"If only I could be so lucky." Jenna fluttered her lashes
behind her black-frame hipster glasses. (Glasses boasting clear
lenses and no prescription whatsoever, but that were very
cute.)

Vere added a date, put the form aside and picked up the next
one. "Year Book Order Form. Yay! We will finally get to have
the bigger pictures! And we'll get to be near the front of the
book. I can't wait for that! We. Are. Big-time. So awesome!"

"Big-time, yes. Insignificant, still. And why are you *reading*
the stupid registration forms? Just fill them out and sign."

Jenna was going through her pile of forms by bending the
stack, scribbling her name on the bottom lines, and dating
each without looking.

"Jenna, you're missing half of the form information lines.
Hello? It's only Spirit Week and you are already failing."

"I have a plan connected to this." Jenna flipped her blonde
braids behind her back and adjusted the Peter Pan collar on
her back-to-school, red-checked, button down shirt. "I'm
going to turn these forms in all jacked-up to see how long it

takes someone to call me down to the office."

"What? Why?"

Jenna beamed, her green eyes glittering with mischief. "Maybe I'll get pulled out of some lame quiz next month. Maybe for a couple of days! And, *FYI,* there are no grades this week, you brown nosing, teacher-pleasing-missile."

"I'd laugh at that comment if it weren't so hot in this room. I need every drop of extra credit I can get. If only perfect forms could count for AP Biology." Vere groaned and flexed her fingers before signing the last one in her stack using Jenna's method. It was something about sports and after-school activities. A new head-injury safety plan for all students in sports, clubs or student council.

She and Jenna did Drama Club. Not so they could be in the spotlight or anything insane like that.

They did stage tech.

Sets, costumes, lights, sound, special effects and props—all while wearing the 'invisible' black outfits that came with the job. Lighting was her favorite.

Vere's phone buzzed against the table.

"Who dares text you besides me?" Jenna wiggled her brows. "I mean, *who e-ffing dares?*"

"My mom." Vere flashed the screen to Jenna so she could read: VERE—VERE ARE YOU THERE?

Jenna laughed. "And you can't *eff-ing* ground your mom for texting you at school?"

Vere grimaced. "Jenna. I hate your new *geek-street* persona. You sound and look," Vere paused, glancing at Jenna's outfit with an affectionate grin. "Like a Hello Kitty hipster, crossed with some trash-mouthed prairie girl."

Jenna grinned. "I know. I'm *ahhmazing* cute, huh? And yet I still hang out with a girl who's sporting her dad's jeans cut down to shorts from nineteen-eighty seven. AGAIN. Matched with her big brother's monstrous, grubby hoodie. AGAIN.

Plus the same brown, twisty bun? A look you've held on to since eighth grade. At least my whole outfit can be found in a magazine."

"Please. You know you love my look. And, as someone who truly loves you, I claim the right to veto the fake-cursing thing."

Jenna grinned. "Maybe you're right. I'll *e-ffing* re-think my *e-ffing* potty mouth. But it's so *e-ffing* fun to feel like a bad-girl."

"You're not even close to bad if you can't say the real word. *E-ffing stop.* It's going to backfire and force us into an even lower social status."

"Is there one lower than ours?" Jenna grinned.

Vere's phone buzzed again. She pulled it under the table so she and Jenna could read the next text together: VERE? ARE YOU GETTING THESE? ARE YOU THERE?

Vere typed into her phone: *Mom. Jeez. What's up?*

The phone buzzed a third time just as she hit send.

YOU AND CHARLIE COME STRAIGHT HOME. PROJECT TO DISCUSS. SOMEONE TO MEET. ALL WEEKEND. UP AT THE LAKE. MAKE NO PLANS. NONE. AND NO. TELL JENNA, SHE MAY NOT COME ALONG. SORRY HONEY. DON'T EVEN TRY. NO.

Jenna frowned. "Your mom's psycho with the all-caps. Does she not know she's constantly text-yelling? What does she mean by project? And why would she not want me to come? It's a *three-day* weekend. That hurts where Band-Aids can't touch." Her frown turned into a pout as she added, "Your mom always wants me to come to the lake." Jenna leaned her chin on a fist. "The last time she had 'someone for you to meet' you guys got that Ukrainian exchange dude for spring break. Remember?"

"How could anyone forget? Thank *God* that was only for two weeks."

Their gazes met, and they both grinned and said, "Lexi. *Not SEXY.*"

They cracked up all over again.

"Her text sounds doomish," Jenna added.

Vere tapped her pen on the desk. "UGH. I smell me and Charlie stuck at some church thing passing out cookies. Remember when she made us wear white gloves and stand around guarding hanging blankets for a whole weekend because of that quilting competition?" Vere shuddered.

Jenna gathered her papers into one crumpled pile but then dropped them with a short gasp. "Alert. Alert. *The Wish.* Entering our airspace."

She'd glued her eyes to a spot just beyond Vere's head.

Vere choked. All air sucked out of her lungs.

Jenna lowered her voice, speaking through a smile, "And the summer was good to him. YUM. ME. I love tans on boys. I love boys—and OMG! He's with most of the football team. *Varsity.* Football. Team."

Vere reached up to check her bun, straightened her back, but didn't turn to look. "If you make a scene, I'll kill you. How close is he and...*ugh.*" She put her hand over her racing heart. "Why are the seniors in here with us? I thought we were safe. I checked. They register from two to four."

"Juniors and *all* sports are now." She wiggled her brows. "I checked, too. They've got some sort of special info-assembly. He's setting up camp on the next row of tables. You're safe enough. He'll never spot us in this sardine can."

"Should I look? Is it worth it to turn around?"

Vere had seen Curtis yesterday on her very own front porch. Because the guy had been her brother's best friend since kindergarten. He'd been riveting with his fresh, new hair cut. So riveting, she'd hidden in her room feeling sick for two hours.

Am I the only one in the whole world with a crush that makes me physically ill?

Jenna shrugged, flipped her long braids around again and gave her a pitying look. "I'll let you know if he does anything worth turning colors and stuttering for, okay?"

"Thanks," Vere said, trying unsuccessfully to find Curtis's reflection in Jenna's wide eyes, but even that activity had her stomach cramping and sent a warning tingle up the back of her neck.

No need to fire the cherry-bomb-cheeks for everyone's entertainment. Stupid blushing.

Vere wasn't a natural when it came to school. But she'd learned if she worked hard (sometimes really hard) she could make the grades and hit the goals she wanted. She'd taken that idea and applied it to her blushing problem. Only, the world (and her face) refused to cooperate.

What works in one area fails in others.

Where Curtis was concerned, Vere had studied, researched, and followed all the rules. But when he was near, she couldn't shake her textbook cases of chronic shyness and social anxiety.

She knew these terms, because she'd looked herself up hundreds of times, searching for a cure that would help her. She'd tried textbooks and any psychology websites she could find.

For the most part, Vere had discovered she was a classic case.

A person who was simply shy and who turned red because of it. Not a major thing.

Vere had also pinpointed her shyness would ramp into what was called *social anxiety* when she was around boys—*guys*—she didn't know very well. Also totally normal for her age. And, a condition that calmed down once she knew the guys better.

Again, all normal.

But what hit outside normal was how Vere's social anxiety spiked to uncontrollable levels when she thought she had a crush on a guy.

Enter Curtis Wishford. Her forever crush.

The only guy Vere had ever cared about.

As though her crush could read her thoughts, Curtis's shouting laugh fired off somewhere behind her. In response, Vere's cheeks fired off the burning-red feeling all over again.

Stupid. Dumb. Crush.

She slouched into her lab stool as low as possible, turning away even more while she worked to cool down her red-hot ear tips in this two thousand degree room.

She would only have to survive forty minutes of this pain and then she could escape.

Please...please...let him NOT see me.

Before the crush, Vere, Curtis, Charlie and Jenna used to be inseparable. They were all neighbors. Their parents had been close friends before any of them had been born.

That meant there were whole photo books filled with photos of them all drooling at each other while in diapers.

From there, they'd moved on to sword fights, mud pies, dressing up in costumes, army battles, decorated hundreds of cookies, attended birthday parties, hung at the neighborhood pool and walked to school together on the first day—all that.

All together.

Every. Single. Year.

But all normal hanging out, normal conversations between Vere and Curtis had completely ended in middle school.

Died. Double died. In front of everyone.

This was thanks to two things:

1. Seventh grade and 2. *The Incident.*

Seventh grade was when Vere had decided that she had a real live *crush* on Curtis Wishford. In her classic style, she'd taken her crush to her usual high level of dedicated excitement and commitment. Her 'hard work always pays off' thing was out of control back then.

Worse, she'd upgraded her crush to include visions of

grandeur. (A term she'd also learned off the online psychology websites.) People who did that were usually also flagged as crazy.

But everyone is crazy in seventh grade.

At the ancient age of twelve, Vere decided she was in *love* with Curtis. Major, huge, obsessive, seventh-grade *mega-love*.

She'd written his name on her binders, had countless journals filled with pages and pages of things like: *Gwenivere Juliet Wishford*, or *Vere Juliet Wishford*, or *Mrs. Vere Wishford*.

She'd made up the names of their kids (Claire and Mara). Planned their entire future lives, including their matching careers as world famous, cat and dog rescuing veterinarians.

Ugh. Middle school madness.

Vere felt the back of her neck heat up all over again, remembering how insane she'd been those years.

The evidence of those notebooks had been burned in the family fireplace on a sleep-over. A night spent bawling, because of thing number two. The famous 'incident'.

Jenna still called it: *The Incident That Can Not be Named.*

As in, Vere's personal Voldemort.

She and Charlie called it one, sad, out of control moment that no one would let her forget. If she had advice to pass on to other middle school girls heading for that 'first love', she'd say straight up: *don't knock out the boy you love in front of everyone —and their parents.*

Ever since that day, her shyness around Curtis had grown steadily worse. The guy was also always around. Almost as inescapable as the snickers and snide comments that had followed Vere year after year.

Because of Charlie, Curtis was always in her very own house.

She had become so epic with her public *blush-and-stutter* tricks, no other boys seemed to look twice at her.

Maybe it was because she simply steered clear of them.

Which is just fine. Other boys don't interest me.

I'm still in love with Curtis Wishford, so there! And it's going well. Curtis and I...oh yeah...very well...

Vere put her head on her arms, trying to see if she could catch a glimpse of his feet under the tables. She had become a master at avoiding Curtis while admiring him from afar.

If he came over to hang out with Charlie, Vere could be found hiding in her room. Feeling queasy.

Queasy, but desperately gluing her ear to the door while listening for the sounds of Curtis's voice to float up from the basement.

Vere had also perfected peeking through curtain cracks so she could watch Curtis walk up the front steps, stare at his truck engine or toss the football around the yard.

If they were in the kitchen or doing homework at the dining room table, she could listen to his voice perfectly by sitting on the stair landing, pretending to read on the window seat.

Curtis had the most beautiful baritone. Plus a loud, travelling laugh that separated him from all of Charlie's other friends.

Curtis couldn't be beat.

Not in her house vents, anyhow. And not in her heart. Ever.

She had no problem admitting her situation made her pathetic. And yes, *fine*. She'd reached some serious low points of possible stalking where Curtis was concerned.

But is it really stalking if the guy comes over to my house?

Hangs out in my front yard? Lounges around in my basement, eats dinner with my family, at my table?

I think not.

It wasn't like Vere had plans to lurk around his locker. Nor did she drive by his house or deliberately try to be face-to-face with her crush like other girls did with theirs.

After the incident, Curtis had made things easy on her.

He'd mastered the art of politely ignoring his best friend's little sister. He was never rude or harsh—just painfully and completely *distant*. There was also the part where the guy

♥ 17 ♥

always had a fresh (swapped out like every two months) girlfriend by his side.

Yeah...that helps. Ouch. Helps so much.

At least he's single this week. That's something.

She sighed, dangling her foot under her chair, wishing she could at least hear his voice one more time above the increasing noise in the room.

Vere had been pretty good at keeping her feelings hidden for all these years—behind her constantly flaming cheeks, that is.

Only Jenna and Charlie knew her deepest secrets about her crush. How crippling her shyness and anxiety around Curtis had become. How much she simply longed for the guy to drink some magic forgetting potion and fall in love with her right back.

If only.

Vere didn't care. The cards she'd been dealt in seventh grade had been played very badly by her. And in front of too many people. All she had left was awkwardness and her incurable crush. At least her chronic blushing meant she wasn't dead.

It also meant she was still in love with the cutest boy in the whole school. The feeling of being in love was better than everything else, anyhow.

Even if he didn't feel the same, no one could take away how she felt inside. Maybe, when Curtis went to college next year, her blushing would finally stop. But Vere secretly hoped she'd still get to have a few butterflies hanging around her heart when she thought about him.

Stupid, dumb crush.

3: black italian coffee

HUNTER

The limo's passenger door swung open before the chauffeur could make it around the side, startling both Hunter and Barry.

His mother, a blur of lavender silk, shopping bags, and clicking heels barreled toward them.

"Hunter...oh my. You've lost a ton of weight. Oh, and that long hair...hmm. Might be a good thing." She looked him up and down but kept her distance as though he were contagious.

"That's all you can say to me? Really? *Really?*" Hunter tried to meet her gaze, but her eyes seemed glued to his shoes.

"You've got the outfit on perfectly." She nodded.

Hunter tensed as he waited, wondering what her next line would be—*hell*—hoping for any next line.

As usual, she didn't engage.

Without another word, she turned her wide, blue-laser eyes on Barry. "Barry. Darling," she started.

Blink. Blink. Blink.

No one could resist his mother when she made the blinky-blinky face.

"I need a bathroom—one with a sink. What I need to do to Hunter could get messy."

Barry's expression changed from loyal golden retriever to nervous Yorkie. "I don't have much staff at this hour. How messy?"

Hunter's mom dug deep into a plastic bag marked SuperDrug Center. She pulled out a square, gold-foiled box with a head-shot of a beautiful woman on it and tossed it to Hunter, still not meeting his gaze.

Hunter read the gleaming gold words on the top of the box

aloud: "Venus Permanent Hair Color: Black Italian Coffee. What the...?"

His mother had moved closer to Barry as though she were afraid Hunter might flip out. But Hunter wasn't going to engage either. Not this time. Not ever again.

Two could play her game.

When Hunter's obvious lack of response made the air thick and awkward between them, Hunter's mom nodded nervously toward the box. With an odd catch in her voice, she finally spoke again to Barry, "Hunter's never had dark hair before. He's got to make it through the flight to Denver without getting spotted. We—Martin and I—" She paused, finally looking at Hunter's face before continuing, "We've modified our plan."

"In what way?" Barry asked.

"Hunter has to be in disguise. Starting now—well—at the airport, that is. Then he's going to keep his disguise while in Colorado. We're going to 'unmake' him. We've worked hard to ensure the press doesn't find out where Hunter's been, or where he's going. What do you think?"

"Disguise? Good. Great!" Barry blinked at his mom as though he'd been hypnotized again. "It makes a lot of sense. Without press sniffing around, Hunter could have a chance to rest so much more. I love the idea."

Hunter blinked at them both, feeling as though the concrete under his feet had just fallen away, but managed to keep his face straight and his mouth shut.

Disguise? WTF?

Holding his face completely impassive, Hunter glanced at his mom and realized he shouldn't have bothered.

Her poker face was as good as his. She was dead-on mirroring his placid, calm expression.

Hell, she'd taught it to him after his real father had passed away when he was six years old and it had been up to him to support them.

"Never let them see you're upset, Hunter. No matter what, keep your face very straight, " she used to say back when he was ten and had his first jobs working commercials. *"You'll get fired for even the slightest tantrum. We can't afford it. We'd have to move back to the apartment. Do you understand, Hunter? Now that we don't have Daddy anymore, it's only you and me. Do you understand how serious this is?"*

Hunter tried to crack her on a stare-down.

She didn't even blink.

He'd inherited her same eyes, same pale skin with contrasting dark eyebrows and her same photogenic face. But unlike Hunter's unruly hair, his mom wore her white-blond mane ironed straight and far below her shoulders. Right now, her zapping blue eyes made her appear every inch an evil ice queen.

One who'd never heard the word *no* from anyone. And one that would not budge even if Hunter broke down and bawled.

Which he was not going to do. Ever. Not to her.

Hunter had thought he'd get to apologize, or at least she'd give him the chance to say *something*. But now, analyzing the grim determination on his mom's face, he realized trying to get her to change her mind was futile.

This was a done deal.

Her voice rocketed through is head: *Do you understand how serious this is?*

Hunter looked away. He got it. He understood.

He let out a long breath of air and pulled in another. This situation was his fault. He'd really messed up. Taken things between him and his mom way, too far.

And then he'd taken them further.

Done some really stupid, scary shit. Even scared himself.

He pulled his hands deep into his sleeve cuffs.

His mom was obviously still pissed off. And he was not about to whine and cry, or ask her how much time would it take for her to forgive him. This made things pretty even, because Hunter couldn't imagine forgiving her for sending him away. With dyed hair.

Again. W.T.F!

"Let's get this going, then. Shall we?" she urged, when Hunter still wouldn't—*couldn't*—respond.

His head had started to pound. He wasn't able to breathe because his lungs had turned to pure lead. He pulled at the neck of his white hoodie. The thing was choking the hell out of him.

His mom was already up the marble steps. The sliding hospital doors swooshed and held open, awaiting her entrance.

"I'm going to need some towels," she said to Barry, who'd followed her up the steps like a devoted puppy.

Hunter didn't blame the guy for switching sides.

His mom had serious magic. Brainwashed people with the blue blinks. Apparently, people said Hunter could to it, too. But he didn't want to. He hated people who manipulated others like his mom did.

He just wanted to be left alone. Mostly...

Hunter turned the box of hair color over in his hands. It was curiously heavy. Its mysterious, loose contents shifting and bumping inside.

Did Martin really agree to this? Why?

It was a big deal to mess with the *GuardeRobe* branding. They'd need some sort of approval from corporate. Hunter was the token blond kid in the band.

You can't just un-blond the blond kid! Can you?

Plus, this junk was from a drugstore! Shouldn't his stylist be involved? Hunter zoned out like he always did when he was stressed. The brown-eyed girl on the box seemed to stare directly back at him.

She looked so alive. Friendly.

Like someone he could talk to.

Black Italian Coffee...Black Italian Coffee...it's a nice color. Solid. Dark.

Does the color refer to the coffee beans or to the brewed drink? Either way, it's dark as hell...almost black compared to blond...

The buzzing sound from the broken sign returned and filled his whole head. His body grew hot and shaky, and Hunter thought he might self-combust.

Black Italian Coffee. Colorado. This is all so messed up...

"Hunter!"

His legs started in automatic response to the sound of his mom's voice. He moved up the steps, but his gaze remained riveted on the model. Her little half-smile...the kind, deep brown eyes.

He imagined her encouraging expression was just for him.

You can do this. You can.

It's just like another costume change. You've had billions of those. No big deal.

"Hurry up. That takes time to process and I refuse to be late to the airport."

4: sexy chip eaters

VERE

Jenna let out a long, dreamy sigh. Her eyes were still locked over Vere's shoulder. "How is it possible our whole football team is this hot? Even Charlie looked all sizzle this morning. Too bad he's not in here."

Vere sucked in a huge breath and elbowed Jenna's arm. "OMG. Don't joke about my brother. Makes me puke."

Jenna laughed. "You know how I adore the jock look. Any boy in any uniform works." She shrugged. "In the right light it even works for your brother."

"Ew. Ew, and EW."

Jenna laughed. "Let's go back to staring at your Curtis. I swear the guy took hot vitamins this morning and they really worked."

"Shut up! Someone's going to hear you. And he's not *my* anything. Not even close." Vere choked on a giggle.

"Well, today he's also in a brand new football jersey. Mmm. Mmm. Mmm. Number seven. As in, 'lucky number seven'. And he *is* your Curtis. A little bit, anyhow. He just doesn't know it. That's why he's so *lucky*."

Vere's phone vibrated on the desk again.

VERE. DID YOU GET MY LAST TEXT? THIS IS IMPORTANT. ACKNOWLEDGE YOU WILL COME STRAIGHT HOME.

The phone rapid-buzzed again: YOO-HOO.

And again: VERE. THIS PROJECT IS SERIOUS.

Vere text-yelled back: OK. GOT IT. STOP TEXTING ME AT SCHOOL. I DON'T WANT TROUBLE.

"That's the first time I've ever seen *yoo-hoo* on a text screen." Jenna propped her fake-glasses on her forehead. "Creepy. But

I think I'm going use it. She better let me go to the cabin for Labor Day in two weeks. Can I? Will I? Me? Choose me."

"Of course. That's a given. You've never missed it since birth."

"Tell that to your mom. She's all but forgotten about me," Jenna complained, re-reading Vere's texts. "She sounds positively mental. I can't wait for you to tell me about the project."

"Maybe I'll die from heat exhaustion before I ever have to find out."

"*Ohmywow.* Maybe we're already dead. Maybe we're in heaven." A wide grin of admiration spread across Jenna's face as she was distracted again by the football guys. "How can boys make eating chips look like a slow-motion commercial of crunching-perfection? I wish I were brave enough to film this on my iPhone. Instant replay...would be so good."

"That's cruel and you know it. Or...is it worth it to look?" Vere swallowed.

"Possibly. Curtis shared the bag. Now they're *ALL* sexy-chip-eaters. This is an awesome day. I feel like I'm dreaming this! Which one should I be in love with this year? Can I have a crush on them all?"

"Stop. You know I can't look. You also know you'd die if any of those football guys noticed you."

"Die happy."

Vere felt her own cheeks flush.

Jenna's expression turned goofy. "Do you think we'll be asked to prom this year? I mean *senior prom?*"

"Can you even imagine?" Vere smothered another giggle.

"If so...I'm having a prom party. Inviting the whole football team, and serving only chips. Corn, potato—heck—even pretzels! Football guys eating all kinds of chips, in tuxedos, at a party. It's my new fantasy. This is so *perfect*. Vere, it's totally worth it. Turn. LOOK!"

Vere turned, locating Curtis immediately in the middle of the laughing, relaxed group of guys draped in the school's colors: orange and black.

Yep. Perfect. Number seven...and...sigh.

"Someone should give them all an A+ for chewing," Vere whispered.

Everything flipped to one of Vere's slow motion, imaginary moments.

How could it not?

With his sun-blond, curly hair, his angled cheekbones. God... and his square shoulders, square chin, square forehead. Ahh-boy-beauty.

And Jenna was right about the new jerseys. So cute.

So handsome. Again. Still. Always.

The guy was perfect.

Perfect torture. UGH.

And yep, insert cheeks of flame because I can't erase the image of me twirling around and around in Curtis's arms as his future prom date.

"*Wow*," Vere whispered again when the butterflies surging in her throat allowed more words to escape. "Love it when he doesn't shave. He's got that manly, sandpaper hotness all over his chin today. He looks kind of like a biker dude and a jock combined. You know? All good-boy-bad-boy...and..."

And Curtis is a perfect dancer. No grinding. He's pulled me close. Face-to-face. So he can run his cheek against my ear. He whispers how much he loves my dress. And me...

Then, he brushes a soft kiss on my lips.

I rest my head against his wide, warm shoulder. His arms wrap me tighter, and I feel safe...so happy. We dance and dance under the low lights until...

Jenna shoved her face into Vere's line of vision.

"Intervention starts now. Don't go closer to the light, little moth. You'll get burned. I shouldn't have told you to look. I'm the worst friend. I suck. HE SUCKS. Look at *me*, Vere, not at him. Okay? Come on. Train those big, brown peepers over here. On me. Right here." She snapped her fingers and waved her hands in front of Vere's face.

"No. He and I could still happen. Maybe," Vere muttered, tearing her gaze away from Curtis. But she couldn't stop imagining how it might feel to have his arms around her.

"Did I mention that I suck as a friend yet? I'm *so* sorry. We need to find another boy for you to have a crush on this year. We will."

As the butterflies and dreams floated away, Vere's heart felt as though it were made of wet clay. "I don't want another crush. This one has almost killed me." Fully dejected now, Vere met Jenna's gaze. "Can you imagine, going to Senior Prom with him? It would be so awesome. If only I could."

"No. It's impossible dreaming. Reality check starts now. School dances are not for us. Especially prom. Not unless we both win one of those makeover contests where we become suddenly fabulous. Or, unless your brother ticks off your mom to the point where he's forced to take us as his dates, that is." Jenna scrunched her forehead thoughtfully. "Which might not be such a bad idea. Charlie could use some chaperones, don't you think?"

"What? *Jenna,* that's sick. *Prom with my brother?*" Vere glared into her friend's bright, green eyes.

Jenna smiled, letting out a breath that sounded relieved. "That's the girl I know. I knew *that* idea would have you snapping out of things. Almost lost you there."

Vere rubbed her eyes with both hands. "Too late. I actually feel sick."

"Sick from *Curtis*. You know it's that. Forgive me for bringing him into focus?"

Vere nodded as her head started to spin. Every time she dreamed too much about Curtis this happened.

She needed a way to stop her crush. But how?

"You do look extra pale. Need some water? Air?" Jenna glanced around the room. "Why do they think starting school in the middle of August, *with no air conditioning,* in an all-glass school is a good idea? I should call news reporters about this." She frowned at Vere's outfit. "Why did you wear that huge hoodie?"

"It was cold this morning. And I've only got a thin undershirt on under here," Vere moaned. "I can't take it off."

"Do it."

"No. I'm not the half-naked-at-school type. Give me your awesome shirt, and you walk around in *your* underwear. I swear, Jenna, my head is actually spinning in the opposite direction of the rest of my body."

Vere sighed and laid her head on her hands, wishing for a breeze to blow through the long row of open windows. Not one branch, not one needle moved on the pine trees shading their lunch quad outside. Just looking at the motionless trees made her body temperature jump another ten degrees.

Jenna was right. The hoodie had to come off.

Because if it didn't, she'd pass out in front of everyone. She'd get wheeled out of here on a stretcher.

And wouldn't that be the perfect way for me, the infamous Vere Roth, to begin my junior year?

Incident Number Two: Knocks HERSELF out.

No. No. No.

5: crazy ain't sexy

HUNTER

"Hunter. We're at the airport."

Hunter jerked awake. He'd forced himself to sleep for the long ride. Sleep (or pretending to sleep) is what he did when he didn't want to deal with shit. And that's what this ride had been.

Complete. Shit.

Closing his eyes was also easier than 'not talking' to his mom. Safer than instigating a fight. He yawned and stretched, acting like he still didn't care that she'd refused to talk to him. Not at Falconer while she'd ruined his hair color, and not once during this whole damn drive had she attempted to wake him.

He tried to bait her again, hoping she'd slip up and say something. "What's next in your psycho, ridiculous plan?"

"Put on this hat. We can't let one strand of your new hair show," she said, her voice was as closed as her shuttered expression.

"Why? The dark color kind of makes my eyes pop, don't ya think?" Hunter's attempts at a careless sounding quip had come out in frog croaks. Worse, his throat was trying to close completely because he'd realized a huge crowd of press waited for him to exit the parked limo.

Really?

His mom watched while he put on the white knit skate cap, then she tucked away every strand of his new hair. "Do not let this hat slip or the whole plan could be blown. You aren't officially in disguise yet. Okay?"

"You and *this*—" He pointed to the crowd outside. "Suck so much right now."

"Just follow my lead. Martin and the guys are waiting. Take

these sunglasses and this matching bag, too." She tossed him a pair of ultra-dark, white-framed *HK* glasses and a poorly made drawstring pack. With silver glitter all over both accessories.

Hunter was grateful for the glasses because he loved hiding behind any and all dark glasses. He put them on and peered out the window. "Why and *how* did the publicist manage a press conference at this hour, at this tiny airport?"

"It's all part of a bigger plan. Don't mention Falconer or Colorado. You've been in Paris. Okay? That's all you need to know for now."

"Okay. Paris. Check." Hunter's head pounded from the effort it took to hold his expressions steady; but then he broke. *"Jesus, Mom.* Tell me a little more. I feel like you're sending me in blind."

"I am." His mom's gaze caught his.

He thought he saw her eyes float a glimpse of regret—or sadness—or *what?* This was definitely an expression he didn't recognize. She looked almost desperate. He also thought for a moment she might say something real—something that would allow Hunter a chance to break in and plead with her not to go through with this.

The driver opened the door, distracting them both.

"Don't blow it, Hunter." Her unrelenting voice turned icier as she went on, "You have no idea how important this is." She stepped out slowly, acting as though this were some sort of red carpet event.

Hunter followed her lead but couldn't resist one more dig. "Important? Do you mean important to your bank account?"

She responded so quietly over her shoulder he almost couldn't hear, "This plan is about you. About me making things right. Just follow along. And for once in your life, please stay quiet. Behave. You don't believe in me, but I *do* know what's best."

"Isn't it a little late for you to run for *Mother of the Year?*" he muttered.

"Yes. Yes it is." She froze and looked back, catching and holding his gaze.

Shit. She's visibly shaking.

Shaking a lot!

Shouldn't I be the one shaking right now?

"Have a good trip. Please try to stick with the plan. No matter how hard it seems." Her voice broke. "*Please.*"

He raised his eyebrows as she stalked away.

WTF? Had his mom just agreed with him?

Had she been crying?

Before he could process more, part of Hunter's entourage—his publicist, manager and three hulking bodyguards he didn't recognize—emerged from another waiting limo and moved in around him.

"Hunter!" His agent's voice shot up from a crowd ahead while his mom's back was swallowed in the crowd. "Hunter! *This way!*"

Martin, along with his band-mates, Royce and Adam, had been trapped against the windows by a throng of reporters near the entrance. They were wedged in, but safely surrounded by their own bodyguards.

Martin jumped up and down, waving his arms. "*Hunter Kennedy.* We're over here!"

Hunter recoiled slightly before he caught himself.

His pulse increased as the crowd's excited energy, plus the eyes and cameras of the greedy press mob, pushed toward him. His closed limo door blocked any retreat.

It took only seconds for Hunter to be engulfed in flashes and the pressing mass of paparazzi. Some he recognized behind their giant lenses and some he didn't.

He froze and squared his shoulders, hiding another flare of panic. Martin knew Hunter hated to be mobbed, yet it never stopped the guy from flagging the press onto him.

Hunter forced his expression into one of practiced, cool nonchalance.

Follow along and behave.

And of course, remember to breathe.

"Hunter! Hunter Kennedy! Hunter! This way. Turn this way," a man shouted. "Hunter!"

Another voice, this time a woman's, called out from the clicking, shoving press-mob. "When did you return from Paris? How long were you there?"

Hunter smiled his biggest grin. At least these bastards still didn't seem to have a clue as to where he'd really been.

A plus.

He busied himself with his silver pack as though he hadn't heard any one question.

"Is that outfit one of the new *HK Originals?*"

Hunter knew that was safe to answer. "Yeah. Check the new shoes."

The photographers immediately aimed their cameras down and took shots of the matching freak-show shoes as though they were rare art objects.

"Hunter, Hunter, turn around. Just one shot, this way. Here! Here! Hunter!" Hunter turned, posed, smiled and turned back.

"Guys!" Martin shouted again. His louder-than-life, New York accent carried over the crowd. "Let him pass through to the rest of the band so we can get inside. We'll give you all a chance at some good shots and maybe a *meet-and-greet* before we go through security."

The photographers parted, and Hunter headed toward Martin, Royce and Adam. They both sported similar, ridiculous, white outfits with silver accessories.

They looked tense, tired. And as sparkly-stupid as he did. As they made their way inside, Hunter tried to loosen them up. "Nice wardrobe, snowflakes. Do your boxers itch as much as mine?"

Royce glowered, apparently not amused, but Adam shot him a wry, almost apologetic smile.

Before either could respond further, a number of new onlookers saw the chaos and crowded around as well, halting their progress.

The new people were mostly curious airport staff and tired looking executives. Business CEOs with private jets and early commuters were not their target market.

At this hour of the morning, their core fans—high-school and college kids—would be fast asleep, and not at the Van Nuys Regional Airport, located just outside Los Angeles.

This meant they were not going to be suffocated by a mass of random screaming, crying girls either.

A second plus.

After all his time alone inside the quiet rooms of *Falconer,* Hunter was not ready to face any screaming. And, even on a good day, crying girls simply terrified him.

Martin looked more than pleased with the press coverage.

Normally, Hunter tried to avoid all photographers and gossip parasites, but he didn't want to screw this up. *GuardeRobe* probably needed to get some catch-up shots to compensate for his absence.

Hunter wanted to make it all right—make the guys and Martin understand he was fully on board. If they had some sort of a plan in motion, messing up in front of cameras would mean sudden death. He worked to play his part.

Along with the guys, he smiled, took off his sunglasses, signed a few autographs, flirted with the cameras and avoided the odd questions about Paris.

Royce and Adam handled those. Blabbing about how they loved seeing the Eiffel Tower. Royce also answered that Hunter had missed going out much in Paris because of a stomach flu?

Nice cover.

It made perfect sense they would create press halfway across the world to divert the attention from Hunter's true, lame location.

His vision glazed to a thick fog. Barry had told him over and over that he was *well enough to move on,* but Hunter didn't feel well enough at the moment. Not even close. He wanted to run back to Falconer and crawl back into the small, silent hospital room he thought he hated.

Shit.

Faces in the crowd pulsed in front of Hunter. He swallowed, yanked down on the knit cap and checked the sleeve cuffs on his hoodie. When the inevitable 'what are you working on next' question shot out, Hunter managed another fake grin and pointed to Martin, who'd finally joined them.

"*GuardeRobe* is heading back into the studio," Martin answered, using his smooth-talker voice. "You won't be seeing much of the band until late spring. They're about to hop a charter to New York and get to work. We have an album to deliver."

Hunter vaguely wondered if the guys were really going to be in New York? If so, he figured suffering through his mom's orchestrated time-out in the boonies seemed a bit less terrible. Martin was a slave-driving ass when they had to pay for studio time. Plus working in a studio required huge vaults of concentration and energy. Hunter admitted he might not have either of those on board. Not this week, anyhow. His gaze fogged out more. He broke out into a cold sweat as his thoughts sunk in.

But...wait. If GuardeRobe has studio time lined up in New York, who is going to write their lyrics? I write those.

Has anyone considered that?

Trying not to openly freak, he looked around for his mom.

All signs of her possible *crying-moment* were long gone. She stood far in the background, arms crossed, watching him. A ball of fury swelled in his chest. Why had she kept all these details silent?

He should have insisted. Begged harder.

But he'd been too hung up on pretending he didn't care. Besides, he'd never had to ask anything before.

People—his mom above all—had always told him everything he needed to know. Told him what to wear, where to go, how to stand, what to eat, when to sing, what to say, and most importantly *what the hell was going on!*

Hunter wiped his hand along his pounding left temple. He was bound and determined to play along. He could afford no more mistakes. He had to prove to his mom, *hell*, to all of them, that he was sorry.

This could be his last chance to get these people to believe that. Hunter continuously checked his hat to make sure it stayed low, hiding the damn dyed hair, hoping his mom noticed his efforts.

Within minutes, Martin had deftly pushed the entire group, minus the reporters and the business travelers, through security and into the *Ages Airlines Diamond Club*.

Once sequestered in the back, Martin directed Hunter to get a bite to eat.

Feeling completely hollow and empty, he watched Martin usher his mother and the guys to the far corner of the large room. It was apparent they did not want him in their conversation.

Should I try to eavesdrop?

Hunter hadn't come up with any excuse to follow them that didn't involve screaming, yelling and throwing things. That behavior would not help his cause. He'd tried it once at Falconer and ended up with hours of additional therapy couch-time with Barry.

He walked over to grab a plate from a sideboard. Not an easy feat, since his hands were shaking and he could still hardly see straight.

This upside down situation will right itself if I can hold my ground. It has to.

I'm Hunter Kennedy for God's sake.

Without me, none of them can pay their bills, right?

Right?

Hunter swallowed, pulling in as much air as he could hold.

Time and patience is all this will take.

He turned toward the small buffet, forcing his eyes to focus on the food. He filled a plate with hummus, pita bread, Greek olives, Feta cheese, grapes, and he grabbed a bottle of water.

This was no breakfast. This was all his mother's favorite foods. She and Elliott were always counting carbs and calories.

Feeling a bit more in control, Hunter pulled off the evil-medieval-sword necklace before sitting. He shot a glance at a tall, familiar looking, blond guy, eating apart from the bodyguards and the rest of his entourage. Each and every person in the room seemed to be avoiding Hunter's gaze except for this kid.

The kid actually seemed to have no problem meeting his gaze or staring like a wide-eyed fanboy.

Hunter shook his head, trying to place him.

I've seen him before. Maybe someone's son? Nephew?

Could be a new intern. One who had not received today's IGNORE-HUNTER memo?

The kid had his elbows propped on the mahogany conference table. He was demolishing a large plate of food that contained only red grapes and crackers.

The dude motioned to Hunter's plate. "What is all that junk? I'm scared to eat it, so I only took what I recognized." He grinned. A large piece of grape skin had stuck to his front tooth, making him look like a whacked hillbilly.

Hunter bit back his own smile and tilted his head—still trying to place the guy. "It's Greek food. Hummus, goat cheese?" He pointed to the kid's tooth. "Dude—you've got something stuck right there..."

The kid flushed slightly and wiped his tooth with a napkin. "Oh. Thanks. You're Hunter Kennedy."

"Yes. Yes, I am." Hunter squelched a grimace. It wasn't this kid's fault he was meeting him on the worst day of his life.

"Nice to finally meet you."

"Thanks." Hunter sighed, hoping the kid didn't want him to chat longer, or worse, sign autographs. Before he could make a polite escape, the kid reached across the table and picked up Hunter's necklace.

He let the chain dangle between them and spun the sword until it became a whirling blur. "This is *nice*."

Hunter snorted. "And sharp. Be careful."

"I guess we're supposed to swap outfits soon. I'm going to catch the plane to New York with *GuardeRobe*, but you have to hand over the matching outfit first." His toothy smile almost blinded Hunter. "New York! I can't wait. I've heard it's so awesome. What size shoe are you?" The guy shoved three crackers into his mouth and continued, "I hope eleven, because those new sneaks are sweet. I'm psyched to have them."

Hunter coughed. An olive had lodged in the back of his throat. He forced it down and stared at the guy, trying to process what he'd just heard.

"If that's okay with you, I mean. You don't need them back, right?"

The dude's grin was now so big Hunter wondered if it would fall off his face.

The kid blabbed on, "Can I keep that hat, too?" He studied Hunter's head and his grin faltered when Hunter still didn't respond. "If you don't care. It's as cool as this necklace!" He dropped the chain over his neck.

Hunter blinked, unable to respond, or breathe, or think.

"They let me keep the other outfits so...I just figured..."

♥ 37 ♥

Hunter gripped the sides of his chair for balance as his mind spun out of control.

Hell. No way.

NO WAY.

They've replaced me!

Hunter couldn't believe his life had morphed into this.

Well aware the room had just gone completely silent, Hunter unclenched his hands and grabbed a handful of grapes.

Methodically putting them into his mouth one at a time, he stapled his expression into *extreme press mode*. He concentrated on chewing, swallowing and willing the buzzing fury in his head to dissipate.

He shot another hooded glance at the huddle in the corner and noted everyone had turned to watch him, except his mom. She was obviously pretending not to notice the exchange.

Typical.

His entire life was spiraling out of control because of her stupid need to punish him, and the woman didn't even have the courage to watch anymore.

I have to think. Shit. I have to breathe.

He let air in through his nose and popped in another grape, biting through the skin. It tasted like dirt.

The effort to swallow almost did him in, but he knew he was winning when he managed to throw in another, chew it, swallow again and add in more breathing.

Hunter surveyed the guy top to bottom. The kid looked almost exactly like him.

How I used to look six weeks ago, with shorter, blond hair. Minus the dorky, shit-eating-grin, of course.

Damn...this guy has so many teeth.

"Dude. Hunter? We cool?" his clone asked, frowning.

Hunter felt his legs start to shake, but managed to flip on a smile and a nod. "Just starving," he muttered. "You know how it is."

"Oh, yeah. Me, too. We have *so* much in common!" The guy shot him another overlarge grin. "I'm always hungry, too!"

Hunter shot Martin a desperate glance.

Martin nodded, but made no move to come talk about this.

Hunter decided he was not going to do what they probably expected him to do.

No way was he going to blow up. Not even a little.

Though he had every right.

He took in another big breath and looked back at the goofy guy in front of him and cracked his own smile.

A fake, *dumbass* smile that matched the other kid's smile. One that hurt so bad he felt like the insides of his cheeks were cracking all the way to his soul.

"Dude. You can keep the whole outfit. Forever. My shoes are an eleven. Are they paying you a lot?"

"Tons! It's the best deal ever. Thanks for—uh—the job— and the trip to Paris too."

"You actually *went*? To Paris?" Hunter's heart dropped. He was mostly amazed that he could still be surprised at this moment.

"Yeah. Me and the guys. When you were...sick? Didn't they tell you?" The blond kid nodded toward Royce and Adam.

Hunter shook his head. "No. They didn't."

"I had to keep mostly to the hotel, but the hotel was sweet. So deluxe. And they got me anything I wanted—room service, video games, movies, French pastries—anything, even wine. No drinking age over there!"

"Right. Lucky you." Hunter wondered how long it had been since he'd found unlimited room service or the accessibility to alcohol exciting.

He studied the kid close up.

Shit. My twin. Eye color, not as blue. Everything else—dead on. As long as he tones down his smile a bit...

"This gig will more than pay for my college or anything I

want to do next year. It's cake acting too. No lines to learn. All I have to do is keep my face down, wear sweet clothes, and not talk."

"Well, at least one of us has a solid future," Hunter said, hating that he'd been unable to hide the utterly desolate tone in his voice.

The dude noticed, and at least had the grace to dim his smile to a sincere frown. "Oh. Right. Well, I'm sorry about you know—that you're *sick*? But they told me it wasn't like— *fatal*—or too major? Is it?"

"Apparently it's more serious than we all originally thought," Hunter managed.

"Oh. I'm really sorry." He leaned farther across the table and continued, "I totally love *GuardeRobe*. It's an honor to help you out. Really. I hope you don't have to go through anything painful like surgeries? Or—well—I'm hoping there's some sort of bright side for you."

"Are you always this chatty?" Hunter unclenched his fists.

"Yeah! I am. My name's—"

"No! *Don't*." Hunter stood abruptly, picking up his plate. The guy sat back, startled.

"I don't want to know your name. Too weird. I'm sorry. I can't."

"Oh. Okay. Sure."

The guy had stopped smiling at least.

"Shall we—get this over with?" Hunter motioned to the rest room signs behind them, as a wave of extreme exhaustion hit him low and heavy across his chest.

His body felt as though it weighed thousands of pounds. He had no idea how he made it to the other side of the room.

And then it was done.

They'd traded out everything but their boxers.

Truthfully, Hunter couldn't have been happier to ditch the white and silver hell-suit for the other guy's plain Levis, white under shirt and his wrinkled, long sleeved, light blue button down. It all fit him like a glove. The freakish skate cap had been replaced with a faded, black and purple, Sacramento Kings ball cap. The offensive white sneakers had been upgraded to surfer flip-flops with dark red canvas tops.

Hunter pulled nervously at the shirt cuffs. The sleeves were long enough to do the trick.

After they'd changed, they made their way back to the table where Hunter's band-mates were now sitting and eating.

Unlike before, everyone was now openly staring, but they all seemed jumpy.

YA THINK? TRAITORS!

I'M ALSO A LITTLE JUMPY OVER HERE!

Hunter wanted to scream. Flip tables. Throw a chair or two. But he didn't.

Instead, he let Adam give him a low five and sat down like this was an ordinary day.

Royce hadn't spoken, just ate his hummus and stared away from him like he was all pissed. And Royce was supposed to be his *best friend.* Truthfully, despite what Twitter, the blogs and the magazines said, the three of them rarely hung out when they weren't working.

He couldn't blame them for being pissed. His exit was risking all of their jobs, too.

"Dude. How you handling—all of this?" Adam asked, grimacing at Hunter's new outfit.

"What do you think," he evaded. "Tell me you guys weren't in on thinking up this ridiculous plan?"

"Hell no!" Adam whispered. "Just get better, or get back home soon. It's so freaking weird without you. We hate your stand-in. He's a total tool. We can't even be mean to the guy because it makes you feel like you've kicked a puppy. He's so damn friendly and *nice.*" Adam shuddered.

Hunter cracked a small smile.

Royce finally piped in, "They wouldn't let us call or email you. Not once."

"Why? I knew it! Damn Martin and Mom. I'm sorry about all this, guys. I really messed things up." Hunter adjusted his ball cap.

"Martin said if we left you alone, it would help you to—recover. You know, to have some distance from us. So...you're feeling okay? Strong, or better or—whatever now?" Royce added.

"Yes. *I am.* I don't know why I did all that shit. You guys have to talk to my mom. Tell her I'm fine. I handled things so badly. That's all. She won't talk to me. If you get the chance, let her know I'm sorry. See if you guys can crack her. I only want to come back to work."

That was all he got out before they were swept away by Martin. Within seconds his agent was back at the table just as Hunter was hit with another wall of exhaustion.

He tried to concentrate but he felt as though Martin's lips had detached from his face. The voice droning out at him sounded like a robot with low batteries. "Thanks for not flipping out. I've got a lot to say and not much time," was all Hunter heard clearly.

He focused on making an internal list of Martin's words so he could recall them later, when he could think.

1. Get to Colorado and hide your identity at all costs—the press can NOT know.

Check. Press can not know. I'm already on that.

2. Don't tell anyone about spending time at *Falconer*, or the details of what you did to yourself.

As if I'm going to take out an ad in the paper about any of that.

3. Scar cream. Use lots of scar cream.

What? What?

Martin shoved a huge brown paper sack under his face. Hunter nodded just in time when Martin asked if he would apply the cream three times a day. He managed a deep breath and checked himself back into the odd, impossible conversation in time to hear Martin's last sentence.

"Hopefully they'll fade out, man. This prescription stuff works miracles." Martin grinned expectantly at Hunter.

"That's what I thought when I gobbled down all of Mom's antidepressants," Hunter volunteered. "Miracles. You know?"

When Martin flushed, Hunter knew he'd said the wrong thing.

Whatever.

What exactly is the right thing to say anymore? Ever again.

Shit.

"Your Aunt Nan will be the only one outside of our private circle who knows about it," Martin finished.

"The scar cream?"

Martin's face changed from red to purple, and he lowered his voice even more. "*The suicide—the suicide attempts, dammit! Ramp the hell in!* We had to tell Nan, in case you need more—help. Someone to talk to? You can call Barry directly any time, or your aunt can find you a local shrink. Your call."

"I'm not going to need any more help. I didn't try to off myself. *I didn't.* I'm not that person."

"You were that night."

"You don't know anything. It was all those pills plus the wine. I'd never been hammered like that before." Hunter looked away. Martin had never spoken to him like this. Like they weren't on the same team anymore. He went on, "A bad fight between me and Mom, plus some mega-stupidity on my part made for a prank gone sour. I'm *fine* now, and I was pretty much fine then. Ask Barry, he'll back me. I only needed monitoring while I tapered off the anti-depressants I shouldn't have been taking. You've got to save me from this Colorado thing."

"Believe me. I'm on it. Just give me a little more time to try to work on your mother." Martin leaned even closer. "Look. Hunter. This secret—what we have worked so hard to set up— it's flipping beyond serious. You can't deviate from the plan. You have to hit every mark, or all is going to be lost."

"I know. I know. I won't piss off the mom. And I won't let anyone find out who I am. Did you not notice how I didn't strangle my replacement or shave off this dyed hair yet? I'm doing my part. What's your problem?"

"That's only half of it." Martin's voice turned even more relentless. "The car thing, the vandalism charges—if they come out in the press—all of that is marketable. It's standard rock-star activity. But your reputation will not survive this *cutting* business."

Hunter's voice was stony. "I'm not a cutter. I cut myself. Once."

Martin shrugged. "Whatever you want to call it. It can't come out to the press. And you can never, ever do it again."

"Christ. Back the hell off! I have no desire to do it again. What part of the whole picture are you missing?"

Martin's eyes narrowed to a squint. He gripped Hunter's shoulder. Hard. "Crazy ain't sexy. And it sure won't sell tracks off iTunes. That's *MY* whole picture. Got it?"

"Got it." Hunter yanked his shoulder out of Martin's grasp, unable to feel anything but the bastard's words slamming into his head.

Crazy ain't sexy. Crazy, crazy, crazy...
Shit...is this what they all think about me now?

Seemingly satisfied, Martin softened his tone. "If I can't get your mom to let you come back early, I'll execute my *Plan-B*. Make sure your phone is charged at all times. Check for my text messages and emails at least once a day. Ignore all others. I'll set up a special email for the duration. I'll text it this afternoon. Do not call your mom. Let me handle that madwoman. Email or texts. Whatever you do, don't contact the rest of the band."

"Okay."

"You're going to be a kid called *Dustin McHugh*. Remember, you aren't really 'gone' according to us. As soon as I get your mom convinced to change her mind, you can fly back. All right? It could take a few weeks. Maybe longer, but hopefully not much."

Hunter nodded, finally meeting his mom's gaze across the room. She was simply standing there with her arms crossed. Would she even come over to say goodbye? Did he want her to? Hunter blanked out all over again.

Was this whole thing really going down like this?

His body couldn't, wouldn't move. Hunter could only stare at the kid in the white outfit—at his mom's closed-off expression—at the way Royce and Adam were staring at the wall—at what an ass Martin looked like right now.

Crazy ain't sexy...

God. My chest hurts. Bad.

Breathe. Breathe. Remember to breathe.

He sucked in some air.

Martin shook him. "Hunter. You're looking ghost-pale. You've made it this far. Colorado isn't going to be forever. I need you to stay cool. You *are* the band. Without you *GuardeRobe* is toast. You freak permanently, and we're all unemployed."

"Martin, are you sure?" Hunter gulped, almost blacking out from the exertion it took to suck in another breath. "It looks like you've got the band and everything handled fine. *GuardeRobe* is completely intact and it's right over there." He jerked his head angrily at the fake Hunter, who was currently admiring his new sneakers as though they were the best things he'd ever seen.

"Christ. This is total bull." Hunter pulled his eyes back to Martin.

"The kid's only for limo rides and paparazzi shots. Smoke and mirrors, man. He can't even sing." Martin handed him a plane ticket, a credit card, and a flimsy, laminated card that read, *Palmer Ridge High School.*

They all bore the name *Dustin McHugh.*

"Shit." Hunter stared at the cards. "For real?"

"Yes. Your school ID. And don't forget to sign the credit card with the right name. Memorize it as yours. "

"I hate my new name. It's—totally lame. This photo's not me at all. It's so blurred. Hell, it's not anyone."

"That's the point. BE someone else. Anyone else. Wait for me to contact you. Don't even think about playing the guitar or singing in public, either. Do nothing but hide out, go to school and rest."

"Tell me again. It is not going to be for long," Hunter whispered.

"It's not going to be for long. We called in a huge favor with the school district superintendent. Luckily she's a huge fan. She has the school principal completely on board. The credit card is for clothes, a better disguise, and emergency supplies only. Your Aunt Nan's involved another family—some kids— to help you blend in. The kids have also promised to drive you around. Anything else?"

"Nope." Hunter stared again at his mom's unrelenting back.

"I'm going to need you to swap out your backpack too." Martin held out a plain, navy, canvas pack. "You have two duffels marked Dustin McHugh that match this. Don't forget to pick them up when you land."

Hunter pocketed the cards and shoved the bag of scar cream into the main pocket of the new pack. His other two belongings he treated more carefully. He placed his iPhone on top of the flattened hair-color box, making sure the smiling, brown-eyed model was face up as he zipped her into the front pocket.

He handed over the white and silver, *HK*-encrusted backpack without meeting Martin's gaze.

He was done talking.

"Flight's in two hours. Gate A36. Don't leave the Airline Club for at least one hour. Don't talk to anyone who comes in here after we leave. Eat some more food. Looks like you could use it." Martin scanned him up and down. "Maybe lift some weights while you're there, huh? Your Aunt Nan will be waiting at passenger pick up in the Denver airport. I'll communicate as soon. Promise."

And that had been it—for him anyhow.

Within seconds the entire group rushed out the door.

Martin forged ahead, drawing the attention with his booming voice and pushing Adam and Royce ahead. His mom trailed behind the fake Hunter Kennedy, messing with his hat, hair and sunglasses.

She'd glanced back once, her expression still unreadable, before being swallowed up in the camera flashes and noise of a new crowd forming in the terminal.

Hunter floated just outside his body and very deep into his own head as the opaque, glass door whispered shut.

Finally he'd sat, staring first at the points of blue, black and grey in the tightly bound carpet. And then at his toes flexing in his new flip-flops.

Exactly one hour later, he'd walked unnoticed to his gate and boarded his plane.

6: howie rutherford sucks

VERE

"Okay. Quiet!" Mr. Peterson, the chemistry teacher, barreled into the crowded lab holding reams of paper. "I said, *quiet*."

He sounded as hot and as irritated as Vere felt.

"I want the new *Concussion Management Form* on top of your piles. They have to get entered into the office database today or you aren't allowed to participate in the assembly. Football team! This means you! Or no scrimmage this afternoon. *Concussion Management Forms* ON TOP. Now stop fooling around in here and get your packets completed."

Vere turned toward the wall to take off the hoodie. Instead of the graceful move she'd told her arms to create, she got tangled up and trapped by her double-weighted bun.

The hoodie wouldn't budge up or down.

With her face completely wrapped in black cotton, she scoured her melting brain, trying to take stock of the situation.

All is not lost.

My cami is at least cute, and from the feel of things, it hasn't ridden up. THANK GOD.

She struggled harder. At least twenty baby hairs at the base of her neck pulled out from her efforts.

"Ow. Uuuf."

Her head spun more. It was either her or the bun.

Fine. The bun.

She yanked as hard as she could. More hairs popped out.

"Ow! Jenna, help. Please. Help! Help!"

Within seconds her hoodie came up, then off.

Vere gasped in two long breaths. "Another minute and a new *epic-fail-moment* would top my list. Thanks," she said, turning with a smile.

♥ 48 ♥

"No problem. I can't resist when cute girls ask for help."

Curtis Wishford stood in front of her, holding her crumpled hoodie.

"Um," Vere managed, choking back the remaining syllables: *bla-durd-yah-bla.*

Curtis seemed to be biting back a grin as he handed over the hoodie. "Vere, I'm kidding. I knew it was you under there."

What is he kidding about?

Am I cute or not?

Maybe I'm so low on the totem pole, he doesn't consider me a real girl?

Bla. Bla. Bla. Dug-bla.

Curtis went on, "And don't worry. No one saw you stuck in the hoodie. You won't have to update that *list.*" He chuckled. "Do you really have a list?" he added.

Vere blinked. And blinked. And blinked. And blinked.

OMG. Try to speak. Try.

"Uh...yeah. I mean, no. I don't. Joking. Thought you were Jenna." Vere felt the back of her neck burn. Her stomach had started to twist and roll.

"Oh." He shifted his feet. "I wouldn't put a list like that past you, though. You always seem to be taking little notes."

"I need extra study notes—sometimes."

"So do I. I make flash cards."

"You do?"

His gaze was warm. "It's a secret."

"Right." She laughed, biting her upper lip to keep her mouth from dropping open again. She quickly glanced around for Jenna. She seemed to have vanished.

When Curtis didn't say more, Vere risked another glance at his face.

His eyes are so nice close up. Half green and half brown with all kinds of bright specks in them.

Seems taller. He's wearing cologne! Mmm...

"So...thanks for saving me," she managed finally and looked away, wondering if she'd stared at his face too long.

"Sure."

When he didn't move, Vere entered a strange, floating time-warp. She grounded herself by focusing on the white swoosh on his black sneakers.

Go on now, sporty shoes. Walk away. Please.

When the sneakers didn't budge, Vere busied herself by shoving the sweaty hoodie into her bag.

His feet turned finally; but before she realized what was happening, her bun slipped to the side and came completely undone.

"Wow." Curtis's sneakers turned back.

"Yeah. I know. I'm a mess," Vere said, darting him a glance through her hair before looking back down as her cheeks started to ache and burn even more.

"No. You have beautiful hair. I never noticed it had grown out so long. Really, really long."

His voice had been soft. Kind. Admiring?

Did he just call my hair beautiful?

She recovered her hair band and grabbed at the mass of hair, trying to pull it all back together, now terrified to look at his face.

Please don't let him be laughing at me. Anything but that.

When he didn't say more, Vere forced herself to talk to his sneakers again. "My hair—it's hard to manage so...I...uh, wear it up. Probably should cut it."

She deftly scrunched her hair back into its bun, wishing she'd said something else. Anything else. But she gave herself a mental pat-on-the-back, amazed she'd said any intelligible words at all.

"I wouldn't cut something so pretty. You should wear it down more. It's a nice look on you. Different."

Vere met his gaze.

A second compliment, and no snarky, teasing remark?
Was this an actual conversation happening here?
Answer him. Answer him!

"Oh. Thanks. Yeah, maybe." This time it was easy to smile at him. Until he smiled back and collapsed her lungs!

"Cool. I love long hair on girls. It's my favorite."

She realized it was her turn to talk all over again. "Yours is pretty too. Not so long and very shiny. Cool black curls—and all that, too."

Lame. Lamest thing I've ever said.

Curtis gave her a strange look as if to confirm her thoughts. She had to recover—fast. "Handsome. Not pretty, of course. It's handsome. And—dark—short, black hair like yours is my favorite on guys, too. So...yeah."

Even lamer.

"It is?" He laughed.

She bit her bottom lip, wondering if he now thought she was insane. Her whole stomach rolled up and over her heart before dropping back down to her knees.

Oh, please walk away, Curtis Wishford. I can't possibly think of another thing to say. I can't breathe anymore, and I can't leave because this is my seat!

Please. Just. Go. Away.

But he didn't.

Still grinning, he crossed his arms as if he meant to stay longer. "Charlie says your mom's got some huge project for you two this weekend. I hope she lets you off for Saturday night's bonfire. You thinking about going to that? How come you never go to school stuff?"

What? Is he asking me to come to the bonfire?

Or does he want me to admit that I'd die if I had to chat with people—with HIM— at school stuff?

She shrugged, focusing on answering his questions in complete sentences this time. "We can't do the bonfire. Mom's

♥ 51 ♥

making us go to the lake. But...I do some school stuff. Drama things mostly."

"Oh, right. That's where you hide. I always pick weights for extra classes."

"I know." Vere nodded, hitting a whole new level of painful-blush-burning at the tops of her ears. "You lift with Charlie. He tells me you guys have fun," she covered.

Curtis didn't seem to notice her ears because he was intently studying her cami. What was *in* her cami!

Maybe he's checking out the chest that doesn't fill out my cami? Help. So awkward.

Where in the heck is Jenna? I need a rescue.

In horror, she watched as his eyes traveled lower then back up. He didn't seem repulsed.

His gaze seemed almost appreciative!

But then, a glint in his eyes suddenly gave her the urge to deck him. And deck him really hard.

The heat plus the stress of him talking to me must be making me bonkers. As if I'd ever publicly deck Curtis Wishford again.

Even if he deserved it.

Which he might right now...if he doesn't stop.

She sought solace in the fact that she and Jenna had done the exact same thing to Curtis for years. They secretly stared him up and down any chance they got. The *chip-eating*, prom-dreaming conversation was just a snapshot of years and years of inappropriate staring plus commentary about this one guy.

Karma in action.

But why hasn't he stopped looking yet?

If he won't end this madness, I will.

Curtis and I both know we don't talk to each other.

Why would he break the rules?

"Have your legs always been that long?"

"Since seventh grade," she reminded him, grabbing her binder to hold it in front of her like a shield.

"Seventh grade feels like ancient history to me."

"I wish..." she started, but then changed her mind. There was no point in continuing that sentence. She looked away, determined, this time, to never look back at his beautiful face.

"Vere, you're so—" Curtis stopped mid-sentence when Howie Rutherford, his teammate, stood and knocked over a stool, distracting everyone in the room.

"Mr. Peterson!" Howie called out.

I'm so what? So what?!

Vere gritted her teeth and figured she didn't want him to finish his sentence.

She could guess what he was thinking: *So hopeless. So pink and red? So weird. So challenged in every way?*

"Mr. Peterson!" Howie hollered again. He was one of those kids who didn't know how to speak, only shout.

"What is it, Howie?"

"You're going to have to give an extra one of these head injury forms to Curtis Wishford and maybe to Vere Roth too."

"Why?" Mr. Peterson sighed and tapped his foot. Everyone was used to Howie's classroom antics.

Vere locked eyes with Curtis and hugged her binder tighter. Her heart had officially stopped beating one second ago.

Curtis shot her a half-smile, one that couldn't hide his obvious regret. Regret that had to stem from him approaching her at all.

The classroom grew silent as Howie continued, "Does the person who *CAUSES* the concussion have to sign the form, or is it only the person who *RECEIVES* the actual injury?"

Howie had turned an innocent stare to Mr. Peterson, who'd zeroed in on Vere and Curtis.

Vere figured it was medically impossible for someone to blush black. She tried not to care that she'd reached this extreme status and with a maximum audience.

She couldn't do anything about that, but she could at least

keep her face straight. "I hate you, Howie Rutherford," Vere called out just before biting down on the insides of her cheeks. Hard.

Howie grinned.

"Vere? Curtis? Do you—or do you NOT—have the Concussion Form?" Mr. Peterson waved the forms in the air.

All remaining chatter ceased. Every eye in the room swiveled to them.

"You're so lame, Howie." Curtis placed his hands on Vere's table, glowering at his friend. "Let it go," he added, shooting Vere an unreadable glance.

A few students giggled quietly.

"Howie, you have two seconds to explain yourself," Mr. Peterson bellowed. "Or all three of you can hit the principal's office."

"Curtis needs one of those forms in case Vere knocks him out with a head-butt again." Howie bobbed his head like a chicken for effect. "Get out of range, Curtis. She's dangerous. We have a game in two weeks."

The entire room erupted into laughter.

Jenna materialized out of the sea of staring faces, her expression appalled. She held up two ice-cold, dripping water bottles.

"Don't let them see you sweat," she whispered, sliding in to her seat. Ever protective of Vere, she shot Curtis and then Howie her *back-the-hell-off-my-bestie* glare.

To make the moment even more memorable, a drop of sweat slid off of Vere's head and smacked onto Curtis's hand.

Perfect.

Vere stole a glance at Curtis through her lashes. Under Jenna's glare his smile had faded to a pained grimace. He retreated back to his seat, rubbing the back of his hand on his shirt.

Attempt at ever charming Curtis Wishford: FAIL.

"Oh, Mr. Peterson. Don't let Vere hurt me. She's scary,"

Howie whined, mock cringing in his seat.

Vere looked away from the sea of staring faces and twisted a lock of hair at the base of her neck as she memorized every single scratch etched on the surface of her lab table.

More laughter echoed around her and then, whispers.

She figured the few kids who hadn't heard about her and Curtis were getting filled in on details. She glanced again at Curtis, who'd chosen to ignore the entire scene. He was now busily signing his pile of forms as if the world had disappeared around him.

Who could blame him?

Vere pasted on her best poker face and tossed a weak shrug to Jenna, but she couldn't meet her best friend's gaze for long. Grateful for the water bottle because it gave her something to do while everyone continued to stare, Vere opened it and took a long drink.

No matter how much water she swallowed, the lump in her throat would not wash away.

Her phone buzzed and rattled against the desk.

VERE MAKE SURE CHARLIE COMES HOME WITH YOU. ALONE. REMEMBER. NO DILLY-DALLYING. I REALLY NEED YOU KIDS TO BE READY TO HELP ME.

"Miss Roth. Are you texting? You may bring that phone up here. I'll return it after you collect and sort everyone's forms for me."

"Yes, Mr. Peterson."

7: landing

HUNTER

"Flight attendants, please prepare for landing." The captain interrupted Hunter's thoughts as the plane circled outside Denver to avoid some giant thunderheads.

He let his forehead rest on the oval shaped window, peering at a small pod of city skyscrapers and highway interchanges framed on one side by a long strip of distant mountains, grateful for the pair of plain, boring, sporty looking sunglasses his imposter-twin had given him.

Crazy ain't sexy. Crazy ain't sexy.

Martin's words still consumed his thoughts.

Am I crazy? No. No. Barry said I wasn't.

Said it more than once, and he's a professional.

"Sir? Sir. *Young man.*"

Hunter jumped and pulled away from the window, trying to make himself disappear into his seat. A woman in a red scarf and navy suit stood there looking at him expectantly.

His stomach clenched in white-hot fear.

Does she recognize me? What am I supposed to do? I have zero bodyguards.

Please don't let me get mobbed.

Please no screaming.

He looked around for a pen.

Maybe she only wants an autograph. I could ask her not to tell. I'll beg. After today, I'm all about not waiting to beg.

The man next to him bumped his arm. "She wants your trash, bud."

"And you need to pull your seat back up from the reclining position." She blinked at him as though he were an idiot.

"Oh. Right. Sure." He pulled a soda can, napkins and his

squashed plastic cup out of his seat pocket. He held it out for the woman to take, risking a breath.

"Drop it in the bag, *please.*" She rattled the white trash bag.

"Right." Hunter reached over and released his pile into the sack.

She stalked away in a huff.

The man shook his head. "Bet she lives alone."

"Ya think?" They shared a smile.

After they'd handed out the snack and drink, Hunter had determined his seat mates were not *GuardeRobe* fans. When no one else around him had given him a second glance, he'd relaxed enough to curl up against the window and sleep.

Now the guy next to him was packing up his laptop, and the woman in the aisle seat had just placed her Kindle into a leather bag.

Both still seemed blissfully unconcerned with him!

Hunter marveled at the idea that they had been sitting next to him for two hours and knew nothing—*thought nothing*—about him. The flight attendant had actually scorned him!

Hunter counted back. It had been at least five hours since he'd been recognized.

This was some kind of record.

For some reason he suddenly wanted this disguise to hold. At least for a little while. It was kind of cool being one of the nameless, faceless many.

The lady in the aisle seat leaned over the middle guy to peer out the window. Hunter had to steel himself from flinching. He hated when strangers came too close.

"These darn afternoon storms. It's going to be bumpy on the way down. Going home?" She leaned back, but continued to eye him curiously—but not in an way that threatened him.

"Sort of. You?" he answered, trying to keep his voice quieter than normal.

"Denver's home. Been away on business. Where's home for

you?"

"Uh...Monument." The word sounded strange on Hunter's tongue. "I'm moving there to live with my aunt. Haven't seen it since I was little. Do you know it?"

"I call it Little Siberia," the guy in the middle seat said.

The lady smiled. "It's beautiful, but you always get extra snow during winter. Nice good-sized town these days, though. Beautiful views of Pikes Peak."

"Oh." Hunter tried to remember the town all over again, but could only visualize his Aunt Nan's smiling face. He actually couldn't wait to see her. Maybe get one of her hugs. He could never forget those.

The plane bounced and jerked. It shot though the edge of one of the giant clouds. Everything shuddered and the carry-on bags shifted overhead.

Why do the people next to me look so calm?

A ray of yellow-white sunlight blazed through the windows on the other side of the plane. Hunter gripped the sides of his seat as the plane bounced again.

This time, there was no cloud to blame for the turbulence.

"Is this a normal landing, or should I be nervous right about now?" he choked out.

"This is pretty par for the course in late summer. Hot air meeting cold over the mountains. You got a name?" The man held out his hand.

Hunter nodded.

Feeling like a total fraud, he peeled his right hand loose from the death grip he had on the armrest and gave the man's outstretched hand a short shake. He had the strangest urge to smile—probably because he was about to *lie* to this guy—so he sucked in a half breath and cracked the grin.

"I'm . . . *Dustin*. Dustin McHugh."

8: spotting panic

VERE

Vere slammed the screen door. "Mom! Charlie ditched
me. I sat in the parking lot for twenty minutes waiting and
waiting, and he never showed up or called. I had to drive home
ALONE."

Her brother's shout blasted her eardrums as he slammed in
right behind her.

"*UNTRUE.* I texted her during last period but she didn't
check her phone. I grabbed a ride with Curtis! We were right
behind her in Curtis's truck, so technically she was never
alone."

Vere glared bullets into her brother's eyes. "Do you hear him?
Mom! He just admitted to disobeying."

Charlie laughed, lowering his voice. "Kiss kiss. Don't be all
mad. Curtis drove away. But not before he asked about you.
What's up with that?"

"Shut up." Vere shoved past him. "I'm not an idiot. I'm
actually positive he won't bring up my name again." Vere hung
her backpack on one of the mud-room hooks.

"Vere. Honest. He did. Whatever happened today had him
all sappy and weird. Kind of creepy."

Charlie blinked his large brown eyes innocently—eyes that
matched hers—before throwing his hoodie and backpack into
a heap on the floor.

"He also asked me if you were going out with anyone. Ha. As
if."

Vere shook her head and gave him her most scathing glare,
refusing to let him tease her about her crush. "*Mom!* Charlie's
too cheap to call me on his cell and text messages have a really
long delay at the school. And he knows it!"

💙 59 💙

"I only have eight hundred minutes of text-and-talk time each month. Bought by me and not budgeted for you," Charlie whispered as he stalked past her, heading for the fridge.

She followed, grabbing the orange juice first. "Seriously? That's why you didn't text me?"

"Yes, seriously." Charlie took the juice carton right out of her hand, opened it and took five huge gulps. "I'm not made of money." He smacked his lips and slobbered on the spout as though he were making out with it or something. Charlie was famous for this move. "Mmm. Mmm. My juice."

"You are so disgusting." She hid a smile.

"I know, right?" He grinned.

The door to the fridge hung wide open while Charlie held out the carton, wiggled his eyebrows ridiculously, and invited her to take it. "Want some? I'm done."

"*Mom!*" Vere reached around him and took out a cold water bottle. "Charlie's contaminated the whole juice carton!"

"Guys! Come in here, please." Her mom's voice drifted in from the front living room.

"Coming!" Vere motioned to Charlie. "After you, big brother."

"Hell, no. You go first. Figure out what hellish project she has in mind and report back." Charlie dove into a bag of pretzels.

"Do I look stupid?"

Charlie fluttered his eyelashes. "Do you really want me to answer that? Because I will."

She rolled her eyes.

He glug-gulped the last of the juice and packed a pile of pretzels into his mouth. "Ready?" he said, spitting bits of dry pretzel everywhere.

"Let's agree to stick together. No matter what it is."

"Deal." More pretzel dust flew in all directions.

Vere was about to crack up. The guy could *joke-charm* anyone out of being angry, even her.

They headed single file toward the front of the house. "Hey, Mom!" Charlie hollered down the hallway. "Vere tried to get a boyfriend today. Howie told me she propositioned Curtis in the science lab. Turned all red and purple. Offered to clock him and drag him back to her cave. She even got her cell phone put on probation!" He laughed, glancing back at her.

"Lies! Rumors," Vere gasped out, horrified the news of how she'd made a fool out of herself had already spread.

Most probably that's what he and Curtis had been talking about on the ride home, not about *her.* Not if she was dating anyone, that's for sure.

"Stop teasing me about Curtis. You know I've sworn not to like him anymore. For real." She launched onto his back and pummeled his shoulders.

"Please." Charlie hooted, securing her legs under his arms. "Despite your first failed make out session—and even though you don't believe me—and even though I think he's nuts to consider you—I'm pretty positive the guy is tracking you on the crush radar. He *did* ask me about you on a serious level today. HE DID."

Vere landed a good karate chop between his shoulder blades, but her brother was so huge he didn't even flinch. "Just shut up about him. It's not funny. You know I'm broken where he's concerned. Even if he asked you stuff about me, it's not going to happen. You know I can't function."

He stopped and spoke over his shoulder. "I wish you wouldn't think that about yourself. You just need a little practice. Curtis told me you had a whole conversation this afternoon. A *cute* conversation. I puked when he described it."

She stopped punching him and tried to keep her elation— her hope—out of her voice. "Honest? He did?"

"He did. You have potential, but you first have to believe you have potential. I'm going to help you work on this. After I make *you* puke for revenge."

Charlie trapped her legs tighter and caught her into an inescapable, spinning piggyback ride. As he reached their wider front foyer, he was going full speed.

They shot into the living room like a tornado.

Vere clutched Charlie's shoulders, fighting for balance.

Her gaze landed on their neighbor Nan first, then her mom's huge, disapproving frown. On the next turn, she locked on to a guy she didn't recognize. He was sitting on the couch—wearing *sunglasses*?

One more turn and she'd taken in a black cap, dark brown hair, and that he was staring at them. Unless he had his eyes closed behind those glasses, which she doubted, considering the spectacle she and Charlie were creating.

"Put me down," she uttered in Charlie's ear.

Charlie, oblivious to the company, wouldn't quit spinning.

On her next time around, Vere caught a direct glimpse of the guy's face, and it was not lost on her, even dizzy, that he was good looking.

Vere felt her cheeks tingle but the blush dissipated instantly thanks to Charlie, who'd started spinning her so fast she lost track of the entire room. She kept her voice steady in an attempt to play this cool. "Uh, Mom? Any time you want to step in? Permanently ground him? Take away his car privileges and give them to me?"

"*Uh, Mom,*" Charlie spun faster, mimicking Vere's higher voice with a girly voice of his own. "*Any time you want to step in and help Vere with her man skills? I've decided to launch her into popular society.*"

"You mean skills like me launching you into the carpet?" Vere grabbed at his ears and yanked.

Charlie grunted and fell to the floor.

She landed in a dizzy, triumphant heap on his back.

"Sadly, these are my children. Vere, Charlie, meet *Dustin McHugh*. *Dustin* is—he's Nan's nephew. And he's moving here.

Isn't that *nice,* kids?" Her mom's tone had changed to Mary-Poppins-bright as she continued, "And *Dustin* is our project. He will start school with you on Tuesday after the three-day weekend. He's going to need our help getting adjusted."

Charlie, still face down, groaned, "I'm the one who needs adjusting. Vere almost killed me. Severed my spine with her bony knees. Get off. Someone call an ambulance."

Vere dug her knee deep into Charlie's back as she clambered off her brother and teetered into a chair. "Whoa. Dizzy," she mumbled.

The new kid laughed.

She shot at him a look and their gazes met. This time, Vere didn't lose focus. He took off his sunglasses and Vere had to bite back a gasp. The guy's eyes were such a blinding bright-blue they disoriented her.

She felt the back of her neck tingle.

Jeez. Not good looking. Try drop-dead gorgeous.

Before she could get a second glimpse, he'd turned away and pulled down the brim of his baseball cap.

She stayed seated and made an effort to control the tingle that was rapidly spreading from her neck to her cheeks, but continued to eye Dustin curiously.

Nan stood, blocking her view as she helped the still groaning Charlie to his feet, and then leaned down to hug Vere. "You two always make me smile," Nan said, before she turned to address her nephew. "Vere and Charlie will kick this unmaking plan into gear. They'll also be great friends for you."

"Really. Well, then. It's nice to meet you all, I suppose," he said, crossing his arms in front of him and ducking even lower into his cap.

Vere went on alert.

His voice had been super-soft. Low. He'd spoken like he was way older than they were. But that wasn't what had caused Vere to pause. It was because he'd also sounded bored and possibly sarcastic.

Is he...sort of pissed off?

She peered around Nan, hoping for another sneak peek at the guy's face, but he was still slouched, arms crossed, hiding in his hat. He didn't look pissed off. She got the odd sensation the kid wanted to curl up into a ball and hide?

What the heck?

"Not to raise a flag too early here, Aunt Nan, but these two just might need their own unmaking. Or, makeover. Look at them." He flicked a glance at Vere. "They don't seem capable of helping me."

Vere shot her mom a *what-does-that-mean* look, but her mom wasn't paying Vere any attention. Instead, she was signaling Nan with some type of strange sign language, and they both looked beyond nervous.

Something's up. Major.

Charlie wandered over to the kid using his *man-to-man* challenge swagger. Vere figured her brother hadn't liked the kid's last comment or the tone of his voice, either.

"I *suppose* it's nice to meet you, too," Charlie said, layering on his own sarcastic tone.

The kid stood and shook Charlie's offered hand. He'd moved with smooth, athletic grace and looked to be about two inches taller than Charlie's six feet.

"We have a few things to tell you," Vere's mom jumped in.

"You mean they don't *know*? They have no clue? I was told they were fully ramped in," Dustin said. He'd backed away from Charlie. She thought she'd seen a fleeting glimpse of panic cross his features before he'd shuttered his eyes.

Charlie followed him, not giving the guy an inch.

Dustin went on, "This is ridiculous. Aunt Nan, Mrs. Roth, no offense, but I don't want to do this. Not with—*them*—not at all."

"You have no choice," Nan said, giving him some sort of

secret look.

"In on what?" Vere scowled. "Do what?"

"Yeah. What?" Charlie stepped closer and Dustin grimaced and turned his face to the side.

Dustin might be tall and gorgeous—and the nephew of a woman the whole family loved—but this kid was now acting like a definite weirdo. She was about to address the fact that he might also be an ass, but her brother didn't give her a chance.

He let out a low whistle followed with: *"OH. MY. GOD! YOU'RE—YOU'RE—YOU'RE—OH-NO-SHIT!! DUDE! HOLY CRAP! DUUUUDE."*

Charlie then launched into a stream of screeching, unintelligible babbling and random cursing.

Vere could only stare as she watched Charlie jump up and down like a squawking chicken in front of Nan's nephew.

He ended with: "Holy crap. Holy crap! *Dude. Dude. DUDE! OHMYGOD DUUDE. I'M DYING HERE. WHAT-THE-FAAK-IS-GOING-ON?"*

Vere's chin hit the floor.

She rocketed Charlie a questioning glance, before looking at Dustin to gauge his reaction to her brother's freak-out. But Dustin seemed to have no reaction at all.

None! Zero.

He simply stood there straight-faced. Looking at Charlie as if he were some annoying, screeching insect.

"I'm just *wow*. WOW. This is so damn cool. HOLY SHIT."

"Charlie. Watch your mouth!" Mom yelled finally.

"Let us explain," Nan added.

Vere turned back to stare at Dustin.

His ultra-bright blue gaze had burned toward her as though he waited for her to do something off the wall as well.

It was then she saw the expression cross his face again.

Yep. Absolute panic!

What is wrong with this kid?

"Oh. My. God." Charlie started up again. "OH. My. GOD!"

What is wrong with my idiot brother?

"This is the absolute coolest thing ever! *No. Shit! No. Shiiiiit!* Dude! So amazing!"

Dustin took off his cap and ran his hand through his hair. Nice, thick, wavy hair. His mask dropped again and she caught his shoulders slumping a little. He looked almost deflated— and somewhat sad?

Vere darted a glance at Nan. She looked sad too.

And her Mom looked as if she might faint!

Poor Dustin McHugh.

Poor Mom and Nan.

They must think the worst.

She and Charlie had been so rude: arguing, yelling, wrestling, and now Charlie's lost it to the point of cussing in front of strangers and old ladies. Vere had to fix it before they both got busted. She was not going to lose car privileges the first week of school. Even if this *Dustin McHugh* might be some sort of a sad, strange—*jerk.*

Time to re-start the politeness.

Vere checked her bun and forced herself to walk over to Dustin. A major flush put heat on her face.

So what? It's not as if I can change the color of my cheeks. I'll just get this over with.

Her ear tips burned as she went for it. "It's nice to meet you, Dustin. I'll be happy to show you around our school. Whatever you need. I know we seem unreliable, but we're not. We can help you with anything. Or try. Honest." She added what she hoped was an encouraging nod.

Unfortunately, that move had the bun bobbing all over the place on top of her head. Hoping it would hold, she held out a shaky hand and slapped on her friendliest smile as she looked up at this Dustin McHugh's face.

Way up.

And choked on her own eyesight.

This guy is beyond, over-the-top, stunning! Like a live model. A model with no pores, and really long lashes, and a sexy, pouty-man-mouth, and broad shoulders with nice biceps. And he's really tan. And...and...the eyes...wow.

Seriously. Wow.

She swallowed.

Whatever! He's abnormal.

If she weren't biting on her top lip to keep the blush under control, her jaw would have gaped open wide as she took in his perfectly square chin.

Cheekbones and muscles and...are boys allowed to be this beautiful?

Her hand wobbled in front of him like it had turned into a rubber chicken.

His eyes scanned her bun, then her face, before he stepped away as though she'd burned him. That same flash of panic shot through his gaze before he cringed and took a step back.

Ugh. Ugh. Ugh. He totally cringed. He did!

Vere shoved her hand behind her. She wanted to die. If she had any remaining doubts that she wasn't complete boy poison, they'd all just been instantly erased by this guy's response to her.

I repel all guys. Now I have proof. PROOF.

Wait till Jenna hears. Maybe I need a different deodorant?

She ran her tongue over her teeth.

Or toothpaste?

"Vere—you dork!" Charlie dissolved into fits of laughter. "She's clueless. She has no idea who you are!"

"What do you mean? Have I met you before? I don't think so." She scowled at Dustin, then Charlie.

"Charlie. Take it easy," Nan said.

Vere's afternoon headache returned full force.

She'd thought the day couldn't get worse. At least Nan's

nephew had evened out the rude points for their mom by blatantly not shaking her hand in front of everyone. And one better, *Mr. Pretty* had managed to make her too angry to blush. Her red-hot cheeks, neck, and ears faded back to fine.

Because I'm not bothered one bit by handsome, rude boys.

"Seriously, Mom, Nan, can you please explain?" Charlie asked.

Vere crossed her arms. "Yeah," she added, making sure she sounded cranky and annoyed, like her time was being wasted.

Because it was. I should be upstairs calling Jenna to tell her that Curtis talked to Charlie about me. I've got things to do!

She caught Dustin's gaze and glowered bullets into him, reminding herself again that she was not at all affected by his looks or hurt by what he did. If he pulled creepy elevator-eyes like Curtis had done this afternoon, she would not hold back the punches. Curtis could look all he wanted, but this guy did not have any staring rights.

Just try it buster. Go ahead. Try it.

She intensified her glare.

She stopped her bun from slipping, but refused to break his gaze. "You can quit staring at me any time," she hiss-whispered, tightening the band on hair.

"It's you—staring at me," he answered quietly, as though he totally understood exactly how beautiful he was.

"I am not! I don't stare at guys. What are you? *Crazy?*"

His dark, arched brows shot up as though she'd surprised him. "Truth? It's possible that I am."

"Well join the club and get in line." She rolled her eyes calling his bluff. "Our whole family is nuts, if you haven't figured that out already."

One side of his lip twisted up into a small smile. "You're still staring."

"You are," she sassed back.

Feeling like a fool and a liar, she stared harder.

It was a standoff now, and she was determined to win.

She scrunched her brows and added a frown.

He cracked a small smile.

"Hilarious! Vere, you really don't recognize him?" Charlie's voice, holding at ten decibels louder than normal, was getting really annoying. Charlie turned and hollered again. "Dude. You rock! I have all your tracks. Every single album complete!"

Tracks? Tracks? Albums?

"I'm glad to know you're a fan," the guy responded woodenly, sounding as though he were on some strange autopilot. His gaze never wavered from skeptical and held Vere's fast.

Vere tried to match Dustin's expression as a taunt, but that backfired. For some reason, her attempts to mock him had made him smile wider.

She tripled her glower. He tripled the smile.

"Vere." Charlie stepped between them, breaking the stare down. "He's Hunter Kennedy." Charlie chose to yell in her face this time. "The Hunter Kennedy. Lead singer of *GuardeRobe*. DUH! And he's in Monument, Colorado."

Gasping for breath Charlie flip-turned to Hunter and got way too close to the guy's face all over again. "Holy Crap! Hunter Kennedy! Dude, you're in our living room! Is the rest of the band here, too?" Charlie looked around the room his eyes darting in every corner. "This is impossible. Nan, how can you be Hunter Kennedy's aunt? Did we all *win* something? Is this for MTV? Where are the cameras hiding?"

Vere frowned and peered around Charlie as she tried to place the guy in front of her as the blond, clean-cut, boy-band singer she'd seen a few times on TV.

Charlie had owned a poster of *GuardeRobe* for a while now but she honestly didn't recognize *this kid* as the blond, guitar-holding, pimped out guy on Charlie's closet door.

When he'd had that panicked look earlier, it had made him seem so real, but Hunter Kennedy wasn't a real person. Was he?

Not in her world.

"This is not a TV show, Charlie." Nan shook her head. "I'm Hunter's *great* aunt. I don't tell people about him. Too many odd requests for favors," she added.

"He doesn't even look like Hunter Kennedy." Vere turned to back to him. "You don't, you know? Do you? Are you really *him?*"

"Apparently not anymore," he answered, sounding very cynical again. "You're only supposed to know me as Dustin McHugh. So it should be easy to forget the famous part about me right away. Because that's the goal here. Let's try again. Say it with me: Nice to meet you, *Dustin McHugh.*"

His sarcasm had returned full force.

"Okay." Vere crossed her arms and tried her best to copy his annoyed-looking mouth twist and ultra-low voice.

"Nice to meet *you, Dustin McHugh.* Happy?"

"Truth? Happier than I was a few minutes ago," he answered, smiling. "Because you've been cracking me up."

"Great." She rolled her eyes.

It was then Vere realized she'd been talking to this guy minus all her usual stuttering and general color-changing weirdness. Somehow she'd managed to keep her anxiety in check. But how? Because he'd made her angry? By imagining she was talking to the poster in Charlie's room?

Is it because having a rock star in my living room is so beyond all normal thought functions that I (or HE) broke my broken-ness!

She thought of a question, testing the situation and her reactions to him. "Why is it you're here and not with your band?"

"And why do you need us all to use a fake name?" Charlie added. "Is that why your hair is brown?"

"I'm—I need—" He broke Vere's gaze and looked at Nan. Nan nodded. "Tell them."

He crossed to the other side of the room but kept his back

to them. The silence stretched as his hands moved lightly over the family photos lining the top of their upright piano. "I got into some trouble in Los Angeles. My mom thinks I need to be here...for a rest. She and my agent think I can't do that well if people and reporters are swarming me as Hunter Kennedy."

He pulled in a very long breath and turned back to face them all. The look in his eyes seemed so bleak it made her heart clench. Vere sensed he wasn't lying, but he also seemed to be hiding some of the truth.

Hunter went on, "They decided I could hang in Colorado best if I could be sort of—*unmade*. You know, completely disguised? Aunt Nan can't coordinate the home-schooling and tutoring I'd need, so I'll be attending your high school until they let me come home. Which should be soon, I think."

His eyes caught hers before he rapidly looked away. This time, Vere was sure she'd seen a glimpse of pure desolation flicker behind the depths of his gaze. Despite his size, his fame and his beautiful face, he seemed somehow vulnerable.

When he looked back again, the sadness she'd seen was hidden behind another one of his sarcastic lip twists.

"So, yeah." He said, resuming his bored and annoyed tone. "You two are also supposed to drive me around and hang out with me so I blend in better."

"You've offered us to do what?!" Charlie interrupted. "Damm, Mom! It's cool to meet this guy and all, but we've got real lives to live here and—"

Mom took Charlie's arm into her death-grip. "No. Stop. Not one more word out of your potty-mouth, young man. You have pushed me to my limit!" She and Nan dragged him out into the hall. "Hunter, Vere, we will be right back."

Charlie was going down. Way down.

9: gnomes and tumbleweeds

HUNTER

"You're staring again," she said finally, but this time her voice seemed forced. Tight, as though she suddenly had to struggle to speak to him now that they were alone together.

Worse, she was dead on.

He had been staring. Mostly at her lips. He liked the way she chewed the pouty upper one once in awhile.

"Fine. I'll own it. You caught me. Sorry," Hunter said, but kept staring, despite her obvious discomfort.

Hell.

He couldn't *stop* staring at this girl. Not since she'd entered the room spinning around on her brother's back. Right now, it would be impossible for him to look away because his words had caused her to blush again.

Up close, the effect turned her lightly freckled, apple-round cheeks—not to mention practically every inch of her skin—a fascinating pink. It had also made her large, dark brown eyes seem deeper, luminous.

Girl was cute with that pink face.

"Would you stop?" She shifted her feet.

He went for honesty again. "I'll try but your cheeks! Makes you look like a little gnome."

"Original."

She was glaring again so he squelched the temptation to reach out and run a finger tip over her cheekbone to test the level of heat hiding behind all of that red and the few freckles.

So...cute.

He crossed his arms, pondering the fact that he'd never been glared down by a girl before. Not counting his mom, of course, but this girl was obviously way more charming than his mom.

He couldn't resist teasing her again. "It's that—*you*—are just so interesting to watch."

He choked back a laugh when she turned even redder.

Her eyes positively snapped with that one.

"Back at you, *boy-band-freak*. You're the one who came from another planet, not me. But don't wait for me to swoon at your feet. If this is your attempt at flirting, you won't make much progress with the girls around here."

"Ooh. Claws," he teased again, laughing.

Instead of the added pink effect Hunter had been hoping for, the color went the other way. The blushing thing seemed to fade in and out.

Out—when annoyed.

In—every other second.

Funny.

Mrs. Roth and Nan marched back in with Charlie.

"Hunter—er—*Dustin*, we have the driving thing settled. Consider these two your willing chauffeurs."

A direct order, not a statement.

Hunter threw Charlie an apologetic glance. The guy's tight expression tagged him as beyond unwilling to participate in any of his *unmaking* crap. Hunter got that it might be awkward for Charlie at school. To have a new guy hanging around 24-7 during senior year was a lot to ask. Mrs. Roth must have threatened something huge to make him comply with such a straight face.

Hunter could relate. Moms were a force few could beat.

"Once they get over the shock of this, they will also *act normally*." Mrs. Roth was obviously threatening him still.

"Fine. Hunter. I'm sorry." Charlie turned to Hunter with a half-eye roll Mrs. Roth could not see. "I acted like a jerk. But don't wait around expecting my little sister to act normal, ever."

Hunter smiled down at the still glaring Vere. "Normal is boring, on my planet." He moved his attention back to

Charlie. "And the name is *Dustin McHugh*. Please. How about you and I start over? I'm sorry if I came off as—"

"An *ass?*" Charlie finished for him, crossing his arms.

"Charlie Owen Roth, if you utter one more curse word, or say one more rude thing to poor Hunter—*Dustin*—" Mrs. Roth had turned as red as her daughter.

"It's okay, Mrs. Roth. I was a complete tool when I met him. And I am sorry, too. I've been really tired and planning this last minute move to Colorado has been a bit much. You can imagine this day is not up there on my top ten list."

"And you did scream in his face, Charlie," Vere said. "Tons."

Hunter bit his own lip. Was the gnome girl defending him? "We can figure out a way I can be low-impact on both of your lives. I won't try to hang around with you if it's not easy or natural, okay? I'll happily be a loner."

Charlie seemed to relax. "Appreciated. I apologize again. I did kind of go from screaming at you to dropping the ball on your situation. So, without screaming in your face, *Dustin*—it's nice to meet you again. For real. Or...whatever." Charlie flushed and shoved his hands in his pockets.

The kid was jumpy as hell—reminded him of Martin.

To Hunter, jumpy meant difficult to trust.

Hunter nodded. "Thanks...we're cool. You're not the first fanboy to lose it like that on me. I've had much worse."

"You have?" Vere asked, widening her already too big eyes.

"You don't even want to know. Let's not talk about that stuff. Stories about the person I'm not supposed to be anymore will throw off our focus. I only want you to think of me as just another kid, like you. If that's possible." Hunter sighed. "And Nan is probably right, I'm sure I can't do this without you."

"I don't know. Dude. I don't know." Charlie shook his head, his expression still not convinced.

"Mom, why didn't you tell us about all this—*him*—sooner?" Vere asked, her expression also holding at skeptical.

"His identity has to remain a secret. Nan and I have known for a month. I didn't want to tell you too early in case one of you slipped."

"Well, the too-late option bites," Charlie muttered under his breath. "This is no small assignment to pull off in one long weekend."

Mrs. Roth rewarded Charlie with another *hell-to-pay* glance. His Aunt Nan walked over and took Charlie's hand. "Please, Charlie. We need your help."

Charlie shifted uncomfortably. "I know. I'm in...if it will work, and even if it won't, I'll try." He parried his mom's look. "Mostly because I don't want to be killed."

Hunter's attention was distracted again by Vere. Her right hand floated up in the graceful, unconscious gesture she used to check her *Mad Hatter* bun. A gesture Hunter had already grown used to. It was a movement the girl executed like clockwork every five minutes.

"We will both try...but *what* can we do with him..?" She trailed off, pulling her delicate brows together, frowning as she examined him from head to toe for another long moment. "How tall are you?" she asked, her gaze stopping at Hunter's eyes.

"Six three." He bit back a laugh at Vere's new, all-business tone.

"What year—or age?" Charlie added.

"Seventeen."

Mrs. Roth came over to examine him as well. "But he's to be in with the junior class, even though he's the same age as you are, Charlie. His mom thought a grade swap would also help hide him." Mrs. Roth patted Hunter's arm like he was some sort of pet. "You'll be in all senior-level courses, though so you won't have to worry about being bored."

Hunter held back a groan, tracking Vere's expressive, darting eyes as they'd moved around his face again. He could tell that she'd noticed his unhappy reaction to his demotion.

Vere shook her head. "You want us to hide this six-foot-three, positively gorgeous, famous rock star—one who has sports-drink-blue eyes BY THE WAY—and who is absolutely PERFECT looking, at Palmer Divide High? In this town? In *my* junior class?"

"Yes," Mrs. Roth answered. "Why is it such a difficult concept for you and Charlie to grasp?"

"Because guys who look like *that*." She pointed a finger at him. "Do not come from this town. In addition to the face, he's too tall, and he's got the posture of some Russian ballerina! And did you *not* notice his voice?"

"What's wrong with my voice?" Hunter frowned.

"It's all, *extra low.*" She modulated her voice down, trying to sound like him. "And, *super-manly-amazing.*"

Charlie cracked up and Hunter had to bury his own laugh.

Vere frowned at her brother. "Nobody sounds like that! Mom, Aunt Nan, it won't work. No way is he ever, ever, ever going to blend in. And his...you know...his shoulders are all wide and he's all tan and looks Superman strong...and..."

"Anything else? Should I turn around?" Hunter intensified his smile, hoping for another blush, but instead drew a glare from Charlie.

Vere threw up her arms. "And he's a compliment fishing egomaniac to boot! "

Hunter laughed. "Wow. I am not. Swear." He laughed again.

Vere shot him a look that said she did not believe him while she re-tightened that rubber band holding her giant bun together again.

He laughed one more time, unable to stop himself.

Damn, but she's hilarious.

This entire ludicrous situation had gone way beyond insane. And Vere Roth's odd antics were the frosting on his whacked-out cake.

Hunter had never really hung out with a girl near to his own age who hadn't been acquainted with his music. Or one who was at least obsessed/impressed with him to the point of gushing over his star status. After eleven years in the public eye, he'd just taken it for granted that every teen just sort of knew who he was.

Vere was on a whole new level. She hadn't even recognized him at first. He wondered if she'd ever listened to *GuardeRobe's* music at all. Hell, five minutes ago she'd actually acted as though she might not even want to stay in the same room with him. Now she was sitting here, calling him hot and conceited in the same sentence.

Total entertaining novelty!

Charlie spoke up next. "Vere's right. This is impossible. Just look at him. He'll be an attention magnet."

"It is not impossible." Mrs. Roth's voice was tight. "We have four days to figure it out. I want you to come up with a real disguise. You two will take him shopping right now to buy some things that will hide him better. We can teach him how to speak differently, mumble maybe? And Hunter?" She frowned. "Do you think you can learn to slouch? Vere's right about the posture thing. You do stand out."

"I'll try my best." Hunter shrugged.

Mrs. Roth continued, "I thought he could get away with borrowing Charlie's clothes, but now I see that won't work. He needs something less mainstream. Something—probably a lot of things—that will make him much less attractive. Take him to a store somewhere, but NOT one at the mall."

"I can't be in on any shopping." Charlie backed away. "Curtis is on his way. You can't expect me to get kicked off the team for this project. If I miss, I get benched. *Dude*, I'll help you with the slouching or whatever later. We'll meet up at the cabin. Deal?"

"I'd take you," Aunt Nan said. "But my arthritis won't let me walk much. Besides, I'd have no idea what to pick out so I'd slow you down. I'll just gather our things and meet you up at the cabin as well?"

Hunter shrugged, suddenly wishing he could run away and sleep for a year. All this forced politeness was exhausting him. *They* didn't want to do this as much *he* didn't want to do this. "I'm sorry I'm so much trouble," he said feeling beyond lame.

Mrs. Roth's expression wavered. "Vere? Do you think you can take him alone?"

"Uh..."

Hunter watched as all of the color drained from Vere's face as Mrs. Roth went on, "I'm going to need to get some things ready to bring up to the cabin as well. You will know what he needs to blend in at school way better than I would."

"You mean *un-blend-in*," Hunter reminded them. "I'm hoping to be some kind of invisible?"

"Yes. Right. Vere has good instincts for acting and costumes. All that stage stuff she does at school is going to have to come in to play here so...she is the best one to help you."

Vere's face had gone from pale, to registering shock, then a hint of bug-eyed fear crossed her wide brown eyes before she met his gaze and turned completely pink and awkward again.

"Vere? Honey? What do you think?" Mrs. Roth said.

Vere didn't answer.

It was like she *couldn't* answer.

"Mom. Vere can't just go and—take a strange guy shopping!" Charlie paced over to the window, obviously trying to cover for Vere's lapse.

Hunter was struck again by the bond that seemed to exist between the two siblings. He also liked how they seemed to love and respect their mom. From the photos he'd seen lined up on the piano, it appeared they were the perfect, made-for-TV, family of four. The kind his network, *NewtNet*, always featured in shows. He could only imagine their dad as some sort of ultra-chipper, lawn-mowing, barbeque-tending, friendly-guy stereotype.

Who knew families like this really existed? Bizarre.

Mrs. Roth looked as though she might kill Charlie again. "He is not a strange guy. He is Nan's nephew. We've introduced you, and *my goodness*, we've known Nan so long this boy might as well be your *cousin.*"

"No way! Seriously. He's a complete stranger. And he could be some sort of girl-playing creeper!" Charlie crossed his arms. "And we don't need any more cousins!"

Really? Well I don't want any damn cousins either!

The shouting escalated, and Hunter's head was about to implode. As much as he found Vere *interesting*, it was time to set the record straight.

Hunter held up his hands high in surrender. "Okay. STOP. Hold up! Everyone just *chill!*"

They all stopped arguing and looked at him.

"Look. This whole conversation is ridiculous. No offense intended here." He tossed Vere a shrug before he continued in a more controlled voice, "I'm used to girls who are...well... more...um. Let's just say stick-legged, milk-fed tumbleweeds aren't my type. They aren't even on my radar. I'm not desperate, *Jesus!*"

Charlie laughed, and Hunter felt bad for that comment because it caused Vere to flush red again. Her mouth had also dropped open in what appeared to be shock.

"Whaaat? I ought to—oh-no-you-did-not and, *really?* "

What was her deal? The girl must be whacked.

Maybe as whacked as I am.

Hunter couldn't take his eyes off of Vere's flushed face all over again, trying to figure her out. She might not make sense, but he could tell she was pissed off at him, that was certain.

Charlie piped in with a quiet laugh, "I can only imagine what kind of girls you're used to. Vere would knock you flat if you tried to make a move on her. She's famous for that."

Vere seemed to choke. Then sputter. "Charlie—you—suck. Just—don't *EVEN* go there. Just stop. Stop. Wait."

They all fell silent.

Vere finally seemed to reagin some control and held up her own hands in front of her, all while aiming a small, ball-of-death-glower onto everyone in the room. "No. Offense. Back. But I can take care of myself. I can certainly drag this spoiled, *rock-and-roll-prince* shopping for ugly clothes and drive him to the lake cabin without getting mauled or pregnant!"

Mrs. Roth gasped.

Hunter bit back another huge laugh.

Double entertainment.

Vere turned to Hunter and wrinkled her mouth in another one of her charming attempts at a mean scowl. She was breathing all funny. Puffing air in and out like she'd just run really far.

"You should be so lucky, *Mr. Model-Magazine-Cover*, to even catch my eye. You aren't my type, either! I'm used to guys who don't require so much attention and personal—grooming. You are the last guy on earth I'd ever go for. I'm not desperate or into pretty boys, either. So—yeah!"

Hunter's gaze tangled with Vere's. He had the feeling she couldn't look away from him as much as he couldn't stop staring at her expressive face.

She seemed to lose it again as she tried to go on, "And, and—I wouldn't look twice at you at—your—well—your— *you know*—all of your—*YOU*. And all that—"

He inturrupted to save her. "Okay. Okay. You win! Touché again. I'm glad that's understood. If we're meant to be hanging out together it will help the situation to note to all involved: *we are not each other's types.*"

"Good. Great. Let the record show. Not at all. And never. So let's stop all this wierdness," Vere added, rolling her eyes.

"That goes for you too, Charlie," Hunter teased. "We'll all agree to be *just friends*, with zero weirdness. Okay?"

Charlie snorted. "Sure. I just became insta-friends with one of the world's most famous rock stars. ZERO weirdness from this point forward. Check" He shook his head. "And, you're not my type either, dude."

They all cracked up at that. Vere's temper seemed to wane as quickly as it had come.

Hunter crossed his arms tightly against his chest. He forced himself to stop staring at how Vere's eyes crinkled at the edges when she laughed. Demanded his brain to stop noticing that he might really like the sound of that laugh...

He turned away from her and pretended to examine the details of the living room while an odd barrage of misplaced butterflies ripped around his stomach like someone had shuffled cards in there. Everything in the room melted to a blur.

He never got butterflies—just like he never looked twice at girls like Vere.

Hell. But I've looked at her way more than twice...

And hell again... Butterflies?

Probably just nerves. Nothing but that.

If he could place a bet, he'd put two hundred toward the side that said Vere Roth had probably never even been kissed. His head started to pound because that thought had him thinking about how she bit her lip.

She called me a pretty boy! Girl doesn't even know me, but thinks she does. Shit. I swear I'm dizzy. This has to be some of that high-altitude sickness Aunt Nan warned me about.

He turned back and studied the light dusting of copper freckles on the bridge of Vere's nose, trying to analyze what drew his attention so strongly to her. Even with the soft smudges of eyeshadow and mascara she sported, she looked much younger compared to the girls he'd known.

Maybe he was simply fascinated because Vere's entire look mimicked a long legged, big eyed, bobble-head doll who was hiding in a giant hoodie?

Yeah. And, who wouldn't stare at that? She's like a mini-circus. No need to freak out that you find a person highly amusing and slightly cute.

Not my type. Not in a million years. But very appealing to watch. No crime in that, right?

As if to confirm his thoughts, she adjusted her incredible bun and hiked up her baggy shorts all over again. It was all he could do not to bust out grinning like a fool.

At least holding back laughter had lightened the weight in his heart. It was also a bonus to think that Vere, plus her wound-too-tight brother, would ensure his time here wasn't going to be boring.

"The guys are going to be here soon. Let's hear where you're taking him, Vere. I've got to change for practice."

"He's right. We don't have a lot of time. What's your plan?" Mrs. Roth added.

Vere had slapped on the comical *down-to-business* persona again. "I want to take him to Dad's office first. I think he can jump start the disguise."

"I'd already thought of that, too." Mrs. Roth nodded. "Go there first. Dad's working through some ideas already."

Hunter let the noise and the impossible conversation in the room fade out as he grabbed his backpack and pulled out his phone. The battery marker read full.

He'd set it to vibrate, but so far, nothing had been texted.

No emails either. He figured there wouldn't be any phone calls from the guys. Not yet, anyhow. They probably were just getting settled at some rented house or taking over a hotel floor in New York. That always took time...

Vere walked forward, her expression guarded.

"Oh, do I have some good ideas. Promise you'll let me choose the overall theme of your make-over? No arguments."

He pocketed his phone and tried to concentrate on anything but the stupid butterflies that would leave his stomach. "You have a *theme*?" he managed, wondering if he was really going to let this disaster virgin pick his outfits and drive him around?

"Yes. But you'll have to trust me." She crossed her arms, waiting.

He didn't trust her, but he gave her the answer he thought she'd want. Mostly because he hoped it would bring on the eye-crinkling smile again. "Okay. I trust you."

It worked. Vere's smile matched the look in her eyes.

Open, happy and *nothing else*.

Meaning, it was cool how she didn't seem to *want*, or expect, anything out of him at all.

I'll let Vere Roth drive me straight into hell if she keeps smiling at me like this.

He smiled back. He couldn't help himself.

It was like her happiness—her irrepressibility—was rubbing off on him. Not like he was going to start skipping around or anything like she seemed to do, but he realized he felt calm around her. At the very least, safe.

That feeling felt different enough to make him hope this whole experience might not crush him. It also made him wonder if he *should* try to trust her. If the possibility of being friends—and nothing else—with someone his own age could be a reality.

He'd give it—give *her*—a chance. Maybe.

Plus, he didn't want to think of how to disguise himself alone. There was no reason to fight any of this. He'd just roll with everything. See what came next. Like Barry had suggested he do.

One hour at a time.

"Why do we have to go see your dad? Does he own a clothing store?" he asked finally, trying to grasp one shred of the conversation flying over his spinning, Vere Roth filled head.

"Well, like I said…" She stepped forward.

He had to lock his knees so he wouldn't pull away. Any possibility of him concentrating shredded to bits when he caught some of how she smelled.

Flowers or lavender…or sage? Or hell, I have no damn clue.

Smells amazing. Like her own brand of friendly-happiness… whatever it is…whatever she is…

Everyone seemed to be talking at once. Hunter gave up trying and breathed in the air around Vere, zoning out on her completely with his relaxed meet-and-greet-smile and mask secured on his face.

Vere chattered away with Charlie, Nan and her mom. Hunter's eyes had locked onto the curve of her upper lip again. She chewed lightly on it every time she paused in her speech to listen while analyzing him at the same time.

She must be worried when she does that.

Is she worried about me?!

His chest tightened at the thought.

She doesn't even know me…and from what I can tell, no one here is being paid. Could they all really be this nice? Simply help a guy they've never met?

She stopped talking again and blinked expectantly up at him, still chewing on that damn lip.

Hunter shot a glance around the room. Everyone seemed to be waiting for him to answer. He crossed his arms and hid his clenched fists under his arms, forcing himself back into the conversation.

"Great, sounds like a good plan." He blinked, adding in a convincing smile. "I'll do whatever you recommend."

When they all just stared at him as though they were surprised by his too jovial response, he concentrated on what he knew he was supposed to do next. Go shopping with Vere, then, meet everyone up at the cabin later.

"And thanks, everyone. For being so cool. Mrs. Roth, I'm really looking forward to seeing this lake cabin and hanging in the mountains. I think I could use a few days of true hiding out. Whatever happens, it's very kind of you to host me," he added, using his most polite voice.

They all still just blinked at him, like he'd eaten the family dog or something.

Do these people even have a family dog?

They probably do. A really cute and perfect Golden Retriever or something.

He shrugged helplessly. "What? Let's get started. Where's the car?"

That worked.

Everyone moved at once.

10: lying to jenna

VERE

Vere headed to her room to gather enough stuff for the long weekend. She dialed Jenna on her cell as she ran up the stairs.

"OMG! What's the PROJECT?" Jenna yelled as soon as the call connected. She never answered with a simple, *hello*. "Have you recovered from your day?"

Vere chose to ignore the second question because there was no recovering from this day. Not with Charlie swearing Curtis Wishford had asked about her on the *crush* level! And not with a famous rock star waiting for her downstairs somewhere.

This day had exploded all normal realities.

"The project is not an exchange student. Not at all. It's worse. It's uh...Nan's nephew. Moved in with her."

"Nan has a nephew?"

"He starts school with us Tuesday. I mentioned him to you, I think? Do you remember?" Vere rolled her eyes at herself in the bathroom mirror.

Let the lies begin.

"You did?" Jenna sighed, sounding miffed. "What's he like?"

Oh, sort of exactly like Hunter Kennedy?!!

Vere bit back a giggle, shoving her toothbrush into her weekend bag and answered, "I don't know yet. You know how it is. Hard to break the ice at first. Awkward mostly."

At least some of what she'd said wasn't a complete lie. Vere's heart sped up and then clenched and twisted with guilt.

Best friends tell best friends when famous rock stars moved in next door, don't they?

GuardeRobe was one of Jenna's many rock-band-religions.

She probably followed Hunter Kennedy on Twitter! Half of her Tumblr blog was devoted to the guy.

If Jenna ever found out Vere had kept this information from her, she'd make Charlie's reaction to Hunter Kennedy seem puny and quiet.

She'd also murder me. Never speak to me again. EVER.
Which would be easy, because I'd be dead from the part where she'd murdered me.

"Did you work on your mom to relent and let me drive up to the cabin? At least for Sunday night?" Jenna whined. "It's such a long weekend."

"No. You're banned. Mom's convinced that Charlie and I are going to be this guy's new besties. That's the project. She wants us to bond with him minus any other *friend* distractions. She says you and I would disappear and ignore him. Probably true."

"Gah. Bummer. And you? Bonding with a guy? Has your mom forgotten exactly who you are? Is the guy hot at least? What's his name?"

"Dustin. Dustin McHugh."

"He sounds hot. Scottish last name hot." Jenna's tone had turned hopeful.

Vere laughed. "Yeah. About that. You'll have to see him for yourself. He's not...your type. And he's *sure* not my type." She snorted, not needing to fake the annoyance in her tone, remembering how he'd called her a gnome-stick-tumbleweed-girl. "He's more of a—"

"He's ugly. Admit it."

"Not ugly—just—different. Kind of tall. Seemed nice once we broke through the stiff introductions. Charlie's not into it though. He and Mom got in a fight about Dustin's presence screwing up *Charlie's precious senior year.*"

"Gah. Guy must be hideous if your brother had to battle."

Vere sidestepped the lies again. "However he looks, I think it will be good for me to try to make friends with him. You know, to have a guy best friend."

"Are you serious?"

"Yeah. It might help me get over my problem. And we could use him like some kind of bodyguard. Um...he'd be good for that."

Jenna sighed, "What would a bodyguard do for us? Battle our invisible boyfriends?"

Vere laughed. "Heck-yes. Invisible boyfriends can get really out of hand."

"Hmm." Vere could hear the pout in Jenna's tone. "As if you need friends other than ME. You're lucky I'm not feeling jealous. I can tell from the sound of your voice that you're serious about his potential—and that he's a total, hideous, geek whom you will probably never love more than you love me."

"Hey. That's not nice. You haven't even met him."

"Fine. But I reserve the right to veto this new friend. We have enough problems trying to be cool without you adopting a social charity case into our lives. Your parents and Nan can't expect us to hang out with him all the time, can they?"

"Yes. They expect us to hang with him. Hopefully he will be half-cool because I'm not going to hurt Nan's feelings, or his. Nan says he's here for the year, but Dustin hinted it might only be for a few weeks. I'm not sure of his exact deal, but I'll find out."

"Ugh. You do that. And tell your mom she sucks for not letting me go."

"I'm sorry." Vere was surprised how quickly Jenna had bought into the idea of Dustin McHugh, the possible freak. Maybe everyone else would do the same.

She yanked a small duffel out of the hall closet, grabbed her swimsuit off the bathroom rack, added some other favorite hoodies, and shoved the whole pile into the bag. "What will you do without me?"

"I'm going to sit here alone, eating ice-cream, Jello, cookies and stealing my little brother's stash of Skittles and reblog depressing junk and beautiful cupcake photos on Tumblr until you come back. Tell your mom that, would you? If I become a depressed diabetic this weekend, it's her fault."

Vere planted one last line on Jenna: "Just don't call and text everyone, telling them that Dustin McHugh is an ugly loser. Give him a chance. Not everyone can be all...*normal*...you know?"

"Pffft. NOT making me feel any better about him."

Vere smiled and went on, "*I'm* trying to have an open mind. However he looks, I can tell being friends with this guy will take us way out of our comfort zones. Remember how we always talk about doing that?"

"Oh God. Now, you're scaring the shit out of me. I'm not hanging out with him. This is not happening to us. Do not make him any promises."

Vere bit her lip to stop a giggle. Jenna had epic gossip-networking skills. Her fearful anticipation of *Dustin* plus her over active imagination will send her best friend all over Facebook and into *text-landia* with red-flag chatter that will spread like a grass fire.

On the way down the stairs, Vere added a bit more, "Remember. It's what's *INSIDE* a person that counts. The heart?"

"Not in our high school." Jenna sighed. "Tell Charlie he sucks, and not to miss me," she added.

"As always. I'm sure Charlie will be heartbroken to not see you all weekend long," she said extra loud so her brother, who was in the back hall getting his football gear together, would hear.

"What?" He frowned, taking the bait.

"Jenna says, '*Hi,*' and, '*Don't miss her too much*'."

Charlie raised his upper lip in a disgusted sneer. "Tell that girl they still have a few spots at the special high school for creepers, and that she should go there and stop stalking me."

"I heard that!" Jenna giggled, completely not offended. "Your brother so wants to date me."

Charlie paused. "What did she say?"

"Something about how you know you want her bad."

Charlie answered with a round of loud, dramatic dry heaving.

Jenna, hearing him, laughed louder. "He's such an ass. I'm going to die without you, Vere. Text me when you make it back to town."

"I promise."

Charlie threw his sports duffel onto the kitchen table. "Call the freak back later," he said.

"Did he call me a FREAK?" Vere held the phone away from her ear so Charlie could hear Jenna. "I heard that, you EGG-HEAD-UGLY-JOCK!"

He paused to roll his eyes while shooting Vere a hilarious, co-conspirator eyebrow wiggle. He covered the speakers on Vere's phone and spoke in a really quiet voice, "Dustin has been in the car, waiting this whole time. If he messes with you, say the word and he's dead. *Okay?* I don't care if he's famous. I will trash him."

"Shut up. And shut up!" Vere pulled her phone out of his hand, shaking her head at Charlie's endless, overprotective impulses.

"Are you telling me to SHUT UP?" Jenna's voice squeaked through.

Vere turned back to her phone. "No. Not you. Charlie. Gotta go. Call you when I can. Promise." She glanced at the waiting Charlie and couldn't resist. "Oh, and Charlie says, *bye beautiful.*"

She hung up fast before Jenna could hear Charlie yell, "I DID NOT SAY THAT. I said, *BYE FREAK,* that's what I said!"

11: my new bestie

Vere made it to the garage and flung her bag into the back seat of the white VW Bug she and Charlie shared.

Dustin McHugh was there, sitting ramrod straight. As she got in, she noticed the guy was so large that he seemed to fill every extra inch of space inside the car.

"Hope I didn't take too long." She smiled. "Can you try to slouch or something? I don't want anyone to get a good look at you until you're ready, or fixed, or..."

"*Unmade.* That's the official term."

"Yeah. Unmade." Her confidence had wavered at first but his dark tone had also made her sad for him again. She tried to cheer him up. "I'm sure this is going to be all kinds of fun. Why do you look so terrified?"

"Maybe because you appear to be too excited about frosting the cake that marks the end of my life?"

She fiddled with her braided key chain hanging out of the ignition, but didn't start the car. "Oh. Is that what this is? I'm sorry. I just love doing costumes, that's all. I guess I didn't think about what it all means to you..."

He sighed. "Maybe I'm simply afraid of you. Are you sure you're old enough to drive?"

"Ha. Ha. Now let's see if you can slouch."

Dustin tried to slide down, but his knees bumped into the glove box. He met her gaze. "I think you're faking that you're happy to do this. Are you?"

"What?" Her cheeks flamed, and she looked away.

"I saw you choke when your mom asked you to shop with me."

Ugh. Figures.

How could she explain her brother's earlier comments—and her freeze-up without sounding like a total mental case? She tried the truth. "That wasn't about you, personally. It's...I don't hang out much alone. I mean—I don't often hang out with guys—alone. They usually make me...uh..."

Panic, turn bright red, feel dizzy, want to vomit, stutter, stop breathing, drop things, die from the inside out, and let's not forget head-butt the people I truly love until they require hospitalization.

"Nervous," she finished. "I'm...shy...or whatever. Sometimes I choke. That's what you saw."

He nodded as though he'd already made his own pile of assumptions about her. "You seem to be relatively fine hanging with me now. Do I make you more nervous than most guys?"

"No. Less, actually." She shot him smirk.

He laughed, appearing to relax a little. "Damn, girl. That's a first. What the hell? Why?"

"I think it's because, in my mind, I've decided to believe forever that you aren't a real guy."

He raised his eyebrows.

She grinned wider and went on, "Not really real, anyhow. Not to me. If that's not hurtful to you. I know, of course, you're a *person* and all that. But to me, I'm determined to think you're a *fake guy*. Dustin McHugh, normal kid. Like you said," she managed, feeling stupid now. "Does that make any sense at all?"

He laughed again, shifting in his seat. "Yeah. It's perfect, actually. I don't feel real. Not even to myself. Would you believe *they*—my mom and my agent—hired a stand-in for me? A guy to wander around and hang with the band while I'm here?"

She blinked and moved her hands over the bumps on the steering wheel. "Wow. That's weird."

He grimaced. "You should have seen him up close. My perfect twin. Totally weird."

"Almost as weird as you having to come here and disguise yourself so you can go to my high school?" she asked softly, her heart wrenching as she watched him work to mask his emotions.

"Ya think?" He shook his head, and let out a long breath of air.

Vere did the same, catching another round of darkness crossing though his clear gaze. This kid was supposed to be Charlie's age—only one year older than she was—but he suddenly seemed ancient in comparison. She let her hands drop from the steering wheel and turned toward him. "God. I'm so sorry—"

"Don't be. It's my fault. Things in my life got out of hand. No matter how much I don't want to be here, I think I need this rest. I do. For what it's worth, I'm not hating it as much as I thought I would."

She frowned, biting her upper lip, not sure what to say.

He went on, "I like your idea of pretending I'm not real. I'll try to do the same. I think it will make it easier for me to get through all this."

"You sure I didn't hurt your feelings?"

"Yes." He tugged at the sleeves of his hoodie and then crossed his arms over his seat belt. "Are you always this entertaining?"

"I'm not sure what you mean."

He laughed again.

"Are you laughing at me?"

He laughed more. "No. Not at all. You just—make me laugh. I honestly don't know why. I find myself wishing I could read your thoughts, though."

"Well I'm pretty glad you can't. And back at you, fake guy from the planet Los Angeles. I'm sure I'd love to read your thoughts, too."

He grimaced. "I'd hate that, actually."

"Yeah," she added. "Scary to think about, huh? Mind-reading." Vere pushed the button on the sun visor that opened the garage door. A telltale tingling moved up her spine as a blush threatened to take over. If the guy ever read her thoughts, he'd run fast and far away from her when he figured out what a total mess she was.

In the meantime, he was stuck with her.

Fake. Paper. Poster. Guy.

With fake, plastic blue eyes.

That seemed to work to calm down the blushing until she darted him another glance and her attention riveted on the very real pulse beating rapidly in the side of his neck.

Her breath caught.

Holy help.

You are sitting alone in a car with a living, breathing guy.

Living breathing HUNTER KENNEDY!

No. Living, breathing, fake guy. Dustin McHugh.

Don't blow it. You were doing well.

She let out a slow breath, and gripped the steering wheel. Closing her eyes to get her head together, she willed herself to find some control. As she pulled in a full breath she realized she there was a strange smell coming off him.

God. You're smelling a pretend guy.

HOLY COW, you're smelling Hunter Kennedy!

He's Dustin McHugh. Not a real guy.

Just a guy who's going to be your friend.

That's all. A friend.

"Please don't tell me you drive with your eyes closed," he drawled. "And, uh...to make this thing work, you've got to turn the key?"

She reacted instantly to the sarcasm in his low, rumbling voice and knew right there, she was going to be fine. She snapped open her eyes and wrinkled her nose.

"Right. Ha.Ha." She turned the key in the ignition. "And... do you smell like...chemicals?" she asked, looking for a way to tease him somehow, a way to stop her blushes from increasing.

He nodded. "Hair dye. A few hours ago I had blond hair." He uncrossed his arms and smoothed the waves of brown hair near the base of his neck. "I think it looks okay, though. Fits the new me, don't you think?"

"Oh. Sure. I like it. I do," she said lightly, pretending that his answer hadn't caused her heart to twist—hadn't sucked any and all teasing comments out of her lungs. Poor guy. She could only imagine the series of events that had led him to sitting in this car, counting on HER to help him.

Popping the car into reverse, she rolled it back out of the garage and almost fainted.

Curtis Wishford and that stupid Howie Rutheford were both leaning on the hood of Curtis's red truck wearing their practice uniforms and waiting for Charlie.

"Oh, no," she muttered before she could stop herself. Like an addict, Vere had to stretch up in her seat to try and catch a better view of Curtis. She couldn't get enough of him.

And holy cute on the new practice uniforms. Sigh.

Guys wearing shoulder pads, cleats and football pants worked for her. Her entire face flamed unchecked to a bright cherry red. She looked away, realizing that she'd allowed Dustin McHugh front row seats to her personal Curtis-longing-lifestyle.

So what. Sigh. Sigh. And sigh. Curtis is worth it.

"Do you know them?" Dustin asked.

"Charlie's friends. They're like interchangeable clones," Vere evaded. She tied to squelch the butterflies rushing around her stomach as the memories from the afternoon poured in.

Did Curtis really ask about me? Really?

"Face the street, in case they recognize you. Are you worried that they might?"

Dustin watched the guys from under the brim of his cap. "Nope. Are you? Worried about me?" He met her gaze. "Nice of you to care, gnome girl." He tapped his cheeks, grinning now.

She rolled her eyes, annoyed that he'd brought up the blushing. "I'm sure they won't make any connection. Who would expect *me* of all people, to be sitting in a car with the lead singer of *GuardeRobe*?"

"Not me, that's for sure." He laughed a little.

Vere tossed him a lightning-fast glance.

She wanted to tell him that he could do a lot worse, but she knew for a fact it wouldn't be a true statement. The idea of the two of them even sharing the same space on earth was so ridiculous.

But that idea made Vere realize that disguising this guy might actually work! No one would ever believe *Hunter Kennedy* had moved to Monument, Colorado and was hanging with her.

Not ever!

Not if there was a decoy Hunter, hanging in New York!

"Seriously. Hide yourself a little more, please...somehow," she whispered, heart racing. "Like it or not, you're stuck with me."

"No need to whisper," Dustin whispered back with a little mocking grin. "They can't hear us. And I think I like the part where I'm stuck with you. Just not all the other parts of my situation."

"Please. No need to lie. The truth won't hurt my feelings."

He met her gaze and smiled before looking blatantly back at Curtis and Howie. "The dark-haired one seems to be very interested, though, doesn't he?"

"Watch your ego," Vere quipped. "That's Curtis. He, like every other unthinking, sheep-following, music fan, loves *GuardeRobe*. So please. LOOK AWAY!"

"I work 90 hours a week on *GuardeRobe* stuff. I won't lie to you, but if you're going to constantly insult my life's passion, maybe you *should* lie to me." Dustin sighed and turned away from her, Curtis and Howie.

Vere's heart twisted all over again. "I'm sorry. Totally uncalled for statements. Please don't be mad. I won't do that anymore. Promise. I'm nervous, and when I'm nervous I say insane thoughtless things. Forgive me?"

"Forgiven." Hunter's shoulders shrugged, and he slouched away from her a little more. "Besides, that dude was not looking at me. He's trying to catch your eye."

"Really?!" She accidently hit the brakes and jerked the car to a skid-stop.

Dustin cringed in his seat and shot her an accusatory glance.

Vere caught a glimpse of Curtis and Howie laughing at her in the side mirror. "Sorry again." She threw another forgive-me-grin at a now very pale Dustin. "Backing up is my only bad steering skill. I *swear* I can drive forward with no problems."

"Oh. My. God. Let's hope so."

She eased up on the brakes, letting the car continue to roll backwards down the slanted driveway, watching Curtis. He *did* have his gaze trained on her!

Yay!

Pulse escalating to six billion beats per minute, Vere managed to back up enough to turn her head, smile, and wave at Curtis as though she didn't care that she'd made a complete fool out of herself in front of him only hours before.

She swerved a little when Curtis smiled and waved back.

Success! Sort of...

Vere steadied the steering wheel, grinned once at the side of Dustin's head, and drove off, wondering if Curtis had taken note of the fact that she had an actual *guy* in the car with her?

How cool would it be to make Curtis a little jealous?

Ha. Imagine...

12: dangerous driving

Hunter tried to make sense of the scenery around him.

They seemed to be finally approaching an interstate that led out of the endless, winding seventies neighborhood where Vere and Nan lived.

They'd been driving (or Vere had been swerving) for twenty minutes. Every other turn in the road showed houses boasting their own meadows. Little red-dirt pathways were everywhere. He could swear he'd spotted at least ten rabbits too. Real, wild, rabbits, munching on front lawns. Even a couple of deer.

The place was like Teletubbie-Land meets the suburbs plus mountains. "Uh...I think you can stop hiding your face now." Vere seemed to be struggling to make conversation again.

"Sorry. Zoned out. I wasn't hiding, just checking out the scenery. My zombie state is one of my many paparazzi-taught life skills. If I get too quiet you have to bring me back." He turned forward in his seat and glanced at her out of the corner of his eye.

"I understand. Sometimes, I need to be brought back, too," she mumbled, chewing her upper lip again.

What is she worried about now?

"It's not a bad thing, spacing out. Is it?" Hunter kept his tone warm and his expression placid, but when she didn't answer he got a little nervous. The car careened through the curves in the road as her tension seemed to increase. If she gripped the steering wheel any tighter it was going to explode and turn to dust.

He figured if he could keep her talking, she might relax. Might not kill them.

He tried again to start a conversation. "Your mom told me

you and Charlie will drive me back and forth to school and to school functions? What exactly is a school function?" he asked, working to keep his tone calm.

"She actually called them that?" Vere grimaced. "She makes it sound so clinical. Dances, club meetings and football games— all that kind of stuff. You'll love school functions! They're the best part of school because they don't involve school!"

Hunter smiled when her glitter-bright enthusiasm returned full force. No matter how endearing she might be with that, he didn't want her to think he was going to join her *golly-Pollyanna-pep-squad* any time soon. He answered carefully, "I'll pass on that stuff. Being driven around like a little kid is already humiliating enough."

She nodded. "I hear you. I'm so glad Charlie and I have this car." She glanced over, then back at the road. "You never learned how to drive, huh? Is it because you're so fancy-famous and have a limo? You should be used to being driven around. Don't be embarrassed," she added. "Maybe you can get your license while you're here. Or do you need me to teach you how to ride a bike first?"

He bit back a laugh, enjoying that she did not hide her disdain for his Los Angeles lifestyle. He told her some of the truth: "I don't have a license because it's been revoked. And yes, I have a driver and a limo. But I can drive. I'm here in Colorado because of a—car accident—thing."

"Oh. Oh." She frowned.

"Yeah. Big, *oh*. In addition to needing a rest, my mom's holding me hostage here in Colorado because she's pissed about some damage I did to my car and also our house. She's punishing me for a bunch of other prank stuff I also pulled."

"Like what?"

His heart clenched while he decided what to tell her. "I participated in what some would call a one night binge of teen stupidity. The legal terms my mom's attorney slapped on me

were *reckless endangerment* and *vandalism*, among other things."
He'd kept his voice deliberately flippant as he continued,
"Enough about me. Let's hear more about you. Your mom told
me you're really named Gwenivere."

Vere rolled her eyes. "Yeah. She's really proud of my awkward
name."

He added in a teasing tone to his words because he knew
that would set her off. Off of him mostly. "*Gwenivere*, my cute,
gnome-girl, chauffeur. I love King Arthur, and Shakespeare, by
the way. Gwenivere is such a classic name. I'm with your mom.
Why don't they call you Gwen, though?"

Instead of making her blush as he'd thought she would, she
rewarded him with one of her snapping glares. "No one teases
me about the name. I'm Vere because my mom liked it better.
What are you? Some kind of literature expert?"

"Yes. It's my favorite subject. Poetry especially."

She raised her brows, surprised. "This is good. Jenna and I
need a friend who can help us study Lit. And don't think I
can't tell you're trying to change the subject away from deeper
topics."

"I'm not changing subjects, I told you what I could about
me," Hunter stalled, pulling at his sleeves, wondering how
much more he should tell her.

"You told me only enough to make me curious. Keep going
on your story."

It was nice to spill some of his secrets, but he'd promised
Martin absolute silence. Plus he'd only just met this girl. It
made no sense to bring up things he hadn't told Barry. Even if
those things were now on the tip of his tongue and ready to fall
off like a waterfall of *too-much-information*.

Besides, he didn't want Vere to think she had to feel even
more sorry for him. Or worse, believing he was crazy. Enough
people already held that assumption.

"Ask me questions and I'll see if I can answer them," he said finally. Figuring he could skirt the truth where needed.

"Okay. If you did all that extreme vandalism stuff, shouldn't you be in jail instead of here? I'm not an idiot, you know? I overheard Mom mention some major drinking was involved. Level with me."

To cover, he pretended offense.

"Wow. Nosy much? I don't have a DUI, if that's what you think. I drank some wine after the car thing. *After*. And this." He motioned to the woods outside his window. "Is my jail, Gwenivere. *You* are my jailer."

He'd taunted her with her full name to distract her again, and it worked, because she'd shot him a bullet-glare before turning back to the road.

He continued, "My time here is actually part of a court agreement. I have to go to your lame high school. Worse, I'm not allowed to work. It's a suck-ass situation that I'm not happy about and that's all there is to it. You now know all. No more questions. The bits I've left out are between me and my mom. And none of your business. Deal?" He looked out the window again.

"Okay. Charlie busts on me about being nosy all the time. I suppose it isn't easy for you to lay the truth out for me, so thanks for telling what you did. I'm sorry if I sounded all mean again. I keep doing that to you!"

She looked so completely contrite, Hunter felt guilty that she was the one apologizing. "You weren't being mean." He sighed. "It was all me."

"No. Me. I think I've been sort of mean to you since we've met." Her voice softened. "I'm not usually like this. It's something about *rock-star-you* that sets me off. I have this strange urge to treat you like I treat Charlie."

"With zero respect?"

She laughed. "Yeah, maybe. I don't know what it is, but I feel somehow comfortable around you."

"Well...same for me," he admitted. "And remember, there is no 'rock-star' me. I'm Dustin. Dustin McHugh. Once you settle on that idea, possibly you won't need to loathe me so much," he teased, but immediately regretted it. He could tell he'd flustered her.

"Some friend I'm going to be. If I already have you thinking I hate you, when, like I said, I'm pretty sure it's the opposite..." She'd trailed off with another self-deprecating laugh, the red color of her cheeks reigning high and flooding the rest of her face.

"You think we're going to be friends?" he asked.

Her expression wavered then, as though she expected him to give her a major rejection.

"Oh...well...we're going to be spending a lot of time together. I thought that we would—eventually—become friends. I mean. Yeah." Her glance was confused. "That's how it works. Right?"

Hunter didn't know what to say. This was out of his area of expertise.

Her face flooded double. And not in the cute way he'd grown used to. He felt really bad for causing it, because she looked positively like she might die inside her own skin.

Worse, it had affected her speed. Her driving had spiraled out of control as she zoomed them up the off ramp with zero slow down.

"I mean. I mean—I—thought we we're getting along. And so—I—thought we—" She seemed locked there, staring at the road, not noticing she was going to kill both of them by barrelling through the stop sign at the top of the ramp!

No way am I going to die at some odd Colorado crossroads.

He spoke quickly. "Vere! Of course. Of course we're getting along. It's only that I don't have many friends. Or any friends outside my band—friends that are girls—that's for sure. It's why I paused. I have no idea how to proceed, that's all."

Hunter shook his head, wondering why he'd told her the truth.

"Oh. Oh! Great!" She took in a deep breath and beamed at him as she rolled the car to a safe stop. "I thought you didn't want to. You know? Be friends with me. Which is cool because you're all famous and I'm just me."

He sighed. "How about you're possibly amazing and I'm just an ass? And I'm not famous. Remember? You will have to stop slipping up with comments like that."

"Right. Me, possibly amazing. You, a nobody-ass. This whole thing is making me feel crazy." She took a hard left and sped up into traffic.

His heart did a double flip. Mostly because she was unbelievably cute at that moment, and he could swear she was now going to ram their car into the pickup truck directly in front of them!

"Jesus. Vere! Could you please watch what you're doing? Slow down! You're dangerous on the road."

She pulled back from the other vehicle and Hunter could breathe again. He shot her a harried glance.

"You didn't have to shout." She pouted. "It's not my fault I'm driving so badly. It's yours."

"What? You have got to be kidding. You swore to me you were good at it."

She stopped at a red light and turned to face him. "Look. You must know your eyes are truly distracting, and you keep LOOKING at me. I've also never talked to anyone who sounds like a movie trailer announcer before. Your voice is so cool. I'm sure you know that. It's probably part of your *famousness*. But here in this car it's unsettling, because I have this sensation you might suddenly begin sentences with some dramatic start like..." She lowered her voice. "*IN A WORLD, FAR, FAR AWAY...*"

He laughed all the way down to his belly. "You're beyond

hilarious. You know that, right?"

The light turned green and they drove on. "I've heard it before, but don't get your hopes up. Your compliments will get you nowhere with me, player. No matter how pretty your face might be to others, it's not real to me. Though it does startle me off and on, know my heart belongs to a huge crush that takes up all my time. So beyond the voice thing—you can rest knowing you don't affect me one bit."

"So you've said. The part where you don't fangirl on me is a huge relief. And, aside from your bun, which startles me every time you move, you also hardly affect me at all so...yeah," he finished feeling lame and well aware he'd fully lied about his level of attraction to her.

"Hey, no jokes about my awesome bun. And again, I *so* don't care that I'm not your type. Jeez. How many times are you going to bring it up? I'll call you if I ever get implants, dye the bun platinum, start wearing stilettos, red leather zip suits and hire myself out for cash. Okay?"

"Deal." He laughed again. "Come on. Give me some credit. Only half the porn stars I've dated looked like that. The other half wore *black* leather zip suits? They were also gingers not blondes. Besides, I never have to pay my women."

She gasped as though she totally believed him. "Really? Porn stars?"

"No. *Hell no!* I've never once dated anyone remotely similar to your ridiculous description." He shook his head.

"Well good. You scared me."

"Scared me that you believed it. It's really refreshing to hang out with you," he added, contemplating her profile.

She shot him a skeptical glance. "Why?"

"You don't take me seriously. I like it. If I ever seem defensive, know it's a reflex. Maybe you've been treating me like Charlie, but I've been treating you like you're some prying reporter. As for you not being my type and me not being yours...let's drop that. It is what it is. But that doesn't mean we can't hang out. I do want to be friends." He raised his brows. "If you're willing to take me on—baggage, voice, and all," he paused to lower his voice. "I could be an asset to you. *IN A WORLD WHERE BUNNIES RUN WILD,*" he finished in his best movie trailer impersonation.

She laughed. "Seriously. You could be so famous with that voice."

"I am. Remember?"

She flushed. "I finally forget, and now you ask me to remember? Pick one."

They both laughed.

"Final truce?" he added, pretending not to notice her blush.

She kept her face averted. "Truce. Do you mean it about the friend thing? I've never been friend with a guy, either. I most probably will botch it, so be warned."

Her reply had been so quiet that Hunter wondered if she'd said it at all. Maybe she was giving him an out, a way to take back the offer. He could sense this was really important. Now that he'd spent a little more time with her, Hunter didn't think he was capable of hurting this girl's feelings—not on purpose. "If we mess it up, it won't matter."

"Why?"

"Because I don't truly exist," he said with more confidence than he felt.

"Yeah. I've been dwelling on that fact. Fake guys seem to be much easier to communicate with than real ones."

"Really?" He laughed. "Good."

"If you're serious, I accept. You, *Dustin McHugh,* newly born fake person, can be my *BGF. Best Guy Friend,* here and at school. For as long as you exist in Colorado!"

He shook his head, bewildered. "Sounds like a truly awful job title."

"Come on...*BGF* status is awesome. We'll share secrets,

advice, gossip about girls—and guys—and stuff." Her eyes were sparkling sunshine again.

"Fashion tips allowed?" He eyed her shorts.

"Maybe." She glared. "After I'm done *unmaking* you into social oblivion!"

He grinned. "I'm in. Aren't we supposed to prick our fingers and seal it?" He was rewarded with another one of her funny half eye rolls as he explained, "I was in a made-for-TV-movie where they did that. Is that not what *real-best-friends* do?"

"If we were ten. You have one mixed-up view of the world, don't you?" She smiled, and he could tell she was truly pleased with their tentative pact.

"Yes. Get used to it. It's the root of my problems. I'm not even close to normal."

"You're normal enough."

He smiled, turning back to the scenery. As they drove along, Hunter realized this was the first comfortable silence he'd had with another person in a long time.

***

They pulled up to a three-story brick office building. Vere parked the car in the half filled lot, cut the engine and turned to face him. "Before we get out, I have a bunch of questions. Working—*unmaking*—kinds of questions."

He met her gaze dead on. "Fine. Shoot."

"Well." She flushed slightly. "Um. These are really awkward questions."

He bit back a grin. "Ask me anything. Go. I swear I'm not easily embarrassed."

"Please confess what on your person is plastic, washable and hopefully removable."

"What?"

She swallowed, and rushed on in a flurry as she'd done before. "Okay. Fine. *First.* The eyes. I'm figuring you are wearing colored contacts. Only dolls, the Caribbean Sea and neon glow-sticks have that insane, pure-color blue. *Second.* Your *lashes*...are they false? I read in a magazine that stars have fake lashes stuck on somehow—with glue that can blind you—glue your eyes shut? If that's the case, and it won't cause permanent damage to you, those feathery things need to come off ASAP. And your tan. Is that sprayed on?" She blinked. "All the fake stuff has got to go. It will really help our cause."

He shook his head and swallowed down his urge to bust out laughing. She had to be kidding.

"The lashes are real. The color is genuine. The tan was carefully acquired on a deck, using real sun. You sure like noticing my assets, though."

When she looked over at him he winked so she would know he was kidding.

"God—you're—so—stuck up," she stuttered. "That ego thing is going to have to stop. As is the disconcerting, show-off, winking thing! Honestly!"

He raised his brows because she actually sounded somewhat pissed-off. "I swear. I'm not stuck up. Why do you think that?"

"Only stuck up people talk about their *assets.*"

He blinked. "Ah, I see. I'm sorry if it came across that way. If you could take that comment from my point of view, maybe you'd understand."

"I'm listening." She crossed her arms.

"You already caught on to the eyes and the voice, but that's not all of it. See, I have entire websites devoted to my hair alone. And well, there's my height, my melodious singing voice, my wild musical talent and don't forget my perfectly sculpted biceps, wide shoulders, six-pack, and ass."

Her mouth dropped open.

He shrugged, working to make her understand. "There's whole YouTube montages and gifs all over Tumblr, playing live motion shots of my butt to music. Or not to music. I don't take credit for it. My mom's been paying a trainer for years. Oh, and my six-pack won a Fan's Choice Award called the *SixPackAttack*. Three years running. It's a cool trophy."

She clamped her mouth shut using her hands as though she needed the extra help to hold herself back, raised up one of her arched brows and rolled her eyes.

"What? You seriously don't believe me?" He pulled halfheartedly at his shirt so she could catch a glimpse of a perfectly flat, washboard stomach. "Want to give it a fist tap? It's solid."

"No! No. And no!" She gasped. "Oh. My. God! Keep that shirt down. Please." She choked out an embarrassed sounding laugh. "And the part where you aren't stuck up begins...UH... *when*? Who says stuff like that? You're a complete bragger."

"I'm not," he protested. "I'm listing my products. You did it too. Just now. Though no one has ever brought up my eye lashes! My manager and my mom go through my 'products', taking notes and suggesting changes every year."

"No way!"

He nodded. "I'm not stuck up about that stuff. I actually feel very disconnected from myself on the *asset* level, *hell,* on every level. I consider all the bits of me are like a bunch of specialized car parts. People are obsessed with each singular item but they never go beyond that. I make fun of it all, I suppose."

"This is your attempt at making fun of it?"

"Yeah." He shrugged, watching as a flurry of changing expressions crossed her face, ranging from horrified to confused. "Is it not funny?"

She giggled then. "I guess. I don't know. It must be really freaky to have your entire body chopped up and made into websites, huh?"

"It's part of my life."

"I think I'm beginning to understand you a little. But you have to know, your perspective is completely twisted! You could possibly be a very messed up person."

He smiled and met her gaze. "Trust me, it's not a possibility. It's a fact you should be aware of about me."

She smiled back. "Who knew we had something in common. Don't worry, you are in good company, BGF! I'm completely messed up too."

"Please. I'm a total broken disaster compared to wholesome, good-girl you. You've only scratched my surface stuff. The information on me only goes downhill from here," he added, testing the waters on her reaction to that small truth.

"Duh. You're assuming that I buy into your strange, sob story. There is no way you could possibly be more pitiful than I am. Your assets alone float you higher by default."

"I'd disagree, but hmm..." He eyed her hoodie, shooting her his most skeptical look, hoping she couldn't see through how attractive he thought she was.

She bought it. "Okay. Hold. We are not going to start a list on what I don't have in the way of assets."

He reached forward and fiddled absently with the stereo buttons, wondering why she was so hard on herself, but left it alone. It was not his place to start calling this girl pretty, so he changed the subject. "I don't know why I'm trying to explain myself to you. I guess I'd feel better if we could re-start all this with you believing that I'm not a complete jerk, okay?"

"Fine. I won't jump down your throat for your random, stuck up sounding comments without giving you the *whacked-childhod-star-raised-by-wolves* grains of salt. But you are going to have to keep all of your clothes on, okay?"

He laughed, tossing her a teasing grin. "Okay. You too, though. We're in the friend-zone only."

She shook her head. "Whatever. Yes, Dustin McHugh." She smiled and gestured to the building in front of them. "This is my dad's building. Let's go in."

Hunter located a small sign that read Roth Orthodontics and

he freaked. "Your dad's a dentist? What are you planning? Hell no. No way. I am not going in there. You'll have to drag me out of this car. What are you going to do? Pop out one of my front teeth and make me a hillbilly?"

She laughed again, a burst of pure sunshine giggles that he found himself wishing would last longer.

"This is Colorado, you dork. There are no hillbillies around here, only cowboys and hippies."

"Really? None?" He frowned.

"Really." She flung her arms wide. "For a guy who's supposed to be worldly, you sure seem like you've never been outside your own back yard. Weren't you listening back at my house? We *told* you my dad was an orthodontist!"

She bit her upper lip.

He tore his gaze away from her face.

No I wasn't listening back at your house, because I was ogling your list of adorable assets like the complete ASS I swore not to be. Now, as your proclaimed BGF, I can't seem to take my eyes off your lips. So please stop chewing the plump, pouting upper one because it's distracting as hell.

Vere continued on, not expecting him to answer. Thankfully, she stopped chewing that lip.

"We have to do something major with that ridiculously perfect smile. Asset number one—or twenty—or wherever you've placed it on that twisted list of yours. If we can't hide that line of sparkling perfection then the whole disguise will be sunk. Like you said, your smile is the stuff of teen girl dreams so we need to turn it into a nightmare!"

"Oh, well that makes me feel much better," he sighed.

She frowned. "Hey, don't worry. Dad's not going to hurt you. He's going to fit you with a huge, ugly retainer, that's all. When we're done, I'm going to buy you a milkshake to cheer you up."

"How do you know I'll need cheering up?" For some reason her sympathy had caused that damn twisting pain to return somewhere behind his heart.

"You've needed cheering up since we met. I've been staring at your sad face all afternoon." Her tone had switched to cajoling encouragement, and her smile reminded him to breathe.

"Things might get a little worse before they get better. But... like...you're not going to be alone anymore," she added.

What will get worse?

The twisting pain in my chest, or the strange way I feel like I suddenly can't breathe without you helping me?

He blinked at her, feeling stunned. Grateful she'd said that, and more grateful that he could tell she'd meant every word.

He let a cryptic laugh escape. "I'll be fine. But I'm holding you to that milkshake, though. I haven't had one since I was ten. I'm thinking Dustin McHugh is allowed to ingest way more calories than Hunter Kennedy ever was."

"That's the most depressing thing I've ever heard anyone say." Her eyes were solemn and thoughtful as she shot him another sympathetic smile. "Luckily, my *BGF Dustin* loves milkshakes. Rumor has it, *he* always has. Trust me?"

"Maybe I do," he answered with a smile that reached all the way to his soul.

He took in another huge breath and let a small part of his heart be pulled into her deep brown eyes.

Maybe I do.

13: shopping with hell's princess

HUNTER

If Hunter wasn't convinced he'd landed on another planet after meeting Vere's jolly-dentist-dad (who'd helped him order one hellish, neon-green retainer) the signs painted all over Rick's Western Emporium & Feed Supply nailed his new reality down for good.

The sign appeared to be hand painted and read: Quality Western Ranch Wear, Oats, Fencing, Kitchen Cabinets, Feed, Tools and General Tack Supply. The sign duct taped to the larger sign was best of all: PLEASE BAG YOUR OWN MANURE OUT BACK. FREE.

Hell.

I'm about to go shopping in hell.

Hell that sells poop.

"We're going in the back door."

"By the manure pile?" Hunter shuddered.

"Yes. Follow me and stay close. Your wardrobe will be epic coming from here." Vere pulled him along.

Shopping with hell's princess.

Hunter had to force himself not to drag his feet.

Rick's Emporium was housed in a giant metal barn the size of a mega-shopping mall. A building, Vere had proudly informed him, that had once been the state's snow-plow storage unit back in the seventies. The whole thing looked as if it might collapse at any minute.

Vere led him through a wide barn-looking door, and then ushered him through a giant aisle that boasted every possible type of chicken farming product he'd ever seen.

Chicken food, and chicken feeders, chicken coops, and chicken wash—not to mention chicken bedding and chicken vitamins and eye drops.

Hunter froze in front of some hats, T-shirts, and bumper stickers that read: *Get Your Chicks at Rick's*. "Wow. Is this where guys go to hook-up?"

Vere shook her head. "In the spring, Rick's sells baby chickens. They set up the whole back of the store with self-enclosed heated pens full of fuzzy baby chicks. They have tons of breeds. All colors. Even ducklings and goslings. Sometimes they let you watch them hatch. It's so cool when that's happening. I'll bring you back in April, if not sooner. This place is addictive."

No. You are addictive.

He smiled, hiding that thought with a skeptical eye roll.

She walked ahead, looking right then left at the end of the aisle. "Wait here. I'm going to do a crowd check." She dashed into the larger aisle ahead.

Hunter loved the way her eyes had been sparkling when she'd talked about the baby chicks. It was like Vere Roth enjoyed everything on the whole planet to some sort of maximum high.

She'd almost freaked out over the fresh peaches in the milkshakes they'd eaten. Hunter admitted the late summer peaches were better than usual, but according to Vere they'd been *beyond perfect*.

"All clear." She skipped back down the aisle, bun bobbing all around.

"I've decided I need one of these chick shirts," he said, wondering when he'd be able to stop staring. Eventually he'd have to get used to her.

"They go half price when the chicks are hatching. We can wait?"

"I won't be here. If all goes well, I could be, will be, home in a few weeks," he reminded.

"I guess it makes no sense to stay her longer so you can watch some chickens hatch." The light from her eyes dimmed and her hand snuck up to straighten her bun.

"Yeah. No."

He felt bad to have rained on her excitement. For a moment, he wished he could come back here with her. Mostly only so he could watch her gush at the baby animals. She'd probably be maximum-cute that day. But April was when final songs for the album were due...so...by then he'd be lifetimes away from here.

"This is why I must have one of these awesome shirts *now*. For the memories and for my new persona. Dustin McHugh loves baby chicks."

He grabbed a size XL and tried to focus their conversation back to the task at hand. He went on, "Maybe I can be disguised as a farming kid or a farm-dude or...heck...what do you even call farm kids?" he finished, feeling disoriented.

She giggled. "Kids. Who live on farms? How about *farmers?*"

"Right. DUH. Lost my mind for a second."

She giggled again and his heart jumped. He turned away as though to study the chicken feed display.

"No way would you be able play off a farming disguise. Too many people will call you on the details. Farm kids know farm equipment inside and out."

"What do you mean?"

"Like if your family raised chickens." She swung her arm wide like a game show hostess. "You would know every single product here by heart. And, by the time you were six. If your family raised wheat, you would be able to talk about droughts, seasons, trucks, harvest, pesticides and everything John Deere. Get me?"

Hunter shrugged, pretending he was on board. He did not want to let on that he had no clue who or what John Deere might be. "I could do horses. Be a cowboy?"

"Ha. You wish. Data ramp-up on that is even worse. Besides, cowboys are hot. For real hot. You're trying to be for real not-hot?" She scrunched her nose and looked him up and down. "Dressing *six-foot-you* in cowboy boots and a hat, even with the new retainer, would create a riot. All the girls in our neighborhood who own horses would stalk you."

"Shit. Are there lots of those?"

"Tons. Half our county is zoned for horses. Besides, the products and skills needed for equestrian and saddle knowledge would be epic. You don't have that much time to memorize stuff. And I bet," she shot him a smug, teasing glance. "You don't have what it takes to sit on a horse without freaking out."

Hunter shuddered. "I forgot about the cowboys going with horses part. Please say your family doesn't have horses. Please say I don't have to *ride* horses. I'm actually afraid of livestock animals. Cows, miniature goats, pigs, and even some dogs freak me out. As a kid, I once flipped out at a petting zoo. Not my proudest moment."

Vere shook her head and laughed. "No horses. Too expensive. In the summer, we're mountain lake lovers. Boating, fishing, hiking, all that kind of stuff. Winter, we ski."

Hunter grimaced. Mostly because he didn't want to encourage an invitation to any of the activities she'd listed.

Hunter was a city boy, and he wanted to stay a city boy.

Vere took his Rick's Chicks tee out of his hands. "Let's go to the general clothing section and start there. This shirt is giving me a good idea. Come on. They're only open for another forty minutes."

She led him past feed troughs, giant water buckets, weird goat feeders and an entire section of pig fencing before ushering him across another brightly lit aisle and into what was apparently the clothing area.

Designated by the wooden, split rail fence surrounding the section. The entry into this section boasted two hand-carved logs holding up a knotty pine sign that had been burned to look like a brand. It read: Duds.

Hunter looked wildly at the racks.

"Duds? You can't be serious."

Vere had frozen in the entryway and was scanning his face. Her brows had drawn down, causing a little crease to form in the center of her forehead. She spoke in a low—almost desperate sounding—whisper. "Lower your voice, and yes, I am serious. They've got tons of options here. If anyone comes near, turn your head and pull down that cap? Okay?"

"Jesus, okay. Why are you freaking out?"

"You—the darn eyes—look like moonbeams or light sabers under these lights." She paused and shook her head.

Hunter teased, "Is this your twisted way of calling me handsome again? Don't worry, I've got sunglasses." He laughed, pulling them out. "Ironically, blue light sabers are for the good guys. Don't let the color fool you."

"Oh shut up, would you?" She closed in on him way too close and peered up at his eyes. He couldn't stop himself from staring at the little line of peach milkshake running near that damn perfect upper lip.

"I swear I can still see the color behind your sunglasses. There aren't going to be eye-glasses dark enough. We're going to have to pay double *and* probably special order you a trash bag to cover your whole face."

"Maybe if we're lucky I'll suffocate to death and then we won't have to do this?"

"Don't joke about stuff like that. Don't. Ever." She sucked in a breath, her anger apparently evaporating as quickly as it came. "I'm sorry. I'm being totally mean to you again. What is it about you that makes me act crazy?"

Safe behind the glasses, Hunter shot a longing glance at that line of peach milkshake again. "It's not you. It's me. I habitually drive people nuts. I'll stop baiting you. I'm doing it on purpose. I'll stop."

"Good." She stalked ahead and gestured to the clothes. "This place sells specialized ranch clothing. It's not cheap. We can also hit the thrift store to keep costs down. You're going to need shoes and everything. If it's too much, my mom and dad will help buy the glasses, I'm sure. And Dad will never let you pay for the retainer, so you're good there."

"What?"

She frowned. "This project is going to break your bank."

He shook his head at her in wonder. No girl had ever worried about him spending money before. Most had expected he would spend tons of it, and mostly on them. She'd also paid for their milkshakes!

Hunter basked in this new, unfamiliar feeling.

Vere was actually watching *over* him instead of *watching* him like everyone else did. He liked it. Her. A lot.

"Look. I'm good for the money, okay? I get paid. Tons."

"Oh...yeah. DUH."

Without thinking, he reached out and grabbed her hand. She froze.

He could feel her arm tense up, so he loosened his grip but did not let go.

"Vere. Um. You have something on your face." He turned her toward him as gently as he possibly could. He sensed that he'd freaked her out, but now that he'd committed he'd have to follow through, or she'd think he was a freak for grabbing her hand like this. He reached forward to wipe the stripe of ice-cream away, resisting the temptation to explore the shape of her upper lip with his thumb.

"Food on my face? Could you not have brought it up sooner? I'm such a disaster." She closed her eyes but not before Hunter read pure mortification shooting through the brown-green depths of her eyes.

"One small strip of milkshake does not scream, *disaster*. You'd do the same for me, right? I'm also disaster." He pointed to spot where a whole peach slice had hit and left a mark. "Look at the stain on my shirt."

She opened one eye and found the spot, seeming to relax when she confirmed he wasn't lying, and then closed it again while he worked the dried ice cream off her upper lip.

"Helping people with food-face is the mark of a truly nice person, you know? This could ruin your reputation."

"What happens after the milkshake shop, stays at the milkshake shop." She didn't answer, so he went on, "Why do you close your eyes all the time?" He studied the ginger-brown curve of her lashes.

Eyes still scrunched, she grimaced. "I'm trying not to blush. In case you haven't noticed, my face, off and on, catches on fire. Especially in extremely awkward situations. LIKE THIS."

Hunter let her go and stepped back. "I like it when you change colors. It's charming."

"Shut up. You promised not to bait me." She opened her eyes, her expression shooting bullets and crossed her arms in front of her. "Luckily, when you make me mad, it doesn't happen. And calling the blushing *charming* makes me mad! It's anything but that. Now let's get back to the topic of money. How are you going to pay?"

He swallowed, trying not to remember the soft feel of her skin. "I have a huge budget for this unmaking, and a credit card to boot. I don't want you worrying about me. About that. God. Never about that."

"I can't help it. If you're my friend, I'm going to worry about every bit of you. A perk of being in the Vere friend zone. Just in case, we'll stick to the sale racks when we can. Deal?"

Hunter laughed. "I've never even seen a sale rack. Do they really put little red stickers to show the price has been marked lower or is that just on TV?"

"Wow. You're truly clueless, aren't you?"

He laughed out loud, unable to stop himself because she'd used his own thoughts about *her*, right back on him! "How could you, a girl who's apparently never even stepped outside

Colorado, think I'm clueless?"

"As if. I've been to Utah, Kansas, Idaho, New Mexico and Disneyland, loser."

He laughed louder which seemed to make her mad again.

"What? Stop laughing so loudly. The voice, *DUH*. Someone is going notice you before you're properly disguised! None of this is funny, and we're running out of time." She paused and glared. "And...I've also been to Michigan, for a wedding, so don't make me deck you."

He couldn't control the next belly laugh that burst forth.

He let it envelop him. It felt so awesome to let loose.

For some reason, hanging out with Vere had made him happy. Better, he couldn't remember having this much fun, ever.

Hands on her hips now, she squinted and looked as though she wanted to do battle. "You are totally doing that on purpose. Do you really need the attention from strangers that badly?"

She pulled the brim of his cap down halfway over his nose as she dragged him by the arm toward the back of the clothing section. "Not another loud sound comes out of your mouth until after we've got your disguise figured out."

14: clueless

As a joke, Vere held up a bright orange, *RodeoDare* brand western shirt. One with paisley fabric, purple piping, white fringe dangling from the armpits to the cuffs plus rhinestone buttons and a row of fringe on the back to boot. "How about this?" she whispered with a look that warned him to whisper back.

Dustin blinked once and considered the shirt, his face impassive. "I'm an extra large. That's too small. Do they have another size?"

His perfectly contrite whisper meant that he was apparently trying to appease her after his laugh attack. But his lack of response to the ugly shirt astonished her. "I'm kidding about this shirt. Can't you tell?"

"No. I can't tell. Don't joke around. Pick what you think is appropriate. Is that shirt not a good choice? It looks like decent disguise material to me."

She tossed the hideous shirt back onto the rack and felt guilty for trying to tease him. "Clueless. Like I said."

He shook his head. He seemed stumped by the different options. She watched his expression warring between confusion and bewilderment.

She went around to the extra-large side of the shirt rack. "How about we start with a few things you are drawn to. Then we can build from there."

He gingerly fingered some of the shirts on the rack. "Hmm. I don't know. I've never picked my own clothes."

"Never?"

"Nope. I have a personal shopper. The stuff shows up in my room. My mom or stylist decide what outfit goes on me each day."

"Whoa. You're like a Persian prince!"

"Not even. I have no harem and worse, no servants help zip me into the ugly outfits they pick."

She rolled her eyes and pointed to a stack of flannel and plaid button down shirts. "Do you like these?"

He shrugged, not even giving the shirts half a glance. "I'll like them if you like them."

Vere was floored again. He had no opinions at all! About anything, or at least he didn't seem to know how to discuss them.

Vere shot a hand up to check her bun, tightening the rubber band so it wouldn't slip. She caught him watching her as though intrigued with how she made her bun or something, and she almost had another blush attack. She looked away, embarrassed, remembering the feel of his hand on her upper lip, his other hand holding hers as he'd wiped away that ice cream.

Her stomach flooded with little butterflies.

Ugh. Focus. Kill the butterflies.

Those were not real hands, only the hands of your new best guy friend. Perfectly appropriate that he would get the ice cream off your face.

Friends don't let friends have food face.

"We're going to have to turn this into a game," Vere said.

She brought the Rick's Chicks tee-shirt forward and hung it in front of them. "What does this shirt remind you of?"

"Chicks? And not the baby kind."

"Ha. Ha." She sighed, pretending he was not funny. "If you saw a *guy* wearing this, plus the retainer you ordered, then what would you think?"

"Extreme but intriguing dork?"

"Exactly what I thought! It's a good idea, isn't it?"

He smiled, chuckling a little. "I suppose there are no specific products I would have to memorize in order to qualify for that, huh?"

"Nope. Dorks are dorks. It's all in the perception of others! I want you to pick what kind of dork you want to be. You could make this fun, like being in a play. *Dustin McHugh* is your character, and you're going to have to live in his pants and walk in his shoes—so to speak. So start with pants."

His brows shot up and he looked slightly scandalized. "What? *Girl*, you are freaking me out. Stop talking about my pants!"

Vere sighed, and double rolled her eyes. "Do you see my patience levels going away? What kind of pants do you want to wear for the next few weeks?"

He looked away. "Vere. I can't do this. Just choose some dork pants for me." He pulled off his cap and rand a hand through his hair.

"Nope. I want you to *pick*. Walk around. See what's here and go with your first gut feeling."

"You aren't going to help me at all?"

He looked pitiful and lost, but Vere held firm. "I'm here to make sure whatever you chose fits within proper dork limits, that's all. The rest is going to be up to you. It's like my drama coach says: Be the character, don't ever let the character be you," she quipped. "That's bad acting."

"*Be all the dork that I can be?*" he tried.

Her turn. "Hamlet: *To dork, or not to dork, that is the question.*" She smiled proudly, thinking of another. "*The apparel 'oft proclaims the man.*"

He chuckled. "Hamlet again, but this time with an English accent: *Though this be madness, yet there is method in it.*"

"You weren't lying about getting A's in Lit."

They shared a smile.

"And who knows Hamlet this well? Dorks like me!" He grinned wider.

She beamed back. "Yes! My new *BGF* is an awesome Hamlet quote guy! You'll have to pull that messed-up accent on my best friend Jenna. I can't wait to see her face when you launch into it!" She giggled.

After that, Hunter seemed to head into the clothing racks with purpose. He wandered until finally stopping dead in front of the Tough Mountain clothing display.

Holding up a pair of dark gold, heavy canvas pants with huge, square front pockets and a large compass sewn into a front belt pull, he beamed. "My gut says these are the pants I want to live in for the next few weeks."

Vere walked over to get a closer look and had to laugh. "Oh yeah. You're totally on to something." She read the Tough Mountain label aloud. "Heavyweight canvas clothing. Sewn from the exact same patterns used by pioneers but with a modern technological twist for *today's man*."

"Today's dorky-man!"

"What's the technology?"

"The compass?" He frowned. "Maybe these giant buttons?"

She surveyed the racks of various overalls, pants, jackets, vests and shorts. All served up in Tough Mountain's four distinct colors: brown, gold, orange, and tan. "It's perfect. Really. It's all stuff for ranch hands or lumberjacks. I think the telephone-pole guys wear it, fire-fighters, and those burly highway dudes!"

"Translation being, no human teenager from around here would be caught dead in this stuff?"

She nodded. "Exactly. So awesome."

"I'm getting one of everything in each color! I'll have a compass on every piece." Dustin fingered the heavy front pocket on one of the vests. "Look at all the gadget spots, and metal zippers, and double stitching everywhere. It looks bullet proof! I hate to admit this, but I actually do love it, and I mean for real! Some of this would look so cool on stage."

"Shh. Don't bring that up. It is pretty cool, but in all the wrong ways for high school." Vere frowned, knowing it was also very expensive, but she didn't say anything about that. She'd have to trust what he'd said about the money.

Dustin pulled some orange, road-worker overalls off the rack and slung them hanger and all over his head, letting them dangle down his body. He flipped over the tag, his smile radiant with what looked to be unchecked, silly glee. "It comes with a ten-year warranty. Who wears clothes with a warranty!?"

"My uber-dork best friend, *Dustin*. That's who. Now what's your size? We only have twenty minutes left to collect the rest and check out."

"I'm a thirty-two waist, thirty-six length in pants. XL shirts. I'll try on a couple. If it's a go, we'll pull the rest without trying stuff on. I'm usually an easy fit."

She nodded, taking up a pair of size thirty-two canvas shorts and some basic pants. He picked up a few of the whacked out vest things.

"Now. Shirts. Choose," she said.

"I did like those plaid ones you pointed out." They made their way back to the flannel shirts and he started picking out some of the button downs in various colors.

"These are all long sleeved. You'll need to get some short sleeved ones, too. We have a month or so of hot weather left."

"Never. I don't care. Dustin McHugh likes only long sleeved, flannel shirts. Always. And forever."

"No. No way. Our school is a furnace. I was almost a heat-stroke casualty this afternoon."

"You said I get to pick. I only like these shirts. Besides isn't it dorky to dress off season?" He smiled wide and she felt a bit light headed.

"Yeah. Well, it's your funeral."

He shrugged happily. "Let's make plaid, canvas and compasses my absolute trademarks. Dustin McHugh. All plaid.

All canvas. All the time. And I'm never lost. What say you, dork judge?"

"Total A++! I'll pick some additional accessories—trucker looking ball caps, lumpy sweaters, that sort of thing."

"What exactly is a lumpy sweater? I'm a hoodie guy."

"Hoodies are in the past. My *BGF* wears only old-man sweaters with zippers. And to shake things up, possibly a hand knitted, gramps vest." She giggled, catching his eye, grinning wider when he smiled back and laughed with her.

"Hell, no. I mean to be long gone before I have to wear shady woolens."

They headed toward the dressing rooms. "Dustin McHugh, this new wardrobe will send you straight into high school insignificance."

"Ahh. My dream come true."

"We aren't done. Next is footwear, socks, underwear and a few oddball school supplies. I think Tough Mountain makes a few backpacks. You'll be so perfectly *matching*!"

She nodded to a back wall that housed the accessories. "How about the pack with the safety whistle?"

He dashed in front of her. His eyes alight with excitement. "Not dorky enough. And did you notice? NO COMPASS. Move over. I see one I like!"

After that, Dustin started picking things right and left as though they were collecting rocks, or finding pennies, and adding them to an ever growing pile on the counter. She tried a second time to convince him to purchase some lighter weight shirts, but he steadfastly refused.

Well, everyone has something.

Jenna hates all things red. I don't like earrings. And Charlie only wears sports jerseys. What's the difference if Dustin McHugh loves shirts with long sleeves?

Maybe it's a good thing.

She knew firsthand dorks were super-proud of their odd

looks and ensembles. She'd have to train him how to be extra smug about his new gear and his new *self* in public.

When she was finished with him, any insults to his person would be taken as huge compliments. It drove the bullies wild with frustration. This always led to more outcast backlash. In the long run, though, it would ensure he had permanent, extra-solid, geek labeling.

Once the label stuck Dustin would be tagged as untouchable and un-dateable. Until he was allowed to go to college, that is, where she was sure dorks reigned supreme.

Didn't they?

She sure hoped so, or she was going to spend her life alone.

15: loyalty, trust and a haircut

HUNTER

Three hours later, after a trip to the *SuperMart* optometry center and a long car ride, Hunter and Vere made their way into the Roth Family cabin.

"Oh. No. You. Didn't." Charlie burst out laughing as he opened the door. "Work boots! Priceless. *Dude.* You are going to get brutalized with those."

"I know!" Hunter put down his shopping bags in the entry and stomped his boots, completely psyched. "I love these things. So much so, that I had to wear them out."

Vere pushed in behind him, her arms also filled to the brim with a load of his brand new wardrobe. "They only had the orangey color in his size. Aren't they magnificently hideous?"

Hunter didn't miss Charlie's gaze systematically searching his sister's face as though to check if she were okay—safe—or something.

What?

Charlie seemed satisfied with what he saw in his sister's smiling expression and appeared to relax. After a short pause Charlie spoke up again. "And I said it couldn't be done. You two have pulled it off. Possibly gone too far. The boots are messed up and ugly."

Hunter tried to stay focused on the boots and on Charlie to take his mind off his growling stomach. "You can laugh all you want but I'll bet these boots start a trend. You'll see. I'll take them back home and wear them on stage."

"Yeah, but until then, these bastards are going to solidify you in the lowest social strata of our whole school." Charlie came closer and kicked the toe of one of the boots and shook his head. "Metal toe tips?"

"In case I drop a book on my foot!" Hunter grinned.

Charlie surveyed the rest of him. "Let me guess. The lenses in those nerd glasses automatically tint even darker when you walk in the sun?" He laughed again. "Perfect! You've become a hideous phone sales guy mixed with a dude who's all Wild West. Or no, wait, I've got it. You're Paul Bunyan meets Waldo!"

"Cool, huh? The glasses go dark even when I'm under regular lights," Hunter announced proudly. "The eye center guy sold us the floor model because we told him I had a huge UVB sun ray allergy and that I'd lost my glasses on the airplane."

Vere sighed. "I felt bad because I lied to him so much. At first he was going to make us wait five to seven days. When he said that, I cried all over him, then pretty much vowed Hunter would go blind by the end of the weekend."

"You did?" Charlie asked.

Hunter nodded. "Oh, she did. The guy folded in two seconds. He agreed it was an emergency that I protect my eyes, but we both know it's because he couldn't stand to watch the little pixie tear up."

Vere punched his upper arm.

Hunter went on, "Vere thinks these glasses will be almost black in the school lunchroom and the hallways too. What do you think?"

Charlie nodded with approval. "Brutal. She nailed it. The place is a freaking eighties skylight showroom. Vere, you're an artist."

"Hey. I chose a lot of this look," Hunter protested.

"He's still hugely tall and noticeable." Charlie frowned.

"Yeah, but a giant dork is still a dork. It's a universal state of being."

Vere set down her pile of bags. "Wait till you see his new walk. And that's not half of it. Dad agreed to a retainer with mega wide and double-crossed shiny wires. It arrives Saturday via FedEx all the way from Atlanta. Overnight shipping is so cool, huh? How do they do it?"

Hunter's gaze caught on her happy smile, charmed again by her boundless enthusiasm over small stuff. Who got excited about mail services?

The strange out of body feeling from this morning suddenly returned along with a massive headache. He was hitting a wall, and suddenly felt two hundred years tired. Every bone in his body ached, but he realized it was mostly aching with relief. Relief that no one had recognized him? Or, was it relief that this plan might actually work?

He caught a whiff of what he hoped would be dinner. It smelled like pure heaven. The milkshake had been great, but now he needed food. And hopefully, soon, a bed.

These people made Martin's demands on his time seem easy.

Charlie flung his overlarge, football player frame to sit on the stairs that led upstairs. "Dude. I have one request before this goes any further."

"Shoot." Hunter tensed, waiting. He hated the word *request*, as much as he hated the words *favor, borrow* and *press conference*.

"When this year is all over, I get your autograph on every *GuardeRobe* T-shirt and swag I own. It's got to be signed, *to my best bud, Charlie*. If I'm agreeing not to rat you out for millions of dollars to Media Channel Today, I gotta have something to prove you were here after the fact. Deal?"

What little air Hunter had left in his chest swooshed out of his lungs. "Sure. That's no problem. If you keep your mouth shut."

Breathe. Breathe. Remember to breathe.

Charlie kept babbling on, "I wonder how much cash I would get paid for this story? Would anyone believe me if I told them Hunter Kennedy was at my lake house right now?" Charlie chuckled.

Hunter swallowed, annoyed with himself.

This is what happens when you let down your guard.

He felt Vere's wide-eyed gaze on him but he didn't want to look. Didn't want to see her face change as she speculated what she could get out of him. His heart crumpled into a tight, leaden ball.

What will she want?

How quickly he'd forgotten these two kids were like everyone else. New people always wanted a piece of him. A takeaway. It hadn't even been one day and already it had started.

"Dustin, he's not serious!" Vere put her small hand on his arm and gave it a little squeeze, allowing him to pull in a long, full breath.

"Charlie's the most loyal person I know. He defines himself by it. If you have his word you have it forever. He only pretends he's a jerk. We've promised our mom, Nan, and now you. Believe me, the last thing we'd ever do is blow your cover. Not after we've promised. Not after all this hard work. We've sworn to protect you, and protect you we will." Her expression had grown fierce and earnest. "Take it back, Charlie. Dustin has no idea you are kidding, and it's completely rude what you said! We're friends now! Jeez."

Charlie hopped up and pulled Vere into a gentle headlock, tagging his knuckles into her crown before letting her go. Vere smiled at the unusual treatment.

"Dude. *Dustin.* That was bad form on my part. I apologize," Charlie said, flushing slightly. "I'd never rat you out, and... what can I say? I'm an ass. Sorry."

Hunter sighed, slowly warming up to the big oaf. If Vere loved him, the kid must be cool, somewhere, somehow. Maybe he needed to relax and give Charlie a real chance. "No. It's no problem. Of course I'll get you both any *GuardeRobe* junk you want. Signed to my best friends. I promise."

Charlie smiled, and Hunter smiled back. And it almost felt

sincere!

"Let's all lay off poor Dustin for a bit," Mrs. Roth said, coming in from the kitchen.

Please let her save me.

She came forward and peered closely at his face. "You already look very different, and completely disguised. I love what you've chosen."

"Thanks." Hunter had meant *thanks* for telling them all to lay off, but he was pleased with her praise.

Mrs. Roth seemed to get that he was tired and feeling really off right then. "Has anyone ever told you what a good sport you are, young man?" She gave him a quick hug, and he didn't have the urge to pull away.

"I'm used to doing what people tell me to do," Hunter answered honestly as he breathed her in. He could swear Mrs. Roth smelled like fresh baked bread and warm blankets.

"This—all of us—it's all pretty overwhelming, isn't it?" she asked, stepping back so she could see his eyes.

He gave her a half-smile. Her questions were the kind he knew he didn't have to answer.

Nice.

Mrs. Roth continued, "Your Aunt Nan's in the kitchen. She's brought your other stuff. Tomorrow we'll let you sleep in, and then, we'll get you into some sunshine. The hard part is over. This three-day weekend you will give you extra time to rest." She frowned. "Learn how to slouch better, cover up your voice and...we'll try to make it as fun as possible while we sort all that out. Okay?"

He nodded. "You sound so positive that all this will work. And exactly like Vere."

She smiled. "I hope you're going to like it here. Do you hike?"

"I now own brand new hiking shoes. Vere made me buy them," he evaded.

"Great. Then you hike. Who's hungry? Charlie, show Dustin the guest room. Vere, wash up, you're sharing with Nan. Dinner is in five."

"Dad said he'd make it here by nine." Vere darted Hunter a smile and trailed her mom into the next room, saying, "After dinner, Hunter's going to let me *unmake* his hair-cut some. Do we have any blunt, terrible scissors?" She looked over her shoulder and shot him one last smirk.

"Dude. You coming?" Charlie called, halfway up the wide, pine stairs.

"Right behind you," he lied. Because without Vere's happy energy pulsing right next to him, he was finding it very difficult to walk on his own.

PART TWO:

BEING DUSTIN
INSIDE & OUT

16: no going back

Dustin

The tapping on his door woke him.

"Dustin. Dude. We're going hiking. You going to sleep all day? Dustin!"

Dustin. Who the hell is Dustin?

His head, groggy and heavy with sleep, wouldn't move. His entire body had morphed into a brick.

"Dustin," Charlie insisted from the other side of the door.

Reality hit him like a slap in the face as he became fully awake. "Yeah. I'll be there. Two minutes."

He rolled out of bed and grabbed the long-sleeved blue, green, and white plaid shirt he'd left on the floor. He pulled it over his white undershirt, taking an extra second to make sure the cuffs were buttoned tightly over his wrists before grabbing his cell.

The charge was complete, but like last night—no signal.

"Still in hell," he muttered, thoroughly annoyed. Martin might have finally texted the contact email, but now it seemed nothing would come through up here for the whole weekend.

He wondered if Martin would flip out when he didn't respond to his texts, then he wondered if his mom or the guys missed him at all. As if it mattered. They'd been missing him for weeks already. Maybe they didn't even notice he was gone anymore.

He felt truly strange as he caught his reflection staring back at him in the mirror.

Shit. Is that me?

He reached up and ran his hand through his *Vere-cropped* hair, fingering the uneven, dark colored clumps near his forehead. Vere had attacked him last night with a pair of mangled scissors. She'd kept his length, but made him look like he'd stuck his hair in a blender.

Worse, as he glanced lower, he remembered what he'd tried to forget. He was wearing tightie-whities.

And he had no other options in his wardrobe.

Yesterday, Vere had convinced him to add the nerd underwear to his new wardrobe all while giggling that cute, irresistible giggle of hers. She'd charmed him so much that he'd bought three packs of these ridiculous things to keep her laughing.

Vere's words still rang in his head. "You have to commit all the way, *inside and out*, or no one's going to believe it. The geek underwear will make sure you don't forget who you are when you're alone."

It had sounded good at the time.

He snapped the double-wide waistband against his stomach and wiggled his butt in the mirror, but stopped when he saw how Vere had chopped up the back of his hair.

He ran his hand through the long, uneven strands.

"Shit. The girl is a menace."

Am I going hiking with this haircut, a plaid shirt, mega-geek glasses and a whole bunch of compasses?

Hell. I guess I am.

Not like I've got anything better to do today.

With a resigned sigh, he pulled on his new brown canvas shorts, adjusted the compass on the belt loop, and shoved his phone into one of the many utility pockets in case he could find a signal later.

He put on the black framed glasses. The late morning sun streaming into the room had already caused them to turn completely black, but he could see surprisingly well through them. In the morning light, they were uglier than yesterday, but they did hide the color of his eyes perfectly well.

He peered closer, satisfied that at any angle, he could not see his own eyes. "Dustin McHugh, you are one freaky bastard."

He grinned, heart lightening as he almost cracked up at himself. Maybe it was going to be fun to be someone else for a little while.

He grabbed his new hiking shoes, a pair of odd socks that Vere had sworn were only for hiking because they *wicked* moisture away from his feet.

He yanked the labels off both and put them on.

The clock on his dresser read 11:08. He never slept this late. As a matter of fact, he usually had a hard time sleeping more than six hours straight.

"Not anymore," he muttered. "I, Dustin McHugh, normal teenager with bad underwear, sleep late all the time!" He laughed as he shoved on yesterday's Sacramento Kings cap, pulling the brim until it almost touched the top of his glasses—exactly how he and Vere had decided last night— would hide his face best.

The scent of maple syrup was coming through the door.

Pancakes? Waffles? French Toast!

Oh, please.

From what he could tell, Mrs. Roth was the best cook in the world. If dinner last night had only been 'thrown together', as she'd said, he could hardly wait for the planned dinner tonight.

Stomach in full grumble mode, he checked his wrist coverage one last time.

Hiking. Shit. Hope I don't die in the woods.

His stomach roared.

Oh, yeah. The smell of syrup is a very good sign.

Dustin opened his door and headed down the hall.

17: guy exposure works

VERE

Vere trudged toward the cabin with a satisfied smile. This morning, the lake had reached her definition of perfect. The water had been crystal clear, reflecting the first golden-yellow aspen leaves. And, after the long, hot summer, it had reached prime temperature. Meaning it would be swimmable up until the first frost. Hopefully that would not happen until after they came up for Labor Day in a couple of weeks.

She wiggled her lower jaw.

She'd smiled so much this morning and yesterday, the sides of her mouth ached. It couldn't be helped. She thought of Dustin's reaction to the herd of deer in the cabin's driveway last night and had to giggle out loud all over again.

The guy had positively flipped.

Refused to get out of the car. He'd told her he'd never seen real deer in 'the wild' before. As if their driveway could ever be described as the wild. *Ha.*

Wait till her new *BGF* saw the bear cross the football field at their school. Their neighborhood also boasted more deer than up here at the lake. Monument was the same elevation and landscape as this lake property, minus the lake and cute old cabins, of course.

But Dustin probably didn't know that. He was under the impression they were 'way high in the mountains' right now.

Vere grinned again at the memory of Dustin preening in the mirror at Rick's. The guy had been pretty darn funny.

Guy exposure. A++!

I should thank him. Tell him how much he's helped me. But how?

The object of her gratitude was sitting on the porch, lacing his brand-new hiking shoes.

Vere sat on the step below him and looked up as she pulled her wet bun into a tighter rubber band. The old panic set in for a moment, but after a quick reminder that this was ONLY *Dustin McHugh*, she settled in and started off with a simple, normal, "Hey."

Dustin stopped lacing and smiled.

Not even a flush or tingle in her cheeks!

"Hey. You missed the waffles."

"I had some. Hours ago, bed slug. You look great, by the way!" She grinned back at him.

Oh, marvelous day! I'm almost cured.

Not. Even. Blushing.

"Not too great, I hope?" Dustin frowned, concerned.

She giggled. "Are you fishing for compliments already? I mean you look great, as in *terrible-dork-perfect*."

Vere checked her the temperature of her cheeks with her fingertips. How could she not have even one blush on the horizon? Her sanity had also stayed completely intact. She hadn't fallen off the step or made a fool out of herself, either. She'd even managed to stay on topic.

Charlie's right, this guy exposure works!

Hunter turned back to his laces. "Where were you?"

"Swimming." Vere pointed behind her. "Do you swim?"

He blinked, as though surprised. "Not in lakes. Ever. Doesn't it weird you out, all those fish, snapping turtles, frogs and slimy plants?"

"It's a sandy bottom lake—eroded granite. There are definitely fish, but no slimy stuff. And no turtles or frogs live up here. It's not a pond for goodness sakes. It's a lake."

"Is there a difference?"

He looked so skeptical that she giggled. "Yes. Oh, man." She frowned. "We didn't buy you a swimsuit. You can borrow one of Charlie's. I'm sure we'll swim after the hike, and you'll see for yourself."

He looked positively petrified. "Not on your life. I think the hike will be plenty 'nature up close' for one day, thanks."

She laughed.

Charlie came out on the porch with a bottle of sunscreen. "Lather up. Unless you want to be lobster-red later."

"Why?" Dustin asked. "I'm already tan. The last place I stayed had this awesome private deck where I tanned every day."

Vere snorted. "Our Colorado sunshine comes with a wicked secret. It will burn right through your..." She glanced up so she could see his reaction to the zinger she was about to let fly, but his lenses, now black from soaking up the sun, had obscured his eyes. Her inability to see his gaze teasing back disappointed her more than she could say.

Dustin crossed his arms and frowned. "The sun will burn right through my what?"

"Oh, um," Vere recovered. "High altitude sunburns are the stuff of legends. You don't want one, that's all," she finished lamely. She smeared some sunscreen across her nose, took a huge squirt for her legs and offered the bottle to Dustin.

Charlie noticed Dustin's glasses as well. "Whoa. Your lenses look like ink. That's a shockingly hideous effect. I hardly remember who you were yesterday."

"Good. That's what we'd hoped for, right?" Dustin smeared the cream onto the back of his neck and started on his face.

"No one at school will ever catch on," Charlie added, shaking his head. "Amazing."

"What exactly am I supposed to do while I'm at your school? I mean, beyond going to classes and all that."

"What skills do you have? Other than standing still, smiling and looking all famous, I mean?" Charlie asked, pulling a face at him.

"The obvious ones, I guess. I can't do anything that would

blow my cover. They wouldn't let me bring a guitar, and Martin, my agent, made me promise not to sing or be on stage."

Vere's heart twisted. "That sucks."

Dustin blinked. "It's not a big deal. I don't mean to be here long enough for it to matter. I'm a whiz at memorizing stuff. Scripts, poems, anything."

"Only that? No sports?" Charlie asked.

"I've never been allowed to play contact sports. Don't want to bruise up the contracted merchandise. I do yoga and weight machines. No free weights. Too dangerous."

"Pisser. You're a lost cause," Charlie said.

Vere leaned back against the steps. "Lighten up, Charlie. All you can do is catch a brown ball, run fast and knock people down."

Charlie shook his head. "Don't get me started on your lack of skills." To Dustin he added, "You're going to have to be a drama dork."

"The people in drama are not dorks! You jocks are the dorks. Besides if we're driving him around, he might as well join something. He'll have to wait for us after school either way. What do you say? Join up?"

Hunter shook his head. "I usually do school solo. My tutors check my work and test me. I'm not joining anything."

"So you're home schooled?" Vere asked.

"Studio schooled. Kind of like home school."

"Have you ever been to a real school?" Charlie asked.

"Not since fourth grade. I don't remember it much. When I was nine I had an ongoing cereal commercial—*Happy Pops*? It paid really well so my mom pulled me out and started the tutoring."

"OMG! OMG! You're the Happy Pops Kid?" Vere squealed. "That is so neat. I loved Happy Pops. I still get Happy Pops on my birthday! SO COOL!"

♥ 140 ♥

Dustin grimaced and shook his head, glancing at Charlie. "Is she trying to torture me on purpose? *GuardeRobe* sold ten million albums last year, and she only recognizes me two days later for her love of a cereal that might be toxic. Dude. I *so* feel your pain. Your sister is unbelievable."

Charlie laughed long and loud. "Yep. I'm aware."

"Hey. Happy Pops is fortified with 12 vitamins and minerals," Vere protested, crossing her arms.

Charlie shrugged. "Told you. Hopeless. What else have you done that we might know?"

Dustin sighed and looked up as though this conversation pained him. "From there I was on a soap. *St. Clair Town*? You know it?"

"I don't," said Charlie.

"I do!" Vere beamed. "Cool. You must have been Doctor Lamber's sickly, long lost son! *Ahhh!* DYING! You were awesome. I bawled my head off over that character on the re-runs last year!"

Dustin scowled but Vere could tell he was biting back a smile. "Thankfully, the kid wasted away after one season, because playing that part sucked. The *Newt Network Kids-Club* job started after that, so I never went back to school."

"I remember that Kids-Club thing. How strange was that? They made you all wear matching knee socks." Charlie shuddered.

"Not very strange. I'm still on it, syndication and reruns on various national and Canadian cable networks. My contract is not up for another three years. It was what I did. What I do. Until now, I mean."

"But what about *GuardeRobe*? How did that come about?" Charlie asked.

"*GuardeRobe* was launched through NewtNet's teen marketing program. Most people don't make that connection, but it's all married to the parent company. It's one huge, intertwined, incestuous machine. Is this some sort of interview? I feel like I'm at a tribunal of pushy reporters."

"Oh. Sorry," Charlie mumbled, not so smug any more. "Just curious."

"Yeah. We're curious." Vere shut down her expanding list of questions. She couldn't help but be impressed. He was really smart, and like yesterday, she had the sensation that he was way older than seventeen. He'd probably had to grow up fast. She could see why he kept calling her *clueless*.

According to him and the world he came from, she wasn't even born yet. Vere didn't envy him, though. She never wanted to grow up. Not to the point where you had to talk about things like syndication and parent companies, whatever those were.

"It is one heck of a weird life you've had compared to ours," Charlie added, his tone apologetic.

"Ya think? Well, it's all I know, so it's not weird to me." He gestured at the trees around him. "I think hiking and swimming in lakes is twice as weird."

"Well, my Dustin McHugh is a great hiker, and he's gonna swim in that lake eventually." Vere grinned, going for a subject change. "So ramp up. I need a *list of things* we did to tell Jenna."

"Yeah. And if anyone's going to recognize you, it's going to be her. That chick is a *GuardeRobe* freak and a freak in general."

"Hey. She's beyond awesome, and funny, and perfect. You're too dense to notice," Vere defended her friend before turning back to Dustin. "Be warned. Jenna is a psycho, channel surfing, music-loving, social-media maniac. If anyone will test your disguise, it will be her."

Dustin shook his head. "I can't wait." He sounded worried, but Vere couldn't tell for sure, because she couldn't see his eyes.

UGH. I hate his glasses so much.

"I hope Dustin can keep up with us on this hike. Coming

from sea level, he might get dehydrated, altitude sickness—maybe we should do an easier trail," Charlie cautioned.

Vere frowned. "Oh, I forgot about that. Do you think he's going to be okay?" Vere jumped up and put her hand on Dustin's brow. "Does your head hurt at all? Is it hard to breathe?"

"Er, yes and yes, if you must know." Dustin grinned before continuing. "But it might have something to do with you and this ridiculous conversation."

Charlie rolled his eyes. "She's treating you like a pet, have you noticed?"

"I am not! I'll be right back with extra water, just in case." Vere dashed into the house.

18: promises promises

Dustin

They both watched her go. Dustin felt a cold rush of air when she'd pulled her hand away from his brow. As the screen door slammed, he had another flood of that strange feeling from last night. It was as if he couldn't function if Vere wasn't right by his side.

He shook it off, took up the bottle of sunscreen, and slathered some on his calves, hoping Charlie wouldn't notice his lapse.

Charlie broke the awkward silence. "We're pretty boring compared to what you're used to, huh?"

Dustin shook his head. "Not really. Your whole family's cool. You're possibly the most *normal* people I've ever met, though. Not going to lie, you're not what I'm used to. It's always been me and my mom. My mom is...kind of cold. After my real dad died, she and I started working together. She became my manager. The lines between her being a mom and me being a son got crossed."

He sighed, remembering how, when he was little, he'd cry to go to bed some long working nights, and how his mom would cry, too. But then she'd order him to stay awake at dinners and events like long award ceremonies they'd been invited to attend, because they couldn't afford any bad press of him looking tired or unhappy.

He went on, "Your mom—I don't know—she's such a real mom. Cooking meals and folding the laundry without any one hired to help her. And your dad was really great about staying late to order that retainer for me. As for Vere, she's—"

Charlie didn't let him finish. "Listen. Before she comes back, I have to level with you about my sister. The fact that she can talk to you like she does has never happened to her before."

"Yeah. She mentioned that some. I don't get it," he said, giving up on the sunscreen.

"She thinks she's truly a freak, as in broken. But she's not. She's really shy, or sensitive. Something gives her these social anxiety attacks. Guys, parties, school, any normal thing where people are hanging out seems to set it off. She stutters, turns colors or worse."

"I've seen some of that."

Charlie nodded. "Sometimes she can control it, but other times...she becomes a total train wreck. And I wasn't kidding about the 'pet' thing. She's acting as though you're some kind of *gift* to her life. It's weird."

"She is? Whatever. No big deal. I'm happy to be her pet, I suppose. For a while."

Charlie glowered at him as he ran his fingers through his dark blond hair. "She told me that you two were going to be *friends*? For real? Are you?"

"What's your point? So what if we're friends? Maybe it's a good thing."

"I don't want to sound like an ass all over again, but...I need you to know my sister has a way of forming huge attachments to people, that's all." Charlie shifted his feet, looking supremely uncomfortable. "I can't have you trying to make a move on her while you're here. If you touch her, hurt her—in any way—I'll straight up kill you."

"Dude! What the hell? I thought we were clear on that. I'm not going to make a move on your sister. I wouldn't even know how to navigate past that bun and all her—virginal—cluelessness. Come ON. Not my type. Never. Not. Happening."

Charlie squared his shoulders. "If she thinks you're *friends,* Vere could get all sappy. I don't want you taking advantage of the situation. My sister is completely stupid sometimes and

♥ 145 ♥

very impulsive and—sweet and—she could easily fall—*shit*, I don't know what I'm saying."

The kid looked him directly in the eyes.

Charlie's point was crystal clear to him.

"Give me a break. We aren't going to be *real* best friends. She hardly knows me. Do you think we'll have sleep-overs, giggle and share secrets until we suddenly find ourselves making out? If that's what you think, then you're mental."

"My sister is the mental one. I'm just being cautious."

"I like her. She's a really nice girl. That's it." He took off his cap and worked to bend the brim into a better shape. "I told you yesterday. Vere—she's—like no other girl I've met. But in all the wrong ways, if you know what I mean. You can stop worrying. Even if she throws herself at me, I'll field that ball and put her back. I'm pretty experienced at deflecting girls. Plus, she's made it clear she's not into *GuardeRobe* or me like that. *Hell.* Not at all. She even told me she's got a crush on someone."

"Okay. Okay. Good. Besides, you're right she's not into you. Vere is in love with my bro, Curtis. Always has been. He's also my best friend." Charlie seemed to relax after that. He smiled and shook his head. "I bet you have some girl stories, huh?"

"Yeah. But it's not my style to kiss and tell. And if you must know, toying with easy girls who treat you like a piece of meat gets old pretty fast."

"Right." Charlie snorted. "I'd sure like the chance to find that out for myself. Lucky bastard." He shot Dustin a knowing look. "You don't blame me for bringing it up, though? I had to lay it out there. It's my duty as a brother."

Dustin shook his head. "I'd do the same if I had a sister hanging around with a guy like me 24-7, that's for sure."

"Man, I'd trade lives with you in a heartbeat."

"You'd get tired of it." Dustin shrugged. "Your family is so stable. I sometimes wish I could have a different life, a family that looks out for each other, goes to a *cabin* all the time." Dustin moved down the steps and sat on the last one.

Charlie took his pack along with him as he followed, dropping his voice. "Speaking of me looking out for Vere—and now that we're solid—I'm hoping you might be able to help me with something. For Vere, I mean."

"Jesus. I thought the conversation about your sister was over. You just told me to stay the hell away from her."

Charlie laughed. "And now that you've promised to do that, I'm enlisting you to be on our *family* team."

Dustin blinked, but didn't answer because there was no way he wanted to be on the family team. He had enough problems of his own. The silence stretched between them.

"So you don't want to help?" Charlie now looked so awkward, Dustin didn't have the heart to shut him down like he wanted to. Plus, he was slightly curious.

"Of course I want to help," he lied.

"I think Vere would die of happiness if Curtis asked her out. Sadly, she can't even exchange more than a few words with him. Not without turning all red, knocking over lamps, and flailing like a psycho in front of him, that is. It's been that way between them for years."

"Okay?" Dustin said, almost laughing as he pictured Vere doing all that stuff. "I just don't see what your sister's crush has to do with me."

"Well, it's a long shot that Curtis would even go for Vere, but I'm going to drop a couple of hints his way. Give him the thumbs up. Vere's going to need major assistance before she will even have a chance with Curtis."

"Still waiting for you to get to the point."

"You're the helper." Charlie flushed, and glanced over his shoulder at the closed screen door. "Look. Like I mentioned, so far, you're the first guy she's been able to talk to that isn't a teacher, or a blood relative. Can you keep working with her? Get her to come out of her shell a little more? I will handle things from the other side. Get her set up with Curtis. Together, we can have her locked and loaded with a real boyfriend by the end of the month!"

Dustin rolled his eyes thankful for the glasses. He didn't know why he felt half pissed off all of a sudden. "I think you're nuts. Vere doesn't need my help—or anyone's help. She's fine. Adorable, funny, and cool—as she is. If *your-man* Curtis can't see the charm in a girl who knocks over lamps, maybe he's an ass?"

Charlie leveled him with a steady look. "Dude. Curtis is cool. He and Vere have a very long, twisted past. You have no clue. You'll understand more when you see how it is for her when she's in front of the guy. It's a brutal scene. She chokes on her shyness. The anxiety makes her freeze up completely. She needs this help. Everyone picks on her about it. Heck, even I can't resist sometimes."

Charlie stood and leaned on the stair rail, dropping his voice to a whisper. "She's already convinced you're going to help cure her; why not bring it out into the open now that she's labeled you her *creepy BGF?*"

Dustin choked, and then laughed. "Christ. She's told you about my new, dumb nickname?"

Charlie nodded. "Yeah. She's committed to you, *Dustin*. And for my sister, that means a lot."

Dustin leaned back against the steps and sighed, crossing his hands behind his head. "Why do I get the vibe you wish it were someone else who could help your sister? Am I wrong?"

Charlie darted him a chagrined look. "Of course I wish you could be someone else—someone more *normal*. Again, do you blame me? You dropped out of the sky as far as we're concerned. And now, after only two days, Vere acts all chatty and happy around you. It has me worried as hell."

"Why? You've got my promise. I'm going to treat her like

glass."

Charlie met his gaze. "If you're gone tomorrow, I wouldn't give a rat's ass. But Vere will care. I'd hate for any of your bullshit to carry over onto her life. She has enough problems without your high-exposure crap making her even more miserable. Exit our scene carefully when you go. We still have to live here after you're gone. Please don't break her—on any level—please. She's kind of fragile. The kind of person you could hurt, well—*forever*. Do you get me?"

"Yeah." Dustin swallowed. He hated hearing the truth about himself. He realized then how much his presence here really did—and could—affect them all.

"Thanks for the honesty." He sighed. "I will do my best to not treat the Roth family involvement in my crap-ass life lightly," he said quietly, meeting Charlie's gaze. "And you're right, I've got a load of bullshit bigger than you can imagine. I won't dump any of it here permanently. I promise." He couldn't help but be humbled by what they'd all already done for him.

Shit.

He pictured Vere cringing in front of a press mob. Then imagined Aunt Nan with her slow-moving gait, trying to get away from a crowd, and he shuddered. Suddenly, his disguise, *working,* really mattered. And not for him. But for them.

"I'll help Vere. Any way I can. Tell me what you need as it comes up. I could ask her directly what she thinks she needs? That might be easiest."

Charlie grimaced, then laughed. "It will be ugly. But yeah direct is best. Ask her about something called *the incident*. She's going to flip, though. Be afraid."

He shrugged. "I've got nothing to lose, and according to you, she's got everything to gain. I'm happy to help. I feel like I owe her a bunch already. Hell, I owe your whole family for helping me, especially Vere. So...thanks for even dealing with me at all."

Charlie nodded solemnly. "Cool. Good. I'm glad you understand." Charlie let out a long breath of air. "Let's stop talking about this. I'm not going to hug you, dude, so don't ask. And don't you dare try to man-hug me, either. You're too damn ugly to even touch in that outfit."

"Whatever." Dustin chuckled. The guy was funny.

Charlie grinned and lightly shoved Dustin's shoulder.

Charlie laughed when Dustin shoved back, not as lightly.

"You know once school is open, our friendship fades to nights and weekends. And only when zero witnesses are present. I will have to brutalize you in public on Tuesday, and every day after that, to make all this believable, *dork*."

"Looking forward to that." Dustin smiled. "Let's hope this costume works."

"Dude, *no one* is going to know that it's you. I promise. And...don't worry, I won't let anyone bully you too much."

"Why, thank you for your protection, Mr. Jock Popular, but I think I can take care of myself on that front."

Dustin hopped back up the steps and walked the length of the porch. "Check the new walk. The slouching killed my back, so we came up with a way to highlight my height to the worst effect."

He swaggered, but with his body rigid and straight, keeping his head high, a little too high, as if he were a robot on some red carpet. "I still have to work on it."

Charlie busted out laughing. "Oh, no. No. Stop. It's perfect. You are one wound-tight weirdo. Once you get that retainer in," Charlie sputtered with more laughter, "you won't even recognize yourself!"

"I already don't. It's kind of fun being someone else." He returned his laugh and took a deep breath.

Vere rushed back onto the porch, hauling four dripping water bottles. The bottom edge of her oversized, shapeless

T-shirt was soaked, as were half of her shorts from the wet swimsuit she still wore.

"Sorry it took so long. Dad had to pull these out of the storage area. I stopped to wash them and fill them to the top with ice. Dustin, this is going to be the best water you've ever tasted. Just you wait. *The best!* It's from the well out back!"

His chest tightened at the elated sound of her voice. Her cheeks were flushed from exertion and she seemed to radiate pure light. Small wisps of light-blonde curls caught the light as they rioted like a sunburst around her face.

Dustin blinked, struck dumb. Something had changed with her, and inside of him. It was a feeling he didn't recognize at all. He felt light-headed and hollow. Like he'd been pumped full of helium. Similar to the thing he'd felt yesterday.

He also felt better. Way better. Like he'd finally landed on two feet in this upsidedown, sideways and backwards universe. Maybe it was because he was now calling himself *Dustin* inside his own head, and it felt perfect. It also helped that everyone had called him *Dustin* all morning long without mistake.

Maybe the feeling had more to do with the smiling girl standing in front of him. A girl who found peaches—and baby ducks—and now plain water—to be *the best things in the whole world.*

Damn! Had she been this beautiful a few minutes ago?

Maybe he felt this great because Vere obviously believed her new bestie, *Dustin,* would agree with her excitement about how everything ordinary was actually extraordinary.

Was that why he couldn't tear his gaze away from her glowing profile? Her smile? Or was it because he was happy the *friends* thing between them seemed to be working out?

Just friends...just friends...but, damn...

I'm feeling way more than the just friends feeling.

Maybe he should call Barry at Falconer to find out what in the hell was going on in his head right now. Barry would gush straight away, "Oh! You're having a *feeling*. Finally, a real *feeling!*"

But what feeling is this? Hell...not something I want to talk about with Barry, that's for sure.

He glanced at Vere again, and his heart jumped, starting back up double time. She turned her smile on him and the thing went even more ballistic.

Shit. Am I getting a crush on this girl? Is that what this is?

He shook it off as impossible. He figured friendship with a girl must feel close to a crush. Since he'd never had a girl that was only a *friend*, he must be simply confused.

The heart beating thing was gratitude to Vere.

He owed this girl for the first taste of raw happiness he'd felt in years. His feelings, getting all sappy like this, must be his friendship shooting back at her. They would lose intensity once he got used to her—this place—and his new self.

Charlie was watching him closely.

Could the guy tell everything he'd just said about Vere—*not being his type*—had possibly morphed into a complete lie? That he had a brand new type? That all he wanted to do was kiss Vere Roth's cute upper lip right now?

Dustin shook his head to clear it.

He might be the newly born *Dustin McHugh*, but thankfully, he still had Hunter Kennedy's press-mode-mask working for him. He also knew deep down he couldn't forget he owned Hunter Kennedy's twisted and jaded heart under this damn plaid shirt.

It didn't matter what he was feeling about Vere Roth.

This girl liked someone else. He'd promised to be her friend.

And that was all his heart and his mind had room to hold.

Plus, she was way too innocent for a guy like him.

She moved closer to him then. He could smell sunscreen mixed with lavender-sage coming off her warm skin. He felt extreme guilt for even thinking about her at all. Like he needed to go straight to a church and beg forgiveness. And right now.

She peered at his face. "Dustin, you're looking really flushed. You're going to die from heat and we haven't even started hiking yet. And I mean *DIE*."

"Everyone dies, Vere," he evaded, crossing his arms in case he suddenly went nuts and tried to touch her.

She moved closer. "Come on. You know what I'm talking about. Take off that long-sleeved shirt. Please, or I'm going to take it off for you."

She did not just say that. Shit. And double shit.

He went on the defensive. "Don't even come near me, you crazy pixie. Worry about your own shirt, if that's what you call that giant, soggy nightgown *you're* planning to hike in."

"Hey. This is my dad's old college shirt, and it's awesome."

"Your words, not mine."

Charlie laughed, heading off the porch steps. "He tagged it, Vere. You've got to stop wearing all of Dad's Goodwill pile."

Vere's gaze had never left his face.

"I know you're trying to change the subject, Dustin. Hand over the shirt. It's a matter of personal safety. Honestly. Don't be so stubborn."

He pushed away from her, grabbed his pack and headed down the trail, following Charlie. "The shirt stays on. Bury me in it. Is she always this bossy?" he asked Charlie.

"You have no idea," Charlie answered.

Dustin's mind had gone wild with images of Vere's delicate fingers working on his shirt buttons. Blood surged in every area it shouldn't. Luckily, the heavy canvas of his shorts, and the fact they were walking single file, hid all of that.

But how am I going to hide the fact that I think I've truly got a crush on this girl?

Behind your dark glasses, dumbass. She'll never know.

How hard could it be? You'll be gone in a few weeks.

Live with the feeling. It's cool, and it makes you feel alive.

💙 153 💙

He put a hand over his racing heart.

Does it? Because I kind of feel like I also might be suddenly dying right now.

"Wait up!" Vere called after him. "Your legs are too long. If we walk this fast we can't talk or search for cool rocks."

He slowed his pace even though he wanted to run as fast as possible in the other direction.

When she caught up, half-gasping, he'd recovered his control. "Promise to not bust on my shirt?"

She rolled her eyes, and softly punched him in the shoulder. "Promise. But let the record show, you're being stupid."

He grimaced. "You're still indirectly busting on my shirt."

"Fine!" She fell into step beside him. "What should we talk about, then?"

Hunter stared down at her and sighed. "According to Charlie, sometime today, we should talk about a kid called *Curtis Wishford?* Charlie thinks I can help you with him."

She flushed so immediately red, he felt kind of bad for bringing it up.

"What? What?!" She gasped, her eyes going wild. "Charlie— *you jerk*—I'm going to kill you!"

Charlie disappeared around a bend in the trail, and Vere tossed Dustin another wild glance.

"What did he say about me and Curtis? What lies did Charlie spew!!"

Dustin shrugged. "Tons. But not enough."

Concentrating on his footing as the pathway became steadily steeper, he watched the dust settle into his hiking shoes. It made them not look so new. Like this wasn't his first time out in the woods.

She startled him when she cupped her hands to make a small megaphone. "Charlie...you suck! *OH-GOD-WHAT-DID-YOU-TELL-HIM?*"

There was no answer from Charlie. He waved as he hit one

switchback above them.

"Come on. How tough could it be to talk about this Curtis with your new *bestie*?" he cajoled.

Vere made a strangled cough-choke sound, and her face flamed even brighter. "No! No! It's not the appropriate time or place. We're hiking." She stopped walking then, blocking his path.

"Ehem. We aren't hiking now. Did you notice that?"

"Why do you have to use that voice on me?" She crossed her arms and blinked at him accusingly.

"I wasn't using any voice. You're going to have to get used to it, I guess. It comes with me everywhere I go."

He smiled and took off his glasses to wipe the sweat off the bridge of his nose, and cleaned the moisture off the lenses with his shirt. He paused, catching her gaze.

When she didn't move, he leaned closer, scanning her face for some response. She appeared to be trying hard to breathe. He remained still and acted as though her behavior seemed completely normal. He totally got how it sucked when you were simply trying to breathe and people refused to wait for it to happen.

Is this what Charlie had meant about Vere having anxiety? Could I have set this off with a couple of simple questions?

"Vere?" He'd asked it softly, trying to break in to her head.

Her eyes widened all huge and round, just like the deer that had been caught in their car headlights last night. The girl was miles from him at this moment and showed no signs of coming back.

Charlie wasn't kidding.

This had to be brutal if it happened to her in public, and it sure as hell would scare off any guys.

Guys who were possible jerks, that is.

Vere made the same strangled sound and blinked as though it were starting all over again. Her face hit licorice-red and her bun had slipped far to one side.

Unlike all the other times, Vere's hands remained uncharacteristically motionless by her sides while her expressions ranged from doubtful, to trusting, to completely freaked out.

Damn. But she's so adorable like this.

Girl has killed my heart.

Dustin's throat went dry. He had the sudden urge to hug her...fix the bun for her. Anything to help her out of this. But he wasn't allowed. And after yesterday's hand-holding moment—plus today's secret-crush admission—he no longer trusted himself to go near her.

He tried talking again, still pretending her lapse was perfectly normal. "So. We were on the topic of *Curtis*?" He said the guy's name clearly, to remind himself of the guy she really liked. He went on, "Your crush. Can we please come up with some ways I can help?"

With what looked like a huge effort, she finally moved, and started walking. Then running! Away!

Hilarious.

He thought she uttered, "Maybe-don't-know-probably-maybe," as she bolted further ahead.

As she reached full speed, her voice grew clearer. That's when she hollered back to him, "After I kill my brother. Maybe."

Charlie was now three switchbacks above Dustin. Probably running for his life. Kid must have known Vere was going to come after him and that's why he took off in the first place!

Dustin grinned.

As Vere hit the higher switchback, she stopped to call ahead, "I HATE YOU CHARLIE ROTH. REVENGE IS COMING. AND YOU SUCK."

Charlie shouted back from way above, "I love you, little sis. It's for the best! Start by telling him about what happened between you and Curtis."

She gasped. Freezing again.

Dustin looked up at her as she'd stopped in the spot one switchback directly above him.

He raised his brows. "Your incident thing sounds so epic. Any idea what your mom packed for our lunch? Have I mentioned how much I appreciate your mom's cooking?"

"SHUT UP," she gasp-yelled.

Dustin wasn't sure if she was talking to him or Charlie.

She looked so freaked out and mad, he wasn't going to ask. She glowered down at Dustin, then and added, "Please...put your glasses back on. Those eyes. You'll—get—an eye sunburn! *Unbelievable!*" She stomped away.

He heard her mutter something about how his *liquid-blue-assets were just too much for her to take right now.* Dustin replaced the glasses and pulled his cap low, watching as Vere's skinny arms flailed into fists as she started running all over again when she made the next switchback turn.

Charlie was long gone. Vere would never catch him.

Dustin hit the second switchback and placed one hand on his chest, trying to catch his breath. An impossible feat, because the first switchback had been steep as hell.

Besides, his heart was busting out of his chest and he was laughing too hard to move at all.

19: the incident revisited

VERE

Hike abandoned half way, they'd stopped to eat lunch on a sloping rock. Vere, worried about Dustin, had begged to turn around after they ate, vowing that she was too tired from being stupid and running up the trail.

Neither of the boys fought her on it.

"Come on, Vere. Say you aren't mad anymore," Charlie pleaded, eating half of his turkey sandwich in three huge bites.

"I'm not mad. I'm completely humiliated." Vere glanced at Dustin, who was also eating his sandwich without chewing much like her brother was, but thankfully, minus the talking-with-his-mouth-full part.

"Come on," Dustin added, after swallowing another bite. "Don't be embarrassed. Take advantage of the situation. You said your complete disdain for me and my career makes it easier for you to talk to me. So talk."

"That's not true. I totally respect musicians. I simply hate *GuardeRobe* and—"

"Easy—" Dustin wrinkled his nose. "You've never listened to one song. Don't hate the awesome music that is *me*."

"Bragger." Vere smiled, finally relaxing under his kind, warm gaze.

Charlie finished his sandwich and swung his legs over the steep side of the angled rock. "Dude. It's not about the music. She hates *GuardeRobe* simply because *I like GuardeRobe*. It's a sibling thing. When one of us announces we like something, the other must then vow to hate it forever."

"Is this true?" Dustin frowned. "You guys *do* that? Is that normal in families?"

"Yeah. Universal behavior." Vere nodded. "I've refused to

listen to *GuardeRobe* for two years. So blame Charlie for my disdain. His fault for discovering the band first." Vere shook her head, somewhat ashamed at Dustin's crushed look.

"Damn, that's so messed up. If I help you get with this Curtis Wishford dude, then my payment is that you have to at least listen to one or two tracks. If you can't stand the music, then read the lyrics because I wrote most of them. Deal?"

Vere hid a smile. "That request crosses a line that was made years ago when Charlie chopped the hair off my dolls and dressed them like army guys. I don't think I can agree to your terms," Vere lied, vowing to listen to every track *GuardeRobe* ever released when she got home.

"Hey, I also *undressed* the over-developed dolls, too."

"You did that? Hilarious." Dustin took an apple out of his lunch bag and held it up. "How did your mom know to pack my favorite apple? The Granny Smith rules." He took a huge bite. "I've always wanted to cut off doll hair. Too bad I never had a sister." He grinned approvingly at Charlie.

Vere glared. "Traitor! Me, listening to *GuardeRobe,* will not happen unless you and Charlie memorize a few Katy Perry songs word for word."

"Already done." Dustin chomped another apple bite. "I'm a huge fan."

Charlie laughed. "Back to the topic at hand. The incident. Spill it, or I will. Don't you want to be cured? This guy's offering to help. Stop creating drama and swapping subjects."

Vere looked away from both of them as the tips of her ears caught on fire. "If I tell this story, you *Charlie Roth,* can never, ever tease me about it again." She turned on Dustin. "And you, *Dustin McHugh*, can never *start* teasing me about it. Okay?"

Charlie nodded solemnly. "I swear, from this day forward. No more teasing about Curtis or your past. All other topics are still wide open though, right? If so, then I promise."

Dustin bit his bottom lip as though he wanted to laugh and

answered, "I promise, too."

"Fine." Vere took a long, shaky breath. "I've wanted to be with Curtis Wishford since I was old enough to know what *girlfriend* meant. Before that, I simply wanted to marry him in the *Prince and Princess* style."

Charlie rolled his eyes. "I hated living in the room across the hall those years. She sang the stupidest songs."

"Whatever. Your spit-shooting gun battles were worse."

Dustin laughed. "Back to Curtis, please."

Vere went on, "Before that, I wanted to play house with Curtis and hand him plastic cookies. Something I did often, because we always played house together, long before things got really awkward."

"And playing house isn't awkward?" Charlie snorted.

Vere tossed him a glare. "You promised!"

Charlie held up his hands and gasped out, "I know. I know. It's just not easy." He bent over and turned away, shoulders shaking, until a full belly laugh escaped him.

Dustin started laughing, too.

Vere stood and threw her apple at Charlie. She missed her mark and it bounced off Dustin's head instead. Both guys jumped up to get out of her way, laughing uncontrollably.

"P-p-pplastic cookies. She's not kidding," Charlie choked out, holding his stomach. "We played house all the time."

"Haa. Stop. No more details." Dustin, still laughing, pulled off his glasses and rubbed his eyes.

"You both suck! Why did I even try? And, Dustin, if this is you, teaching me self-control after *years* of acting classes, now we all know why you have not yet received an acting award! You've got work to do."

As though that insult didn't even touch Dustin, he laughed louder.

"He's got two Mega-Music Awards. Isn't that enough?" Charlie shook his head.

"You do?" Vere blinked at Dustin while she contemplated throwing rocks at Charlie.

"I don't have any awards. I'm just Dustin. Charlie, stop bringing all that shit up."

He met Vere's gaze and laughed again.

"Ugh. Stop laughing at me." Vere winced, wishing she could disappear.

"No. No!" Dustin laughed louder. "I swear, I'm not laughing at you. I laughed at Charlie, because he was so funny trying *not* to laugh. I swear. The kid's face cracks me up."

"And I only started laughing because I remembered the time Curtis actually *ate* one of those plastic cookies. Then I remembered, that cookie was the first time you'd sent Curtis to the emergency room." Charlie made his eyes all big and round. "*The incident* was the second time!"

"I'd forgotten about that." Vere shook her head and bit back her own small smile.

"Vere, you're like his fatal attraction!" Charlie doubled over, howling again.

Even Vere had to crack up at that. "I'm glad you've been keeping track. Please don't pass this information on to anyone outside the three of us, you *ass*. No need for people at school to know."

Vere met Dustin's smiling eyes, and realized the plain, fleckless, burning blue color had hardly shocked her at all during this whole conversation.

"Curtis used to eat everything. He ate rocks out of our front yard once," she explained. "Some tree bark too, and every quarter he could find." She giggled. "The kid was always heading to the hospital for stuff like that.

"Are you sure you want to get with this guy? He sounds... challenged." Dustin grimaced.

Vere giggled again. "He's amazing."

Dustin arched a brow. "Of course he is."

"And nice. And beyond good looking. And *yes*, I'm sure I want to be with him. I've been in love with him forever."

Dustin sighed. "Okay, good, as long as you have your goal straight."

"I do."

"Then tell me about this *incident* thing. What could possibly be holding the two of you, ultra-nice, creepy love-birds apart?"

They all sat back down. Vere leaned her back against the rock. She glanced at Charlie, hoping for help.

Charlie sighed and started for her, "It was at a neighborhood summer barbecue. Seventh grade. Everyone we knew was there. The whole middle school, practically."

"And everyone's parents. Let's not forget them." Vere shuddered. "If you're going to have a major incident, you should never have it in front of parents. Because they overreact, right? Especially if there's a ton of blood."

Dustin nodded as though he completely understood, which gave her the courage to go on, "Well, I had this best friend back then. Kristen Hodjwick. Only she wasn't really my friend. Does that make sense? She was like a 'frenemy'. Nice on the outside, evil the rest of the time?"

Charlie pulled a frown. "Dude. She's still brutal. Like a sinister, manipulating brainwasher. This chick's worked her spell on half of the football team. You'll meet her. Be afraid. Very afraid."

Vere went on, "Kristen and I, with a bunch of other girls, had done this sleep over the night before. We were all supposed to share our deepest, darkest secrets. And, stupidly, I went first. I told everything. About how much and how desperately in love I was with Curtis. I even told them about the way I did 'homework' every night by writing his name in my journals, and like how I totally couldn't wait for him to come over and see Charlie. *Everything*."

"Damn." Charlie grinned. "I always wondered what you were

scribbling. Girls are such disturbing people." Charlie wrinkled his nose.

"Go on, it's no big deal. I'm still not seeing how this was anything major," Dustin said.

"Just wait, you haven't made it to the game of Truth or Dare." Charlie moved to sit on the rock next to Vere.

"Yeah." Vere pulled her knees up to her chest. "That's where it all went wrong. We'd all huddled up on the side of the house to play. Kristen called on me. I was stupid enough to pick *dare* because I thought she'd make me admit that I liked Curtis in front of the whole school if I chose *truth*."

"Makes sense. What was the dare?" Dustin asked.

"Kristen hit me with one worse. She dared me to *kiss* Curtis Wishford. In front of everyone."

"Sounds like the perfect chance to start something in the right direction?"

"Yeah, if you're not Vere, and it's not seventh grade," Charlie chuckled.

Dustin raised his brows. "Tell me the rest. What did you do?"

She swallowed, remembering. "First, I was excited, right? So happy. I'd waited for this moment my whole life. Practiced on my pillow thousands of times."

Charlie grimaced, obviously biting back another laugh. "Please. Hold off on more freak details. I swear to God, I've lost the urge to even sneak a peak at your journals if this is the drama that's in them."

Vere shot her brother a glare, before sneaking a peek at Dustin through her lashes. If Dustin was about to laugh or be disgusted, he didn't show it, so she kept talking, "And Curtis, well, he didn't seem against the kiss idea. He was smiling and acting all good about it. So...like...yeah..."

Vere felt her face finally grow hot.

She stared away from Dustin's eyes and focused on the black specks in the rock under her hands before continuing,

"Everyone made a circle around us, mostly so the parents couldn't see. And as I moved in, I kept staring at his lips and thinking about finally kissing *my Curtis*. Then it shifted to total anxiety. I got pissed that Kristen outed me with this secret, private thing. And so I stopped moving." She looked up. "Because everyone was staring at me—it was like I couldn't move."

Dustin shook his head. "Wow. Awkward."

"Yeah. She was seriously frozen in mid-pucker with her eyes bugging out," Charlie added.

Vere rushed on, "When I stopped moving Curtis decided to go for it. He came at me fast, which made me totally flip out and lose my balance. My hands went all crazy and I clocked him so hard in the head that he actually fell down."

"Chin, actually. She hit his chin. With a closed, fast moving fist," Charlie said. "A perfect upper cut."

"Woah-no-you-didn't!" Dustin's eyebrows shot up.

Vere nodded. She could hardly swallow, let alone finish the story.

Charlie kept going for her. "Vere looked like some sort of elbow-knees-and-fists tornado. Curtis was just in the perfect position to go down hard. He'd been slightly bent over, because Vere's so puny. He'd also puckered up big-time. Scrunched his eyes closed right before Vere went, *SLAM, BAM, KA-POW!*"

Charlie flung himself around, doing his best rendition of Vere on that day, and Vere couldn't even fault him for one move.

When she could finally speak again, she said, "And let's not forget. This happened. In front. Of everyone."

Dustin let out a long, low whistle. "So how did you draw the blood?"

"Curtis bashed his whole face into some huge garden rock when he fell." She shrugged.

"No shit?" Dustin looked at Charlie for confirmation.

He nodded. "Knocked out cold. Blood spurted everywhere. From where his face hit the rock."

Vere sighed. "Kristen was the first, and the loudest, screamer. Everyone and everyone's parents came running, of course."

Charlie piped in again, "The whole time Kristen was howling: *Vere did it. Vere killed him. Poor Curtis. Poor Curtis tried to kiss her and she went crazy and attacked all of us. Vere beat Curtis up like a maniac!*"

"No way!"

"Way." Charlie made a face.

"So, Vere and Kristen weren't friends after that?" Dustin asked.

Vere caught Charlie hiding a pitying look as he nodded. "That girl didn't need friends. Somehow, she brainwashed and then *dated* Curtis until the end of freshman year. Almost killed our bro-friendship forever."

Dustin let out a long whistle. "*Eee-vil.* Beyond evil."

Vere looked up and gave Dustin a resigned shrug. "Turns out, Kristen had liked Curtis all along. She'd been really jealous after the sleep over. Kind of planned the whole thing to get rid of me." She sighed again. "All's fair in love and war, I guess."

"Worse, Curtis had double black eyes for months. Everyone teased him even more than they teased Vere," Charlie added.

"I know that made him hate me. My blushing and stuttering act started shortly after. It's never stopped. Obviously. Do you think there's hope for me?"

Dustin nodded. "Yesterday, we all thought you couldn't *unmake* me." He put his glasses back on. "And look how I've changed. If we can sneak me into your high school, then turning things around between you and Curtis should be cake. Let me gel with this. Get me through my first week of school and then we'll come up with a plan. I'd like to observe you two in action before I solidify anything, though? Okay?"

"Yeah. Okay." She reached into her pack and passed out the

water bottles.

Charlie gulped his down. "Damn, that's good water. Like you said, Vere," Charlie smiled, heading down the trail. "Let's get home."

Dustin was blinking at his half-empty water bottle and finally met Vere's gaze. He looked kind of stunned. "It's true. Best water in the whole world. Damn, but you weren't kidding!"

Vere beamed at him, completely thrilled that she'd managed to hold—what she was certain—had to be—the longest conversation she'd ever had with a guy besides Charlie, ever!

Dustin shook his head. "Why are you standing there grinning at me like that?"

"I don't know," she evaded. "I guess it's because I'm so happy you came—to our house—to our lives."

He sighed and seemed to tense his shoulders.

"What? Did I say something wrong? Now you know my whole life story and you didn't even judge me—so we must be at official trust levels now. Talk. I can't be happy about having a new friend?" She bit her lip, worried she'd messed up.

He looked at the sky. *"Hell.* I don't know. I don't want to rain on your parade, but could you please try to remember that I'm not exactly thrilled to be here? This is not just about *you.*"

"Oh. Right." She swallowed. "Of course."

He softened his tone. "I know I said I'd help you out, but I hate being used. Maybe it's me—being paranoid—but I feel like somehow, somewhere, you mean to do that to me before this is all over. You're acting like we're all signed up for some sort of happy-camp. I didn't want any of this. I was forced to come here."

Vere's heart twisted.

She shook her head, almost running into him as he cut in front of her to start down the trail behind Charlie. "Dustin, wait. I'm sorry. You're right. I was using you. I guess I still am." Her voice wavered as her throat got all tight. "I suck."

"Shit! That's not what I meant, and you don't suck." He stopped and turned around, his huge frame blocking the whole path. "Please don't make that face—like you're about to cry."

She pulled in a breath. "What face? Jeez. I want to understand you, that's all."

"I was trying to be honest. To tell you how I *feel*. Only, it came out bad. I'm terrible at talking, and worse at talking about *feelings*. My therapist said I should try to do it more. Obviously I just failed."

She stared at his feet, pushing away her tears and trying to focus on what he'd just said. "You have a therapist?"

He tucked a finger under her chin and brought her face up. She could see her horrified expression reflected back in his dark glasses. "Everyone in Los Angeles has a therapist."

"Please. I'm not stupid. They do not."

He shrugged and shuttered his expression. "Vere—let me start over. I know you aren't using me. You aren't the type to be like that. And now, I've volunteered to help, so I can only blame myself if things get strange."

"You volunteered because we *made you*. And I have been using you! All along I've practiced talking to you to see if I could do it without blushing. I *did* do that without your knowledge."

"Well I used you to help me come up with a disguise."

"I wanted to help you." She frowned.

"Yeah, but I didn't want you. Not at all. Not at first. And it's not like you're getting paid for all these hours of baby-sitting me." He pulled his hand away from her face and his eyes darkened. "Wait. *Shit?* Are you getting paid?"

She blinked. "No. What is wrong with you?"

"Vere. Don't you get it? Everything's wrong with me and my life. I've left my home, my band, my career—and there's the matter of my 'stand in' to worry about. Plus, I can't get through to my agent. The guy is supposed to tell me when all this madness will be over."

She flinched. "I'm sorry. I got too fired up. I didn't think."

"You didn't know." He finished his water and put on his pack.

"What about your mom? Won't *she* tell you when you get to go home?"

They started walking together slowly. "Mom and I are not on speaking or texting terms. Not even close."

"Oh. Now that you lay it all out there, I guess it could seem like I was dancing on your grave there a little," she said, trying unsuccessfully to mask the pity in her voice. "I don't know how to act around you yet, because I don't *know* you."

"Vere, there's not much to know beyond I'm the closest thing to the dark side you'll ever meet. Which is why I don't know how to act around you yet, either."

"Please. I'm not buying it. If you're representative of the dark side, then it's probably an awesome place!"

He laughed. "This is what I mean. Only *you* would find something good to say about the world melting into magma. You're like a random ray of light. Brightening up everything in every direction. I can hardly keep track of you among the other crap I'm dealing with in my head. I guess you, that brightness, just freaked me out."

She nodded. "I get you. I'm overwhelming. Charlie vows daily that I exhaust him. My parents also say it. I'll try to chill until you're used to me."

"Don't. I like how you are. But if I get short tempered or act weird—it's about me—not you. Know I'm dealing with my own personal garbage and don't get your feelings hurt. Okay?"

"Okay. And thanks for telling me all this. Being completely honest." Before he stepped ahead where the pathway narrowed to single file, she grabbed his arm. "Wait." She was suddenly fully aware that her touch had caused his muscles to tense.

He has a lot of muscles. And a very large forearm.

From guitar playing probably...

Sadly, that thought fired her cheeks to red. "Uh, so...yeah. If you want to back out. If it all gets too awkward, I'm sure I can get Curtis to notice me on my own. I don't really *need* your help," she lied, holding her breath.

When he didn't answer, just stared at her hand gripping his wrist, she let go and rushed on, "Okay. Fine. I do need you. It's not going to be strange. I'll try to tone it down. I promise. But...maybe we can do some more 'practice talking' sessions before we head down the hill Monday? Like talking about real, live—boy—girl topics? We've got two whole days left to cure me before school re-opens on Tuesday. I want this year, *me*, to finally be different. "

He raised his brows high. "You promise to take me to town tomorrow so I can try to find a network for my phone?"

"Yeah. Of course, but don't get your hopes up." She stabilized her bun before it toppled to the side. "Please say yes to the other stuff."

He smiled softly, as though she'd somehow amused him all over again.

"You don't need me, Vere. But how could I deny you when you ask me like this? I'm not backing out. For as long as I'm here, *Dustin McHugh* is your go-to-practice-guy. Or, whatever you need me to be until you wake up and dump me."

She let out a long breath and grinned. "As if. Can you imagine me doing that?"

"Yes." He smiled. "I can."

She laughed and rolled her eyes.

Charlie's voice came from far below. "Losers. What ARE you doing? Come on. I want to go swimming."

Vere shot Dustin a hopeful look.

"Not on your life. I will not swim in that lake!"

20: the first test

Dustin

"This is the *town*?" Dustin groaned. "It looks like a movie set. And not a good one."

"Car windows are still open. Shh!" Vere commanded. Her face had gone slightly pale.

"*This* is my promised *metropolis* of Buena Park? The main street is still a dirt road! How? Why?" He reached into his utility pocket to pull out his phone. The lack of bars had him panicked, horrified and hugely disappointed. "Dammit! No signs of a network. How can places like this still exist off the grid?"

Vere shook her head as they both got out of her VW. "I warned you. Cheer up. I did deliver on the cute promises," she added. "The historical society actually re-built the boardwalks so you can really get the old-west feel. Do you love it?"

"Only because you love it," Dustin answered, making Vere smile. His new favorite activity.

"So far, no one seems to notice me," he said, checking out the tourists. "They're looking at you and your epic outfit way more than looking at me."

"Yes! I know. I'm distracting them."

"Is that what you're doing?" Dustin laughed.

"Duh. Yes." Vere pulled her shirt down. "This outfit wasn't an accident. I wore it to dazzle people's attention away from you."

Dustin laughed, surveying her. Vere had worn what appeared to be Charlie's old football jersey. Long before she'd met him, she must have thought it a good idea to tie-dye the monstrous thing grape-juice-purple. Like all of her other clothes, the thing swallowed her small frame.

She'd *un-matched* it with some denim capris, which he could only see from below her knees to her calves. Because, yes, the purple jersey was THAT huge. Add in her cluster-clump-bun, some neon running shoes plus her pink cheeks, and the overall effect was that of a shapeless, crazed-looking circus clown.

She dashed in front of him and scanned the street. "Do you feel nervous? I feel really nervous? Stay behind me."

An adorable, nervous, circus clown who thinks she needs to protect me.

He took in how the hiking and her time at the lake had brought out the ginger color in the freckles across her high cheekbones. They now matched the reddish-blonde tips of the curling hair wisps that always snuck out of her bun. He never tired of watching them weave around her expressive face.

Vere glanced quickly around again, the straight set of her lips looked beyond stressed. "Let's stick close to the car for a bit, just in case. Remember, this is only a test. Dress rehearsal."

Dustin tried to lighten the mood by mimicking the American Broadcasters voice: "This is a test. This is ONLY a test."

Vere gasped, turned and slapped her hand over his mouth. "And, please don't talk above a whisper until we get the voice thing figured out. Are you *insane!*"

Dustin smiled down at her. "Sorry," he said from under her hand.

She glowered. "And delete that grin until my dad fits you with the retainer tomorrow. You promised. We walk around. You don't talk. You don't smile. We go home and we re-adjust the disguise where necessary. What is wrong with your memory?"

"Omfkay. Move your hand."

"Not until I can feel your smile disappear." She pushed her small hand farther against his mouth.

"I can't. Your cracking me up major right now." He laughed

behind her palm.

"Stop it! Don't even start. Just keep that voice under wraps, along with all the other amazing *assets*—okay?" She slowly removed her hand.

He leaned forward and whispered, "You keep mentioning the assets, *fangirl*. I think you find me amazingly attractive and it's killing you not to tell me."

She shoved his shoulder as they started down the boardwalk. "A corpse would find you attractive and you know it! It's natural human selection. We're both of the same species. I'm bound to react to what biology set up so very well for you. Stop fishing for more compliments. People who look how you look..." She paused and considered him.

"Yes?" He bit his smile back into a composed expression.

"Well—you all must be ruined from gaping at your own beauty in the mirror every morning—aren't you? That's what I would do if I had your face."

"You're calling me beautiful now? Throwing out more compliments, just when you swore you'd never. Do you want me to become permanently stuck up?"

She shook her head. "These are personal facts, as you said. Part of your marketing package. And you forgot to lower your voice again," she hissed.

He chuckled, taking in the lay of the little tourist trap. The town boasted the following disgustingly quaint shops marked: Soda Shop, Toy Shop, Book Shop, Antique Shop, Wood Shop, Taffy Shop, Wild West Saloon and The Museum.

He tried to remain calm as families and even a bunch of teenage girls passed him by.

Vere wasn't doing as well.

He could swear she was actually holding her breath until the girls turned the corner, which took a very long time.

"I feel like we're cast in a spy movie," he whispered.

"Yeah, right?" She gasped, pulling in some deep breaths.

"Thanks for braving the test run with me. Where first?" He'd whispered extra quietly so he could move a little closer to her.

"I don't know. Antique shop? It's right here." She jerked her head toward the window. "And it's the only one with a wide door in case you draw a crowd. It's got a straight line to my car."

"Wow. You have excellent paparazzi skills. Before we go in, I'm going to test something. Watch." Dustin boldly stared at the next teenage girl that walked by with her family.

Vere tugged at his arm. "Don't. Don't do that. I'm not ready. You aren't ready. Abort the test. Abort the test. Please!" She sounded so panicked he allowed her to drag him into the dark, cool entry of the antique shop.

He pulled off his glasses so he could get a better look at her face. She was breathing like she'd just run two miles, and looked so stressed he had the urge to wrap her in his arms; but instead he settled for picking up one of her hands.

Shit. She's really shaking. Shouldn't I be the one shaking?

"Vere. It's cool. The disguise works. It's all good. I'm okay." She squeezed his hand back, hard. "I know. I know. But what if—what if someone—does—recognize you?" She continued to whisper, "How will we ever pull this off at school? This is going to be impossible."

Hunter shrugged. "I have to pull it off, not you. And I was just fine out there. My cover is bound to crumble eventually."

"I hope not." She frowned. "We've worked so hard."

He let go of her hand. "I'll stick it for as long as it holds, I guess. After that, who knows what will happen to me?"

"I don't want to find out. I hope it works for a really long time. I already don't want you to go back home." Her hand drifted gracefully up to check her bun. Color pooled in her cheeks while she bit her lip to hide her worry.

He gazed down at her, soaking up her elfin, heart-shaped face—memorizing the way one curve of her lip twisted slightly down when she was sad and up all other times.

But only on the one side.

Cute.

Very cute.

He had to force his fingers not to reach out and touch that spot. Force his hands not to grab her and try to kiss the sad twist back in the other direction.

But, he knew that would completely freak her out.

Damn my crush. It would completely freak me out.

She thinks we're both of the same species, but vultures don't make friends with hummingbirds.

"I'll keep in touch after. You could visit, with Charlie and Nan. If I'm not too busy." He couldn't meet her eyes.

He knew it would be impossible to keep in touch with her after he went home. It was for the best. He didn't want anyone from here to see his other life.

She flushed bright red under his scrutiny, but seemed to recover a bit because she tossed him a little eye roll. It was as if she knew he'd been lying. "Of course we'll keep in touch. I know it's only been three days, but you probably already wonder how you survived seventeen years without me. Am I right?"

Her tone had been so self-deprecating, he answered without thinking, "Yep. I almost didn't make it before I met you." He pulled at his sleeves and quickly folded his arms, turning his wrists under his oddly aching heart.

"Can I help you?" An older, white-haired lady came out of the antique shop's back room.

"Is it okay if we look in back? I wanted to show my friend something," Vere asked.

The lady smiled. "Sure, honey. Just ring the bell if you need me." She disappeared into the back room again.

Vere led him past some old tricycles and single wooden school desks, then around a towering high section of books on creaky, wafer thin shelves.

As they passed a fan, Dustin was hit with a warm wave of her clean, lavender-sage smell. It mixed with the dust from this place plus the mint gum she'd been nervously chomping since they parked the car.

He breathed her in like she was water and he'd been in some sort of long, terrible drought.

"Look." She pointed to a far wall. "On the hook, high up."

His eyes scanned through the chaotic mess. "It's an old guitar," he said, placing his glasses in his front shirt pocket. His fingers curled in anticipation as he stepped forward to pull the guitar off the wall and examine the neck.

He let out a long, appreciative breath. "A *Strat*. Beat up and battered, but not one bit warped. No strings...but, damn. She's a beauty."

She moved in close behind him. "Is that a good guitar? You're smiling like it's good."

He flipped it over and tossed her a grin. "Yeah it's awesome. Old Strats are some of the best guitars in the world!" He laughed and flicked her another glance, wondering if she'd noticed he'd suddenly sounded all giddy and goofy like she did. But this was no delicious, cold water bottle. It was a Strat!

He watched her eyes taking in the guitar.

"Pretty, mother of pearl inlay on the twisty things," she said.

"They're called tuners. And these are deluxe. The wood looks like Poplar. Neck is made out of Rosewood." He felt her staring at his hands as he ran it over the back and the sides of the guitar's curves. "Some harsh scratches but not one crack! Amazing. Just needs strings and an amp. How long has this thing been back here?"

She shrugged. "As long as I can remember. I could buy it for you? Do you want it? Like, will it help you?"

His throat closed up, and he felt his knees start to shake. "Help me with what?"

"Help you not seem so sad? You explained some of your stress yesterday. All that you left behind. I think there's more. Like...how can you just leave behind your guitars? You said before you came here you worked hours and hours a week on stuff. But how can you do that without a guitar? Aren't you freaking out?"

He blinked, stunned. Amazed that she'd seemed to memorize everything he'd said. More stunned that she'd been so perceptive about all he hadn't said.

He pulled a fake smile. "Don't get me wrong. I'm touched you care. But I promised not to go near any guitars while I'm here. I've already crossed the line messing with this old thing. I can't draw any attention to myself. If we strung this baby up, well, I'd be tempted to—" He glanced at her lips. "Tempted to go all-out and lose control. I'd play it from the rooftops and I'd never put it down."

"That's why you should have it."

His heart twisted with longing as he stared at her face. "If that happens, little *bestie*, it would not be good for either of us. You just told me you wanted me to stay here awhile. And believe it or not, I'm curious as hell to try your high school after hanging with you. That means, in disguise, and in control. This guitar would blow us both out of the water. Got it?"

She flung her purple-sleeved arms wide. "Yeah, but promises are made to be broken!"

"Are they?" He frowned, considering the huge promise between him and Charlie while he stared at her lips all over again. "I disagree. I'm all about being honorable. My mom and my band mates are really pissed at me. I need to prove to them that I'm sorry. It's partly why I'm here. I've got to stick with the plan they've laid out. At least for a while. I made the promise, I'm keeping it."

"But what if the promise means life and death? What about

bliss? Saving your soul? If all that is at stake, then promises need to be broken."

"Vere. Nothing's at stake. Not on that level."

She pushed closer. He could read the excitement in her eyes. "You should see how you look holding that thing. Like it's already yours." She glanced around. "There's no mirror here for you to see yourself, but I swear, that guitar looks perfect when you hold it in your hands. Like somehow you know every bit of it, even how it's going to sound."

"Yeah, well I've picked up thousands of guitars, so that's easy."

"No. I swear. This guitar wants to belong to you—even now—how you hold it in front of you. It's like you two are dancing!" She grinned. "Don't you think that's worth breaking a promise over?"

"Um...I'm not one to put feelings and emotions onto an inanimate object. It's weird."

She stomped her foot. "Well I am. Other examples, then." She breathed up, puffing the escaped curls off her forehead.

"Do we have to?" He grimaced, wishing she would stop.

"Right now you look how I feel when I get a new book. Or, when it's opening night of a play and they've just turned down the lights. Your eyes look like they've snapped into that perfect *moment.* That breathless second when the first page is turned, or when the audience in the theater gets all quiet and the curtain hasn't opened yet. Your face, while holding that guitar, is a beam of total, blissful anticipation. There's no more perfect thing than that."

"To you, Vere. Not to me. I'm not like you."

"I can see that you are," she insisted, still defending him even though he was deliberately misunderstanding her.

"If you, touching an old guitar, gets the expression I'm seeing now to hit your face, I can only imagine how you'll look playing it. Don't you get it? You're the luckiest person in the whole world to have already figured out what you love. And you'll be, quite possibly, the stupidest person in the world—if you don't hold on to it."

"You're insane," he breathed, pretending her words hadn't made perfect sense. Hadn't moved him. Hadn't made his hands tighten desperately on the neck of the guitar as though it were a life-raft and he might be drowning.

"I'm not." A small, stubborn grimace set her chin completely straight, and she flushed bright red. The first time she'd done so since yesterday. "I can tell the guitar makes your heart sing, and that playing it will make you happy. Don't you want that? I bet if your mom or your agent saw you holding this Strat, they'd take back the stupid promise they forced you to make. They would let you break the promise and—"

"No. Stop!" Bringing up his mom and Martin gave him the reality check he needed.

He loosened his grip to flip the guitar one more time. "Maybe you're right about how much I want this old thing. But stop pestering me. I can't have it."

"You can't or you won't?"

"Both. Vere! *Dammit.* Just back off! You don't understand." She winced.

He felt really bad because he thought she might cry. In a softer voice he said, "I'm here in Colorado to get clear. To live a different life. To think things over. *Hell*—I don't know, actually. But I do know I'm supposed to be hiding and doing exactly what my mom and agent have sent me here to do. I've become someone else for awhile. Inside and out, just like you helped me to be. And I think I might like it."

"Yeah but—"

He shook his head, stopping her. "I'm worried there's a possibility I'll lose who I'm trying to become if I start playing the guitar. Any guitar."

"Well I'm worried you'll lose yourself if you don't."

"My choice to make, Vere. Let's stick to the plan. Dustin McHugh doesn't know how to play the guitar. Okay?"

He hung the guitar back on the hooks, trying not to care that his tone had pulled the light of her eyes.

She shook her head, clearly still not agreeing.

He glared at her.

Afraid she'd start up again he added, "Not. One. Note."

21: awkward topics: a++

VERE

"Anyone else want to ride down with Nan and me?" Vere's dad came out onto the porch followed by Nan. Her standard, tight, white curls were slightly rumpled. She looked years younger without her glasses on.

Vere greeted her with a smile as she tried to stifle a long yawn.

"Anyone?" Her dad tried again.

No one responded.

Vere had sprawled next to Charlie and Dustin in one of the six Adirondack chairs on the double-wide, enclosed sun porch. It was everyone's favorite morning gathering place at the cabin. This morning was no exception.

"I can't believe we have to shut this place down in two weeks. How could Labor Day sneak up on us so fast? It's so sad." Vere sat up.

"What's sad is the Colorado Public Schools make us start in the middle of August. That's what's sad," Charlie muttered.

"What is wrong with you three?" Nan glanced at Charlie's and Dustin's prone forms.

Dustin pulled off his glasses and placed them in his front pocket as he rubbed his eyes and groaned. "Mrs. Roth forced us to eat second helpings of bacon quiche and strawberry muffins. I'm not digesting anymore, I've died."

"Ah. Well. That explains it. Your mother just attacked us with the last of the French toast on the way out here. From the look of you three, I'm thinking you should take one more hike before you head out."

"Good idea. Who's in?" Vere struggled out of her seat and stood.

"I'll go. I need to see if I can get my legs working. Nothing extreme. Please." Dustin hauled his tall, lanky frame forward and stared at his feet as though he couldn't move another inch.

"Hold up." Aunt Nan stepped in front of Dustin. "I have something for you. From your mom." She handed him a letter. Dustin took it and glanced up at his aunt, his eyebrow raised in question.

"It's a letter."

"That's obvious, Aunt Nan. From who?" Dustin blinked.

"Your mom."

Dustin quickly handed it back. "Keep it. I'm not going to be all manipulated from afar. Not interested. Can you send it back?"

Everyone seemed to be unable to stop staring at the envelope in Nan's hands.

Vere's dad broke away first with a cough and wandered to the window, pretending to admire the view.

"I'll put it in your desk. Okay? I promised to make sure you had it right when you got here, but I forgot. Delivery completed. Officially, and in front of witnesses." Nan sighed when Dustin seemed to take too long to meet her gaze. "Okay?"

"Whatever. Fine. If you speak to her, tell her I'm not opening it." Dustin glanced at his aunt then looked away, but not before Vere noticed a flash of unguarded pain in his eyes.

Her dad coughed again.

Charlie appeared to have gone back to sleep, but he hadn't fooled Vere. Her brother avoided all awkwardness by feigning sleep.

Vere had to say something before her dad coughed again.

"Hiking. Let's go, then. But you chose the route, Dustin. Don't want to hurt you this time."

Dustin stretched one leg forward and cringed, causing Vere to laugh. "Two days later, and it's still funny," she teased him but he didn't respond. His eyes were trained on Nan as she headed back into the main part of the cabin.

Charlie stood and stretched. "I'm coming with you, Dad. This is as much quality family time I can take. Vere, Dustin, it's been—weird." He winked, but Vere could tell he was still uncomfortable with her hanging out alone with Dustin. "Weird but fun," Charlie added. "Dad, give me a second to grab my stuff."

Dustin grabbed one of the bags Mr. Roth had piled onto the porch and headed toward the car to help him load. "Mr. Roth, I already told your wife this, but...thanks for everything this weekend. The place, the food, the retainer. All of your help was great."

"That reminds me, son. Stop by later tonight and we'll get the thing fitted properly. I'll pick it up at the office on the way home."

Vere followed along with their cooler, smiling the whole way at Dustin's back.

The guy is really so darn nice. And helpful.

Dark side. I'm so sure.

He'd worn the polyester green trucker cap backwards today. As though he knew she was staring, he turned back and shot her a smug grin. His eyes caught in the sun, a wild flash of blue light streaked her direction.

When will those things stop yanking the air out of my lungs?

She shook her head, watching him walk toward her. She'd have to remind him not to wear his hat that way because it showed way too much of his perfectly rectangular forehead.

And, of course, he needed yet *another* reminder to keep the glasses on. If she brought it up now, he'd accuse her of admiring him again so instead she said, "How can you not be dying of heat in those long sleeves? You are so stubborn."

"Stubborn like you, maybe?" He grimaced. "Would you please stop busting on my awesome shirts? I love these things."

She frowned at the obvious line of sweat that had formed on his forehead. "I will never understand you."

"You shouldn't try." He shot her a look while her dad piled the bags into the trunk, filling it to the brim.

Vere scowled and dragged the cooler around to the side of the car.

Her dad was doing his man-to-man voice. "It's been a pleasure getting to know you, son. I hope you come back next weekend for the close-up." Her dad nodded to Vere. "Don't be too long. Make sure the place is locked up if Mom and Nan are gone when you get back from your hike."

"Okay." Vere shoved the cooler into the back seat. "I'll take Dustin around the lake trail. We can head out now." She pulled her head out of the car and shut the door. "What do you say, *BGF*?"

Dustin looked around. "Without supplies? Don't we need water bottles or sunscreen? A pack full of food? How about some giant guns in case we run into wildlife?" He looked more than a little nervous. His nature phobia thing was so cute.

Dustin and her dad circled back and picked up the last bags. She pulled her gaze away as he approached again.

Is it cheating on Curtis because I really like the way Dustin McHugh's back flexes when he picks up heavy things?

"What? Something wrong?"

Her entire face flooded with tingles as he drew nearer.

"No. It's just I think after all this awesome progress, I'm having a total relapse. I'm kind of shy to go hiking with you alone."

"Back to the snide witty comments! You can do this. You took me to town yesterday *alone*, and we had a full on argument."

She followed behind him as he piled the last bags next to the car. "Arguing is easy, but today, I'm hardly hating on you at all."

"I can fix that by pissing you off. Would that help?" He laughed.

She nodded, staring at his chin. Up close, it had this cute blond stubble on it. Total opposite of Curtis's dark coloring but equally as appealing. And something they'd have to watch. Guys with blond stubble did not have dark hair. Lucky his eyebrows and lashes were freakishly dark. Nature's way of making his eyes explode off his face so every other guy's eyes seemed boring, of course.

She swallowed.

What were we talking about...

Her mind had just been wiped clean with guy stubble plus back muscles plus thinking about dark lashes?

Vere Roth, curing the anxiety jitters. Day three: F-

And just LOOK at him. Whatever. Let the blush fire full force. It can't be helped. I'm not dead, right?

She hoped he wouldn't notice, but how could he not? She was at scalp tingle level already. Ears burning bright.

She must look like an idiot.

Dustin tapped his cheeks as though to tease her a little.

Ugh. He noticed.

He gave her an odd look, shook his head and smiled. "Check back in, little gnome girl. What about our hiking supplies? Mr. Roth, do you have any sunscreen on you?"

Vere's dad chuckled, not noticing Vere's blush attack. "You won't need any if you are only hiking the lake trail. It's shady, and short."

Annoyed with herself and with him for calling her a gnome again, she grabbed Dustin's arm and tugged him into step next to her. "Bye Dad! Come on. The lake trail starts just over there."

"So close?"

"Had you gone swimming *once*, city-chicken, you would know this. It is only one mile around the entire lake loop and as flat as a pancake."

He had to duck low under the branches. "I hope the entire trail isn't like this. I'm not a *Hobbit* like you."

"Ha. Ha. It widens at the lake. We're almost there."

"Whatever."

"Hey. Are we fighting again?" She stopped and he turned around to face her.

"I thought you wanted me to make you argue." He pulled off his cap and ran his hand through his thick hair. "I'm coming across wrong. I feel totally off. Stressed all over again. I think I don't want to go back to Aunt Nan's house. It makes the idea of school, this disguise, seem all too real."

Vere shot a look at his face. "Or, maybe you don't want to face the letter?"

He sighed. "That thing is so like my mom. Dealing with our relationship—or lack thereof—with some disconnected words. I know what to expect in that envelope. I have no intention of reading it. I'm sure it's lines and lines of her guilt-dipped, sob-story crap. I'm way more afraid of going to your homogenized high school tomorrow than that letter."

"It's your school, too. We won't abandon you when the bell rings."

"I hope not."

He was trying to play it off but she knew he must be flipping out. After yesterday's trip to town, she wouldn't want to trade places with him.

They made it through the trees and turned toward a wooden dock. The surface of the small lake glittered jet-smooth in the morning light. It reflected the bright yellow aspen trees, mountains, clouds and tall pines in the distance.

"Wow. This place is a living postcard."

"The flat rock by the dock is my favorite spot to nap."

"Where?"

"It's kind of behind that huge bush. You can see the edge of it." Vere pointed to a the tip of a flat, granite boulder that was hidden behind a low scraggly shrub off to the side of the dock. "The dock is where we dive in, of course."

"Oh no. Not 'we'. Not ever."

She frowned. "A good deep spot is on the left side. Next time we come up you *will* swim."

"See? Stubborn. Dustin McHugh does not swim."

"Focused and determined." Vere grinned, taunting him. "*My* Dustin McHugh does swim."

He shook his head. "Annoying and single focused."

"Charlie always tells me my inability to lose focus is what gets me all freaked out, especially where Curtis Wishford is concerned."

"Why?"

"He says I've got Curtis on some kind of pedestal, that he's just a guy, like any other. I try to see him like that, but I can't. He's just too built up for me in my own mind. What do you think?"

Dustin stared at the sky and thought for a long moment. "I haven't seen you with this slice of manly perfection, nor have I met him, but your brother might be onto something about the source of your behavior."

They'd made it to the dock and Dustin stepped up onto it with a groan. He bent and rubbed his calf. "Do you mind if we just sit and put our feet in the water instead of hike?"

"I'd love to. Wish I had my suit." Vere sat and kicked off her shoes and socks. Dustin did the same.

She put her feet right into the water but Dustin held his just above the surface. He glanced at her and wrinkled his brow.

"Uh. What are you doing?" she asked, feeling her heart bubble with laughter.

"If one fish nibbles my toes I'm going to lose all testosterone and scream like a little girl right in front of you. They won't, will they?"

"No!" She grinned.

He held his feet even higher. "And you swear, there are no snapping turtles in here. Not one frog? I'm terrified of all amphibians."

Vere laughed openly, leaned forward and pushed down on one of his knees and then the other until his feet were in the water. "Come on, relax. I'll keep you safe. I'm an expert fish wrangler, you know?"

"Why do I feel as though I can't do anything in Colorado without your help?" He looked right into her eyes, and Vere felt the cheeks tingle full force.

"Uh. Because you can't?" She shrugged. "I could move to Los Angeles and pretend to be a rock star with way fewer freak outs than you're having here just pretending to be *normal*."

"So you think. I'd have you in tears at your first sushi bar. I wrangle *raw* fish and wasabi. You wouldn't last one day as a rock star. I'd like to see you make your way through a nightclub. Handle Ibiza, or ditch crowds in Times Square on New Year's Eve, for that matter."

"Okay. You win. I don't even know what kind of food Ibiza is."

He grinned. "It's an island. Off the coast of Spain where people party, and party, and then party some more. Our band has gone there to play the past two summers. In Spain, the restaurants don't open till 9 P.M. And the nightclubs don't fill up until after midnight. Way past your bedtime."

Vere stared at her toes wiggling in the water. "Still makes you seem helpless to me."

He'd relaxed and leaned back on his arms. Vere's eyes riveted to where his shirt had tightened over his upper body.

Holy mother of ripped-gorgeous.

Get over the assets. Get over the assets.

It's an award-winning six pack. SO WHAT? Get over it.

He's just your friend. Your Dustin McHugh.

Think about Curtis.

"Water's warmer than I thought it would be. Not bad," he said, splashing his feet. Making small waves.

When she didn't answer, he glanced over, and she realized she was still staring—at his abs, at his arms. At his everything.

Think about Curtis. Curtis...Curtis...

"Having a hard time again? Come on Vere, it's just me."

She nodded. "Right. I know. You just suddenly look different. Like...more rested. Mom's food must have done you some good. And you aren't wearing the disguise. With only the green hat and the plaid shirt, well, you look completely—"

"Easy there, girl. Save it for Curtis, would you? I've heard it before. I know I'm pretty. Remember? You already told me."

She glowered, annoyed that it felt again like he could read her mind. "Please. I was going to say you look normal, that's all."

He laughed, the sun catching how the smile lit his eyes brighter. "Normal, huh. Whatever that means."

Curtis...Curtis...Curtis...

She went on, "Of course. And you know that I could care less about your *pretty*," she lied, tearing her gaze away from the pulse beating in the base of his neck.

He grimaced. "You've made that clear enough. So tell me, then. If *looks* are the last thing you notice in a guy, then what is the first?"

Vere leaned back on her arms as well, pretending to study the water. She let her feet splash out in front of her, forcing her voice to remain steady. "I notice nice. Niceness."

"God. Yuck." He shuddered. "So, this Curtis Wishford guy... is he some kind of extraordinarily sweet, door-opening, snow shoveling, goodie-goodie, *nice* person?"

She smiled. Thinking of Curtis had made her tummy flutter. "I'm not sure if he's nice—not on that level. He's always been nice to me, though. I think he's nice, and I want him to be nice. Full of niceness. Does that count?"

Dustin snorted and took the weight off his arms to settle flat onto his back. He crossed his hands behind his head and closed his eyes. "Girls. You're all the same. You just want to imagine someone is something, without even knowing them first."

"What do you mean by that?" Vere felt slighted.

He shrugged.

Vere pressed on, "Come on. Give me the inside guy info. You've probably had a ton of experience. Did you—do you— hook up—with like, groupies?"

He turned, and gave her a measuring gaze. "I have. Yes."

She felt her eyes grow wide. "Do groupies really do what they say groupies do?"

"Yeah, and more."

"Wow. Have you ever had a girlfriend?"

"Nope."

"What! How can that be? You're positively perfect boyfriend material. I think you're full of..." She tore her gaze away from his washboard stomach for the third time and contemplated his perfectly sculpted face. "Full of—niceness—among other things."

"Watch it. My ego, remember? I prefer the aloof, bad-boy persona I've worked so hard to acquire."

They laughed together.

After a long pause he added, "You haven't ever had a boyfriend. And I think you're positively perfect girlfriend material, yet, you are single." He opened his eyes and regarded her solemnly. "Possibly you have a tad too much of the niceness thing, though. Could be why. Scares them away."

She didn't blush, because obviously the guy was lying. "Oh, shut up. As if. I've never even been approached for my number. Once, this amazing hot guy asked *me* for Jenna's number though. That was fun."

"Criminal." Dustin sighed and looked up at the sky. "Seems

impossible. Girl like you should be locked down."

Vere's heart did a strange little flip. "Ugh. Back to you. Tell me why you never had a girlfriend. It's only fair. You know everything about my dating and social-disaster situations. Why have you never had a real girlfriend?"

"I've never thought about *why*."

"Think now. What was the problem with all those girls? Were they not pretty, or nice, or—what?"

"The problem wasn't from the hooking up. It's never that." He grinned, wickedly.

Vere felt her whole face flame up. But even a snowman would have blushed and melted instantly with the look he had in his eyes. She called his bluff. "If you're trying to make me bolt and change the subject, I'm not going to. Go on. We were on the topic of you hooking up and '*why*'?"

"Damn. Okay. Hmmm." He let out a long breath. "No denying that all the attention from girls wasn't a rush at first. And it was good for my education—to say the least." He shot her a funny grin and then looked back up at the sky. "A guy likes to know he has it all-together and functioning with enough left over. Plus the talent to please—if you know what I mean." He finished with a wink.

Vere giggled at that. "Ha. I'm sure, " she managed to choke out even though she was dying inside.

He gave a little self-deprecating laugh as though he thought she were mocking him. "What? I have skills. What of it?"

"God. You are so full of yourself. Someone really said that to you?"

"Easy. You asked. And I will have you know, my skills have been complimented more than once."

"Uh. Eew?" She giggled all over again and punched his shoulder. "It doesn't make it less funny!"

"My stepfather's assistant said it most, and that was a couple of years back."

"Woah. Really? When you were fifteen?"

He nodded.

"Are you trying to shock me or simply scare me?"

"Both? If we are going to be friends you might as well know I wasn't kidding about the dark-sided stuff."

Vere laughed but had grown utterly uncomfortable. Again, she had the feeling he thought she was about to make fun of him.

"Whatever. That assistant was on the dark side. Not you! Shouldn't she be in jail?"

"No, she was seventeen at the time. Turned eighteen, broke up with me and took off with my stepfather. Mom pays him not to contact me. Not that I want him to. The assistant is long gone."

"Jeez...and wow!" She wanted to lighten the mood so she used a lighter voice so he wouldn't notice how creeped out she was by his story. This, plus all the other stuff he'd told her, was over the top. "How could that assistant girl know so much and be so young?"

Dustin shot her a wry look, picking up on her joking tone. "No clue. Look at you. Sixteen and you've only made out with a pillow. Isn't that your claim to fame?"

"Whoa. Okay, okay. I resent that and so does my pillow."

He grinned so wide he almost blinded her, then bit his bottom lip like he was holding back a laugh.

"Anyhow." She had to look away. His smile had sort of made her chest ache. She suddenly understood that he was an expert at hiding his pain behind a huge mask. "We all know I'm behind. Way behind," she added, hiding her own pain.

He glanced over and regarded her with a solemn expression. As though he knew things were getting way sad and serious, he shot her a too-knowing smirk. "Feel free to let me know if you ever need any best friend or coaching pointers on that subject. Maybe you're doing some stuff all wrong with your pillow?"

He flicked her another challenging glance and a comical brow wiggle. "Coach Dustin is here to serve."

"Please! I made that pillow very happy. And you won't believe the feathers it put in my ear. Still does, and I haven't made out with it in over a year. You aren't the only one with mega-skills," she joked, amazed that she didn't even feel embarrassed about this conversation!

Better, she was well past blushing when he'd winked at her! *The cure is back on.*

Her heart soared with the knowledge that she trusted him not to go there. "Curtis would kick your ass if he heard you."

"We'll see. Call me after he's asked you out, and I'll set up a fight date. Kid should be kicking your pillow's ass, anyhow. Not mine. I'm not a threat. I wish him luck."

"Whatever back. I hope your next groupie is *nice*. Which takes the conversation right back to you." She smiled.

He groaned. "No. Can't we stop? Hasn't this been enough practice yet?"

"Nope. Tell me a little about what you think about *girls*. In general terms, I mean. If you're truly my coach—then keep talking. I need this male insight. You said I could ask you anything."

Dustin rolled onto his side and faced her.

She had the oddest sensation he was staring at her lips.

"God. Not this topic," he said.

"Yes," she demanded. "Please. I need to know what goes on inside guys' heads so I can change. Charlie only tells me so much, you know."

He shook his head. "Why do you think you need to change? You're great the way you are and—"

Her stony, determined glare must have stopped him because he shook his head again and sighed as he lay back again, breaking her gaze.

"Fine. I've got some ideas about you and Curtis—and what's

not working."

She gasped. "Really? Go...talk...what?!"

"You know what Charlie said? About you putting Curtis up on a pedestal, and how you shouldn't? There's a lot to that."

Vere's heart soared. She couldn't believe how cool this was. She was twelve inches from a guy and talking about girls, and boyfriends, and making out, and life. And it felt normal.

She could hear Dustin's feet splashing in the water somewhere next to hers but didn't want to risk a look at him. Her tummy did another little flip.

He went on, "I can only speak for myself, but I've spent my fair share of time on some huge fan pedestals."

"I can imagine, but...isn't it cool to be admired?"

"No, and yes. But the pedestal thing bites. The girls, the ones that have me on that pedestal, are all the same. They even look weird. Scary. It's their eyes mostly. I feel like I can spot this hungry, glazed over, excited gleam when they look at me. Makes me want to crawl out of my skin. It's the wrong kind of excitement. It's so strange, but they will do whatever I ask them to do when they are like that. It's a total turn off."

"Why? I thought all guys loved it when girls were easy—or whatever."

"It took me a long time to figure that out. The weird part comes from the fact that the girls aren't meeting me, they are meeting who they *imagine* I am, you know?"

Vere nodded and closed her eyes, enjoying the sound of his rumbling voice as it floated over her. "Yeah. I've done that. Stared at posters of guys, or movie characters and imagined totally what they'd be like if they were with me. Everyone does that. It's what fans do."

"Yeah, but fan adoration is impossible to live up to. No one can be that perfect. So if you have this Wishford guy on a pedestal, maybe you're doing that weird *fan behavior* with him. If so, it could make it difficult for you to have a real conversation with him and so—you freak. That's what my fans do. They just scream, and cry, and babble stuff like, *oooh-my-God-I-love-you-so-much* and act generally insane when they meet me."

"Impossible. I've known Curtis forever. I'm sure I'm not imagining what he's like. I must already know. He's the perfect guy for me. Is that putting him on a pedestal?" She opened her eyes and looked for his response.

Dustin shrugged. "All girls—the ones I've managed to get close to anyhow—seem to have this messed up fairytale idea. They all imagine, universally, that they were *THE ONE GIRL* that I was going to just fall in love with, simply because we'd made it to the hooking up stuff. They acted as if I was going to start calling them or emailing them every day when I got home after we'd—you know...Why do girls *go* there?"

"I can't answer that past knowing that every guy I hang out with is...just...too dreamy? She met his gaze. Can you answer why guys *don't go* there?"

He shook his head and looked away.

She went on, "You must be onto something, though. I can confirm that Jenna and I are beyond fangirl goofy like that about movie stars. Like, if Leonardo DiCapprio were 25 years younger—and he met me—I'm sure that he'd fall in love with me on sight. Heck, I'd even consider marrying him without the 25 years younger thing. He's so cute."

"You are such a twisted person. Leo is older than your dad!"

"But not in the Romeo and Juliet remake. He's forever young there. And he loves me. ME. I *am* Juliet," she joked, but then sobered when he looked slightly ill or, was he afraid of her now? "Sorry. Go on. Tell me. What's it like then, from your side. If the famous person doesn't fall in love with the adoring fan what happens?"

"I can only speak for myself. But...after awhile, the whole scene fangirl scene bummed me out. I knew I wouldn't fall in love with any of them. The longest I'd spent hooking up with a girl backstage was for a few hours. We locked ourselves in a cleaning closet and she had so much stamina that we..."

"Okay, coach. *TMI.* Stop on the specifics. I'm sorry I asked."

Dustin smiled up at the sky. "Right. Sorry. I wouldn't want to be responsible for taking little Vere Roth from a G rating to an R."

She scowled at the sarcasm in his voice and was rewarded with his flash of teasing, light blue eye twinkles.

"Hey. I'm at least PG-13."

He laughed again. "The official definition of PG-13 includes foul language and kissing and you haven't crossed either boundary. Do you ever use foul language?" He'd used a stern, comical voice.

"Yes. Of course. And just because I haven't done—stuff—doesn't mean I don't know stuff. I read books. And watch MTV. Movies."

He raised one brow really high.

"Oh—never mind. Stop trying to change the—the—*damn* subject," she said in an attempt to prove she could curse. Her cheeks had flushed to mark her a total fraud, and he chuckled.

"Ugh." She turned away in frustration and he laughed louder.

"I bet you led some of those girls on." She already sensed that he probably hadn't, but she wanted to dig at him a little for embarrassing her.

"No. I did not. I made sure the girls who were—willing—were also well aware I wouldn't call them afterwards. I made that very clear."

"Ew. That's weird and creepy. Especially the part where the girls still stuck around for the hook-up after you'd told them all that."

"Well, they did. But I felt bad about it, so, like six months before I..."

He stopped and looked away, taking in a deep, almost shaky sounding breath before going on, "Six months before I came here, I'd stopped hanging out with girls all together. I'd sort of given up on them. Given up on trying to make a connection with anyone. I'd worked so many hours. And the thing with my mom—I got tired. I sort of turned into a hermit."

Vere looked at him as she readjusted her bun so she could rest her head flat on the dock. "This whole story of your dating life—or non-dating life you could call it—makes me go back to that idea I have of you that you're from another planet."

"I am. Compared to you, I'm a jaded, black-hearted, dark-sided, cold-bastard ass. That's the truth. I feel like some type of innocence despoiler for even hanging out with you and telling you my stories."

She glanced over and he was regarding her as though he believed what he'd just said. "Oh, please. Unless you're going to tell me you're secretly a vampire and your wealthy, gorgeous family is hiding in the woods wondering why you don't just bite me already, you can just leave your 'big bad wolf' front for someone else. You aren't fooling me. I think you're just afraid, like me. Like any, normal, *anyone* is afraid. You simply didn't give any of those girls a chance to be your girlfriend."

"Hear me right, it's not a front. I never went into any of those hook-ups wanting a girlfriend. I wanted to hook up. That's it. I did not, nor do I today, ever, want a girlfriend."

She flushed again. "But why?"

"To me, a girlfriend is just another person who would want me to perform for them in some way. At the end of my days, I don't seem to have any performing left in me. After the sex, it's too much damn trouble to hold a conversation with any of them."

"WHAT?" Vere sat up straight and brought her legs under her, crisscross. She glared down at him. He hadn't moved. "Aren't you just inspiring! I wonder if all guys think that?"

Dustin stretched and sat up. "I don't know. Maybe you know guys who are coming from a more normal place. All I know is that boyfriends are supposed to be able to make their girlfriends happy for more than one hour. I do not have that capacity."

"Duh. And duuuuh! Yes you do. Everyone does." She had the strangest urge to clock him just then so she yanked out her bun and remade it back in its normal spot to keep her hands busy. She could not randomly smack him, no matter how stupid he sounded. "*This* is what goes on in guys' heads," she ranted.

Wait till I get Charlie alone to confirm his thoughts on this topic! Wait till I tell Jenna! Ugh. Wait. Can I even tell Jenna? UGH.

She threw her arms into the air, trying not to yell. "But—but—having a girlfriend—being a couple, and all that—it's supposed to not feel like work or like an imposition. It's supposed to just happen, easily and naturally. Isn't it? Why do you make it sound like that?"

He frowned. "Like what? I was just being honest. *Damn* girl, you asked me. I told you what I could."

"You made it sound empty. Void. Terrible. And so...cold. You've lost all the romance."

Dustin shook his head. "God. *Romance.* You would go there. Romance is every girl's messed-up fantasy involving flowers and poetry, and piles of fake crap. I—*guys*—don't know how to handle all that. Anyone who does is *so* faking it. Any girl who falls for it—I'm sad for them—because they're victims of marketing!"

"What? What?" Vere sputtered. "If there are flowers and cute stuff, it's because the couple cares about each other and they want to do sweet things to show their love *to* each other. It isn't a job. As for the poetry—you're a songwriter! Are the zillions of love songs on the planet not real? Jeez."

"*GuardeRobe* doesn't have any love songs. But you wouldn't know that, now would you?"

She gasped, and her heart twisted painfully. "Well there you go! Another reason *not* to like your band. I'm sad for you. It's a total waste of a whole band if they don't sing love songs, so there!" She shot his words back at him. "I think—if you've only had the hook-ups—then you've missed all the good, sweet stuff. What about the everyday kisses? And making out on the couch? Or the hand-holding where you don't even make out but you're just daydreaming together?"

He sat up too. "Is that what your pillow taught you? Or is this all coming from the favorite books and movies?"

Vere glared huge bullets into his stupid, blue eyes. "What about the butterflies in your stomach? Do guys not have the butterflies, at least? Come on. I know those are real for me because I've felt them. Please, say they are real to guys."

His gaze caught hers in a tangled, confused, half-angry way and he turned away. When he didn't answer, only stared at the lake, she felt her cheeks flush.

She wondered if she'd hurt his feelings." I—I shouldn't have yelled."

His voice sounded rough, sarcastic, and somehow lost when he finally turned back to her. "I can confirm the existence of guy butterflies. But it's not something that's advertised. Okay?"

"Well...that's something," she said under her breath, all of the fight going out of her.

Vere pulled her sneakers next to her, unable to hold her thoughts in order, as a huge, random blush-attack set in. She tried to talk her way through it. "Boy. This *BGF* thing is a total eye opener. As if. Well, I don't know anything about guys, you're right. And...I guess I'm sorry I asked. I'm glad you gave me a reality check, though. Maybe I am like those groupie girls. Too caught up in the fairytale versions of love."

"Vere—I—"

She couldn't stop herself. "No. It's good for me to hear this. I need a friend like you. See, butterflies are the only thing I've ever had when it comes to romance and guys. And mostly, you're right. I've found them in books and movies—and all over the casts of Teen Wolf and Supernatural." She shot him a sheepish smile. "Not going to lie. What I'm trying to say is… that I love those butterflies. I search for them endlessly. Real or not, I have to imagine they are going to lead me to something real. And awesome."

Vere could feel her flush deepening but she couldn't stop her mouth from motoring on, "Maybe I believe all this junk because I'm a total dork. A real one. Not like you—*pretending* to be a dork. You wouldn't understand what that feels like. I live your hellish disguise every single day and it's permanent."

"Vere, you aren't a dork. Not even close. You're just shy."

"Whatever. I'm not ashamed of it. And being shy puts me smack in the outcast-dork-nerd category. If we are truly going to be friends for the next few weeks or months, then you need to *get* this about me."

He shook his head.

"No. Don't say anything. You've only seen and known me here. But back in the real world? I know my deal—*my assets*— just like you do. I've got no magic-hat and glasses trick to pull off where I return to *fabulous*. I can't stop a whole room of people breathing because of my eye color. I'm the one who's already fainted on the floor and made a fool out of myself because I *saw* your eye color. Get me?"

"So why does that make you sound so angry? Are you mad at me for how I look? For trying to be totally honest from my own heart?"

She shrugged. "No. Of course not. I'm only mad because I thought I was waiting for some boy to come along who believes in romance. If I ever find him, well then, it's going to take him a really long time to get me out of that dead faint before he can even find my lips to plant a first kiss on them."

"Vere—I didn't mean to—"

"No. Let me finish. What if I wait—and I think I've found that guy—and he turns out to think exactly like *you* deep down inside? What if that guy just wants to sleep with me and *pretends* he's happy he got me roses. And that he did all that romance crap for one singular goal and not for—for love and butterflies?!! Then I've been waiting all this time—and for what? Maybe—I—"

"Okay. I'm going to stop you here, before you blow a fuse." His low voice grounded her.

She sucked in a deep breath, relieved he'd broken into her endless chatter.

He'd also done that yesterday.

It was as though he understood how she couldn't stop herself when she got like this, and he somehow knew exactly how to help.

She blinked at him and tried to replay what she'd just said in front of him. Hopefully nothing too humiliating had bumbled out. She gave him an apologetic and very grateful smile. She had to admit it was nice to have a friend who didn't judge her for exploding like that. "Thanks. I lost it."

"Yes. But it's partly my fault. I flooded your brain with my mad life, and I egged you on." He smiled back and kindly didn't address her still flaming face.

"Did you? Well, then yeah, it's all your fault, you jaded romance-bubble-buster."

He moved a small piece of hair out of her eyes. "I don't know what's real when it comes to love and romance. I've never had either, okay? But I do know I wouldn't recognize the sweet stuff you talk about if it were a bus running me over. My exposure is too skewed. I'm permanently broken in that area."

Dustin pulled his feet out of the water. He pushed himself

back and stretched his legs out to dry them in the sun. "Your—untried version of what dating should be seems way better than what I've been doing. My *BGF* advice to you is to carry on and believe. I'm sure I'm wrong."

"For the sake of the whole universe, I hope so, *Mr. Vader.*"

He smiled and shot her a sidelong glance. "I'm glad you finally believe me. After this, I think we're well past formalities. Please, call me Darth."

She couldn't even laugh because his expression seemed so forlorn.

She felt utterly sorry for the guy sitting next to her. He seemed so lonely. He'd just told her so much about himself, she now felt like she'd known him for a really long time. "Your toes are all wrinkly," she told him.

"Yours too. They're so tiny compared to mine." His voice had turned quiet.

Vere darted a glance at his face again. She leaned to the side and bumped his arm with her shoulder. "Look. If I don't have time to say it before tomorrow, I just want you to know this weekend and all the time you've given to—talking to me and helping me through—my issue—has meant a lot."

He laughed low, as he pulled on his socks and shoes. "Vere. It's been a pleasure. Truly. You are the one who deserves the thanks, for helping me suit-up and hide-out. You're really an awesome person—for a dork."

He stood, and when she was finished with her shoes, he helped her to her feet.

"You're awesome, too. Despite the part where you should probably keep hold of your therapist's number forever," she added, tossing him a light smile so he'd know she was joking.

"Oh, I will." He grinned.

She was so filled up with this strange gratitude toward him that when he turned back to face her she just needed to hug him.

So she did.

"Oof." Dustin staggered back. "Thanks. I think."

Warm sunshine had heated his shirt and it felt soft against her cheek. It mixed with his fresh-soap smell that was enveloping her. She breathed in. His chest was so solid. She could feel his heart beating near her ear.

He hugged her back for a second—or—was it a lot of seconds? She'd heard hundreds of lightning fast heartbeats inside his chest before he'd set her away from him.

It must have been lots of seconds.

AWKWARD. Hopefully he didn't notice.

Ugh. What was there to notice? It was just a hug. That's all.

Mortified, she avoided his gaze completely and walked ahead so he wouldn't see her flaming cheeks. As she jumped off the dock she chose a flippant, confident voice in case he'd noticed anything was off.

Because nothing is off. Not at all.

"Come along, my Dustin McHugh, let's head for home."

"Can you do *me* a favor?"

"Sure."

"Stop calling me 'my' Dustin McHugh. It's sort of— distracting."

"It is? Sure. Sure. Sorry." She stopped and turned to look at him with a frown, feeling sad about his request. And then she really looked at him. His cap was off and his badly chopped up hair had softened into thick, dark, curling waves.

Somehow, that made him look even more handsome than the first time she'd seen him, with his fancy salon haircut. His perfect chin was more pronounced thanks to a slight tan and the fact that his lips were now serious and frowning.

As he strode smoothly along the path, minus his long practiced dork gait, her Dustin McHugh looked slightly like a blue-eyed panther.

If there are any blue-eyed panthers...and...whatever.

I can still call him 'mine' inside my own head.
Because he kind of is...mine...

"Can you do me a favor back?" Her voice cracked. She had to look way up into his shuttered gaze, as he closed the distance between them.

He stopped in front of her and quickly locked his arms behind his back. Maybe he was afraid she'd hug him again.

"Anything, like I said. Ask me anything." His voice seemed different, gravelly deep as usual, but it sounded wary and slightly perplexed. His gaze also seemed to be travelling all over her entire face. She had the oddest sensation he'd been staring at her lips exactly like she'd been staring at his.

Well, I'm not looking at his perfect lips anymore, that's for sure.

Her heart thumped oddly against her chest, and she realized she had little goose bumps on her arms. As though her own body and brain now betrayed her, she was flooded with butterflies, erupting around her stomach.

She clamped her arms across it.

These aren't real butterflies.
They come with his package-er-his—assets.
This is a totally normal response.
Ugh. Not real butterflies. Say something, Vere.

Vere had the feeling that this time he was not going to bail her out if she lost it. "Could you—put your glasses and hat back on—for the ride back? You, minus the disguise, is distracting, too. Don't want to be all dangerous back on the road."

He raised his eyebrows and shook his head.

"Fine. Yeah. Of course. I'll wear them from now on."

22: test bunnies

Dustin

Dustin leaned into the backseat of Vere and Charlie's VW. They were on a long stretch of road Charlie had called 'the 105'. Apparently, the high school was somewhere along this stretch. From what he could see, there was nothing here but trees, hills, and tall grass. Aut no high school, that was certain.

He might as well be in a modern episode of *Little House on the Prairie*.

His phone lit up the time. 7:10 AM.

He accessed his email again and reloaded all new messages. *Nothing.*

The text message box still showed one message, sent to him Friday afternoon at 5:43 PM, from Martin—about the same time he'd been driving up the hill to the cabin with Vere.

It contained only the new email address information plus his mailbox password, as promised.

If Dustin wanted to get in touch with his agent he was supposed to email or text to NYjuice77@gmail.com.

Martin said he'd do the same at to Cojuice99@gmail.com. They were such lame email addresses.

Martin loved fresh squeezed juice and his Maxi-Juicer. He was obsessed with it. Drank it 24-7. He must have been drinking juice in New York when he'd made them up.

Dustin reloaded the mail again.

Still. Nothing.

He got that his mom wasn't going to email him. She obviously wanted him to read her suck ass letter and get choked up and call her. But like he'd vowed, he hadn't even touched the thing. Well, not beyond looking in the drawer next to his bed and noting it was in there, that is.

Maybe he was expecting too much from Martin and the guys. Everyone was probably busy and distracted getting the band settled in New York. Getting everyone situated in the studio. Locking up the freakish imposter guy.

That had to be it.

It had been only four days.

Only four days, but for some reason, it felt like a lifetime had passed him by.

He glanced up.

Vere sat in the passenger seat in front of him, silently chewing her upper lip while Charlie drove. The long road leading to nowhere still seemed to stretch out in front of them in more endless curves.

Where is this freaking school anyway?

Unable to stare at the road anymore—or Vere's damn upper lip—he quickly typed an email message to Martin:

— *Yo-NYJuice.*

Where r u? 2day is 1st day school!

I DON'T WAN2. GET ME OUTTA THIS ASAP.

Plz. B4 I flip.

No signal all wknd. No msgs from u or Mom? WTF?

FYI, hiding in dorklnd.

Me + glsses + retainer + amazing newly invented lisp.

Plans going OK. No one knows. Family helping is cool. Kids helping me r cool 2.

High hopes my cover will stick.

Where R U? Tell Mom 2 call Nan. Is Mom w u in NY or still in CA? More l8r. WRITE ME BACK.

Dustin McHugh. —

Dustin zipped the phone into the side pocket of his canvas pants. The pocket located *above* his knee, not one of the two rectangular pockets *at* his knees. So many pockets!

He needed to get some more dork stuff to fill them up.

He'd get candy dispensers, a calculator, ruler, tons of pencils and maybe even a sharpener and his very own tiny stapler. Maybe he should suggest another shopping trip. He could just imagine Vere's face lighting up as they chose more odd accessories for his disguise.

When he looked up, he locked eyes with Vere, who'd turned in her seat and was eyeing him.

"How you doing?" Her wide brown eyes were heavy with worry.

Dustin gave her his biggest smile to show off his giant retainer. "Thsuuper."

She giggled. "That thing is so—"

"Amattthhhing, I know."

She giggled again, and even Charlie cracked a smile.

Dustin ran his tongue over the retainer on the roof of his mouth. It felt strange, as if he'd stuck the bottom of a melted plastic water bottle in his mouth or something. He hated it, but loved it because the thing made Vere laugh every time she looked at it. Every time he spoke.

He already knew he liked making Vere laugh, so he'd made a point of showing it off to her any chance he got.

Vere's dad had run the wire across the front like any normal retainer, but then he'd added a second, larger wire that twisted and crisscrossed over the first, giving the him the appearance of braces. It truly looked like he'd eaten a bunch of soda cans. Since there was no need for the wires to be tight, it was only mildly uncomfortable.

Vere had finished texting something into her phone and turned again to level him with her most serious expression. "Listen. We're only two minutes from Jenna. She's meeting us in the parking lot."

Charlie spoke in a perfect evil Russian-spy voice, "If she vill-not be fooled, veee-must abandon zee-experiment and assimilate her. Or better, vee-should murder her—"

"Charlie! Shut up! Why do you always have to take things

too far?" Vere protested.

Dustin couldn't help but chime in, "Ssssheee vill-doo as vee-sayyy, or she vill-be very, very sorry." It was easier to laugh about the situation than face the true stress of it all.

Vere rolled her eyes. "Okay weirdos. Stop. We need her. Jenna's our canary in the cave, our litmus paper, our teen-test-bunny. If she catches on even a little, I'm thinking, at that point we spill it to her. Jenna's safe. She wouldn't tell. She might scream and dance around worse than Charlie did. But eventually, after we took off the duct-tape we'd be forced to wrap her in, she would relax and simply be a pain in your butt for the year. But she wouldn't tell."

Dustin swallowed. "Great. Can't wait to meet her."

"God. Dude. She's a freak, like I said. Good luck with that girl," Charlie added as he turned into a long driveway leading to a huge parking lot. "Vere's right though, she's loyal to the cause, but I hope to hell and back she doesn't find out. She'd come over to visit even more than she already does."

"You are so lucky you are driving right now. When I punch you later, you'll know why," Vere said, flicking a glare at Charlie, and then, "Look. There's the school."

Dustin surveyed the long, two-story brick building. Tall windows made up each of the building corners. He spotted the evenly spaced skylights that ran across the entire length of the sloped metal roof, glinting in the sun. The center of the building was obscured behind the pine trees planted in front of the school, but he could see the entire front of it was made of glass. His new peepers would be black as night in there.

But...damn, the place is huge.

Dustin eyed the rows and rows of empty parking spaces that were filling up in an orderly fashion as they waited for their turn to park.

"I suppose I should have asked this sooner, but how many kids go to this monstrosity?"

"Almost three thousand," Vere answered.

"Do this many people live out here?"

"This is the only high school for like four different back-to-back towns. We all had our own middle schools, but share one high school. I thought we'd warned you."

"Nope. But I've never been good at asking questions about stuff. Got a bad habit of guessing and assuming things. It's one of my goals while here—to start asking more questions," he said dryly. He grimaced as he remembered what an ass he'd been when he'd assumed his mom would take him home from the airport last week and not make him come here.

Vere interrupted his thoughts. "Remember, we both have your cell number, and you have ours. I'll keep mine on vibrate. If you need to be rescued, text me first then hide out here in the parking lot. I'll find you. Call me if you end up needing to run."

"What?" Dustin frowned.

Vere blinked, as though this were a perfectly normal conversation for them to have. "There's some good places to hide in the woods behind the school; just memorize what landmarks you're near so you can text us to find you."

"If you get that far, dude." Charlie laughed.

Kid is finding this way, too entertaining.

"Really? Did you really just say that?" Dustin swallowed, pushing back the image of the whole high school swarming him for autographs. But it could happen. It had happened. But he'd also been supported by bodyguards and a waiting limo. Not by pine trees!

"There she is!" Vere pointed to a lanky blonde girl with hipster-white sunglasses, leaning against a white, late-model Honda hatchback.

Dustin eyed Jenna as the car crept toward her in the slow line of traffic. She didn't look as scary as Vere and Charlie had described. That was something, at least.

Jenna had the same wholesome, *fresh-no-make-up*, pretty thing going on, like Vere did. But, unlike Vere, Jenna's outfit and hair were—stylish. Nice jeans, sandals, and a fashionable, tailored blue shirt that showed off her cute figure. She looked normal, even. Dustin felt immediately bad for that thought and risked a glance at Vere in the front seat. She was busily grabbing up her stuff, and still chewing on her lip.

Her adorable top lip. The lip with the little side-twist...

God. I'm going crazy from stress. That has to be why I can't shake my attraction to this tornado of a girl.

She turned suddenly in her seat and caught him staring.

Dustin knew it was easy to keep a straight face behind his dark glasses because he'd spent hours practicing in front of the mirror last night. He simply held still, and kept his face passive. Hopefully she wouldn't notice the fact that his heart was about to beat out of his chest.

"Don't forget to smile, it distracts from your perfect chin," Vere whispered as she opened her door and swung her legs out of the car.

"You think my chin is perfect?" he asked quickly, knowing the comment would make Vere pause and sass him back.

"Gah! Remember? *My Dustin*—I mean—" She met his gaze, looking guilty, and continued, "Dustin McHugh is not a stuck up egomaniac." Vere's voice lacked its usual bite.

"Dude." Charlie caught Dustin's eye in the mirror. "Remember. I don't hang out with you, I'm never going to hang out with you, and I hated being forced to spend the weekend with you. I only tolerate you out of courtesy to my sister and my neighbor, Nan. It's sealed, dork boy, don't even approach me."

"Check. No approaching." Dustin fake grinned. "As if I would. Dustin is not comfortable around stuck-up jocks."

Charlie grinned back. "Good luck." He turned to his sister. "Vere, if it's a bust, drive him to Nan's. Let me know the deal.

If it's a go, great. I'll meet up with you guys after school. If it bombs..." He swallowed. "Good luck."

"Charlie," Dustin called out quietly as Charlie opened his door. "It's appreciated. All of it."

Charlie glanced back quickly again and, with an imperceptible nod, he darted out of his seat. He shouted, "*Hey, crazy!*" out to Jenna, and took off without a backward glance.

"Hey, loser!" Jenna called after to him. "Did you miss me?"

"Like a corpse misses the plague," Charlie shot back, joining up with a pack of guys in orange jerseys.

"I wish I did not have to..." Dustin muttered.

"I know," Vere whispered. "It's going to be fine. I'll be with you."

Dustin smiled. It wasn't easy to keep the retainer out of sight, and he wanted her to see his real smile. Wanted her to know he was beyond happy to have her watching over him.

Hell. Maybe I am vain.

"Thanks are in order for you, too, *gnome-girl-bestie*." He swallowed the lump of fear at the back of his throat.

Her big eyes softened and she shot him a half smirk. "Remember, it's *me* who's thanking you, *bestie*. We're both on trial today." She pointed at her cheeks. "And look! Zero pinkness!"

"Yeah. You're doing great." He watched her small, delicate hands butterfly up to check the bun.

"I haven't blushed once since we talked on the lake dock. I think your extreme conversation topics seriously desensitized me. I feel like—like—I can talk about anything with any guy now!" She beamed.

"Practice on your pillow first, huh? Just in case," he teased.

"Yeah, yeah, whatever! Now stop trying to procrastinate. I'm giving you two minutes to exit this car," she commanded and disappeared out of her seat, slamming the door, but not before he'd seen the whole back of her neck turn bright pink.

She ran over and hugged Jenna, and they immediately started whispering.

Dustin let his gaze linger on Vere through the window. Today, she'd worn a long, paisley, hippie-ish skirt. She had paired it with another giant hoodie, under which he could see some gargantuan, white tee-shirt peeking out near her knees.

And she makes fun of me in the long-sleeved shirts?

The little hypocrite looked positively swallowed up, like a tiny warrior, hiding in her giant cotton armor. Her strange ensemble combinations were something he'd begun to truly look forward to.

He listened to her excited voice as it slowly rose as if to jerk him into action.

"He's nice, like I said, Jenna. *Super nice.*"

Dustin hid a smile. The girl was actually taunting him.

"He's already got marks against him for stealing you for the whole weekend. He better be double nice." Jenna flipped her braids and turned toward the car.

"Hey. Give him a chance."

"I will, I will," she grumbled. "What's he doing? *Dude.* Dustin, are you coming out?"

Vere gushed, "Wait till you see my guy exposure in action. I can talk to him and almost always, no blush! He's curing me. Wait till you see us together."

He nervously checked his phone again. All good and set to vibrate in case any messages came in. He cracked open his door and grabbed his Tough Mountain backpack off the seat.

His chest was so tight he thought it might explode, and then he remembered: breathe, breathe, breathe.

Damn, get a grip.

Exiting slowly, he launched his heavy work boots so they slammed onto the black-top. The giant *thwack-thud* they let off gave him the courage to get completely out of the car.

"Jenna Riley, most coolest girl *ever*, meet Dustin McHugh.

He's Nan's nephew, my new *BGF*, and newest member of our junior class."

Vere's voice had sounded stiff. Robotic even.

That's making me less nervous. Thanks, bestie.

Dustin shot her a look, then faced Jenna dead on.

Bring it, test bunny. Bring it.

Jenna must have noticed Vere's tight sounding voice as well, because the look she gave Vere was half-terrified, half amused. Maybe she also found Vere Roth's antics to be hilarious?

If so, then they might even get along.

"Hey," she said.

"Hey," Dustin managed.

"All the way from California, huh? How do you like it so far?" She looked him up and down.

Dustin glanced over at Vere. She was behind Jenna, giving him a huge smile and pointing at her mouth.

He quickly stretched his smile wide and bared his retainer to Jenna. "I like it. Lotssth of treessstth."

The test bunny did not answer.

She was too busy flinching and then trying to hide the look of horror on her face.

Dustin had started to sweat. Major. "And I jusstth love the hiking," he added.

He knew he sounded as lame as he looked, but it couldn't be helped. He was freaking out. He tried to smile even bigger.

Come on retainer, don't fail me now.

Jenna, as if finally focusing in on his retainer, executed a full body cringe as she looked at his face. To her credit she finally did manage to paste on a fake smile as a quick recovery.

Dustin could see Vere cracking up out of the corner of his eyes. If the situation weren't so damn serious he'd laugh also.

Hell. How can this screwed-up deal be my very own life?

"What the *heck*?" Jenna reached forward and grabbed the compass sewn into the pocket of the orange canvas vest he'd picked for today. The vest matched with his orange canvas pants in exactly the wrong way.

"You like compassthes?"

"Never thought about them." Jenna frowned. "Do you—do you—um—are you some kind of professional fly fisherman, or deer hunter or...*something*?" Jenna asked, flipping her braids over her back and moving a little closer.

"Nope."

It was all Dustin could to not to take a step back every step she took closer.

"Live on a ranch?" Jenna was almost toe to toe with him now. She leaned in close as though to study him—study his glasses! "Something has to explain that outfit. Man! Oh, man! I've got it. You look just like—hmm. Just like—holy *CRAP*!"

Dustin caught his breath.

Damn. It's over.

He glanced at Vere to see if she showed any signs of panic; her smile had turned to plastic and it looked sort of stapled on, but about to fall off.

She'd pulled out her car keys and had her thumb on the beeper unlock.

Shit! Not good. Not good.

It's only ten feet from here to the passenger door...

Dustin struggled to answer Jenna. "Nope. No horses, no hunting. I'm from Bakersthhhfield, California. Thissth is just normal wear from back home...I guess." He looked back at Vere. They'd decided on Bakersfield just this morning.

Maybe it had been a poor choice.

Jenna ignored what he'd said. "Dude. For real. Vere! For *REAL*?" She walked around him and looked over at Vere, then back at him before speaking again. "Seriously, I don't mean any offense, but you're—you're both kidding me, right? I've been to Bakersfield. No way do they wear this stuff down there. NO WAY, and never on purpose."

"Jenna!" Vere's voice held a higher note of alarm.

Dustin took one step back. He did not feel good at all.

"But, Vere. Can't you see it? He's—he's—the spitting image—of—of—"

The canary, the test bunny, now the evil, bad Jenna Riley waved her hands in the air, and then pointed straight at him. "I've got it! He's—just like that cool eighties band, DEVO! Dead on. Nerd glasses and all! How do you not see it?"

"Maybe because I was not born in the eighties and didn't start seriously listening to music until last year?" Vere's voice was shaking, but Jenna didn't seem to notice.

Jenna went on, "Come on. Everyone knows that band! It's the group with those boots and the matchy-matchy, radio-active fallout looking zip suits? Although, I think they wore yellow, or was it white..."

Vere shook her head. "Nope. Don't know them."

"God, Vere. you're such a philistine!" Jenna cried.

Dustin sucked in a deep breath. "I know the band. Your point about them...?"

Jenna shrugged. "No point. Just searching for reasons as to *WHY* you are wearing this insane outfit? Say you're a fan."

"I am a fan, actsttthually. Yesssth." DEVO was one of his favorite inspiration bands. No wonder he'd been drawn to the zip suits and big boots.

She grabbed at his shirt sleeves, which made him flinch major, drawing a frown from Jenna as she examined him closer.

"Sorry." She blinked, clutching his shirt even tighter. "But again, what's with the flannel?"

"Jenna!" Vere gasped. "You're being so rude."

"Fine, maybe I am, but what the *heck*?"

Dustin quickly crossed his hands in front of him, protecting his wrists and forcing her to pull back a little. He had to work not to flinch as the test-bunny continued pulling on his shirt fabric.

"Hmm. The plaid makes you sort of punk as well as late eighties...so confusing. So boggling...so wrong, yet, I kind of like it." She let him go and turned to Vere, pulling gleefully on the ends of her braids. "I don't even know how to label him, though."

"Then don't," Dustin choked out, holding back a laugh of absolute relief.

This Jenna girl is slightly cool.

Jenna was on some kind of roll because she was still talking to him and he hadn't heard the last ten things that had come out of her mouth.

"Aren't you melting in that get-up? You're a sitting duck for heat exhaustion if you think you're going to wear that outfit into our school."

"Jenna! You are going to hurt his feelings," Vere admonished.

"Not as much as he's hurting my eyes. We can't let him go in like this. No matter how whacky-cool, and I'm all for that, we can't let him go in like this!"

Dustin caught Vere's eye. She was grinning now. This time it was her good, happy grin.

"Dustin, don't you listen to her. You can go in how you want, be who you want to be. I mean, who you ARE."

Vere's relieved smile had grown so large he flashed his retainer smile back.

Vere laughed out loud.

Jenna seemed to find none of this funny. "C'mon. He will be murdered on sight. God. Poor guy." To Dustin, she added, "Vere is not the person to advise you on what to wear around here. Take my suggestion and at least leave the pockety-vesty-thing in the car. Heck, even the plaid shirt. Take all that off. Oh no! Is that a second compass on your pants?"

Time to launch THE WALK, and THE TALK.

Dustin faced Jenna and bent into a deep bow as he worked

up his best English accent. "My dear, lady, Jenna. Dare you offend me, or have you justth paid me the highesthh compliment?"

"I—er—what?" Jenna flushed. "I didn't mean to offend you it's just—"

"Hold!" Dustin interrupted and rose from his bow, grateful to see he had Jenna's full attention.

He risked a glance at Vere.

She had her arms wrapped around her waist and was trying not to laugh again. "I'm referring to your comment about the band, DEVO. It istth my favorite." He continued, "If you know that band at all, it marksth you the most unusual of acquaintances. There are not many our age who are ssstho advanced in their musical tastthes. Please, allow me, in advantth, to invite you to be my date to prom?"

"Er. NO?" Jenna did some strange blinking thing at Vere as though they shared some sort of secret language. "Is this a joke? Are you pranking me? Am I being filmed right now?"

Dustin noted that Vere was trying to ignore Jenna because she looked away. Jenna stomped her foot just then, pissed off at being ignored.

Yep. Secret girl language.

Time to finish this. He took Jenna's hand and brought it up quickly and kissed the back of it. "It istth an open invitation."

Jenna ripped her hand back. "Ask me to prom again, and we are not friends. Deal?"

"Deal." He grinned, toning down the lisp. "And I was just kidding."

"Isn't he fantastically adorkable?" Vere piped up. "Don't you see now why I've adopted him? Really. I'm keeping him forever. With a little more convincing, he's going to join the drama club with us."

Jenna was busily wiping the kiss from the back of her hand onto her jeans.

Worried he'd gone too far, he quickly brought it down a notch minus the accent. "Oh, and the lisp can fade if I work hard at it." He added, already noting that he might forget on that once in awhile. "And, I really don't have an English accent at all," he added, being dumb on purpose.

"OMG, duh!" Jenna cracked up. "You are a good actor, though." Dustin knew he'd won her over when he saw that Jenna changed her glare into a half smile.

"Lucky my best friend thinks you are awesome or I'd sock you in the stomach for that hand kiss. No more smooches, Sir Eighties-Rockalot. That was flipping over-the-top, stalker gross. And no more talking like you just stepped out of a Renaissance fair. That has got to stop, as in, now."

Dustin smiled. "Right. Got it. Sorry. When I'm nervous I always do that."

Vere burst out into a fit of giggles. "Stop. You're killing me."

He could tell Vere had about two million more things to say, but was holding back. This was actually kind of fun! He couldn't wait to try random weirdness on the next round of people.

They trudged up a long sidewalk, heading for the school. Within minutes they were in a crowded front courtyard full of high school teenagers. He pulled his hat down. People were looking at him.

Tons of staring eyes all shooting straight at him. He thought he would be used to being stared at. But this was wild. Everyone was looking, but pretending NOT to look. It was the first time he'd been stared at minus any admiration or adoration.

What he was getting now was simply bad energy.

His stomach rolled. Maybe he should have eaten more breakfast. Dustin moved a step closer to Vere as his heart rate went crazy. "I don't know if I'm ready for this."

He shot her a glance, trying to keep the fear out of his voice, and hoped his glasses hid his expression.

"Don't worry. They aren't looking at you, they are looking at the boots, the glasses, and the fact that you are hanging out with the dorkiest girl in the whole school, *me*. It just isn't done. You'll see."

Dustin gave her a sharp glance, but she appeared completely unperturbed. "Why do you always say that stuff about yourself?"

"Because it's true," she answered simply.

The crowd forgotten, Dustin's panic slipped away as he was distracted by Vere's attitude. Why did she seem so comfortable branding herself an outcast? "It's not. You're so awesome."

She arched a funny look at him and shook her head. "You don't really know me. Not how they know me. Sadly, whether you like it or not, I am the dorkiest girl in this school. I've earned the title."

Dustin opened his mouth to launch a major rebuttal but Vere grabbed onto his arm. Her hand locked like a vice into his shirt as she paled. "Great," she whispered. "Kristen Hodjwick. Weapons ready and shields up. This game is about to get serious."

Vere pasted on the tense, fake smile she'd had on earlier with Jenna.

"What game?" Jenna asked.

"Life?" Vere answered, and shot an apologetic glance at Dustin for almost blowing it by saying too much.

A short brunette approached, followed by a gang of over dressed, over made-up girls. They were currently giggling and whispering to each other. One had the audacity to point directly at Dustin and laugh.

Well, perfect. It's what I wanted, right?

They certainly weren't running up screaming and asking for autographs, so it had to be a good thing, right? Dustin took a deep breath.

Round two. Let's go.

"Hey Vere. Who's the tall guy with the dark glasses?" Kristen asked, her eyes never leaving Dustin. Her tone had been less than flattering. She was wearing a cheerleader outfit, and her hair was cut into a perfectly shaped, upside down, cartoon-style triangle.

Dustin gazed down at the brunette. She wasn't cute or ugly, but standing next to Vere, Kristen came across to him as plain boring. The girl had talent, though. She'd mastered how to ignore Vere while talking to her at the same time.

She reminded him of a double-talking album producer or worse, a studio accountant.

Dustin recognized her name from Vere's incident story. Miss Kristen H. was probably not here to welcome him or play nice.

"His name is Dustin," Vere said. "Dustin McHugh."

Dustin offered his hand for Kristen to shake, but the girl crossed her arms, clearly not in the mood to shake hands.

"He's new. My neighbor's nephew. Dustin, meet Kristen."

"Ooh. Our names almostth rhyme." Dustin said, firing a small glimpse of his retainer smile at the girl and watching her grimace.

"Did Vere teach you how to dress or something?" Kristen asked loudly, sneering at his outfit.

The pack of girls behind Kristen laughed.

Dustin flicked Vere a glance, worried this girl had hurt Vere's feelings. Vere tugged at her giant sweatshirt and checked her bun as if to show she didn't care, but he could tell she did.

Dustin, scrambling for a way to fire-back at this Kristen, stalled by executing the same bow he'd given Jenna. "A pleasure to meet you. I dressth myself. But if you want to help me get dressthed...anytime!"

Kristen Hodjwick pursed her lips; she did not even try to hide her horror at his bow, or at what he'd offered.

This was going to be good.

He'd decided to misinterpret Kristen's interest in him as flirtatious. He flirted right back. "I'm from BakersTHHfield, Cal-I. Forn-I-A." He winked at her. "Kristtthhen. Is that right?"

Kristen made a perfect bitter-lemon face and rolled her eyes. "Uh. Yeah. It's Kristen." She flipped her hair and continued with a mocking voice, "I THuggesstTH you don't memorize the name. I only wanted to see Vere's new *boyfriend* up close."

Dustin preened in front of Kristen. "Oh. She's not my girlfriend. If I could only be sttho lucky. But can I get your number?" He straightened his vest and gave her the full, double-wide, look-at-my-retainer smile.

Vere immediately started to cough.

Dustin knew it wouldn't be long before she had the giggles again. He forced himself not to look at her, because his own lips were twitching.

In the meantime, Kristen Hodjwick had actually gasped at his question. "So gross." Her voice turned acid. "Don't mistake my curiosity for some kind of pickup, because I've definitely seen enough of you. Enough for the whole year." She tossed her hair again. It was so bone straight that it did this insane little flip that looked just like a slap in the face.

Yep. She had talent.

Another few years and she could apply for a job as a Hollywood accountant. It was a relief Kristen was making a point to not look back, because he was hardly able to contain himself.

Wow. Totally snubbed.

He couldn't imagine this disguise working any better.

"Oh, but—Kristtthtten, wait!" He called after her, unable to resist.

Kristen held up her hand to silence him without turning back around.

This gained her another solid round of giggles from the

girls who awaited her return. To them, she was announcing, "I never thought there could be a male-geek version of Vere Roth, but I was wrong. They say everyone has a perfect match somewhere on earth, and now I'm going to have to believe it." She threw a glance at her posse. "Girls, you should get a look at this guy up close."

"Eww. Not happening," one said.

"Yeah. We'll take your word for it," sneered another.

Vere and Dustin dissolved into laughter.

Jenna, not understanding Dustin and Vere's absolute glee, had crossed her arms as though she were holding back on throwing punches. Her venomous stare into Kristen Hodjwick's back could have started a fire.

Dustin was glad to have Jenna on their team and watched his new ally unclench her fists. As if she realized Vere would not assist her in this confrontation, she shook her head, looking somewhat dazed. Jenna shouted, "Yeah. Well. Kristen Hodjwick, the perfect match of you is—is—your *MOM*."

Kristen turned back and laughed. "Ooh. Nice. Last time I heard that one, I was in the third grade, dork!"

"Damn," Jenna whispered so only the three of them could hear. "Kristen's right. I *so* deserve that. Who says 'your mom'? I'm so lame."

She looked so helpless and mad that Dustin chuckled. "You're awesome, like Vere promised."

Vere's laughter started up all over again, her large brown eyes twinkling pure happiness at them.

Jenna glowered at her. "What is wrong with you? You've gone mental." To Dustin, she added, "Vere's usually in charge of excellent comebacks when she's not delirious. They are obviously not my strong point. Vere. Stop laughing."

"Sorry. Once a fit starts, it's hard to stop." Vere stepped in between him and Jenna, and bumped his upper arm with her shoulder. Her eyes were still filled with mirth. She giggled one last time, and he felt like the holes he'd been carrying on his heart had somehow just been filled in with her friendship.

With her...just her...

"We've done it. The *BGF* is on board," he said softly.

"Oh yeah. We've done it," Jenna quipped, still not understanding as they headed for the door. "We've sealed your fate."

"She's right. I hope you weren't expecting to make other friends besides the two of us," Vere added.

Dustin took a deep breath and smiled at his newly formed gang. He felt...slightly...amazing. "Why would I need to do that? I'm good with you two. But on the flip side, I could be too much of a long-term social burden. No hard feelings if you decide to cut and run after today."

Jenna folded her arms across her chest. "We can decide that later. And if you try to dump us, we'll stalk you or something. I like you a little—or I like the compasses—so you're stuck!"

A loud electronic beep cut through the air.

Dustin flinched and glanced nervously at Vere.

"First bell. We have ten minutes to get to class," Vere explained.

Dustin smiled and pulled his lips up above his retainer in reply. Vere laughed again and rolled her eyes.

Jenna grimaced. "I suppose there's no way you can yank that retainer and only wear it at home?" she asked, her expression hopeful.

"Hey now, it issthhhh new technology. The dentissthh says all my teethtths will ssseparate if I don't keep it in."

"But our eyes could separate if you don't take it out—"

"Jenna, can you give him a break? He's only just met you. You can work on his fashion later," Vere said cheerily. "Follow me, Dustin. I'll take you up to the office."

23: invisible

Dustin

Dustin stared at his registration packet.

Vere and Jenna had long since left him alone at the front office with a goat-ish woman called Mrs. Ferriter. She was now leading him along. Each of her steps sounded like hooves, *clack, clack, clackity-clacking* all the way to a long table in the back room.

She handed him a huge pile of strange school safety waivers and forms to fill out. He also had a student handbook, a registration form and a booklet that had yellow sticky notes all over it. Mrs. Ferriter had told him the sticky notes designated which classes had been marked full, and that he was not to sign up for any of those.

There were two other late-start students filling out their paperwork, but after only a cursory glance, they had positively ignored him.

Excellent sign of success.

Mrs. Ferriter had directed him to choose something they called *Advanced Placement* courses for his core math, science, literature, and history classes.

His grades and test scores that had been sent over allowed for that, whatever *that* meant. He dutifully chose Trig. II, Physics, English Literature, and Medieval History, all from under the AP category.

Dustin let out a big, noisy sigh on purpose, and quickly looked at the guy sitting next to him.

The guy didn't look up.

The girl he'd dubbed *permanently-annoyed-girl* shot him a glare from across the table.

Amazing!

A flood of laughter surged into Dustin's chest but he managed to hold it in.

This new teen-invisibility factor had to be the best feeling in the world! He tapped his pen onto the table and tested his dorkiest whistle as he turned back to his forms. When he looked over his choices of electives, drama was the only available option. Vere would be happy, at least. Besides, he sure wasn't going to take any of the P.E. classes. Short sleeves and locker rooms would not work.

"Excuse me. You, with the ugly vest. Stop the whistling bit," *permanently-annoyed-girl* ordered. When he looked up at her a second time, she pulled a face and rolled her eyes while tossing his pants a sneer.

Point for the canvas!

The guy next to him had finished his pile of paperwork and seemed to also be openly assessing his outfit with sneers.

Dustin tried to make contact again. "Thsshthese forms are a big pain, huh?"

The guy raised one eyebrow in what looked like absolute scorn. He leaned back in his chair and gave a little snort and shook his head when he took in Dustin's boots. "What are you? Some kind of inbred?" he asked, finally.

Dustin stopped whistling. It was his turn not to answer.

Even though it was almost impossible to do—he dropped his smile, and turned away, acting all sad.

He glanced again at *permanently-annoyed-girl* but was met again with her hostile, closed face.

Christ. These kids have zero sense of humor.

His initial sense of elation fled, leaving—what?

Was he suddenly embarrassed? Freaked out? Supremely uncomfortable?

Yes.

But, he also felt pretty good, considering. He sucked in a deep breath, imagining Vere's happy reaction to this news.

Dustin McHugh had it made. No one wanted a piece of him. This high school schedule was easy compared to his usual 20 hour days and nights. No one took photos or randomly grabbed him either. Hell, these kids didn't even want to be near him. His heart twisted a little, thinking of his fans. His band, recording songs in NYC right now.

Maybe this wasn't the best feeling in the world.

He imagined entering a classroom full of kids just like these two in a few, short minutes. They couldn't all be this flipping rude. Could they?

He zoned out and stared at the form in front of him and circled a deep groove with his ballpoint pen around and around the words that said 'Drama 300/400 Jr./Sr. only'. The only course in the booklet for upper grades. Vere would have signed up for this same class. Because if everyone was going to treat him like invisible trash, he needed to refuel with his *bestie*, and soon.

Please. Please. Please.

What's that song line? 'If you're loved by just one then you can't be rejected?' No...that's not right...and who sings it? Besides I should switch it to: 'If you love just one but she doesn't know it...'

"Young man. Mr. McHugh."

Clack. Clackety. Clack.

Mrs. Ferriter's face loomed over his shoulder as a cloud of cheap perfume assaulted his senses. When Dustin looked up, Mrs. Ferriter's face had turned even more goat like.

Did her beady eyes seem sort of disapproving or is it the hairs on her chin that are freaking me out?

"Principal Sloan would like a word with you about your file."

Dustin's heart sank into his stomach. He scanned her face for a clue as to the meaning behind her words.

Maybe she knew. Maybe they all knew who he was.

Please. Please. Don't let her know.

Mrs. Ferriter scooped up his paperwork. "You two done?"

She jerked her head at the other kids. They quickly gathered up their things. "Good. All of you follow me out." She waved a meaty hand at Dustin. "You. Head two doors south. Corner office. After you're done, I'll have your class schedule printed."

***

"Mr. McHugh, please come in. Shut the door." Principal Sloan's stern, disapproving voice caught him by surprise as he stood in the hallway.

Dustin entered the office and glanced warily at the man sitting behind a huge oak desk. The principal looked to be older than time. He had on gold wire-rimmed glasses, sported the most unbelievable beige polyester shirt, and he'd oddly highlighted the whole look with an electric blue tie.

Principal Sloan had a file open in front of him. He didn't look up as he studied its contents. "Come closer, son. What do you say?"

Dustin's heart raced double time.

What should I say?

Silence was always his preferred choice when presented with dangerous people, but in this case, he opened with: "Er—nice to meet you, sir?"

Dustin shifted his feet, his heart pounding in his chest. Did this guy know who he was or not? He thought back to Thursday in the airport. What had Martin and his mom said about the school district? Was this the person who'd done the favor?

Dustin scoured his brain but couldn't remember.

Why hadn't they emailed him at least some kind of reminder about all this crap?

"I don't know what your deal is, Dustin McHugh, but your file came down to me from pretty high up. The only other time we had anything this unusual and this hush-hush was when one kid's family was in the witness protection program—back in

♥ 226 ♥

ninety-seven."

Dustin opened his mouth to say he was not a federal witness but the guy held up his hand and stopped him.

"I don't want to know. Get it? For your safety, and the safety of the school, I'm not allowed to ask. So don't tell me. My concerns lie in other areas. The only information I've been privy to is your penchant for vandalism and reckless driving. Oh, and personal endangerment? I also have a note here about your possible depression. If you are depressed, Dustin, we do have counseling available. As for the other stuff, I need to warn you that it will not be happening here. So. Are you? Are you currently depressed?"

"No sir," Dustin almost choked on the words.

"Will you be requiring any counseling at this time? Your file says you're living with your great aunt as guardian. I'll call her to let her know we've had this conversation. I have to return this form to the district this morning to show that we talked."

Dustin breathed a sigh of relief. He had no clue how Martin had managed to hide his identity but he was, at this moment, truly grateful for his agent's abilities.

"So is that a definite *no* for counseling?" He blinked.

"I had a therapist at my...old place. He told me I only needed a therapist if I wanted one. I don't. I'll refuse to go if anyone tries to make me." Dustin hated that he had to justify himself to this guy, but it had to be better than being found out. "I can honestly say to you that I'm starting to realize that since I've come to Colorado, I've never been happier. Really."

"Good. Good. Let's hope it stays that way. Let me know if you need anything." The principal was busily filling out an orange form with the name Dustin McHugh typed in all caps at the top. "The other shenanigans will not be tolerated. Do you have that under control?"

"I do, sir. The Roth family is helping me out. The kids, brother and sister, will be driving me to—uh, to," he used Mrs.

Roth's words, "here and to all school functions."

"Charlie Roth? Really. Interesting." The principal scratched his ear and wrote more on the bottom of the form as he blabbed on, "Charlie's a darn good football player. That kid's got his head pretty much on straight. Hope to work him out a fine scholarship this year. Didn't know he had a sister."

"Vere. His sister's name is Vere. Vere Roth. She's a junior." For some reason it bothered Dustin that the principal didn't know Vere's name.

Principal Sloan hadn't heard a word he'd said. "All right. So long as we're clear, McHugh."

"We're clear."

The principal put down his pen and directly looked at Dustin for the first time. "You're a tall one. But you don't look to be very sports oriented. I'll tell you though, our basketball team is always looking for—"

"Drama!" Dustin couldn't help but interrupt. He could hardly believe the principal had bought into his dork factor. The guy was a total tool. "I'm going to join the drama club, sir." He flashed his retainer, which earned him the expected and hoped for disdainful squint. Dustin grinned even wider and had the urge to laugh because his new power to horrify people was beyond awesome.

"Yes. Yes. Drama." The principal sighed and looked away as though he couldn't stand to look at Dustin's smile. He seemed to lose all interest in Dustin and glanced at his watch. "Don't waste any more time, son. Head out. You should be able to make it to second period."

24: drama class just got better

VERE

Seventh period. Last class of the day.

Vere checked her phone for the time. Ten minutes early.

Drama class, followed by Drama Club.

Mrs. VanDeWirth, followed by more Mrs. VanDeWirth.

Vere's all-time favorite topic, combined with her most favorite teacher.

Pure perfection.

This year, Vere meant to go for stage director, or lighting master. As an upperclassman, she'd have a better chance this year at getting some real responsibilities back stage.

Vere pulled open the auditorium doors. She loved how it smelled in here, some dust, some must, and all the rest pure magic. This part of Palmer Divide High had been around since 1967. The theater still boasted the original red velvet seats, now crushed and worn into a faded pink color. They were still sturdy with metal backs and bottoms and Vere loved how the crunchy springs in the seats sounded when you first sat in them.

The floors were concrete except for the stage, which was made up of a light-colored pine. Today, the huge, heavy red curtains hung open, exposing the stage that now held a ton of students all waiting for class to start. Why had she thought she would be the only one who would want to come in here early?

The school funding had cut Mrs. VanDeWirth's hours back. To compensate, they'd combined the junior and senior drama classes into one larger class. Because of the size, they'd been instructed to meet here instead of in Mrs. VanDeWirth's classroom.

Vere's confidence wavered when she saw how many people

were sitting cross-legged or sprawled around on the stage floor. How would she stand out in a class this size?

Vere slipped silently into the back edge of the crowd and sat on the floor. There had to be at least forty people here already with more trailing in through the side doors.

Her stomach growled. She rummaged in her backpack, searching for snacks.

"Hey, Vere."

A familiar low baritone rumbled at her from above. She startled, pulled her head out of her backpack, and checked her bun as she struggled to swallow the whole pretzel stick she'd just shoved into her mouth.

She twisted and looked up. Way, way up. Her gaze traveled past a pair of tanned legs in sun-faded, khaki shorts. Then it traversed an impossibly white shirt and a perfectly sculpted collarbone and chin. Her gaze had made it all the way to a pair of perfect green eyes with midnight black lashes.

Then she died.

"Uh. Hey, Curtis," she gasped.

The pretzel stick was now suffocating the back of her throat with dry dust and stinging salt.

"It took me awhile to find you in this crowd," he said. "Should have known to check the dark corners of the room first." He smiled.

"Yeah. Corners." She took a deep breath and worked to swallow the lump that now blocked her pretzel from going down. "Are you lost? This is really far from the gym," she said, finally.

Her only solace was that her head wasn't stuck in a shirt this time. She wiped her mouth, wondering if she'd blown any food bits at him on accident.

"Don't I know it." Curtis Wishford grinned down, crossing his arms. A move that fully showed off his nice biceps.

His grinning, dimpled perfect face threatened to make Vere

die all over again. (If that was possible when she was already dead.)

Dead and gaping at him like an idiot.

Help. Help. Someone help me think of something perfect to say.

Crickets. Crickets. Crickets.

Someone help. I've been hypnotized. By crickets!

Curtis's jaw moved steadily as he chomped on a piece of gum as though he had his own rhythm.

Bright, neon-yellow gum.

It bounced around his mouth, two chews to the right, one to the left and back. Crack. Snap. And chew.

Great. Who stared at gum? Dead people. That's who.

"Um. Charlie never comes in here, so..."

"I'm not looking for Charlie. Mind if I sit?"

Her brows went so high she felt them almost shoot off the top of her forehead. But she managed a nod.

He dropped a notebook next to her backpack and sat. As in right next to her.

"I signed up for this class on a whim," he said.

"You did?"

Was this really happening? Could she handle this?

Obviously NOT.

Come on Vere.

You practiced all weekend. You've got it.

She took a deep breath and kicked her brain into gear. "You'll like it. I love this class." He was looking straight into her eyes but she felt too ill to hold his gaze, so she glanced away and pointed at the audience seats. "I love this auditorium, and Mrs. VanDeWirth."

OMG. I think I quake-yodeled that entire sentence. Please don't let him say anything. Please.

"I know you do." He stretched his legs out and leaned back.

"You do?" she asked, completely distracted by the fact that Curtis Wishford smelled like spicy, warm sweat. He must have just worked out. He was always working out or about to work out.

It wasn't a bad smell. But maybe it wasn't a great smell either. Ha. Wait till I tell Jenna this one.

"Yeah. You talk about drama all the time when I'm over for dinners and stuff."

She gaped at his long, muscular legs stretched out in front of both of them. Dark hair covered his calves and what she could see of his thighs.

Vere had her legs tucked crisscross under her long skirt. Her skinny smooth legs would look weird next to his bumped and bruised football-huge shins, wouldn't they? Curtis Wishford always seemed so comfortable in his own body. How could she get some of his confidence to rub off on her?

Keep talking to him. You can do this.

"So...do you know what else I like?" She managed, and she shocked even herself with her next move: she smiled.

"I'm hoping I do know." He smiled back, with what looked like a calm, interested and flirty smile!

Was this conversation working so well because the stage lights were only half up? Maybe it was the long weekend of practice she'd had with Charlie and Dustin, or maybe, she really was truly dead.

Either way, Vere was in control of herself in front of Curtis for the first time in years! She couldn't believe it.

She hadn't even started to blush.

Oh, thank you, Dustin McHugh!

Curtis went on, "I signed up for Drama because Charlie told me it would be the best place to track you down once a day so we could hang out."

"What?" So much for control.

Her cheeks went from zero to two billion on the pink tracker in less than one second. That had to be a record.

"You heard me. I was thinking we could hang out a bit."

She checked her bun again and focused on getting air. She

placed her hands flat on the stage floor and wondered if the vortex created by her empty lungs would eventually suck her through the stage and into the orchestra pit below.

Breathe, Vere, breathe. Don't put him on a pedestal.

"What do you mean by hang out, exactly," she squeaked out.

Thankfully, Curtis seemed not to notice her upset. He'd been tracing a small knot in the wood with his finger the whole time and hadn't looked up.

Wait. Did Curtis seem a little nervous?

"I mean, I don't know. I've just had the urge to hang out with you. I tried to mention it last week, but Howie messed up my mojo-magic. I'm so busy after school with football, and you're so shy around me." Curtis paused his hand and looked up. Looked up and right at her!

Good God. Why do you have to be so gorgeous?

Vere closed her mouth fast because it had opened really far by then.

He ran his hand through his hair. "I was hoping you'd like the idea. Do you mind?"

"Is Charlie putting you up to this or something?" She shot him a suspicious frown. She would have to play this off as funny until she could get a handle on his level of seriousness. "I just want you to know, Charlie's flat broke so whatever he offered you, he has to pay me two hundred bucks first."

Curtis laughed. "No one's behind this but me. Charlie only gave me his blessing, if that counts. I kind of wish I'd had the courage to do this last year. Really. I've had a crush on you for a long time."

Vere made sure her voice was dry and over-skeptical. "Really?" She raised her eyebrows and double crinkled her forehead while she leveled him with her 'don't-mess-with-me' stare.

"You're blushing, Vere, so either you like the idea, or you hate it. Which is it?"

Vere risked a longer look into Curtis's eyes.

Truly, this did not appear to be a joke.

Vere. Say something!

Can't. Crickets are back.

When her silence stretched into an obvious problem, Curtis glanced down and fiddled with the edge of his notebook. "If you aren't into it, into me I mean, I'm dropping this class. No biggie."

"No!" She gasped, his words bringing her out of it. "I like the idea! I mean—it's good...a great idea. And cool. It will be really cool, you know...to just hang out once a day...in here. It seems like a safe place to do that. Not like I need to be safe—from you."

He laughed, his eyes smiling warmly at her. "Oh, I wouldn't say that. Once I stake my claim, *my* girls are never safe." He gave her a strange sideways look as if he might regret what he'd said to her, or regret what she'd said.

Did I hear that right? What did he mean by 'my girls'? And why the plural?

Stop. Stop over thinking this moment.

You've waited for this for so long. Don't over analyze.

And stop gawking at him like he's the Statue of Liberty and you just got off a boat to America.

She willed his lips to move, to say anything, to rescue her. When they didn't, she couldn't stop her mouth from motoring-on a second time. "As for me being into you, well, you'd have to be in a coma or blind to not notice that I've had a crush right back at you. And since I was six. You knew that."

His eyes opened with his own surprise. "Well...I...wasn't sure and..."

She didn't let him finish. "Heck, everyone knows that. What I mean is—if I haven't said it right or clearly—then officially—*yes*. It's a great idea. I'd like...I'd love the chance to know you better. Here...in here and...everywhere...you know?"

Why in the world did you just admit to all that?
In here and EVERYWHERE?
Let's hope HE doesn't overanalyze that. UGH.
AWKWARD. AWKWARD. AWKWARD.

Her recall had returned, and she replayed the whole scene fast-forward in her mind.

Ugh.
Might have been way less obvious to just to rip out your heart.
Stick it on a plate.
How about shove in a couple of tacks and pin it under his shoe?
This guy now has full power to crush you.

She glanced up through her lashes. He was simply blinking at her and chewing his yellow gum. Curtis swallowed hard, and brought his hand up to stroke his chin. His sexy, hot-guy-thinking-pose all but did her in. His gaze searched her face, and she acted as if she didn't notice.

Don't look up again. Just don't. But did he swallow that gum?
She desperately wanted to fidget, or better, run.

Somehow she held still. If Curtis was not going to respond to what she'd said, well, she wasn't going to say another word. Her fire engine red, all over body blush was doing a fine job at screaming her shame.

She pretended to stare even harder at her lap but her gaze traveled from his knee to his perfectly muscled football thigh. How could she not look that over? It was twice as wide as hers and had never been this close to her before.

Even his knees were gorgeous.

Vere forced her gaze away and faked interest in her own knees. Vere shut her eyes for a quick second and opened them, but it didn't help. Curtis still hadn't said anything and most probably he wasn't going to say anything.

The silence had stretched to the point that there was no way she would recover from this moment.

Ever. Ever. Ever.

And then, the most amazing thing happened.

Curtis Wishford, senior star quarterback, and the most perfect of all guys, reached out and turned her chin toward him.

That was when everyone and everything in the entire auditorium just disappeared. The noise, the students milling about, Mrs. VanDeWirth down stage, all of it faded to black. She and Curtis became the only two people sitting center stage.

She stared into his beautiful green eyes, and she felt pretty much just fine. No body shakes. No fisted hands waiting to knock him flat, and her heated cheeks started to cool!

Let the record show, this is happening in front of everyone!

Both of us are still conscious, and there is zero blood. Also, zero emergency vehicles have been called during this moment! YAY!

He smiled and tweaked her nose. "You said it perfectly, and it was just what I wanted to hear. Since you were so honest, I'll lay it all out on the line. Me, taking drama, is my lame attempt to let you know the same. I've been into you all along, too. And well before you knocked me out."

"You did? You have? You are? Really?" She rubbed her nose because he'd pulled it pretty hard. How embarrassing. This had to be some kind of hallucination.

He nodded, his expression still holding at sincere. He tapped the tip of her nose a second time with his most perfect, oversized finger. "We can start slow. Friends. Hanging out. No pressure."

"Perfect. Slow. Slow is perfect."

Like you!

"I'll need you to show me the ropes in this class. I'm also hoping you can keep a secret for me."

"I keep lots of secrets. I'm good at it." Vere swallowed and managed a half smile, thinking suddenly of Dustin.

He gave her his all-American grin and winked. "Really. Then

I'll trade one of my secrets for one of yours."

"Maybe. You first," she challenged, and WINKED BACK!

OMG. This is flirting.

This is ME flirting with Curtis Wishford.

And I'm pretty sure this is Curtis Wishford flirting with me!

Curtis Wishford leaned in. His bubble gum breath moved the wisps of hair that covered her ear. She stared at his lips, but not in a kiss sort of way—she was waiting for him to chew.

Jeez. I think he did swallow that gum!

"I'm scared to death of looking like a total fool in here," he said.

Vere leaned back and looked directly into his eyes. She could feel her cheeks and the tops of her ears tingling hot again, but didn't care. Her heart threatened to burst out of her chest in thirty different directions.

Again, this felt nothing like one of her anxiety moments!

This feeling had to be coming from butterflies. That or she'd swallowed a tiny grenade and it had exploded.

"Now you. One secret," he whispered, keeping his face close his eyes scanning her gaze.

"I'm scared to death this moment might be a dream," she whispered back.

"It's not." Curtis grinned, his expression sort of expectant. He glanced over her shoulder and made a face. "Hmm. Dream or nightmare...for me. I hate having to compete for your attention."

"Ha. As if you ever would." Vere blinked at him. The world crashed back in so fast it disoriented her.

Curtis turned and motioned to the far end of the stage. "Your entourage has arrived. I should have known they would be in here. Why did I think I would have you all to myself?"

Dustin McHugh had entered front and center and was doing his stiff-back-walk. Vere could make out Jenna's light blonde head bobbing right behind. Dustin carved a path right through the center of the kids sitting on stage.

It was like the parting of the red sea as people moved away from him. Cringed away from him, actually. Avoiding all eye contact and everything!

He greeted each and every person who accidently gave him half a glance using his new plastic and metal dork smile, and a loud: "Hey. I'm Dussttthhin."

Priceless.

From the way most kids were acting, Vere could tell the disguise was working better than fine.

Jenna, oblivious always to other people's scorn, and to the fact that she was hanging with *THE Hunter Kennedy*, skipped along, chattering away happily.

Aww. They must have bonded.

"Charlie told me all about the new kid. Heard he's a menace. As for Jenna Riley, when will she give up those goofy braids?"

Vere glanced sideways at Curtis.

What did he mean? Why would he say such a thing?

"I love those braids. And Dustin's awesome. You'll see." She defended her friends, waving so they would see her. She couldn't wait to get Dustin and Jenna alone so she could tell them everything Curtis had said to her! With class about to start, she had to get their attention. "Dustin. Jenna! Over here!" She waved her arms. Dustin nodded, held up his index finger for her to wait, and then pointed toward Mrs. VanDeWirth.

When she acknowledged him with her best eye roll, he countered with the retainer flash.

Vere couldn't help but giggle.

"Shit. Did you see that smile. Charlie also mentioned he's hideous." Curtis groaned.

"Yeah. Poor guy," Vere said, trying to sound somber as she pictured Dustin's real smile. She wanted to laugh out loud. "He's super nice though. And Nan's nephew so we've got to include him," she added gleefully. "What else did Charlie say?"

"None of us can mess with him because your brother feels sorry for him."

"Come on! We're good friends already. He's not that bad."

Curtis grimaced. "Yes he *is* that bad. Look at him. The dude's lucky you and Charlie have him under guard because there's something about him. Something that sort of makes me want to kick his ass."

Vere frowned. "I didn't know you had such a weird sense of humor."

"I don't," Curtis said as he looked away from Dustin and trapped her in a sea of his green-eyed heaven. "Wonder what he's doing in here?"

"Maybe he signed up for this class!" Vere knew her voice sounded too excited, but she couldn't help it. If he were going to be in here, then he'd be around to help keep her calm if she needed him.

Dustin had gone over with Jenna in tow to greet Mrs. VanDeWirth, who checked her list and nodded.

Curtis sighed. "Looks like he did."

Dustin was shaking Mrs. VanDeWirth's hand wildly. The poor lady looked a little sketched out because of that move.

Vere giggled again. How she wished she could hear what Dustin was saying.

"He's going for teacher's pet. Does he have to be so goofy and friendly?"

"I guess it's just his personality."

"What's his deal? Does he act?"

Vere glanced at Curtis. His expression seemed mild enough but she wondered why he sounded so annoyed.

"Not sure," Vere evaded. "He told me he hates drama so it is a surprise to see him."

"Really," Curtis said with an unreadable look. He brushed the side of his index finger across her left cheek. "Well, maybe he has the same idea I have."

Vere's stomach did a flip. "Impossible. We're just friends. And besides." She tossed Dustin a glance. "He's got no chance compared to you."

"Aww. You're sweet." Curtis smiled.

Vere smiled back. She tried to concentrate on Curtis but she couldn't stop herself from tracking Dustin's progress.

Curtis tugged at one of her escaped bits of hair and frowned when she scooted to the side so she could see Dustin better. There was no way to explain to the now scowling Curtis that she just had to watch her protégé do his nerd walk again.

Someday she would be able to tell it all to him. Someday they would laugh about this. Curtis was almost acting like he was jealous.

Imagine.

And imagine she did: homecoming, cheering at football games, Winter Formal, somewhere in there her first kiss, and of course...if it all went well...Prom!

Jenna and I will be eating chips before all school dances after all. I'll make Curtis find her dates, or I won't go!

Vere hugged herself.

Maybe she should calm down. She still had to somehow convince him to really like her first. It was a rocky road traversing the friends stage. There was still the huge chance the incident would sneak up again. He could change his mind about this.

She had to figure out a way to make him really like her, as in for real. Like a girlfriend. And one who would last for more than his usual two-month trial period.

The whole idea was kind of making her head hurt.

In the meantime, she just had to watch Dustin. How could she not? She had her *BGF* to thank for everything she'd been able to say to Curtis today.

Her heart burst with pride for herself and for Dustin's

success. She could tell Dustin was looking directly at her as he crossed the rest of the stage. Because of the low lighting his glasses were only a light grey tint. She could see his eyes twinkling behind the glass with their shared secret.

He seemed to be almost cracking up.

Vere beamed at him, wondering if she'd ever felt this happy.

A++ with bonus extra credit for both of them.

She turned her sunniest smile back onto Curtis, mostly to check if he was really still sitting there.

Jeez. He is. Crisscross applesauce and popping in a fresh new piece of that neon-yellow gum! I will have to tell him it's not a good idea to swallow the stuff.

Dustin clambered up to them.

His work boots made more noise on the stage than an elephant stampede. He clumped way too close and stood there acting all helpless and confused. He held all his stuff in a disorganized lump in front of him.

Jenna followed close behind, squeezing in next to Vere. She dashed a look toward Curtis and bugged out her eyes when she realized who Vere had been sitting with this whole time.

She met Vere's gaze with the silent *what-the-heck* blink.

Vere promptly flicked her subtle *half-eye-roll* plus the quick left-sided grin. Translation: *I know. And OH.MY.GOD!*

Dustin dropped all his stuff in the center of their small circle and took the spot on the other side of Vere closing up the space between her and Curtis. "You must be Curttisth Witsthford," he said. "Vere's told me all about you."

Vere gasped and had to bite her lip.

God. Did Dustin not know when to quit?

She almost exploded into a giggle attack. She held it together long enough to recover and watch as Curtis threw Dustin a disgusted look. She couldn't even could blame the guy. Curtis had been buried Dustin's loose papers and Tough Mountain weirdness. It was as if Dustin had dropped everything on top of

Curtis on purpose.

Curtis shoved Dustin's backpack off his legs. "Well, Charlie's told me all about you. And apparently, he wasn't lying," Curtis said, shooting Dustin a cryptic, snide laugh.

"Oh! Thanksssthh. Charlie'stth been sttho cool."

Vere bit back another huge belly laugh, because she'd caught Dustin's gaze through his lenses. She could tell he was wondering what Charlie had said about him, exactly.

Dustin was absolutely glorious right now. Solidifying his permanent, publicly-played dork-status, all while grinning like a fool. He scooted away from Curtis on his knees, muttering "Sorry, so sorry," to everyone around him as he collected his things. She could tell by his voice that Dustin was also trying not to laugh.

Curtis captured Vere's gaze by tugging on her arm and pulling her back in next to him. He leaned in too, scooting as close as he could and hit her with his gorgeous smile.

Forgetting about Dustin, she suppressed a sigh and smiled back into his eyes.

Yes!

25: BGF is better than nothing

Dustin

From: nyjuice77@yahoo.com
To: cojuice99@yahoo.com
Subject: Hang in there.

Going on one full week without you and regretting ever letting you board that plane. Sorry for the delayed contact on my part. It's been nuts. As for getting you out, it's in the works. Can't seem to get an appointment with the judge. Not so easy to track him down from the NY side.
Once the band's settled I'll head back to LA to lock it down.
I hoped your mom would be more help.
Cheers,
Martin

Disguested, he threw the phone onto his bed side table.

No way in hell was he going to email Martin back. That bastard needed to call *him*.

He sprang up from the bed and pulled apart his curtains to check for Vere's car. She'd promised to come take him hiking. Apparently, there was a place tucked into a neighborhood close by with a trail Vere was *dying* to show him.

One that had a monopoly on *cool-shaped rocks.*

Actually, she'd touted the neighborhood as having "the best, most awesome stockpile of heart-shaped rocks in the whole world!"

He thought of her wide grin as she'd gone on and on about the rocks, while he'd only half-listened, wondering how many neighborhoods in Colorado boasted their own hiking trails. Did the real-estate developers not understand the open spaces were perfectly good, saleable lots? Double for the lot that owned the heart-shaped rock mine.

He laughed quietly to himself. This place was so strange compared to Los Angeles, New York, Paris, the entire world.

Of course he couldn't tell her he didn't want to go.

Because, after her descriptions—and despite the fact he'd have to take another long hike—he really wanted to see Vere skipping around, flipping out and gushing over rocks.

Who wouldn't want to be there for that?

He cracked the window a few inches so he could hear her honk when she showed. Flopping back down on his bed, he sighed, contemplating how quickly his days here had passed.

The email from Martin had felt like a hard slap in the face. It reminded him of his real life. His old life.

He'd almost forgotten everything in just a few short days.

He'd even forgotten himself. Completely.

And I'm going to stay forgotten.

Right now, I don't want to be anything, or anyone else, other than a kid who's waiting for his best friend.

That's it. And that's me.

He also admitted he liked school. Milling around the lunchroom and the courtyard packed with hundreds and hundreds of kids—kids who didn't scream or swarm around him—was kind of cool. The classes with the desks lined up in rows (full of more kids who ignored him nonstop) had also been great.

Drama class was now his top favorite. Not because he liked watching the scenes and working on the skits; but because he loved watching Vere *LOVE* her drama class.

The auditorium was obviously a drug for her. The backstage area seemed a place where she could let herself shine with complete confidence. Just like the lights she loved placing on stage to make things brighter, the whole environment lit Vere in the same way. Inside and out. Of course, this fact made her even more beautiful than she normally was.

To him, anyhow. The bun, baggy shorts and those big brown eyes were what he craved. The girl had started to stun him stupid with a simple smile or one of her little glares.

And every single day his crush got worse.

All while she hangs out, longing for Curtis to notice her more.

He grimaced at that thought. If only Vere were skipping into drama class her eyes sparkling—the edges of her cheeks all flushed pink—looking around for one glimpse of *him.*

He sure as hell wouldn't make her wonder. If he could trade places with Curtis, he would do everything in his power to make her his. Forever.

But he wasn't Curtis. He was the lame *BGF.*

And it was working well for both of their purposes. It wasn't that Vere didn't seem happy to have him near at all times. Heck, she seemed to want to hang with him more and more.

But in all the wrong ways.

If only she'd want me in the right way.

But do I want that? Really?

He let out a long, annoyed sigh.

It's not like she's going to swap crushes on Curtis and publicly hold hands with me in my canvas pants. Social suicide was never her plan. Curtis Wishford is her plan...

He tried to imagine a scenario in his other life. He pictured walking around Los Angeles with Vere, introducing her to the band and his entourage, then showing her his monster-huge, but empty house and he broke out in a sweat.

Hell no. Plus, that place would suck the life out of her eyes. Once she knew everything about our family, about me...she simply wouldn't want to fit there. The stupid BGF status is all I'm ever going to get. Besides, who would I be to Vere back in California?

The same person I am to her here in Colorado: Not. Curtis.

She's kind of made that clear this past week, along with telling me every second of her life story. Her cute, hilarious life story...

Listening for Vere's little snippets of her past and her ultra-normal family had become part of his daily routine. His secret fun, but increasingly, his private torture the more he found out about her.

Because I'm starting to adore every little insane thing that she does. The girl can make pie from scratch. And she comes over to hang out with Aunt Nan so they can watch TV and knit? KNIT. She's actually making me a hat! Who does that kind of granny stuff?

The cutest girl in the world, that's who.

He knew for a fact that Vere's opinion of drama class had also skyrocketed this year. Vere had told him this again only hours before on the ride home.

Why?

He gave the ceiling fan a cynical little smile.

Because Vere tells her bestie everything.

As much as he loved to watch her smile and be happy, he was starting to get—down to his core—that there was a possibility this *BGF* thing could eventually crush him. Crush his heart anyhow, as Vere's relationship with Mr. Jerk-ford grew. And it was happening. Slowly, and surely, right before his very eyes. Curtis was growing more enchanted with Vere every second.

How could he not?

To add insult to injury, Dustin couldn't even show the kid up. Rage on the guitar, write Vere a song, act his assigned parts how he *wanted* to act them, or even go after a singing lead for the musical. He was actually failing drama because he'd sworn he had stage fright and had refused to perform any skits.

He was stuck. Trying to *not* draw attention. Not that it mattered! He had less game than a toad. Vere treated him as though she couldn't even remember he'd ever been anything *but* Dustin the dork, her *slave-BGF*.

Worse, to date, Vere had told him every excruciating detail of her MIND interactions with Curtis.

Everything.

And then, she'd bombarded him with girly, best-friend-gushing like:

*What Curtis had *surely* meant when he blinked that time?

*Or, *if* she should text him?

*What she *would* text him if she were brave enough?

*Or why hadn't Curtis asked for her number yet—and so maybe it was inappropriate *to* text him. (Because she'd stolen his number off Charlie's phone two years ago!)

HELL.

It had started out as comical, and he was happy to try and help her interpret Curtis's moves. But after a few days of it, the whole thing had spun out of control. Mostly because Curtis had no moves—besides being a complete ass—but Vere never seemed to get that part about the guy!

He was totally wrong for her.

Today had been an epic example. She had been all freaked out at lunch because Curtis appeared to be spacing out right in front of her. Like, 'uninterested' spacing out.

She'd kept asking: *Do you think it's a possible BAD SIGN? Do you think it's over before it started? Are my chances ruined?*

He'd had to bite the inside of his cheeks.

Mostly so he wouldn't shout: "THE RAT BASTARD WAS NOT SPACING OUT. CURTIS CAUGHT A BRA SHOT WHEN YOU BENT OVER. YOU PUT HIM IN A COMA!"

Instead, he'd muttered some lame, *bestie* response like, "I'm sure it was nothing. He likes you, he totally, totally does."

Hell. She'd put ME in a coma. Who knew Vere Roth wore a bunch of lace under all those hoodies?

Damn...but, I love a girl in some lace, too...

To rub salt in the whole thing, Vere gushed constantly that her guy exposure and his *BGF's* coaching tips were working. He couldn't escape the fact that this whole, unfolding nightmare was his damn fault.

His and Charlie's.

He'd even *agreed* with Charlie that things couldn't be better. Vere had come pretty far out of her shell this week, and Curtis had taken notice. Way, too much notice.

Whatever. Fine. Whatever they wanted. I'm a short timer. I have no right to be annoyed. At least not with Vere, Charlie or even Curtis.

He flipped over so he could pick up his phone. Stared at it until his head spun. Should he log back in and re-read Martin's email? Should he just call the guy?

He pulled Martin's cell number up in his contacts. The over-bright screen lit up.

Ready to go. Tap it. Just tap it and call. But Martin told me no direct calls. Just in case. Just in case what?

He stared at the number on the screen until it went black.

Would one call bring down the commando, phone-sniffing, pop-star-tracking press? And if it did, would they be able to locate him in this God-forsaken town? Maybe he could leave a quick message. Beg the guy to give him the end-date to all this madness.

That was all he really needed. So he could handle himself— the too-huge feelings around this crush—if he could wrap his head around when it all would stop, he'd feel calmer.

Instead of motivating him to dial, his heart tightened at that thought. Yes, his crush was painful, but it was also the best feeling he'd ever felt. And he couldn't imagine how empty he'd be if it ever stopped. If Martin called him home, then it all would go away.

In an odd panic, he quickly dialed Vere.

"Hello? *OHMYGOD,* Dustin!" Her chatter immediately made him feel better. "I'm so late. Watching this awesome show about how DaVinci might have communicated with— or possibly was—*an alien.* And the signs are hidden in his paintings! SO COOL. I'll be right over."

He grinned. "I can't wait to hear about it. Now hurry up."

When he hung up, the battery flashed a warning.

His charge signal turned from green to red, just as he had the huge urge to make a second call. To dial his mom. He craved the sound of her voice. Even if she were still angry at him.

And that feeling scared the shit out of him way more than his crush on Vere Roth did.

What if his mom hadn't forgiven him yet? If she never would? What if she hung up and refused to talk to him? His heart imploded at the thought. Not knowing felt better than the possibility of the two of them never speaking again.

He tossed his phone into the drawer along with his mom's unopened letter. She would have called by now if that letter had anything good in it.

He heard the puttering sound of Vere's VW outside.

Whatever. I'm not the kid with the messed up life.

I'm Dustin McHugh, hanging at home.

A kid who hikes, and loves drama class, and is now, officially, an orphan who lives with his aunt! An orphan with no cell phone, because I'm not charging it, or picking that thing up again.

If other people didn't like that, then they could show up here in Colorado with their ideas about who I am and what I'm doing.

But for now, he was good enough with this, because it was the only thing that felt good and real and right.

He pulled in a huge breath.

Vere honked and turned up her car stereo. To his surprise, she was playing...*GuardeRobe*?

He grinned, popped in his retainer, grabbed his glasses, one of his vests, the trucker cap and shot out into the hall.

GuardeRobe and Vere? Really? Should be an interesting drive.

26: heart shaped rocks

"Okay. Start looking. This is the spot where I've found the best stuff."

They'd driven just outside of Monument to the Falcon Canyon Open Space. Vere and Dustin had bush-whacked only a small bit behind the parking area, until reaching a dried creek bed that ran parallel to the main trail.

"You can also find major good petrified wood here. It washes out in the flash floods."

He frowned at the cloudless sky. "Flash floods? Should we be standing here at all? What if it's raining up on Pikes Peak?"

"Good question, nature-safe-Dustin."

Vere took his shoulders and turned him to face the mountain in question. Not one cloud floated anywhere near the peak.

He took off his glasses and shot her an embarrassed grin. "Fine. But what about the possibility of huge packs of mountain lions attacking us from all these bushes. I don't think we should be off-trail."

"Stop looking at the bushes. Eyes on the sand. It's perfectly safe here. Look for white quartz or bumps of brown sandstone stuff. The sandstone erodes into these awesome iron concretions that look perfectly round. Train your eyes to search out anything that has the appearance of marbles or superballs covered in sand. They are easy to step right over, and they're so—"

"Amazing?" Dustin laughed, slowing his pace to fall into step beside her. "I'm looking. They all seem to look like regular rocks to me."

"No...you'll see. Keep walking, and staring down—and—there's one! It's a heart shaped quartz!"

She jumped forward and picked up a milky white piece of quartz. "Look. Bottom shaped like a triangle. Top—two distinct bumps connected by slight *v* to make a heart!" She beamed, handing it over. "Now that you've seen one, you'll search for these forever. So addictive."

Hunter turned the rock over in his hands. "No shit. It *is* in the shape of a heart."

"Did you doubt me about this place? I have hundreds of these in a bowl in my room. All sizes. The round ones are harder to find than the hearts."

"I've never seen your room. Is it allowed?"

He'd turned away before she could see if his expression had been joking or sincere.

"If you want. It's kind of basic. Posters. Junk. But if you plan to come up, I need ten minutes warning to straighten up."

"Why? Do you have to take down all your secret *GuardeRobe* posters and framed photos of me?"

She punched his arm. "No."

"Ah. Too bad." He smiled, but for some reason his voice didn't seem as teasing as it usually was.

"I'm proud of the *GuardeRobe* poster I have in there," she added.

"What?"

"Yep. Stole it off the back of Charlie's closet door. The kid has no clue it's mine now. I had to have it. It's a friend-loyalty thing." She left off the part about how she liked having Dustin's blue-blue-eyes smiling out at her. "But, in case you haven't noticed, I've become a bit of new *fangirl*. I know I said it on the ride over here, but I am sorry I made fun of the music. It's really good. Awesome, actually!"

He shook his head, his gaze totally unreadable now. "And fangirl to you, means exactly...what? Are you tweeting them, stalking them, Facebook friends with each individual member? I would prefer a dedicated Tumblr blog that's only about me."

Her turn to frown. "Oh...uh. I stole a poster? I've heard the latest album six times and I *think* I once met the lead singer." She shot him a look. "Is that enough?"

"Not. Even. Close. Call me when you're up for mailing photos of yourself. I'll help you chose which one. Some girls try to send ones minus their clothes. I wouldn't recommend that."

"Yeah. Not going to happen." She punched him again. Harder. "My Dustin McHugh has a nudity phobia," she joked. "Won't swim. Showers in his plaid shirts all buttoned up tight."

He laughed. "That's right, I do. Showering in the shirts saves laundry soap."

He handed back the rock but she shook her head, already scanning the ground for another. "Pocket it. It's your first. If we keep doing this hike, you'll have tons before you go home."

"Done with me already?"

Vere looked up, startled at his tense tone. "What? No. Of course not. It's what you want, isn't it? To go home?"

"What I want is—"

Her phone buzzed against her leg to the sound of trumpets shooting out of her pocket.

She felt her cheeks flame to purple.

"*OhGod.* It's CURTIS. He's texted me. I set a special ringtone. And—"

The trumpets sounded again. Vere's heart soared.

"FINALLY!"

Hunter put his glasses back on. "What did he say?"

They both glanced at the screen together, and read: *hey.*

She looked at Dustin. "This is serious. What should I say back? Get the advice rolling. Hurry."

Dustin shrugged. "You could try *hey* as well?"

Vere tossed him a look. "*Hey,* all alone? Or should I text *hey* and add a smiley? But *which* smiley? Don't want to look too happy. Or too bored. Or too winkey-faced. Oh." She swallowed. "My stomach hurts."

"Jesus. Girl, give me the phone. We are not doing this. It's time to lock some of this deal down."

He quickly typed: '*Hey. You coming over?*'

"Holy cow. You didn't just do that." Vere grabbed her phone back.

Curtis texted back: *Yeah. Your BRO invited me to stay for dinner. Did he tell you?*

Dustin snorted. "He would be in it for the food first."

"He always eats at our house. That's standard." Vere defended him, shooting Dustin a glare. "What's wrong with you?"

"Sorry. Guess I'm tired."

She typed: *Yeah-see you then* into her phone. Then, when the trumpets went off in response, she turned away so Dustin couldn't see, and she typed, *I can't wait :)* .

"Vere, I was kidding. What are you saying to each other?"

The trumpets sounded again. She paused to read.

"He's bringing the last summer peaches from his mom's tree. I told him I'd make us some peach milkshakes!" She beamed. "He'd like that, don't you think?"

"He'd be a fool if he didn't." He shook his head, kicking his feet roughly into the sand of the dry river bed.

"The rocks usually aren't buried that deep," she called out as he moved away from her. "This is killing me. Why won't he text me back?"

"Look at this! I've found one!" Dustin held up a small white rock.

Vere dashed over and examined the rock. "Yep. One perfect heart. See? Aren't they just amazing—"

The phone trumpeted again. Vere laughed, breaking Dustin's gaze as he frowned at her phone. "I guess I better change the ringtone. It's brutal. I know. Stop glaring." She opened her settings, still laughing, swapped out the ring tone, and read the next text.

"He wants to know if you're coming to dinner?"

Dustin raised a brow.

She beamed at him. "You should! You know my mom wouldn't mind. Peach milkshakes. Your favorite."

"No."

"You sure?" She frowned, again wondering at his tone.

"Yeah." He took her hand, pressing the little heart rock in to her palm before continuing, "I've got homework and I'm fighting a stomach thing. Cramping up all over."

She closed her fist over the little heart shaped rock, chewing her upper lip with worry. "Then we should go? Why didn't you tell me?"

"It's been coming on all week."

He turned away, but not before she saw a real flash of pain cross his face.

"Poor you."

"Yeah. You'll want to get ready anyhow. So let's go."

27: what really happened

Dustin

From: nyjuice77@yahoo.com
To: cojuice99@yahoo.com
Subject: Not happy.

Hey—I'm typing this on the fly.

Wish I could fire your impostor. He's turned into a hell raiser.

Afraid if I cut him now he'd spill our deal to the press. Little shit. I gave him a raise and a credit card to calm him down. This whole thing's giving me an ulcer.

Before she hung up on me again, your mom told me you're doing ok. I'm glad to hear the updates, but can you two lay off the chat? The cell phone bill shows she's called Colorado every day. Sometimes twice. I thought I said no direct calls.

Had any time to write some music or lyrics at least? Email me anything you've got. We're starting on the stockpiled stuff soon but will run out fast. We need you. More than you know.

Continue to lay low. Nothing's leaked yet. I can't believe it's working. Another week and I'm back in LA. I swear. I will have you permanently home by Thanksgiving.

Either that, or I'll have a stroke. Since you appear to be talking to your mother so much can you convince her to please take my calls again?

It's been two days of the silent treatment. I need to talk to her. Whatever game you two are playing, I've lost my sense of humor.

We've got contracts. Tell your mom that. We've got contracts and I don't appreciate you plus your aunt messing with me!

—Martin—

WTF? What did Martin mean? Mom had called here?

It had been three days and a whole weekend since Martin's last email. Since the night he and Vere had gone hiking, and she had made peach milkshakes for *Curtis*. Hand made, probably hand cut, fresh *peach* milkshakes—that were not for him!

Worse, he'd hardly seen Vere or Charlie the whole weekend. They'd gone to the football game Saturday. Sunday, they told him *they had something to do.*

Both of them had been acting really strange, too.

Meaning: they'd wanted some time without him. Most probably so they could spend it *with Curtis*. In what felt like some sort of 'consolation prize', Vere had half-promised she'd take him back to the hike with the rocks again this afternoon.

After she'd made it clear her time with her *bestie* now all depended on *Curtis's* schedule. Jenna had also been grumbling about that situation some today.

At least he wasn't the only one suffering.

He forced himself to think about Martin's email. His mind had been spinning so much on Vere's progress with Curtis, he'd all but forgotten about his stand in.

Well, if the fake HIM was wreaking havoc in New York, then things were probably rolling along just fine. He missed none of that scene at this point. He secretly hoped the kid would be caught in a hotel room with two hundred naked strippers, or that someone would catch on that the kid was NOT HIM.

Shit! Let the press fry us all.

Martin deserved what he got for hiring that guy and coming up with this idiotic plan!

He hadn't been able to resist checking his phone. He charged the thing just enough to load his emails. But now he jerked the charger out of the wall. He was pissed at himself for not being strong enough to leave the phone alone.

♥ 256 ♥

He rolled over and yanked open the top drawer of his night stand, catching a glimpse of the bent hair-color box he'd brought from Falconer, glinting from the back of the drawer.

The woman on the box smiled up at him as usual. He flipped it to block out her face, tossed his phone in there again and grabbed out the half-used tube of scar cream from the bag Martin had given him at the airport.

He squirted some of the bright green cream onto his finger and dutifully rubbed it on each wrist as he surveyed his self-imposed damage.

A thick, almost luminous, light pink line was still very visible on each wrist. Most of the angry red color had disappeared. The lines had diminished in width—but not much.

He hated looking at them. Wanted them to be gone.

So gone.

He added a little more cream for good measure and rubbed that in as well. Not one email from Royce and Adam?

Nothing. Nothing at all. Hell, even some forwarded jokes, or those ads that promised to make your junk bigger would have been awesome at this point.

Thanksgiving was a lifetime away. What happened to this month, or October? They'd promised it would be soon. Thanksgiving was not soon.

He sat on the edge of the bed and rested his head in his hands as he glared at the night stand. He resolved to leave the stupid cell phone dead no matter what, from now on. No obsessive checking, no calling Vere this time.

None of that.

He needed to be able to go through this alone.

A soft knocking combined with Aunt Nan's voice came from the other side of his door. "Are you in there? I've been cleaning out the linen closet and I have something—"

He jumped off the bed and yanked open the door.

His lightning fast appearance had startled her because she'd jumped back. "Oh good. There you are—I've got—"

He didn't give her a chance to finish. "My mom has been calling you every day?"

She blinked behind her glasses, speaking over the folds of a down comforter. "Yes. She calls. Sometimes twice."

"What the hell?" Dumbfounded, Dustin froze and could only stare down at her.

Aunt Nan shifted her feet, a sign that she needed to sit down, or that she was nervous. "She didn't want you to know."

He took the comforter out of her hands and stepped aside to let her pass into the room.

She motioned to the comforter. "That's for you. In spite of the long Indian summer we're having, it is going to start to cool down quite a bit in the night."

"*That's it?* Now we're back to talking about the weather? I guess I should clarify." Dustin crossed the room and tossed the comforter onto his bed as he went on, "What the *hell?* What the *hell* is my mom doing calling you every day? What the *hell* does she talk about, and why the *hell* haven't you told me," he said, his voice pure ice.

Aunt Nan winced and frowned as she all but stomped her slippers right up to him. "I'll thank you for not using foul language in this house or speaking to me like that, young man."

"Sorry," he said, feeling bad for making her upset.

She nodded and squinted up at him, making her smile lines show deep. It was impossible to stay mad at this woman. Why should he? None of this was her fault. "I didn't know your mom's calls to me were an issue. I thought you knew we talked. Your mom implied as much."

Dustin's let the fire drain out of his voice. "I haven't even had one call, not one email, or even a crappy text message from my mom, and she's been calling you every single day."

Nan sighed. "I didn't know that. She's calling to check up

on you. To see if you are okay. Depressed. Sad. Heading for a relapse. Anything like that. I tell her daily you are fine and happy so she can make it through her own days. Have you read the letter?"

"No. Don't you see? That woman plays games. She's playing me with that letter and I refuse to play. Why have we never visited you in such a long time if you two are so close?"

"You used to. I think you came out here at least twice a year until you were six. Sadly, it seems you don't remember but I do. Your mom is very protective of her feelings. She's always been a very private person. It's not her style to talk about things that would bring you pain. What happened with your dad dying...bringing him up would hurt you, I'm sure."

"Maybe not bringing him up at all has been worse. Who knows?" He glanced away from her too kind eyes as his throat threatened to swell up.

"As a mom, she's sheltered you. She also never lets anyone into her head about your father unless she trusts them completely."

"Right. That would be why she never talks to me, then. I'm first on her untrustworthy list." He couldn't cover the sarcastic tone in his voice.

"No. She's protecting you. And me. Her own broken heart."

He flicked her an eye roll. "You must be worth a lot of money if she's looking after you, too. Do you have her in your will or something?"

"Easy. Your mom bought this place for me. If she's in my will it's only to give back what support I gave to her after your real father died."

"How many years ago did she buy this house?" He had to know.

"Six."

He shrugged, forcing away the lump in his throat. "If you think about it, then didn't *I* really buy this house for you? It was all my money, my time in front of the camera. All Mom's money comes from me."

"This conversation is totally inappropriate, but I'll humor you." She sounded slightly pissed again. He didn't blame her; it was a rude topic. But money was always rude, wasn't it?

"It was my understanding that your mom pulled her own salary. She's driven herself to the brink of exhaustion as your manager. Until you could afford a larger entourage she worked 80 hours a week or more. You can't deny that." Nan sighed and looked deflated. "You know you aren't being fair."

"Maybe." He looked away. "But let's talk about *fair*. Was it fair for her to pull that pumped up salary off my back? I never asked for my career. It just sort of happened."

"You never once told anyone you wanted to stop. I thought you liked it. Did you want to stop? Do you now?"

That question floored him. "I don't know."

He had no idea how to answer that. He ran his hand through his hair, desperately trying to process. "I like when people are moved by my music. I've never considered stopping as an option. I can't leave my band. They're counting on me. So are Martin and Mom. If I stop how do they get paid? What about the other guys?"

"They'll find something else to do. They were okay before you hit it big, they will be fine after."

He paused and looked skeptically over at her. "Would they? I wonder." He knew for a fact that Martin and his mom would crumble if he stopped working. They didn't know anything else but working with him either. And Royce and Adam... would they care?

"You must not know your mom's whole story. Has she never told you how it all started? You working instead of her? You don't remember?" Nan pulled off her glasses and rubbed her eyes. She put them back on and met his gaze.

"No."

"Your father—when he—died, he didn't leave much behind. You had begged your mom to be on TV from the time you were able to talk. So, on a whim she took you to a talent agency. They signed you, did head shots that were sent out the same day. It was only a matter of days and poof, you filmed that cereal commercial. We were so proud of you."

"Yeah. I've heard the stories. I only remember eating the cereal. Mom never let me have sugar cereal before that job. After, I could suddenly have whatever I wanted. Because I paid for it all, right? She couldn't say *no*."

"Absolutely not," Nan snapped. "It's really hard to deny a kid who's father has passed away. We all just wanted you to be happy so we messed that up. Your career wasn't about the money. Not at first. It gave you both something big to do so you could stay busy and forget how much you missed your dad."

His heart twisted, and he whispered, "When I think of him...I don't remember his face, but I do remember how much it hurt to have him simply there one day and gone the next... just gone."

Nan nodded. "Imagine how your mom felt. Your dad was the love of her life."

He pictured his mom in a space he'd never considered. Tried to think how she would have been, younger, happy and completely in love.

How he felt for Vere right now floated through his mind.

Though they had only just met—and they weren't even near to being 'in love'—his friendship with her was the closest comparison he had.

He played it forward. Pictured them years together and how it would feel if Vere suddenly died. But it was impossible to stay with it. The instant, searing pain it caused in just *thinking* about Vere not being around almost imploded his soul.

"Shit," he muttered, as a wave of goose bumps covered his

arms and moved down his spine. "Mom must have felt so alone. Terrified."

Nan sighed. "She was left all alone with a little boy who thought she could handle things. After, she couldn't bear to be parted from you. Another deciding factor in allowing your career. Your job kept the two of you together every minute."

"But later on...she shouldn't have left it up to me to make all the money. I totally felt that pressure as a kid—still feel it."

"Maybe. But there was no way your mom could have predicted you would make the kind of money you made so easily by hamming it up in front of a camera. Not without putting you into full time school or getting you a nanny. None of us were prepared for your fame, though—or what it has done to you."

He kicked his feet into the carpet. "Fame hasn't done anything to me. It's been great. It's me and mom. We've been on permanent disconnect since *GuardeRobe* hit. She won't even let me apologize to her for what I did."

"Again. She's trying to protect you." Nan shook her head. "It's not my place to discuss you and her. Not without her here to defend herself. To explain the whole story."

"But of course." He snorted with disgust. "That woman is never here. Don't you get the pattern? Never here to explain and never here for me, that's for damn sure. You're totally wrong about her."

He got up and paced over to the desk to scoop up his glasses and retainer and pocketed them. A surge of anger, frustration, and unexplainable desolation shot through him. As soon as Vere showed, he was bolting. If she showed...

Please. Please. Please.

His lungs had grown tight from lack of air. He'd almost forgotten this feeling. He glanced again out the window. To his disappointment the white VW was nowhere in sight to rescue him.

He let his anger surface. "Mom uses the money from my career so she can live like the freaking, *checked-out-on-life*, ice queen. She makes friends, lets them love her, and then dumps everyone she's ever met."

He turned away from the window and shot Nan a challenging look that dared her to disagree. "Now that I've grown to be quite the crazy nuisance, she's dumped me, too."

"She's afraid you think that. I can only vow it's not her intent."

"Oh really, the woman has an *intent*. Regarding me? Let me guess. Ruin my life? *No?* Then she must intend to take away the only thing left that I love. My music. I'm so mad at her. How can she make me stay here, grounded in Colorado like this? Don't you get what it's like for me? I don't even know who in the hell I am anymore."

Nan grimaced. "Is it so bad, *you* being Dustin?"

He didn't want to hurt her feelings. "No. Sadly, it's awesome. Everyone treats the new me like a person instead of some fragile, money-generating freak. Who wouldn't like that? As for living here," he paused and looked around the comfortable room and back at his gentle, loving aunt. "It's nice, perfect, and so are you. Okay?"

She smiled. She continued in that soft, *full of love* voice she'd used every day with him. "It's pretty obvious to me there's a man caught up inside you and he's struggling to breathe. Let me give you some advice. Grown-up men, they talk. Not as much as women, but they talk. Opens up the lungs."

"Fine. Can I tell you what happened that night?" He was afraid to meet her gaze. "What I did? *All* of it?"

"I've been waiting for you to tell me.

"It's gruesome details. I can't have you bawling on me."

She nodded. "I'll try not to."

He stood, pulled the chair next to his aunt and sat on it backwards so he could lean on the back with his arms. He sucked in a painful breath. "When I wrecked the car into the front door," he paused for a long breath. "Mom was upstairs ignoring me as usual. After we fight she can hardly wait to take her next antidepressant. Did you know that she's on those? Does that stuff come up when she calls you? Or do you just talk about the weather?"

"No. I knew about it. She gets really sad when you two fight. The antidepressants, as you know, are something your mom has needed to function ever since your father died."

"Yeah. I know. We've talked about them. The medication really helps her. I'm glad she's taking them. The alternative might be me, with zero parents, I think."

"You could be right. Sadly, depression runs in our family."

Dustin rested his chin on his arm and shot a surprised glance at his aunt. "I didn't know that. On both sides? Dad's?"

Nan nodded. "Your mom's sorry about shipping you off to Colorado, but that fact is the main reason she got so scared. She felt she had no other choice. Someday you'll have to believe her."

"Someday she'll have to tell me that *exactly*, or I won't be able to." He met Aunt Nan's calm, quiet gaze.

She nodded as though to agree. "Tell me what happened."

He pulled in another breath. "I don't know why I did what I did. To this day, I still don't have an answer for why. All I know is I'd started feeling low. Really low. And I felt like I had no one to talk to about it. Hell, it's not like I wanted to admit I was having a problem to anyone. I was embarrassed about it."

"Many people are."

"That's how I came up with the brilliant plan to handle things myself. I snuck a few of mom's antidepressants that week. Thinking they would help me feel better. Like ibuprofen does when I have a headache. The bottle said one a day. So I took two."

"Hunter. I'm not going to lecture you about taking other people's medications. Obviously you know you were wrong to do that. And that it was dangerous."

He shot his aunt a chagrined look. "Ya think! Sadly, that week, it made perfect sense to me. I felt so desperate. I'd taken two a day, for like six days straight. Instead of making me feel better, they'd made me feel like I was flat—as in cardboard flat—two dimensional, inside and out. I thought maybe I just needed more. To jump start it, or something. That night—when it all went down, I'd taken a whole bunch, and all at once. Again, my bad. But I've paid for it."

He didn't meet her gaze this time. "Shit. I'm still so ashamed..."

"Don't be," she said. "Go on if you can."

"I can. It actually feels nice telling you all this." He sighed. "So, I waited, like a whole hour for something to feel *different* inside me after I took the last pills. But when nothing happened, I decided to think of something else to pep me up. That's where the Porsche came into play. Mom and I had just fought. Don't even remember about what. She'd said I couldn't leave the property. So I'd started driving the Porsche around and around the gated parking area—around that big fountain in our portico? Do you know it?"

"I've seen pictures. It's lovely."

"Was lovely." He shook his head. "Huge. The upper part was actually some sort of fake poly-marble. Thank God, or it might have killed me when it fell through the roof of the car."

He shot another embarrassed glance at his Aunt to see if she was judging him or scornful.

She wasn't. Not at all. Only sad.

He went on, "The fountain was fun to corner. And that's what I was doing. Cornering it, at like thirty-five, forty miles per hour. Tight, fast, turns made my adrenaline pump. Around and around until I hit the stupid thing. I was so surprised when Mom didn't come outside to see what the noise was when it all crashed down, I snapped. That's when I drove the whole damn Porsche up the steps and lodged it in the front door. All the while I had been wondering if I'd been loud enough."

"You were really depressed."

"I think at that moment, I was angry. But yes, depressed too. I'd reached this state where nothing mattered any more. And nothing seemed shocking—like driving my car through the front door—that idea had seemed totally legit. Worse, nothing made me laugh anymore. Or cry. The closest thing I can describe to the feeling I had that night is that everything, and I mean everything, all of a sudden, seemed to bore the hell out of me."

Dustin took in another deep breath and glanced again at Aunt Nan. She was just listening. Her face still held no judgment. She sat there, simply waiting for him to go on. And loving him, no matter what. He could tell that for sure.

He shrugged. "Fine. I'll say it again. I was depressed. I wanted to stop feeling the 'nothingness' that I couldn't shake." He rolled his eyes and shook his head. "I was so lost."

She frowned. "Sounds like you were so alone."

"Yeah. But stubborn, too. I should have tried to talk to my mom. Tell her how I was feeling. Admit I'd screwed up and taken a bunch of her medications. But instead, I drank all that wine. I just wanted to sleep. That's how mom handles life when it freaks her out, so I thought I'd give it a shot. But of course I couldn't sleep. And, somehow, I ended up cutting myself."

Nan frowned. "I can't believe you went so far. Your scars are so huge."

He wiped at his eyes. "I know. But not deep. Scratches

mostly." He gasped, and paused. "*Shit.* I was worried unloading all this would make me cry. I hate crying." He sniffed back some tears.

Aunt Nan put her arm around him. "I was so happy when I found out the wounds you'd inflicted weren't serious, that you had stopped."

"*Yes,* I stopped. Barry, all of you, see what I did as this suicide attempt. But I didn't want to die. I only wanted my mom to hear me. To come find me. To *see* that I was sad. To help me, I guess. I just didn't have it in me to tell her what I needed. And fine, I get now that she couldn't read my mind." He wiped his eyes again. "But I didn't get it then. I'm so mad at myself. What was wrong with me that I couldn't just tell her? That I didn't have the capacity to ask her for anything."

"No one likes to ask for help. You aren't alone in that."

He shout her a grateful smile. "I've learned the hard way that it's important, *hell*, even if you have to beg."

She went on, "You need to forgive yourself. Admit the life you were living was not normal. You were so isolated. Sounds like you didn't have any other friends to call. Or anyone around you that would take the time to notice how sad you were. I can only imagine the insensitive response your agent would have given if you'd told him." She snorted, rolling her eyes.

Hunter blinked. "You know Martin?"

"Your mom tells me about him." She looked away.

"Martin would have thought I was whining, you're right. But it's hard not to blame myself. I know after living here, I was beyond lonely back at home. That's for sure. I sat in that kitchen so long, all by myself. I just stared at my own blood all drunk and stupid knowing the whole time I'd made yet another, epic mistake. But I'd made so many. Instead of dealing with it like I should have, I wrapped up my arms in kitchen towels, and then I cried until the wine took over. I fell asleep there like that." Dustin pulled in a shaky breath, his heart feeling heavy but lighter than it had in a long time.

"Oh." Aunt Nan swallowed, smoothing the bed cover under her hands. "I think this is going to make *me* cry again right now."

He moved out of his chair and sat next to her on the bed to give her a quick hug. "Don't you dare. Please. I won't be able to take you through the rest of this story. And I want to. I need to finish."

She nodded and took in a deep breath, obviously trying to keep it together.

He kept his voice light, hoping she wouldn't blow. He rushed to finish, wanting to make her understand he, things, were different now. "Do you get what I'm saying about all of it? I didn't mean it. Dying is the last thing on my mind. But—I have to come to terms with the fact that for one night—I danced with the idea of killing myself. And way too closely."

"Yes. You did." She sniffed. "You scared us all so much."

His heart twisted, and tears threatened to drown him in a waterfall.

"Aunt Nan, please believe me. I can tell you I will never go that route again. It also scared the hell out of me."

She let out a deep breath that sounded relieved. "Are you sure? How do you know you won't do it again?"

"I've at least learned that I have the power to control my own energy. You know, turn it back around when it gets too dark?"

She shook her head. "I don't understand."

"Before, I didn't know I could be this strong. I kept waiting for others to *make* me happy. Waiting for things I bought to bring happiness. Although, I swear my Porsche did make me happy for a little while." He shot Nan a sheepish grin. "Sort of..."

"So happy you decided to wreck it?"

"Hell yeah. Because on that day, I felt betrayed by my own car. Like...how *dare* that awesome vehicle not be ABLE to make me happy? At least now I understand I was simply a victim of marketing. Only *I* can make myself happy."

Aunt Nan grimaced. "I'm supposed to be extra-dancing-around right now, according to the fresh-smelling laundry soap I use. But so far, these feet haven't even started tapping."

He smiled, happy she seemed to get what he was saying. "I had no clue how much I was trying to pull my happiness off all the wrong sources. For me, when I'm sad it's usually because I'm off focus. I'm letting others have my power. Now, I think about doing the best I can. Does this make any sense? I can't control others, but I can control myself and what I produce—what I allow inside."

He tapped his head. "When I go home, no one is going to boss me around anymore, either. Not unless I want to be bossed. I'm going to live life on my terms. Only do, wear, sing, and *be* what makes me proud. Only hang out with people who are there truly for me. I definitely wasn't doing that. I was Mom and Martin's puppet. I know that was part of why I got so sad. I'm done with saying *yes* all the time."

She nodded. "Well, good."

"Since I've been Dustin, I've learned if I want to stay up—*happy*—it's on me. It's not always easy to do—especially when I'm stuck living life as a mega-dork. Falconer and Barry tried to teach me that, but living here has made me see it's completely true. I feel bad about what I did, but despite the oceans of crap I still need to clean up and deal with, I'm happy with myself now. I'm ready to move on and make things right."

She stood along with him and hugged him tight. "I'm glad you told me all this. I like knowing you're okay."

He hugged her back and stepped away. "I am. Would you please tell my mom this information? I'm ready to get back to work. I'm lost here doing crazy things instead of doing what I love. Things that mean nothing! Things that are wasting my time!"

"Are you sure about that? You seem to be enjoying a lot here."

"Aunt Nan! I have to go to a required appointment with a college counselor next week. College. *Me?*"

Nan's eyes widened. "Have you thought about it?"

"Why would I need to go there? I have a paying job already."

"I don't know. You can be one of the lucky ones. Go to college because you *want* to learn? Maybe there are other things you long to explore besides the entertainment industry. College is a blast. Even more fun than high school."

"There is no way high school is fun," he lied. "It's an odd form of torture from what I've seen."

"Why can't you let go for awhile and try to just enjoy the experience? Spend the year here like your mom wants. Stop fighting so hard to go home."

Dustin looked at her and blinked. "Look. I love you. But you have to know as soon as I have my ticket, I'm out. I don't want to enjoy any of this! I just want to be free. This is my whole life on hold. There's no way I mean to spend the whole school year here!"

"You need to call your mom. She should have talked to you about her plans and ideas around you staying here. There's a lot more to this that you don't understand. Go through the letter your mom sent for you to read, at least."

He marched over and took the his mom's letter out of the drawer and handed it to Aunt Nan. "She needs to come here and say it to my face. I refuse to read this unless she and I are in the same residence. Maybe that will get her to send for me."

Aunt Nan took the envelope. "I'll tell her what you said."

He walked back to the window and saw Vere's white VW parked in front of the house. "It won't be long now. They will start missing the money soon. Either she or Martin will have to get me out of here. Simple as that. Only from now on, I'll let them do the work."

She shook her head.

"Aunt Nan, I'm out. Vere's been waiting this whole time. Thanks for listening."

***

As he made it through his doorway he froze, completely taken by surprise. Vere was leaning against the wall just outside his door, gasping for air. She had her arms around a giant, lumpy, newspaper-wrapped package with a floppy bow made out of orange knitted yarn on top.

She looked straight at him and shook her head. Her eyes were luminous, huge, and weighted with tears.

His stomach knotted. He realized she wasn't gasping for air, she was full-on crying, and he knew why.

Hell.

"Did you hear all of it?" His voice had come out clipped.

"Yes." She sobbed. "All of it."

He felt as if he'd been punched. He held his breath, just in case. He was desperately afraid breathing would hurt worse than ever right now, and he didn't want to associate that feeling with Vere.

Not her. Not ever.

"I'm sorry." Her words came out in a sniffling rush. Her face had long since flooded with color. "I...waited outside. And when you didn't come out, I thought I'd dash up. The front door was open. I have a present—for you. It's a thank-you present. For all you've done to help me. You know, for the *BGF* stuff." Tears had started streaming down her face and her voice shook, but she kept on, "Charlie lent me the money for half. We drove up together to the antique shop and back. Got it on Sunday. You still need an amp." She gasped. "He also

❤ 271 ❤

thought it was a good idea. Now that we're all friends. And now that I'm practically...*cured*. We think you need to have this."

Tears poured unchecked like a river now.

He didn't move or answer. He couldn't.

Vere whispered through her tears. "I know you said you didn't want it, but I also knew you were lying. You'll have to fix it up—oh, jeez. Take it."

She lurched forward and shoved the package into his arms just as Aunt Nan stepped into the hallway.

Aunt Nan gave Vere a sad little smile. "More secrets to add to your mix, Vere. Can you manage to keep track of one more? It's a lot to ask. Even your parents don't know this private stuff."

Vere wiped the back of her hand against her nose and sniffled loudly. "Yes. Of course. I won't, I wouldn't." She flicked him a desperate glance. "I'd never tell. I understand. I'm sorry about what I did. About what you did to yourself." Her eyes closed.

Dustin used that moment to finally manage a deep, and thankfully, painless breath.

When Vere reopened her eyes, the tears were still pouring out, but she looked right at him for a second before her face flushed a second time. She didn't glance away. Instead, she continued, her gaze tangling with his as her voice and speech seemed to reach a frantic pitch. "Nan. Dustin. Please. I didn't mean to—but—then I couldn't stop listening."

She shifted back and forth from foot to foot, unable to do her usual pacing thing in the tight hallway. "It was terrible of me. I don't know why. I just stood here. I can't believe what you've been through." Her eyes spilled over again. "We're all a bunch of kindergartners compared to you, aren't we?" She took a long, wavering breath and shook her head, her expression had turned almost accusatory. "You—you've been so generous. All this time, helping me work on my lame, puny problems. I'm such a selfish baby. I can't believe how I've been acting with you about my stupid crush. Like it was the most epic, most important thing in the whole world. While all this time—all this time—you've had *all this* on your mind?" She flung her arms wide.

"Vere. It's okay," he started.

She rushed on, "I'm sorry if you didn't want me to know. And now—" She broke out into a round of rocking sobs. "Now I do know. I know. And that's that. I can't take what I did back. I can't stop hearing your story in my head. I totally, totally, totally eavesdropped and I'm so—"

"Stop. Stop. Please," he said, glancing at his aunt.

Vere sucked in a breath and stopped talking.

But not crying.

"Vere. It's okay. It's not the end of the world," Nan added.

His chest constricted, watching the tears roll down her face. He knew she needed help when she got all worked up. He now felt guilty for not stepping in sooner. She was now two thousand times worse than she'd been up at the cabin that first weekend. He was so moved by her tears, he was having a hard time functioning, too. He had to make her stop crying. Make her feel better. Before she blacked out or something.

And she thinks she's cured?

Girl couldn't be more tragically, bright-red and adorable right now.

"Vere. I'm not mad," he started up loudly over her ragged breathing and sobbing. "It's actually a relief that you know everything. I'm the sorry one."

"What?" she gasped out.

"Don't you see? I'm sorry that now, in your eyes—" He paused, almost losing himself in the wide brown depths of her pure empathy before continuing in a much softer voice, "I hate that you will think I'm way more messed up than you thought I was yesterday."

♥ 273 ♥

She gasped. "I heard what you said. You aren't messed up at all. If anything, you sound more evolved and okay than anyone I know. You're ready to go on talk shows, and speak to kids at high schools!"

He shook his head. "Not even close."

Vere wiped her now puffy eyes and wet cheeks with her sleeve as she went on, "If it makes you feel better, I don't think you're some sort of spoiled party-boy any more. That's what I thought about you yesterday. I actually respect you now," she finished with a double snuffle.

Her body shook as it took in more air.

She shot him a guilty glance. "Um. No. Wait!"

Was there an end to her cuteness?

"Waiting."

"I respected you some yesterday too, okay? I'm just upset...so I'm talking crazy. You know how I am..." She wiped her face against her shoulder.

Nope. Definitely no end to it.

"Yes. I know how you are." A small chuckle escaped, and he let himself breathe fully. His lungs filled with a heady mix of flowers, saltwater tears and her.

He had the urge to take her face into his hands and wipe away the tears still threatening to pour out of her eyes. He was also desperate to plant a kiss on each of her apple-red cheeks, and then her lips.

Luckily, the giant package in his arms saved him from making a fool out of himself in front of her and his Aunt Nan.

The fact that she'd brought him a present—*this present!*

Damn, how she knows me. And damn how I love her for that, way too much.

It was enough to almost undo him into another round of awkward tears himself. He tried to yank his mind and his heart back from her, gaining control with a long sigh.

Teasing is in order here. Better to have her spitting mad than looking so deeply into my eyes right now. And if she doesn't stop chewing that damn upper lip...

"Now you'll stop bugging me about the long sleeves on my shirts. You know? Even when it's hot?" He smiled.

She locked gazes with him and gasped.

She seemed to pull him directly into her soul, and then snapped him back out like a rubber band. She burst into a new flood of sobbing, and tore down the stairs, not once looking back.

Her sobs grew louder the farther away she ran.

The front door slammed and the VW started up outside.

He could hear her drive exactly one house over, cut the engine, slam her car door, and do the same with her own front door.

Sobbing the entire time.

He looked helplessly at Aunt Nan, who didn't seem to be shocked by Vere's hasty retreat. "Any tips on what grown men do in this situation?"

She shrugged and gave him a small smile. "Wait for her to come back. She will. In the meantime, open that thing." She gestured toward the lumpy package in his hands. "I'm dying of curiosity."

"I don't have to. I know what it is."

His heart raced and filled up with an unexplainable feeling of gratitude and excitement. He tested the weight and gentle curves of Vere's badly wrapped present.

"It's a guitar. She's bought me an amazing old guitar."

28: more favors

Dustin

To: nyjuice99@yahoo.com
From: cojuice99@yahoo.com
Subject: WTF? Where are you?

Martin: There better be a good excuse for this zero-communication bull. To be fair, I thought I'd tell you, this will be my last email. This time, for real.
WHY? 1. I'm pissed, and, 2. I have midterms on the horizon. GET IT, BASTARD?
MIDTERMS means I've been here too long.
If you want me, show up or call me directly because I'm DONE checking my cell phone like your little slave.
If you care, I've got a new song worked out. Been practicing my ass off up here on an old guitar while hiding in my room.
I think it's time GuardeRobe branched out into the love song arena. Working in A Minor. Would send you the chords if you didn't suck so much. I'm thinking slow. Adding cello.
Major love ballad. I'LL TRADE YOU THIS SONG FOR MY LIFE BACK IN ORDER. You know you want it.

Cheers back, you ass. WTF?
—DUSTIN (about to lose my shit) McHELP—

***

"You. Dork Boy."

Dustin pulled out of his locker, startled to find his back surrounded by semi-hostile football players.

Charlie stepped forward and tossed his friends an easy grin as he moved up to slam Dustin's locker shut.

Hard.

Curtis Wishford stepped forward as though to join Charlie, but Charlie tossed him some silent command executed by pushing his chin toward the ceiling in what Dustin had dubbed the *universal, Palmer Ridge High, jock salute.*

"I'll catch you guys later," Charlie said and looked pointedly at his pack of friends. "I need a word with Vere's *pet.*"

Curtis got the message and returned the jock salute with a *cool-guy* nod of his own and stalked away with the other guys.

Dustin could tell the guy was not pleased to be shut out of the conversation, but Dustin had already learned from being with Curtis in Drama class, that the fool avoided anything that might cause a scene.

When the team was out of hearing range, Charlie leaned on to his left shoulder against a closed locker to turn his back to his retreating pals. "Sorry about the slam. Wouldn't want any of us to get out of *character.*"

Dustin eyed him and decided to stay silent.

Wait to if this dog meant to bark or bite.

It had been a silent car ride that morning between all of them, so he was certain Charlie was tweaked about that.

Well stand in line. Aunt Nan had said Vere would come back— talk to me—but so far she can't seem to look me in the face.

Why?

"What in the hell did you do to my sister yesterday?"

"Nothing. She gave me the guitar. Said you helped her buy it. Nice gesture by the way, coming from both of you. Aunt Nan's taking me to get an amp this afternoon." Dustin layered on his best sincere smile and wondered if it looked sincere with the giant retainer. He hadn't practiced this look in the mirror yet.

"It sort of seemed like Vere had been crying. Her face was all puffed up. Do you know anything about that?"

"Don't all girls cry about everything? Move off my locker, dude. I need to get one more book."

Charlie obliged and leaned on the next row. Dustin quickly re-opened his locker. He was relieved he could now hide his face behind the open door.

"Vere hardly ever cries. To top it off she blabbed about you all night long at dinner. On and on about how freaking *nice* you are. Then she played *GuardeRobe* on her computer speakers all night long. And not one flipping word about her and Curtis at all. It was over-the-top strange. She was a moody psycho. You sure you don't know why?"

"Not a clue. Maybe she and Curtis had a fight?" He evaded. "I'm bummed she thinks I'm *nice*, though. I hope that label doesn't get around school." Dustin rolled his eyes at Charlie, even though he was secretly elated. "Look. I guess it just made her really happy to give me that guitar or something. She did seem a little choked up when she handed it over."

Charlie nodded. "She would get all sappy about that."

"Again, double cool of you guys to think of it. It's a good one by the way. I love it. I'm psyched to be playing again. Thanks."

Charlie smiled, appearing to relax as though he'd bought into Dustin's denials. "Totally her idea. I only agreed because of personal reasons. It would be a tragedy if certain musical talents, in my favorite band, got out of practice or something. Don't make me wink at you. You know what I'm saying."

Dustin had to laugh. "Yeah. Please don't wink," he said, moving deeper into his locker when Charlie laughed, drawing the attention of a few onlookers.

Dustin spoke to Charlie from behind his locker door. "Anything else?"

"Yeah. Another favor. A huge favor."

"Shoot." Dustin paused.

"Can you keep Jenna Riley away from Vere and Curtis in drama class? For that matter, make *yourself* scarce. My man

Curtis says he hasn't had a chance to be alone in the crowd with Vere, thanks to you two stalkers."

Dustin swallowed. "Sure. I'll see what I can do."

"Good. I also need you to come to the lake for the weekend. I'm sure you don't have any plans for Labor Day, do you? My mom invited you through Vere last night. I'm sure she'll tell you, but in case she doesn't, consider yourself told. And consider yourself going for more Jenna Riley duty."

"What?"

Charlie grinned. "We always invite our friends along for one last blast and to help with the cabin winter shut down. That means the dreaded Jenna will front and center. I've obviously invited Curtis. We'll head up after the football scrimmage Saturday afternoon. Sadly, you'll have to hang with my parents and the giggle-twins for the ride up and all day Saturday until we get there."

"I'm used to them." Dustin's stomach grumbled as he imagined the cabin and Mrs. Roth's cooking. "As long as your mom's in charge of the eats. I'm in. Does she pack car snacks?"

"Again, the point for you coming along is not to gorge yourself and have cooking lessons with my mom. I'm hoping you will create a sufficient distraction. You know, enough to occupy Jenna."

"Dude. You are not suggesting that I like...try to hit on her?"

"Hell no! That girl is a total freak. For God's sake. I can't even imagine flirting with her." He shuddered comically and wrinkled his face into a horrified expression. "I'm thinking more along the lines of a nerd-filled, Uno/Chess tournament or something? Whatever she's into these days. Just keep her engaged and distracted so Vere can have a chance to do some hikes and hang out—as in alone—minus YOU TWO mood wreckers and *with* Curtis."

"Ugh. Why can't you do the Jenna chore? You know her better."

Charlie blinked. His face paled. "If I try to distract Jenna for that much time she will get weird ideas about me liking her. I do not need a stalker, thanks. Plus my parents—they always hint at me about going out with her. *Imagine.*" He shuddered again and looked Dustin up and down. "Doubtful your attentions will get her heartbeat up one notch. *You*, looking like *that*, keeps you safe enough."

"Great. Is that stthupposed to make me feel like a winner? Becausstth that hurtttsh my feelingssth." Dustin smiled and pulled a face at Charlie.

Charlie cracked up again. "Hey. You're the one who begged to lose your mojo. Use your lameness for good deeds."

"Fine. Hell. Whatever you and Vere want."

"This is make or break weekend for Vere's chances with Curtis. The guy doesn't have a long attention span, if you know what I mean."

Dustin gritted his teeth, fully hating Curtis Wishford as Charlie went on, "The cheerleaders have already marked Curtis as a juicy, single sitting duck. They've been sniffing around. One girl threw herself at him in the locker room last week. I won't blame him if he decides on easier game. Some of those chicks are way hot. I'm thinking about getting my own cheerleader girlfriend soon. It's homecoming-hookup time." He winked at Dustin along with a gloating smirk.

Dustin had the urge to deck Charlie right then, but knew he was only wishing he could punch the shit out of Curtis.

How could Charlie want his own sister to date such a tool?

And who wouldn't have a long attention span where Vere was concerned?

Whatever.

Whatever made Vere happy, no matter how much it hurt.

"So, we're understood?"

He sighed and nodded. "You know I'll do what's right for the situation."

Charlie grinned and breached all popularity rules by patting Dustin's dorky, plaid-covered shoulder. "Dude. I thank you. You're truly real."

"Am I?"

29: dreams come true

VERE

"What do you say, Vere?" Curtis asked.

"Hmm?"

Vere searched the stage for Dustin and Jenna. They were totally late. She wanted to catch Dustin alone to apologize and ask him if he'd liked the guitar.

She wished she'd gone back last night once she'd calmed down, but she was just too embarrassed about what she'd done. And then when they were in the car together this morning, she'd botched her chances because she felt like crying all over again when she saw his face.

Besides, what could they have said in front of Charlie?

"So will you?"

"What?" she asked.

Curtis was on her left, idly tapping a finger against her knee. He'd done that every day in class, but today he'd upped his moves.

A few minutes ago he'd drawn small delightful circles all over her knee. It had given her awesome goose bumps, but now he'd switched back to this endless, annoying tapping.

She couldn't concentrate, only she had no clue what she was trying to concentrate on—

Where are those guys? Not like them to be tardy.

"Vere, I'm trying to ask you out."

She slammed her hand on top of his to stop the tapping motion, and then tried to make it look as though she'd meant to hold his hand instead.

As if she would just reach out and hold Curtis's hand in public? Her heart fluttered at the thought, because it was exactly what she'd done! They were now holding hands, all because of her.

Or that stupid tapping...

Curtis smiled, his expression sort of goofy now.

It was one she'd grown to recognize as the confident, *I-know-you-love-me-face*. She'd liked it last week, but for some reason, today, it was playing into her odd mood. She glanced around again for her friends. They would be able to knock her bad attitude back into a good place.

Curtis's expression shifted into a half glower. "I'm going to say it one more time, spacey. I'm asking you to homecoming. The dance? Will you go with me to homecoming?"

"Homecoming?!"

Dream come true. Dream come true! I'm going to a school dance, finally. And with a senior. AND WITH CURTIS. Pinch ME.

"It's in two weeks. Say you'll go."

"You mean it?" she asked, stalling and pinching her own arm just in case this might be a dream.

"Yes! I can't wait to see you in some tight little dress, heels, and without the bun!" He smiled over at her. "Will you finally wear your hair down for me?"

"Yes. Yes!" She beamed at him. "Of course. I'd love-love-love to go with you. This is going to be amazing! Yes!"

"I love-love-love that you said yes," he said, mimicking her using this comical, slightly creepy, baby-talk voice.

She smiled.

Because he was a little funny...sort of...

Vere reached up to check her bun, but stopped halfway, feeling weird about it, and tucked her hand back into his.

Curtis isn't out of line for bringing up my hair, is he?

And I'd wanted one of those dresses with a flowing A-line skirt. But I guess I can look for a straw-wrapper-tight dress instead.

But...no...

Vere. Do NOT over-think this. Curtis Wishford asked you to

Homecoming! BE HAPPY.

It's an obvious fact that her current hairstyle was...unique and possibly not dance worthy. And the straw-wrapper-tight dresses were really hot. Maybe he knew fashion and liked to talk about it. She was just getting to know him on this level. It would take time before they truly understood each other.

"Can you dance?" she asked, trying to joke.

"Among other things." He gave her hand a hearty, almost painful squeeze. When she looked up he had that knowing smile on his face again and this time he added a wink.

She smiled back but dropped his hand.

No need for her to have broken fingers until dance night, plus his hand was too warm. Sweaty almost.

Vere suddenly regretted that she'd told Curtis how much she really liked him that first day. Thankfully, he'd said the same things back to her so it shouldn't be any big deal.

But now, thinking about it, she wished she could have a do-over. She would have waited to say all that stuff, because then, he might have waited to invent that weird *sure-thing* smile.

And heck, maybe he hadn't invented it. Maybe he smiled just like that to all of his *other* dance dates. The ones before her.

She laughed at her thoughts. What was the big deal? She was his sure-thing. And she was thrilled that he knew she liked him, wasn't she? She'd been waiting practically her whole life for him to ask her out, so why couldn't she just be happy about it now that her moment had finally arrived?

But, dreams coming true should not make me feel this cranky.
I must be tired. And I do have a small headache...

"It will be cool, uh, and fun to see you all dressed up too," she added lamely, rubbing her temples.

Vere heard the sound of Jenna's laughter echo across the stage. She looked over and spotted Jenna by the door.

She never sat over there. As in never!

That side of the stage was relegated for freshmen!

Another round of laughter drew her gaze to Dustin, who sat right beside Jenna. He appeared to be entertaining the entire group, including Mrs. VanDeWirth, with some of his antics.

What in the heck are they doing?

"Looks like I get to have you all to myself today. Maybe they'll stay over there for the whole semester."

Curtis moved his backpack and hers to one side. He scooted closer and lowered his voice. "I hope I get some chances to be alone with you at the cabin this weekend. Might be a good habit to start up, you and me, *being alone.*" Curtis reached over and drew a couple little circles on her knee again.

Vere smiled at that and sucked in a breath. He'd given her shivers. She had goose bumps all over now. "Yeah," she whispered. "Alone seems fun," she added, her heart filling with doubt.

Curtis moved his hand higher and shifted it onto her inner thigh. Vere thought she might die. Her heart had done so many flips in the past few seconds she wondered if she was having a heart attack. Maybe that's why she also felt kind of panicky and strange and, really embarrassed all of a sudden. Was anyone watching them?

She blushed, but didn't care, because it was the first time she'd blushed in front of Curtis for days.

And in this case it is totally appropriate!

"Um...maybe like this room is too crowded to be doing that?" She looked deep into Curtis's grass green eyes. Why did it seem as though he somehow sort of enjoyed her discomfort?

"Relax, Vere. I'm not going to bite you," he murmured as he scooted closer. His slowly circling finger did not once miss a turn on her thigh. "This is why, like I said, we need to spend more time alone."

"Yeah. I agree." She glanced at his gorgeous lips and wondered what it would finally be like to kiss him for real. Her heart rushed into her throat, and her mind fled to panic.

❤ 285 ❤

Kiss him? Kiss him? KISS HIM? I can't. I simply CAN'T.
What if I flip and knock him out again or something? Aaah!

There was no way she could trust herself to try touching her lips to his. She knew deep inside she was truly still an awkward mess where he was concerned, especially on the kissing front. Just thinking about it, and the stupid incident had her shaking.

One step at a time, Vere. Don't think about kissing yet.
Just stay cool and enjoy the goose bumps. You like those...

Goosebumps, getting asked to homecoming, and circles on my thigh: A++! Kissing can come later. One test at a time. I'm passing well enough for today.

She pulled her gaze from his face and concentrated instead on the short thick waves that made up his perfectly cut sideburns. Curtis had amazing hair.

Almost as nice as Dustin's...

She swallowed an odd lump in her throat and moved one perfect black curl off Curtis's forehead. It stuck to her finger. She had to work for a second to untangle it without hurting him. "Sorry," she added when he winced.

The laughter from across the stage had reached a new level of hilarity. They both looked over to see Dustin and Jenna performing some odd mime-type dance.

Even Mrs. VanDeWirth was still in on the fun.

Vere wished she could hear them—be part of it.

The curl she'd moved dropped back down.

"I *so* don't miss those two right now," Curtis said, resuming his circles on her other knee.

She glanced one last time at her friends and then back at her homecoming date and smiled. "Neither do I," she lied.

30: lake swimming

Dustin

Dustin McHugh had landed back in heaven.

Mrs. Roth's food heaven.

He felt right at home back in the Roth family cabin. Like he really belonged here. They'd given him his old room. Aunt Nan said she was staying behind to catch up on cutting back her garden, but he knew she probably wanted a weekend of peace without a bunch of teenagers in her house.

Dustin had just gorged himself on Mrs. Roth's famous jalapeño, roasted green chili, cream cheese and scrambled-egg bagels. So damn good, and satisfying. Mostly because Mrs. Roth had left a note on the plate. Just for him.

For our dear, Dustin. Eat up. Fresh juice in the fridge.

He'd pocketed the little slip of paper and done exactly as instructed, eating until his stomach hurt.

Heaven. Definitely. Heaven.

And Mrs. Roth is my real live angel.

They'd all arrived late last night. Jenna and Vere most probably had gone to the lake for a swim. It was all they'd talked about on the ride up. That is, before Jenna Riley, who had taken the center seat, had fallen asleep all over his lap.

She'd drooled on him for the last hour of the trip.

At least it had amused Vere, who'd giggled about it every five minutes.

Girl had the sweetest laugh.

He assumed Mr. and Mrs. Roth had long gone on a hike, doing what they called a *fourteener*.

Vere had explained the term meant a hike that involved a peak at (or higher than) 14,000 feet. Dustin had opted out, swearing he needed extra sleep. Charlie and the *perfect* Curtis had also begged off the hike, and were still sleeping upstairs. He'd tried to read on the covered porch but the late morning sun had turned it into a sauna. He wished he'd brought along his guitar, but he'd left it at home.

He didn't want Curtis or Jenna to know he could play that well, and when he had that beautiful old Strat in his hands he couldn't resist simply playing it well.

After pacing around inside for a good half hour, he dashed up to his room and put on the swim trunks Charlie had lent him last time. He decided to walk along the lake loop to search for Jenna and Vere. And maybe swim or quickly cool off.

Maybe.

It didn't take him long to locate the path Vere had shown him that first weekend. Within minutes he'd made it to the shoreline of the little jewel looking lake.

He scanned ahead and checked out the empty dock.

Perfect. I'm alone.

He made his way over to it, pulled off his plaid shirt and T-shirt, kicked off his shoes, and stared down at the water rippling in the breeze.

Maybe swimming isn't such a good idea. Maybe sunscreen first.

He tucked his retainer and glasses into his discarded shirt, and grabbed up his bottle of sunscreen, slathering some on as he contemplated the dark water again. He hated that he couldn't see the bottom. With a pool, he could always see the bottom.

But this...hell...

He watched as a stringy water plant and some dry, brown leaves drifted across the surface until they slid whisper quiet under the dock.

Creepy.

He shuddered and looked across to the other side. In the distance a large fish, a trout possibly, flung itself out of the water and flipped before it splashed back down.

Double creepy!

No way am I going in...no way!

A movement and a flash of color caught his eye to the left of the dock behind a large scrub oak. He caught his breath.

The lake, the dock, the mountains in the distance, all twisted into a grayish blur, blasting out of focus except for the sight of Vere—who appeared to be sound asleep—stretched out on the hidden flat rock that jutted into the lake.

Her giant sweatshirt had been turned into a pillow. Her hair, unbound, tumbled wildly across the rock and all around her. He had the strangest déjà-vu sensation.

Have I dreamed this? Or IS this the dream?

He shook his head slightly in an attempt to right his thoughts, right the universe that now spun beneath his feet.

How could Vere just be here alone? Was that safe? Where was Jenna? Did the girl not fear being hit with a flying fish?

His clarity slipped again, as his gaze moved over the rest of her.

Hell.

This was not the fashion disaster, one-piece-nightmare swimsuit he'd expected Vere to own.

She was wearing a dark red bikini! A very small, very fashionable, impossibly sexy, dark red bikini.

He ate up the sight of her. She was gorgeous in it. He was dying to get a closer glimpse at what looked like a perfect, definitely oval shaped, tucked-in, super cute belly button in her flat, tan stomach!

Her bikini bottoms tied in a bow on each side.

They stretched perfectly over her hips as though the suit had been custom made just for her. He noted her long, slim legs didn't look at all gawky like this.

Nope. Not in this outfit. Is a bikini an outfit?

Hell.

He felt all of his blood rush into his swim trunks.

He pushed back the sudden feeling of guilt for his uncontrollable attraction to her. Who could blame him?

How could the sight of her, or any girl for that matter, sprawled out in a bikini *not* get him all worked up? He was a guy, right? And she was a girl. A beautiful girl in a bikini.

And he hadn't seen that in a very long time.

Sadly, she was not just any girl. He had no right to think about her like this. He had to remember that, but how?

She'd already exploded his heart last week with the guitar gift and now she'd just blown his mind by simply taking a nap!

Did she not understand the little puff of air from her sweet little mouth had just shattered him into ten million pieces of desperate longing?

You look like a gaping fool right now. Get your shit together.

He looked around.

Who cares. The girl of my dreams is the only one around and she's asleep, not watching me. And it's not as though I'm going to have the chance to see her like this again. I'll look my fill, and then add the memory to my list of torturous things I can never explore further about Vere Roth. And be done.

He glanced around again, but then back at Vere.

Dude. You need to walk away. Right now. Walk the hell out of here. Let her sleep in peace...

The sudden simultaneous throbbing that had started up in his head, combined with what was already happening down in his swim trunks, must have robbed him of half his brain.

One more minute. Just a tiny bit longer...

She sighed in her sleep, a sound which stole away his ability to move one more inch.

He needed a moment to gather his...control. But damn her bikini top...and damn me for being a weakling...and damn that bikini top AGAIN...and how she fills it up like that.

Who knew?

If a bear, or a buffalo, or a mountain lion had trampled out of the woods just then, he would not be able to run or even attempt to save Vere. He was the one who needed saving now. He swallowed and craned his head forward and swallowed again. This was madness. He was full on ogling her like a creepy stalker now—and he couldn't—*wouldn't* stop.

But her skin...

He'd only ever seen her face and neck, maybe some arms, and kneecaps, but this—this girl—with *this skin*, all laid out being kissed by the sun. Plus every single, creamy curve of her? And all in one glance?

A strand of her golden-brown hair caught in the breeze and settled itself across her chest before it whipped up and caught against her lips.

Lips that have never been kissed. Remember that, dude. Remember that.

His own reality came crashing back around him. The facts were that he was millions of miles away from ever being able to make contact, or deserve the kind of sweetness that made up Vere Roth.

He forced himself to look away.

He knew, without a doubt, that he wanted her, but it wasn't his usual understandable, physical kind of want. He wanted what he couldn't have. He wanted her to be his, as in his girlfriend. He wanted the right to *love* her.

He thought back to what she'd said to him on this very dock. How it was all supposed to be *easy and simple and full of butterflies.*

He'd mocked her then, but now he admitted the truth. He'd felt the damn butterflies from the first moment he'd seen her.

So, fine. They did exist for him and in huge amounts.

As for the easy part. That did not.

Not for his life, and not for him. He glanced back over at her and shook his head. Could he ever tell her just how deeply he'd fallen for her? Was he admitting he was full-on in love with her? And, if this was love, he needed to stop it.

It was bad enough that he'd almost seriously kissed her in front of Aunt Nan when she'd handed him the guitar, but now he had this feeling that his heart might implode. Explode.

Whatever. People didn't just fall in love in a couple of weeks, did they? Delete the idea of love from your head.

She loves Curtis. You two are friends—that's it.

Get over it and be happy you get to know this girl at all. You'd rather have her for a friend at the end of this than nothing.

Nothing, he knew for a fact, was never worth it.

But damn...

He wanted to kiss her upper lip first.

The one she drove him crazy with every day when she chewed on it. And then he'd kiss her bottom one, because that poor lip was sorely lacking in his attention. And then again, after a long while of more kissing, he'd make her laugh, kiss the giggles right off her mouth. After that, he'd see if he could try to convince her to take that bikini top off and...maybe...

Maybe what? You ass.

She'd flip out. Take your freak fantasy and walk away.

As he turned, totally shaken now, he accidently dropped his bottle of sunscreen. The bottle *thwang-kathumped*, as loud as a metal drum, rolling across the dock, *thwang-kathumping* the whole way.

Vere stirred and locked gazes with him.

Karma.

He'd been silly to think he could head out after turning into an insecure, stalking ass, sporting a giant woody while ogling an innocent, unsuspecting girl!

Hell no. Now he had to pay.

Instead of shock, fear, or surprise, Vere simply sat halfway up on her elbow, shaded her sleepy brown eyes, yawned, smiled, and said, "Hey. Yay! You're here. Finally going to swim?"

He tried not to groan out loud.

He was now in true, physical pain. Worse, she was about to notice why! Because she'd just doubled the problem in his swim trunks with her beautiful smile.

Hell!

"Thought you were too chicken to try this," she added. Her voice had came out all raspy-sexy. Her eyes were still half closed. A length of hair slid over her shoulder, curling around her tanned hips!

Tangling into the little red bikini bows!

Beyond hot. Shit!

He knew he was going to die, or at least go to hell for each and every one of the six thousand twisted thoughts bouncing through his brain right now.

He couldn't answer her. Only blink like a fool.

"Must have fallen asleep. I need to switch sides or I'm going to get burned." She flipped over to her stomach—totally at ease in front of him—and unaware of his extreme discomfort.

While she settled her head on her arms and found his gaze again, some of her hair slid off the rock and spread like a fan of floating curls just under the surface of the water.

She looked like a real, live mermaid!

The remaining mass of hair billowed around her shoulders and trailed down her back, the ends of it resting just above her waist where his fingers longed to touch.

"What?" she asked, probably ramping in to the fact that he hadn't uttered one word. "It's so hot, isn't it?"

Karma was unbelievably cruel.

Quickly, without a second thought, he took a huge breath and jumped into the lake.

He let himself sink slowly under the surface.

The cool dark water calmed him inside and out.

Plants, fish and other lake creatures were no longer frightening to him at all.

He pushed every ounce of breath out of his lungs and opened

his eyes. Enjoying the silence under the water, he watched as his air bubbles wobbled up, popping at the surface.

He noted the bright, Colorado-blue sky above as he contemplated his new phobias: gnome girls, mermaids and impossible love.

As if on cue, Vere dove into the water, grabbed his arm, and yanked him up.

31: guy language

VERE

"UGH!" Vere shouted, trying to catch her breath. "Why do guys always hold their stinking breath under water for as long as possible? Charlie does it! My dad does it! Every guy I've ever known does it! Guys suck when they swim."

She and Dustin were treading water facing each other. She pushed her heavy, wet hair off her face. She hadn't had time to bun it before jumping in when Dustin didn't surface—in what she deemed—was an appropriate time for him to come up.

"It's what guys do. What can I say?" Dustin laughed, but it wasn't his usual, easy laugh. It sounded forced.

"Not funny." She glowered, scanning his face to see if he was okay. She was relieved when he added his usual impish grin, but realized he wasn't wearing the retainer or the glasses.

How she'd forgotten—how she'd missed—his real smile and his real, over-the-top beautiful face outside of the ugly hats he wore. She felt so comfortable around him. When had she begun to take his amazing looks for granted? Or...had she? Because right now he was so amazingly stunning with drops of water all over him, she was pretty sure she wasn't taking it for granted.

So he's beautiful.

So I notice.

So what? I can't turn off my eyes, right?

"First time to hold my breath in a lake though." His voice sounded more normal that time. Had she imagined the tension in it? "I wasn't under there that long," he added.

She cupped her hand, filled it with water and splashed him. "You were! I bet you knew it freaked me out." She splashed him again, this time harder to show she was serious about the freaked out part.

His eyes suddenly struck her as bluer than she remembered. Maybe it was the sky, reflecting into the lake with the bright sun? Or maybe it was because he seemed to be looking really deeply into her eyes.

She swam closer and scanned his entire face again. "Your hair seems to be lightening up a bit all over. You might want to re-color it soon, before your roots grow out," she said finally, when she realized she'd stared too long all over again.

"Yeah. It's on my list. I've been hiding it non stop. Don't worry." He shook out his wet hair.

Vere was close enough to reach over and move one long, wet strand out of his eyes. "I could trim it again," she said absently.

"Wait." He smiled. "You're going to have to repeat that move in one second. I'm not the best swimmer...so I need my hands to keep me floating." He shook out his hair again, deliberately spraying her face with the water from his hair.

She laughed, and obligingly moved the wayward piece of dark brown hair again. She liked how it stayed put, just where she set it.

"Thanks. Where's your sidekick?"

"Jenna's with my parents. She wanted to bag one more big peak for the season." Vere shook her head, unable not to keep studying the angles and planes of his face, remembering the first time she'd ever seen him.

She figured it was a darn good thing Jenna had decided to go on the hike with her parents because, duh and *holy cow*. There was no disguising this guy in this lake.

Worse, before Dustin had jumped in, Vere's gaze had been stuck on his *award winning six-pack* like a staring fangirl. She had also not missed he should have possibly won awards for his perfect, muscular biceps, and shoulders. And legs...and all of him!

Stupid assets! Jeez.

Encouraging this guy throw on a suit and swim had been a very bad idea. Jenna would have tagged all of that muscular perfection right away. She would have started asking questions. She would have flung herself at him. Or worse!

Mega-bullet dodged.

Vere tried to erase the image of his perfect *assets* from her mind as she taunted him by swimming around in a circle using her best side stroke.

He spun along with her, keeping his shoulders under the water but turned along with her strokes, facing her the whole time. His gaze was pensive. An expression she'd never seen before, and she thought she'd seen them all.

She wondered if he was going to bring up her crying attack and lame eavesdropping. They still hadn't talked about it yet, so she knew it was inevitable.

Does his look mean: Awkward conversation comes next?

Hoping to avoid it, she splashed him with a big arc of water, and paddled backwards away from him.

His brows shot up. "Oh. Oh you want to play that, do you?"

"Yep." Because *that*, Vere could handle way better than how her heart felt when she thought about him being sad for so long without any friends. She added, "But beware. Tangle with me, you'll lose. I've been trained by Charlie at this sport."

She turned quickly and hit the surface of the lake with a perfect hand-to-water slam. She got his head, dead on, with tons of spray.

"Oh...no you didn't!" He swam after her and splashed her back, hard.

Vere retaliated with her epic, two handed water flood. "Ha!"

He coughed, choked and couldn't get out of it. "You want to hold your breath so long, you can start again now," she teased, letting the guy catch his breath as she changed positions for her grand finale.

While he wiped water out of his face, Vere laid her entire

arm flat against the water and held it rigid, digging it just into the water's surface to create a perfect mini-tidal wave. It rose up about three feet and aced him right in the mouth, causing him to choke all over again.

He looked so surprised as he wiped his face a second time she couldn't help but giggle. "What? Didn't think I had it in me?" She giggled again. "You ready for another? Start holding your breath, city boy."

Fun water fight: A++!

Dustin raised his eyebrows high, but instead of retaliating as she'd expected, he sucked in a deep breath and dropped back down under the dark water.

Fine. I can wait. He will not get to me twice. Don't count, Vere. Don't let him win. How many seconds has it been?

She paddled over to where he'd disappeared and peered around looking for a flash of swim trunks or pale skin under the surface.

Nothing.

"You jerk. Come up," she called into the water.

Was he heading toward her in a surprise dunk attack from behind? If so, bring it. Charlie invented that game, and she beat him at it every time.

She dove down as deep as she could to meet him head on, but again, he wasn't there. Why did this always have to freak her out so badly? She resurfaced and glowered.

"Dustin McHugh, if you think you're scaring me...you are. You win. Okay? YOU WIN!" Vere's gaze searched further out into the lake to be sure he hadn't surfaced somewhere out of reach.

"Dustin!" Vere's heart picked up its pace as panic set in. She took in as much air as she possibly could and went under again. This time, she swam in a long, deep circle. Her hands reached through the water in every direction but came into contact with only water. Her lungs felt as though they'd burst, but she stayed down, her eyes wide open in the murky water, looking for any sign of him.

Large, very warm arms circled her waist from behind. She knew it was him, safe and sound, and probably thinking this was all very funny.

She went limp with relief and let him pull her up.

She gasped in a huge breath of air as she broke the surface and turned to kill him.

He did not drop his arms when she gripped desperately onto his forearms for support, treading water along with him.

"Weak swimmer, my ass. You suck!"

"You told me to start holding my breath, so I only did what you asked." His gaze was bright and unreadable. He remained silent, and she felt swallowed up for a moment into the intensity of his gaze.

"Couldn't you hear me calling? What in the hell were you trying to do? Kill yourself?" She glanced down and realized her hands were over the scars on his wrists.

She gasped and looked up into his face, immediately regretting what she'd said so lightly. She could tell from the look on his face, he thought she was reacting badly to his scars.

She felt him try to twist his wrists away from her.

"No!" Her voice quaked. "Please. Wait." She held on to his wrists extra tight. What was she supposed to say to him after she'd screwed up so badly, again? She took a deep breath. "I'm sorry. I didn't mean to say that. I didn't. You know I always talk too quickly and—when I gasped—it was not because of you, it was because of me always being so stupid. And so..."

Her throat was closing up, and she stopped treading water. His hands were gentle, and surprisingly warm on the sides of her waist. Tears had filled up each of her limbs. She could hardly move.

"Vere. *Don't.*" His voice was too low. Too soft. Water, rushing over stones as she sensed he, too, was holding back tears. "Don't say you're sorry for me. I know what you meant. It's okay. Just please don't cry again. Not about me, not about the damn scars I put on myself."

"I'm not."

They both knew it was a lie.

Vere let him float her weight fully. He swam them a little toward shore until they could touch bottom, but didn't let her go.

She couldn't look up at his face, so instead, she pulled his arms off her waist and brought them near the surface and kept them there just under the water. She let her fingers trace the jagged lines crossing back and forth.

He didn't pull them away, but she could feel him tremble at her touches. It felt nice to know he trusted her with this. With this part of him.

She finally spoke, her fingers still on the widest part of his scars. "I'm glad you didn't succeed at this—or even come close. I can't imagine not knowing you." She sniffed back a flood of tears, and whispered, "Since I overheard your story— I've have this terrible flash of how it might have gone. I keep thinking of you not being—just not *being*—in the world. And that's why I haven't been able to talk to you about it. I can't imagine it, and when I do...*God*. I kind of flip out."

"I can't imagine it either."

His voice floated softly over her head, setting off a shiver down the back of her neck.

He went on, "Mostly because I would have never met you. I don't want to sound like a sappy dork, but I really want you to know how much you've meant to me."

She looked up then, her eyes still heavy with unshed tears. His face was so sincere. "I love being friends with you, too. So much..."

"Yeah...I know. It makes me happy when you're happy."

He looked away and took one of her hands to lace his fingers through hers. They were palm to palm. He did the same with the other. He gave her hands a little squeeze and it felt nice, perfect. She could swear she felt his pulse connecting with hers through their palms.

"Poor you. Your poor mom. That whole night sounds like it was total chaos."

"Yeah. I wish I could take it all back. My mom only came into the living room hours later. My lame-ass suicide attempt was nowhere close to nicking an artery, but I guess there was a lot of blood on the floor. I don't remember it clearly."

She kept her hands with his, but turned his wrists to face her again. She wanted him to know—to feel—that he didn't need to hide them away from her. "What do you remember?"

"I only remember my mom's super pissed-off voice, yelling down the hall. She'd found the car stuck through the front door. She was in the middle of screaming something about how I was never going to drive again. And how I was going to have to clean up the mess I'd made without her help this time."

"Sounds like the standard mom-type speech. She should have grounded you for life." Vere met his gaze.

"She did. Remember?" He flashed her a look that was half smile, half grimace. "My mom's voice that night made a permanent impression in my brain. It's like I can't forget one word or how she sounded."

"I can imagine. Were you very drunk?"

He shrugged. "I guess. I spilled most of the second bottle of wine, thankfully. Or I'd have been sleeping in my own vomit. At least I didn't sink as low as that. I keep telling myself there must be a couple of notches lower on that ladder than the place I landed that night. I'm also using those imaginary rungs as a reminder that there are people way more bad off than I am. People with so many more scars than mine to bear. Depressions that aren't as easy to get out of. My mom, she has to take medication to handle her depression every day."

"Why?"

"Ever since my dad died, she's been on it and it really works for her. Nan told me depression runs in our family. I'm lucky, actually. Lucky I know about it now, and that I can track it if it comes back." His blue gaze burned into hers. "Lucky that I'm alive too, of course."

Vere felt like his eyes had just pulled her deep into his heart. He was such a complicated, lonely person, yet he'd seemed to have let her in, and it felt great to be there.

She swallowed a small lump creeping up her throat. "I can help you track it. Check in with you every single week. You seem to be just fine now. To me, anyhow."

"Yeah, well. I am fine now." He smiled. "I'm happy that someone besides me and my over-paid therapist has reached the same conclusion though. But it doesn't erase what went down that night."

"No. It doesn't. But that is over."

"All but the part between me and my mom is over. She and I are still so disconnected."

"But not forever?"

"Maybe. When she finally figured out what I'd done, she called Martin. He came in and handled everything. He also had the crashed car snuck out before sunrise, and a new door installed by 10 AM the next day. The rest of it was so whacked. My mom had her own freaking team of doctors at my botched suicide/nervous breakdown event! Martin ordered private doctors to come to the house to evaluate me, but it was my Mom who needed the most help!"

Vere sighed. "Moms...are moms. I guess it makes sense. My mom would act the same."

He shrugged. "Because I wasn't critical, beyond needing some stitches, they—Mom and Martin—sent me to the residential home the next night. I was there for six weeks before coming here."

"God. I can't imagine being away from my Mom for so long, but I'm glad you went. Glad they helped you."

"They did. A lot. My therapist...he was awesome. Taught me so much. If only I'd known to ask to see someone before I got so depressed."

"Don't look back at what you could have done. You didn't know, and now you do." She tightened her grip on his arms. "Have you talked about it with your mom?"

"Nope." He shook his head and shot her a wry looking smile. "The last time I saw her—I mean before she nailed me to the wall and then dumped me at the airport—a team of Martin's *paid-off-to-be-silent* doctors were giving her some sort of sleeping drug. Get it? I still haven't digested that scene. All the others, I've been able to process. But that one...I don't know where to put it, you know? Or her. Where do I put my mom after a night like that? After she's forced me to come here against my will. For that matter, where am I supposed to put myself?"

"Just be where you are. Right now. Be in this moment only. That's all that really counts. Don't you think? You're here, and you're swimming with me."

He smiled, but didn't answer.

She smiled back. "Everything else—don't let it matter." She smiled wider, trying to convince him. Herself. All the while her heart ached for him. "It will all sort itself out. One breath at a time. It's all we can control, huh?"

He gently tightened his hold on her hands again. "That's the secret, isn't it? Barry said the same. One moment at a time. If I keep it there, then it all seems easy. I know if I think about the days and days ahead, and dealing with my mom, and my future that's currently one giant question mark, then I know I'm in the wrong place."

"Why? How do you know that?"

He smiled softly down at her. "Because it's exactly how I was thinking the night I cut myself."

Vere looked up at him, and fear slammed into her chest.

He was at that moment so beautiful and so forlorn she couldn't hold his gaze. She stared at their intertwined hands and slowly unhooked hers from his, bringing his scars all the way above the water into the sunlight. "Swear. Swear to me you will never try it again."

"I swear. I won't even hold my breath in front of you as long as you promise to never worry about me like this again."

"How can you be sure you won't go back there?" She pushed back the urge to scream at him to make him *promise, and promise, and promise!*

He tried to pull his arms away again, but she held on fast, staring at his scars.

He bumped his forehead gently against the top of her forehead, and whispered, "Because now...I like peach milkshakes and the most *awesome*, icy-cold well water."

"What?" She looked up.

He nodded. "You heard me. I've also only just begun searching the world for ridiculous, heart shaped rocks. And I've started collecting antique guitars. I've got stuff to do, *girl*. Tons of awesome and amazing moments to walk through. I've got this moment with you, and the next. Oh, here it comes already—and the next!" He smiled. "See? I've got it down."

She laughed, smiling up at him. "Good. Okay. Good."

His gaze pulled her in again. She felt his hurt, but she also saw warmth and calm inside the clear depths.

He wasn't lying about being okay.

He went on, in the same low, happy voice, "Besides, I've sworn it to you, little *bestie*. And I keep my promises. Never again. Only these stupid scars remain of the whole deal. Sadly, I'll have them forever."

Relief took over. "The scars aren't stupid. They're a part of your past. So what? Everyone has scars, they just aren't as visible as yours."

"True," he said, not sounding convinced.

She impulsively pulled one of his wrists to her lips and planted a gentle kiss there, and then she did the same to the other. "There. See? All better. We're both completely cured."

Because she promised that she wouldn't cry all over him like she had the other day, she dunked herself out of his arms and swam away. When she surfaced about ten feet over she didn't look back; instead she turned and swam toward the dock.

Oh...help.

Charlie was standing in his swim trunks at the far edge of the dock, arms crossed. Curtis was coming around the bend in the path. Thankfully, he was still quite a few yards behind her brother.

Had Charlie seen them?

Why did she kiss his wrists like that? It was probably such a wrong thing to do. But it had felt so right...

"What have you two been up to?" Charlie called out.

She could tell by his voice that he was trying to not sound super pissed.

Oh, he saw us.

But they hadn't been doing anything. So he could just chill. There was nothing for him to be pissed off about.

"Swimming. What does it look like?" Vere climbed out of the water.

"I don't know? What *does* it look like?" Charlie crossed the length of the dock in two seconds and spoke so only she could hear. "Did that bastard mess with you or something? I thought I saw you two all but—*crap*! Vere, are you crying?"

"Don't be ridiculous. We were swimming. Goofing off, that's all. I'm not crying. I'm wet and I had my eyes open under the water."

"*Bull.* You're major crying," he whispered.

"Charlie. Don't. It's not what you think. You don't understand," she whispered back.

Curtis lumbered up on the dock at his own pace, and interrupted them with a long low whistle that painfully pierced Vere's thoughts.

Instant headache. Why is he so loud?

"Look what Vere's been hiding. Hello hotness! Can you walk that bikini a little closer?" Curtis swaggered forward making that little creepy smile. He'd seemed to miss the fact the she was losing it right now and that she Charlie were about to have a huge fight.

The guy seemed to miss a lot.

She figured it was a good thing in this case.

Curtis whistled again. "Whoa. Vere, you're killing me in that sexy red suit."

She shot Curtis an embarrassed smile. The whole situation, especially Charlie acting so strangely, had started a nice freak attack of blushing. "Oh...yeah...um...thanks."

Vere wiped at her eyes as a few more random tears tried to escape. Curtis still didn't seem to notice any of her upset. Instead he just and stared and stared. It made her feel really nervous, like she was naked or something.

Vere avoided both his gaze and Charlie's as she glanced around for something to cover herself. Dustin's towel was right at her feet so she quickly grabbed it and put it on.

Why did she have to notice how safe it made her feel? And for that matter how great it smelled? Dustin's scent floated all around her skin, baking into her pores from the sun heated towel.

As she wrapped up, she realized Dustin's plaid shirt was at her feet. Worse, his retainer and glasses had fallen out. This was not at all good. She had to get the stuff to him.

"Here Dustin," she called out, her voice urgent. He'd swum up to the dock but had remained quiet. Thankfully he'd kept his face hidden next to the dock. She handed them down.

"Thanks." Dustin had the glasses and retainer back on in less than one second. Vere did not miss his look of worried panic.

"Mind if I borrow your towel?" She kept her back to her brother and Curtis, pretending to make conversation, as she shoved on his cap. Her voice was still a little shaky but she thought it sounded casual enough. She shot a glance at Curtis. Had he seen Dustin's face clearly? Probably not. He was checking out her legs and butt.

"Gladly," Dustin answered with a tight smile. "But can you grab me yourssthh. Off that rock?" He jerked his head toward the towel on the rock where she'd been sleeping.

Vere blushed again and glanced nervously back at Curtis. She'd plastered on her own tight smile. "Sure. Hang tight."

Curtis had that stupid, wolfish grin on his face. As she dashed past, he shot her a wink.

Vere fought to ignore all three of them. Hard to do when she felt as if they were all burning holes in her for different reasons. She whipped over to the rock and back as fast as she could and held the towel up, shooting Dustin a *hurry-up* look. Trying to keep Curtis's attention, she flipped her hair to one side and pretended to squeeze out the extra water to help hide Dustin as he first came out of the water.

Glimpsing the scars on Dustin's wrists again, as he quickly buttoned the plaid shirt, she managed to get control of a new flood of tears and her overactive heartbeats.

Dustin seemed to understand her stress, and so moved as quickly as he could. Before he was fully upright, she'd thrown the towel over his six pack. He smiled his thanks, working to bury himself in his towel and his disguise.

Vere took a second to adjust Dustin's towel so his perfect shoulders and collarbones were also hidden where he hadn't been able to button his shirt yet. She looked nervously at Charlie, who had not once stopped shooting death glares at

Dustin.

To further distract Cutis's attention off of Dustin, she hopped off the dock to head back over to her sun-bathing rock. She grabbed her ponytail holder and yanked on her abandoned hoodie. Within seconds she had her hair bound into her bun and she felt much better. Curtis's eyes had never once left her, which meant her plan had worked.

Thank GOD he kind of likes staring only at me. I guess.

"Aww. Vere. Keep that pretty hair down. Are you done swimming?" Curtis whined, his voice cut lightning bolts into her headache. "Charlie and I were just going in. I'd hoped you at least, would stay and watch us?"

"I—I'll hang out with you guys, but I'm done swimming."

"Well, I'm heading back, totally done." Dustin shrugged, his voice sounded odd again, probably just nervous about getting caught without his disguise. He gathered up his sunscreen. Vere could see he was careful to keep his wrists turned inward. If only she could help him do the buttons...

"Yeah, you're *done*," Charlie's tone was menacing. "You're freaking super-done. You two-faced jerk!"

"Care to clarify what you mean, you pompous, ridiculous *ass*." Dustin returned Charlie's glower.

"Oh I'll clarify." Charlie moved in and punched Dustin right in the face. Dustin's head whipped back and his glasses went flying. He placed his hands over his exposed eyes, turning his face away from Curtis.

"Charlie!" Vere screamed. "Stop!" She scrambled back to the dock. Racing to scoop up Dustin's glasses to hand them back to him. One of the lenses had cracked into a sunburst from the impact. Dustin quickly put them back on.

Vere had swallowed her heart. "Why did you hit him?"

"He knows why."

"Whatever. I do not." Dustin rubbed his chin.

"Dude," Curtis said. "What's the deal? Why did you hit

him?"

Dustin faced Charlie. He looked pissed, but thankfully it didn't appear he was going to punch Charlie or attack him back.

He sighed before he spoke while he straightened his cap with his free hand. "Nothing. Nothing's going on. You're totally out of line, Charlie. I told you. She's not my type. At all. NEVER. We're friends. JUST FRIENDS."

Vere gasped. "What? This is about me and *Dustin?*" She felt as though all the wind had been knocked out of her by Dustin's words. Her heart clenched into an impossibly tight ball and now she couldn't discern if the feeling came from Charlie punching Dustin or Dustin's claim, yet again, that she wasn't his type.

Head still spinning, she placed herself between Charlie and Dustin just to make sure no more punches went flying. "Charlie. You've lost your mind. And Dustin—*whatever*. As if I could care less that I'm not your type. I like Curtis." She shot him a glare. No need for him to know how deeply he'd hurt her feelings. "I'm really sorry, Curtis. I don't want you to think anything's off. Because it's not."

"What?" Curtis was frowning and possibly trying to see down the front of her towel! "Hell yes, you like me—especially over this dumbass. And good that you're finally saying it out loud!"

Charlie still had his hand fisted as though he'd like to hit Dustin again. "I just wanted us all to be clear. That's all."

Curtis finally seemed to be ramping in, and moved his gaze from Vere to Dustin. "Vere, if this dork made a play for you and right under my own nose, I'll be the one taking the next punch outta-him, thank you very much."

"Good man, Curtis." Charlie smiled at his friend. "I think it's settled now."

"You two, loser Neanderthals! Dustin's my friend. Like he

said. That's all! We were swimming. If you two can't handle us being friends, then you can just both kiss off. Nothing's going on besides that."

Vere couldn't make eye contact with Dustin.

Nothing's going on besides I just kissed his wrists like a freak. God. Why did you do that, Vere?

"Good. Because if there were something, our friend Dustin would be so finished. You know what I mean. Don't you, *buddy?*" Charlie and Dustin had not once broken each other's gaze.

"Eat shit, *buddy,*" Dustin muttered.

Vere finally realized Charlie was blatantly threatening to blow Dustin's cover right in front of Curtis. And for what? He was acting as though he'd caught them totally making out or something. And so? If they had been making out, so what! It was her choice whom she made out with. Charlie was not the kiss police!

She almost had to laugh at the direction of her thoughts. This whole thing was making all of them crazy. That had to be it.

"Charlie. You just better apologize right now, or I'm telling mom."

"Maybe I want you to tell mom, Vere. What the HELL?"

"No. YOU, Charlie. *WHAT THE HELL? YOU?* Apologize."

Charlie softened his tone and spoke to Dustin with his teeth clenched and his voice dripping with sarcastic venom. "I'm sorry I punched you, dude. I thought I saw something that apparently I didn't see. You don't blame me, do you, *friend?* I bet you *get,* that if positions were reversed, you'd have done the same."

Vere was too shocked to speak. Charlie had never acted like this, at least not in front of her before. Why did he sound so mean? She knew she'd somehow crossed over into guy-land. And she sure didn't speak the language here.

What Dustin said next shocked her more. "No. I don't blame

you. Let's hope this is really the last time we have to bring this up." Dustin rubbed away the drop of blood that had formed on his lip, and dropped his hand.

His voice didn't hold any anger, and for some reason, she got the impression Dustin was sort of resigned about something all of a sudden.

She glanced at Curtis, who'd turned into some sort of Charlie-copying, stuttering robot. "Sorry Curtis, I'm too annoyed with my brother to hang out. I'll see you back at the cabin." Vere shoved hard at Charlie's chest and he stepped back. Her brother wouldn't meet her gaze.

Good.

Hopefully he was embarrassed for acting like such a freak. Vere bumped Dustin with her shoulder.

Thankfully, he seemed to understand. As if he'd awakened from some strange trance, he hopped off the dock and walked ahead of her along the trail leading back to the cabin.

She followed in silence.

There was nothing to say.

32: love, hate, heaven and hell

Dustin

Dustin couldn't believe how quickly his heaven had turned into absolute hell.

He'd survived the afternoon *lounge around* time, pretending to nap in the sun on the porch with everyone else. And he'd perfectly pretended nothing had changed or was wrong.

But everything had changed!

Everything was now beyond twisted and wrong!

He'd made it through the lie they'd told Mrs. Roth about his glasses breaking on a rock. Luckily, Charlie's fist had connected with his jaw, so there wasn't much of a bruise from the punch to explain. He'd even suffered through Jenna helping him secure the cracked center of his glasses with a fat mass of white duct tape while everyone (except Vere) had laughed at the ridiculous nerdier-nerd-effect.

Dustin had survived the trip to Mr. Roth's workshop along with Charlie and Curtis. Helped clean it out. Helped put up the deck chairs, canoe, oars, and barbecue for the winter without another fight. But now, with the sun completely down, Mr. Roth stoking up the last fire in the moss-rock fireplace, and the damn duct tape itching the bridge of his nose, Dustin was falling apart.

They'd gathered back in the living room. Some sprawled on the soft couches, some on the braided rug, to digest the most delicious dinner he'd ever eaten. They were all now waiting for Mrs. Roth's famous red-velvet cake to cool.

He'd replayed Vere's soft lips on his wrists so many times, and he still couldn't stop picturing it. He'd also re-analyzed every single second of *her* while he and Charlie had fought on the dock. Her expressions had fallen off her face like petals ripped from a flower.

There was her initial shock from the punch Charlie had planted on him. Then that adorable flash of true concern when she'd handed him back his broken glasses. She'd had so much anger at Charlie, followed by her obvious frustration with the whole scene.

But what had anguished him the most as he went over things, was the flash of her expression right after he'd claimed—*yet again*—she was not his type.

For a moment her eyes had told him, without a doubt, she'd believed and accepted what he'd said as a rule. If he could only be free to tell her the damn truth. She deserved to know, and to *believe*, she was the most beautiful girl in the whole world. Inside and out.

He wanted to throw his book across the room in frustration. His arms tingled with the memory of holding Vere in the water. He only wanted to hold her again now.

Hell. What had made the girl kiss my wrists like that? Could she possibly have feelings for me too?

If she admitted that she did, would I tell her the truth?

Tell her I'm in love with her?

What would be the point? I could only offer her a fling until I leave. Unacceptable. And inappropriate. I'd never ask that of her. Never. And she doesn't want me, anyhow.

He sighed in pure torment and flicked a glare at Charlie.

The kid returned it without hiding his anger one bit.

How long had the guy been glaring at him like that?

Resigned, he stared back down at his book. Any attempts at a deeper connection with Vere would break the rules he'd accepted as part of this game. One of those rules was to not hurt or mess with Vere's heart or soul. Any attempts to approach her on the level his heart craved would harm her eventually.

Curtis Wishford, his hair still damp from the shower he'd

taken before dinner, had scooted up next to Vere, who rested with her back to the fire.

Dustin glared at Curtis through his cracked lens.

With the red and gold firelight reflecting on the guy's hair, Dustin couldn't help but visualize two, black devil horns growing out of the top of his giant head. All the slimy jerk needed was a pitchfork and tail to complete his look.

Does one else notice the similarity?

As if to prove his thoughts were dead on, Curtis grabbed Vere's hand in a possessive gesture, and shot Dustin a smirk that of course, no one else spotted.

Dustin looked away from them.

Whatever.

If this is hell, then of course the girl I love is dating the devil. BECAUSE IT'S HELL.

Mr. Roth. The Devil is holding your daughter's hand. Now would be a great time to step up and whack the kid with your fire poker.

When nothing happened, Dustin just slouched lower into his book.

Curtis's voice sliced through the room. "What do you say, sweet Vere. Are you up for a moonlight walk by the lake?" He was obviously trying to be all suave and whispery, but to Dustin he sounded like a megaphone. The guy had no finesse.

Dustin just had to look up again.

Damn. Vere's cheeks had turned that cute shade of pink he liked so much.

"Sure, Curtis. Sounds awesome," she answered.

Dustin slammed his book shut, drawing another huge glare from Charlie.

Bring it dumbass. Go ahead and punch me right here, but I am SO going on a night hike right now. Hell yes I am.

"Can I come? I've never seen the lake at night," Dustin said quickly.

"Oh. I want to go too," Jenna piped in. "I could use a walk. I'm dying of Chicken Alfredo overload." She seemed to melt out of the couch as she stood, and patted her stomach. "Mrs. Roth, this weekend has made me a bit—chubby."

Mrs. Roth smiled.

Dustin grinned double-wide at Jenna.

Go Jenna. I love you right now.

He locked gazes with Charlie, knowing what the kid wanted. He *expected* him to convince Jenna to stay away from Curtis and Vere. But after what happened on the dock, Charlie should know better.

All favors are off, dumbass. Do your own dirty work.

He fingered the sore spot along his jaw, wondering briefly if he and Charlie were even friends anymore.

Were we ever?

The whole thing felt too weird. If Curtis needed to make a move on Vere, he would have to up his game all by himself.

Dustin's thoughts rocketed him to his feet. "Charlie, you coming?" he taunted.

A direct challenge smoldered from Charlie's gaze. "Not a chance. You two *couples* should go. I'd feel like a fifth wheel."

Jenna gave Dustin a strange, almost apologetic look. "Uh... Dustin. I—"

Dustin grimaced.

Touché Charlie.

Dustin spoke up fast to interrupt Jenna, "If we're talking about *couples*, then I should be the one to stay." He paused, returning Charlie's challenge with a small smile.

"What? Why?" Jenna asked.

"Jenna, Charlie's got a crush on you. He told me all about it. I don't want to get on his bad side for stepping out on a walk with a girl he considers *his territory.*"

"WHAT?" Charlie jumped up.

Dustin went on, "You two should go. With Curtis and

Vere."

Charlie fisted his hands and took one step toward Dustin. Dustin fisted his hands back.

Bring it. Just bring it. I am so ready to pound someone right now.

Mr. Roth put down his iPad. "Well, wow. If this isn't news!" He smiled at all of them.

"Charlie, if you even start up anything," Vere shouted, staring at her brother's fists.

"Well. Now you've done it," Jenna said.

"Done what?" Vere asked.

Dustin smirked at Charlie, but it wasn't from the heart.

This whole thing was out of control. Why couldn't he just step back and not care? Vere wanted to be with Curtis. He should just let it happen. And now poor Jenna might get hurt because he couldn't stop making up fake stories about fake lives!

Mrs. Roth saved everything when she interrupted, "Charlie, no need to be embarrassed. How sweet. Dad and I always suspected it. Have you asked Jenna to homecoming?"

Vere's mouth had dropped wide open. "Charlie—Jenna, is this even true?"

It was so like Vere to believe stuff like this. Girl was too gullible.

He searched the back of his mind for a way to play it off and fix what he'd started without any of this impacting Jenna's feelings.

Jenna didn't give him a chance. She spoke up again, "Whoa. Okay now...just hold up." She held up her hand and pointed at Charlie. "You can just sit back down and uncurl those fists Mr. Testosterone. First. Dustin and I are just friends." She smiled at Dustin, and went on, "Mr. and Mrs. Roth, I'm sure you're happy about this finally coming out in the open, but Charlie and I are NOT going to happen. It's no secret Charlie holds a candle for me. He always has, but there is no way I would go to homecoming with him. Even if he begged."

"What the...gah?" Charlie stammered.

Dustin's chin hit the floor.

"As for trekking around the lake as a *couple*? I'm just not sure." She flipped her ever present, long blonde braids back behind her and regarded Charlie solemnly.

"Oh? Why?" Mrs. Roth asked, glancing at her husband.

"What?" Vere and Dustin asked at the same time.

"Yeah. What are you talking about, Jenna?" Charlie managed to strangle out.

Jenna held up her hand again and turned her attention to the adult Roths. "Mrs. Roth, no disrespect meant to your son, but I mean to marry Charlie Roth some day. If he takes me to homecoming, I think it's just too soon. It would mess up my plans. I don't have him on my dating calendar until *after* college."

Charlie dropped back onto the couch. His expression had gone wild as though he wanted to run out of the room. His wide open mouth mirrored Dustin's, only more so.

It had fallen open so wide bats could fly into it.

"Jenna, seriously. You are the most messed up person I've ever met—and—and—I—what the hell—" Charlie choked. It was a desperate attempt to play this off, and it had failed. The guy was trying very hard to act cool, but he'd blown that about two gaping minutes ago.

Dustin noted with cheer that Charlie was acting exactly like Vere. His stuttering was hilarious, and the kid's face had turned a show-stopping beet red.

Well who knew?

Dustin murmured just loud enough for everyone to hear. "People say there's a fine line between love and hate. Hmmm. Interesting." He laughed.

Mrs. Roth seemed to be holding back her own laughs. "Well, Jenna, I suppose it's good to wait. If you think it's best."

Charlie sputtered and flailed his arms from across the room. "You have got to be kidding. *Mom.* I've got no crush on Jenna. And, she's the last person on this entire earth I'd ever choose to marry, let alone take to HOMECOMING. GOD, SAVE ME!"

Jenna sighed as though she could care less what Charlie had to say about it, and continued, "Charlie, it isn't the guy that does the choosing. And I've chosen you."

"Mom. Vere. Make her stop," Charlie moaned. His face had turned even redder.

"Dude. You're looking like spicy-red-hot candy." Curtis laughed too. "I bet you do like her!"

Dustin tossed a glace at Vere, wondering if she'd known about this, but she appeared as surprised as everyone else.

"Statistically, Charlie," Jenna announced, with absolute calm, "the guy usually does the ASKING—with the ring. Eventually, you will have to step up. So, yeah." She shrugged. "Even though you asked, I'm not going to homecoming with you. I hope that doesn't hurt your feelings."

"I didn't ask you to ANY dance! What the hell?"

"Maybe prom, but let's see how it goes." She blinked.

Vere giggled and locked eyes with Dustin, who was having his own difficulties keeping more laughter in check.

Curtis laughed louder.

"Call the cops. Dad, give me your car keys. I'm driving out of here," Charlie cried.

"You're so funny," Jenna laughed. "It's one of the reasons I do like him," she added, turning to Mr. Roth. "A sense of humor is so important." She smiled.

"How did you come up with this 'girls choose' idea?" Mr. Roth asked.

"One of last year's social experiments. I've surveyed about two hundred parents. Their marriages ended in *The Big D* if the man was the one who chose the girl. It's practically a scientific fact that the guys don't know how to select a quality, lasting mate. All you have to do is compare back seasons of *The Bachelor* against *The Bachelorette*. Every time the guy chooses, the couple bombs!"

Mr. and Mrs. Roth burst out laughing along with Vere, Curtis, and Dustin.

Mr. Roth nodded at Charlie. "She's right, son. Your mom picked me, and I did the asking. There could be something to this. You might as well fold. Beg her to reconsider the homecoming thing."

"God. Don't encourage her!" Charlie shouted.

"I suppose I could walk by the lake with you, Charlie, as long as you don't mistake it for a date or do anything untoward." Jenna tilted her head to the side and blinked at him.

"Anything untoward? *Untoward?* Crap. I don't even know what that means!"

"This is why I am not dating you until after college. Your vocabulary is years behind mine. The sense of humor is good, but your temper is just too...loose cannon. I'm sort of waiting for you to catch up, here." Jenna tapped her forehead and gained another round of laughter from everyone in the room.

Charlie pushed his hair back with both hands. "Vere, call her off, or I swear I'm going to—"

"Don't be all insulted," Jenna continued, "I'd like the inside to match the outside." She blushed slightly then. "If you must know, I find you so beautiful on the outside, Charlie. No one's cuter."

"Bahfah-*what*?" Charlie stuttered. "Restraining order. I need a restraining ORDER! Does no one see that she's scary?"

Jenna laughed, not offended. "Okay. I'll walk by the lake with you. Just don't try to hold my hand."

Dustin almost felt sorry for the dude. He'd now turned even redder than Vere's reddest! "I think thisssth istth ssstthoo sweet," Dustin added, unable to resist rubbing some salt into this one. "Lettths's go!"

Mr. Roth put the grate over the fireplace and came to his son's rescue. "You youngsters have just inspired us both to chaperone you. Let's *all* take a walk by the lake, shall we? Charlie, you look as though you need some air."

Bonus!

"Good idea, Dad." Vere seemed to breathe a sigh of relief, probably assuming if her parents were along, he and Charlie couldn't beat the shit out of each other again.

Dustin hoped the same thing.

Curtis did not look exactly pleased with the situation, but seemed to be following along, two steps behind the conversation. With no fight, or personality, as usual.

The slow bit was the only thing Dustin liked about Curtis.

As Dustin passed Charlie on his way across the living room, Charlie sent him a look that could have turned him to stone.

Charlie, unlike Curtis, was at least a valid, thinking opponent. The guy's expression currently promised absolute revenge.

Dustin grinned, unable to hide his delight.

At least I'm no longer entering hell alone.

He spoke low so only Charlie could hear, "What? Aren't you glad you've been picked to marry? Should be a relief, dude. Now you can focus on other things."

Dustin sidestepped Charlie's upturned foot at the last second, and hopped over it with another grin. "Whoa. Watch the feet, *bud*. I can't stheeeee very well out of thttheesese cracked glasses, *remember*?"

Charlie stalked away, his shoulders so rigid he looked about to snap.

Good. Now we both feel just about the same.

Like killing someone, but we can't.

Mrs. Roth hollered from the kitchen. "Pass this way before heading out. The cake is frosted, sliced and ready to walk."

Dustin swallowed a third grin as he followed Charlie into the kitchen.

Mrs. Roth handed each of them huge slices of warm cake.

Dustin bit in to his, rolling his eyes back in pure bliss.

At least hell has great eats.

33: holding his attention

VERE

"Vere. What's eating you? Come out of it. You haven't spoken for thirty minutes. I've had enough silent scenery. Talk to me. Maybe I can help," Dustin said.

Vere sighed and flexed her shoulders back into the driver's seat. She stretched her arms straight against the steering wheel and wiggled her fingers. "Sorry. I'm distracted."

"Just a few more minutes. Shhh. *Mom...please*," Jenna mumbled from the back seat before she fell asleep again.

Dustin turned to look in the back seat. "I love Jenna Riley. She's hilarious. And the coolest friend ever, huh?"

"She's perfect, even asleep," Vere agreed, eyeing her friend in the mirror. "She's had car narcolepsy since we were little. She used to fall asleep on the school bus every single day in middle school."

"You didn't have to take me down early, you know? I could have gotten the glasses fixed tomorrow with Aunt Nan. It would have been a perfect excuse to ditch school."

"I know, but I wanted to get out of there. I just couldn't face Charlie. I'm still so mad at him. I kind of wonder if I messed everything up with Curtis yesterday. Everything feels all... awkward."

"Ya think? Imagine how I feel with this white tape between my eyes. Double awkward." He pulled off his glasses and rubbed the bridge of his nose. "Another hour and this tape would give me a rash."

Vere made sure to censor her words just in case Jenna heard them. "God. I'm so sorry. Sadly, I think our hasty retreat will mess up things more with Curtis and me. He will probably figure I'm not that into him."

"Maybe you aren't that into him?"

She laughed but kept her eyes on the road. "Hello. Yes I am. It's just that Curtis makes me really nervous and jittery. It's hard to hang around with him for long stretches. Sort of tires me out because I'm so worried he will, all of a sudden, not like me. Do you know what I mean?"

"Yeah. I guess." Dustin was spinning his glasses in his hands, but had turned his face back toward the window.

They were almost down the hill and into the outskirts of Manitou Springs, the small town that led into the larger expanse of Colorado Springs. "Dustin. I have a favor to ask. You can say *no*, because you've already helped me so much—"

"Shoot. Anything."

"Could you help me pick a homecoming dress, as in THE RIGHT homecoming dress? And, in the meantime, while I'm waiting for homecoming...I sort of want to do a makeover. I think if I look prettier then Curtis won't get bored with me. I don't know. I just want to *wow* him, keep his attention. The dance is two weeks away. Since you know so much about fashion, and what's hot, do you mind giving me additional pointers? And maybe today? At the mall?"

Dustin snorted and crossed his arms.

"Do you think I can't do it? Like I don't have enough to work with?" Her heart beat tightly against her chest. She hoped he would be honest with her about this.

Dustin snorted again and looked over. It seemed as though he wanted to say something else but he took a deep breath and shook his head instead. "You sell yourself so short. You *wow* and keep the attention of everyone you meet. Don't you know that?"

"Yeah. But I'm tired of scaring people. I'm done being eccentric. I just want to be mainstream." She took one hand off the steering wheel and pushed at her hair. "I think the bun has got to go."

"You are so stubborn. I love that bun. It's beyond perfect. It's your trademark." His eyes trailed up to it and he smiled. "I can't imagine you without it."

"Well, you're the only one. Thanks for always being so nice. I don't know how I survived a day in my life without you as a friend." She shook her head and turned off the freeway and onto Academy Boulevard, a busy six-lane road.

"Stop calling me that. I'm not that *nice*. And that word sets me off. It sucks. Makes me want to break things. Figure out ways to prove I'm not nice."

"Okay. Meanie. Whatever." She laughed. "After we drop off your glasses it will probably take a couple of hours before we can pick them up. So can you please help me, like today? Now? Pick a cool looking dress with me, at least?"

He let out a long sigh. "I'll help you do anything. Anything at all, Vere. Whatever it will take to make you happy. You only have to ask. If it's Curtis you want, well—you'll get him. Heck, you've already got him, but you just don't believe it." His voice had grown quiet as his eyes scanned her face.

"Yeah right. Curtis can have any girl he wants at our school."

"You think that, but it's not true. Besides he's making it pretty obvious that he's after you." Dustin glanced again into the back seat at Jenna. "You helped me—with, *you know*." He tugged at his plaid shirt. "I would love be able to pay you back. My mom, she's really fashionable. It's one of the few things we talk about without fighting. I'll have no problem choosing a good dress for you...and some other stuff."

"Yay!" Vere pulled the car to a stoplight, waiting her turn to maneuver the car into the Chapel Hills Mall parking lot. "What's she like, your mom? You never talk about her—I mean how she is as a person?"

"She's beautiful." Dustin shrugged.

"But is she nice? What hobbies does she have?"

"That word again?" He grimaced. "Like I said, we don't really get along. I wouldn't know about her hobbies. We haven't even spoken since I've been here."

"Wow. Why?"

"I don't know." Dustin's raw tone made her heart twist.

"My mom would just about die if we didn't talk for a week or longer. I bet your mom is sad. Really sad about it."

"Maybe. But so was I."

"You said *was*! Are you not sad anymore?"

"I thought we'd covered that topic while swimming."

Vere pulled into a parking spot and killed the engine. Neither made a move to get out of the car. "Yeah. I know. I know."

She felt her face flush slightly when she couldn't understand his darkened expression.

Please don't bring up the awkward wrist kissing. Please...

"You should call her." She jumped back in to chattering, to get them off the lake topic. "Maybe you miss her?"

"Yeah. Maybe." Dustin pulled off his cap and ran his hand through his hair. "Sure is hot down here. This Indian summer stuff is weird. I thought it was supposed to snow in Colorado. COUGH. COUGH. Done talking about my mom."

She laughed. "Okay. I hear you."

She reached over and tugged a thick strand at the top of his head. "You have got to darken your hair again," she whispered. "With that cap off I can see miles and miles of very pretty blond highlights coming through. Tell me they aren't natural."

"They are. Jealous again?"

"You take what you have for granted. Yes, I'm jealous. The whole world is jealous. It's unfair how naturally attractive you turned out. I'd go on, but I can't have you all puffed up with yourself again."

"Shut up. You *so* take what you have and under-play it. You know your own list of assets is a mile long."

"Yeah...yeah...I have a few." Her ears started burning. "Maybe. Sort of. But it's hard to build up my confidence after hiding everything all these years behind my red cheeks."

He nodded, seeming to understand. "Trust me, it won't take much to knock down that last wall of hoodies you hide behind. It's all there, Vere. You'll see. By the end of today we'll have it handled."

Vere glanced in the rear view mirror. Thankfully Jenna's legs hadn't moved an inch, and she'd started to snore. Vere realized she shouldn't have mentioned his hair dye. She put her finger over her mouth and made a face at Dustin to show she'd just screwed up.

He laughed, glanced behind him and put the cap back on. "Itthhh cool. She's sound asthleeeep." He pasted on his giant dork smile, and she had to giggle.

"So...anyhow." He paused, his eyes still dark and unreadable, drifted over her face again. "This Curtis...being your boyfriend. It's really going to make you happy? It's truly what you want, without any doubts?"

Her tummy fluttered. "If it works. YES! And of course I have doubts. Like, I want to know that he's sure about me. For the long term. That's really important. I don't want be like those other girls he only dates short term. I want the fairy tale romance. Right now, I think he's simply curious, but not committed. That's standard, right? He and I...we're just starting out. Getting to know each other way better..."

"Yeah. It will work out. Hmm." He surveyed her hair, frowning. "While we're here, what do you say to me dragging you to one of the salons? But I get to tell them what to do."

Her heart clenched. "Cut my hair? Maybe..."

"Not much shorter. A trim. To create some movement at your cheekbones and chin-line, frame your face? A few highlights of your own around your crown area?"

"Ugh. What's my chin-line? I don't want any movement there. Do I? Will it help me? Should I trust you?"

Dustin ignored her questions, beaming as though he now had a huge plan. "We can have them do your eyebrows too and a classic French manicure. That should last well till you would have to re-do them for the dance. My mom swears the French goes with everything."

"Uh. You really do know some random stuff, don't you? I'll agree to everything but the nails. I hate the smell of nail polish."

"Whatever. Not the nails then, little hippie. If you are going to pull this off though, you'll want a few other outfits to get you all the way to dance day."

"Okay, yeah. Good idea."

"But you won't fix things with Curtis with outfits alone."

"I know, but at least I'm trying all I can."

"You'll have to at least call or text him tonight. Something short, flirty and sweet with the hint of a *promise*. Then, you'll walk in and stagger-his-eyeballs at his locker tomorrow. It won't take him long to forget that you ditched him today when I'm through with you."

"Oh, please. You aren't a magician."

"Just wait. I am. If some other lucky guy hasn't stolen you away, Curtis will be locking this whole girlfriend bit down in a matter of days. We'll make you so irresistible he'll be scared to lose you. Then you'll be set and happy for the whole year— until you wise up and dump him," he added.

"Ha. Ha. As IF! But...I...my budget is tight. We're going to have to shop smart."

"I'm not helping you unless you agree the whole makeover thing is on me. Sort of a 'thank-you' for all you've done for me. A gift. Payback for the guitar you and Charlie shouldn't have bought for me."

"Maybe..."

"Take it and love it. I did. I really *do* love it by the way. You know I do." His expression softened. "I've been writing some new songs."

She smiled. "Maybe you can play some for me?"

"Sure. Maybe."

"I accept your offer, but don't go over the top, okay? I'll want to pay you back eventually, or I won't be able to live with myself. Makeovers are expensive."

"I've got it covered. Don't worry about it."

"Makeover? Did someone say makeover?" Jenna sat up straight in the back seat. "Are we giving Dustin a makeover? He *so* needs one! Dude, I get to help!"

Vere felt her smile grow tense. Hopefully she hadn't heard them talking about Dustin's disguise. "Not *him.* Me."

Dustin shoved his glasses back on, twisted in his seat and broke out the retainer smile. "Jenna Riley, you do instthult me. I'm the makeover king. I have an uncle in Los Angeles who's a *stthtylist.* And my mom, she's quite the fashion maven, *stthoo* I've offered to help our Vere."

Jenna rubbed her eyes and blinked, finally looking around. "Are we at the mall?"

Vere shook her head. Great. "Yeah, sleepyhead. Waiting for you to wake up."

"Will you make me over too?"

"Of course. Now come on, I'm tired of looking at you two through these dumb, cracked glasses."

34: creating my own demise

Dustin

"Good God," Dustin muttered under his breath as he looked at Vere's and Jenna's transformations. They were sitting side by side in the salon chairs. The stylist was just finishing Jenna's blow-out.

Vere seemed stunned. Her eyes were wide, facing the mirror. Her brow had not once lost its worried looking creases as she stared at her reflection.

He stepped back, farther out of sight, wondering what in the hell he had done? Curtis Wishford's attention span was about to get very, very long. Long on Vere Roth.

He sighed, resigned. Maybe it was for the best.

He'd outdone himself with this deal. He hoped Vere and Curtis fell madly in love with each other and just left him alone after this.

Hell.

He had no idea how to talk to her. The girl he'd grown to know had completely disappeared, and it was his fault! This Vere looked twenty-five, and yet, still sixteen at the same time. She was so beautiful sitting there looking worried and so unbelievably gorgeous that Dustin's heart wrenched.

"Jeez. Help. There is no way I'm going to school looking like this," Vere squeaked to Jenna.

"Why? You look like a golden, glowing Malibu Barbie doll," Jenna said. "Those highlights are so cool. I'm the one who looks like a newscaster. Why did I go for the French look? I thought French meant 'Euro-sexy' but I don't think I'm ready for the big city. It will take till summer to grow back my approachable, Anne of Green Gables length."

She tugged at the ends of her now, shoulder length hair. "I

hope I can still braid it."

Vere shifted in her seat. "Should I smack you for calling me a doll? And you look amazing, Jenna. Look. Your cheekbones are so perfect now. The bangs show off the angle of your eyes. You're stunning, and it's totally long enough for your braids."

"Okay, fine. I'm adorable, it's true." She pulled a face. "And Barbie is beautiful, through and through. It was compliment, honest." Jenna wiggled her eyebrows. "You have to admit, the waxed brows are awesome. We look like we have fairy wings. Who knew all the models in the magazines did this? I always thought they just had special, model eyes. I thought it was the extra, thickening-eyeshadow and gobs of perfectly applied color that made their eyes so cool! I'd never made the waxing connection. I'm addicted to this look."

"All pictures need a frame," the stylist said.

"YES, they do. I'll be back here with my twenty bucks just as soon as these babies try to grow back in. No wonder people grow up and get real jobs. It's to pay for the eyebrows and haircuts. Look at us!"

Vere turned her head to the side, fluttered her lashes and wiggled her brows imitating Jenna in the mirror. "Yeah. Right? Eyebrows: A++!" Vere said, catching sight of Dustin's reflection.

She gave him an accusing look. "How long have you been standing there watching us be vain and ridiculous?"

Dustin came forward, his hands heavy with shopping bags. "Long enough. Like what you see, huh?" He had to force himself to keep his face impassive. At least the voice coming from this beautiful woman's mouth sounded like Vere's.

"What do you think?" Vere gave him a worried glance. "Love or hate?"

Hate. Hate. Hate.

Dustin faltered. He wished he could shout his feelings out to her. But also understanding this little make over would send her farther away from him than he could have ever imagined she would go. And tomorrow, at school, she would go far. He had to let her, and though it hurt, this was the only proper course for both of them.

"Vere. I love it. It's just what you wanted, and it fits you perfectly. Try to get used to it."

Like I will.

Vere smiled at his reflection as he continued, "This will stop Curtis in his tracks. There's going to be a full on line-up for you two tomorrow. It'll be a bloodbath. You two are so beautiful right now." He'd included Jenna in that statement, but his eyes had never left Vere's.

Jenna laughed. "Oh, do I wish, and thanks!"

Vere didn't say anything, but Dustin noticed the worried crease had left her forehead. That was answer enough.

She believed him, and that alone put a band aid on his aching heart.

"What's in the bags, shopper?" Jenna asked.

"What do you think I did with my time and your clothing sizes? I fixed your wardrobes."

"All that's for *us*? Did you rob a bank?" Jenna grinned.

Dustin could tell Vere was not pleased. Looking down at the huge mess of bags he realized he'd probably just drawn a lot of attention to himself with this deal.

Guys from Bakersfield might not have this much change to spare. "Yes. I robbed a bank. Of course not. I have a—a trust fund going to waste," he said using the carefree bravado he'd learned from Vere. "I decided I didn't want to argue with you two over who was paying for what, nor did I want to discuss fashion or tastes, because I am the boss of this makeover. Inside these bags you will find your futures as popular beauties. Down to a homecoming dress for each of you."

"Wow! Yay!" Jenna clapped her hands.

Vere chewed on her lip and tilted her head to the side.

"Dustin. This is too much."

Jenna spun her chair around and around with undisguised glee until the stylist stopped her. "This is awesome. I love you, Daddy Warbucks! But I'm not going to homecoming, remember?"

"Anything you don't like, take it back. The receipts are all there."

Dustin met Vere's troubled gaze and realized he had to get out of here. The stylist had finished spraying Vere with a fog of spray-gel. His thoughts drained out of him like water.

He sucked in a deep breath and just had to stop and stare all over again.

"That should do it for both of them," the stylist said. She handed him a receipt. Also to avoid arguments, he'd paid earlier on his way out to the shops.

"I'll get my mom to pay you back for most of this, Dustin. She's been offering to do this with me for years." Vere stood and peeled off the stylist's cape and placed it on the chair.

"Yeah, me too. I was due for a haircut," Jenna added.

"Whatever," Dustin managed to sound cool and collected but he was desperately aware his brain was about to shut down.

Vere's glorious hair, about four inches shorter now, and cut to frame her face, slid across her back and shoulders in a dry waterfall of sparkling gold highlights. The stylist hadn't added a lot of color, just enough to make Vere's brown eyes stand out and show off the green specks hidden in their depths.

They were definitely not hidden now.

Hell.

He sighed and pulled in a breath of nails. He thought he could handle being near Vere and quietly admire her from afar. But with her looking like this and wasting it all on Curtis, the friend thing was going to be impossible.

His heart hurt, everything hurt. This had gone too far.

He didn't think he could hang out with her any more, not

without causing a scene or making a fool out of himself. His lungs tightened as though they'd turned into a suffocating brace.

Vere, unaware of his terrible disquiet, got out her hair ties and quickly pulled the glowing, highlighted mass back into her bun. "There." She sighed with apparent relief and turned to face him with a smile. "That feels better."

"Good God!" Dustin accidently said that out loud.

It couldn't be helped. The highlights streaked across her crown and her newly shaped, arching eyebrows enhanced her usual pixie look to over-the-top gorgeous! Her bun was no longer a wild and out of balance cluster clump. This stunning, made-over bun had instantly framed her face with wisps of hair that were now too short to get caught in the rubber bands. A few longer, soft looking tendrils had dropped out, and now curled softly against the back of her neck.

"Wow," Jenna echoed his thoughts. She went on, "Vere. You can't even hide in your bun anymore. Now you look just like a Princess Barbie. Highest of all compliments."

Vere turned back to the mirror as though to analyze what they'd said, while Dustin mourned the loss of his cute, blushing gnome girl and her missing tumbleweed topper. There was no way Dustin would be at school tomorrow to watch her launch this look. He'd just developed a huge case of the heartbreak flu.

Jenna jumped out of her chair. "Now show me what's in those bags. I'm dying."

"Stay back. Just stay back!" Jenna froze. Dustin almost laughed because he'd meant those words for Vere who, wasn't even looking at him, or moving.

He figured he was only seconds from losing his mind.

Vere turned to him, surprised.

Dustin quickly gestured to the bags to cover his outburst. "Uh. You two will have to check out the loot on your own. I'm done with the mall. I have to get back for some—stuff. I've called Nan. She's meeting me out front in like...five minutes," he lied.

Shit. It's going to take her forever to drive down here. Where will I hide?

"Sorry, should have warned you," he added.

Vere raised her (now perfectly distracting) brow as though she sensed something was off.

Well it is way off! So! Way! OFF!

"Oh. It does feel like we've been here for hours," she said.

"Three hours and fourteen minutes, to be exact," he choked out, heart racing.

Shit. Why did I say that?

I sound like I'm going crazy.

Oh. Whatever. I am.

"One more thing—about the dresses," he tried to cover. "In case I forget." He couldn't drag his gaze away from Vere's.

"What?" Jenna asked, as she jumped up and down in front of the bags. "OMG. Dresses!"

Dustin broke Vere's gaze and forced his eyes to stay on Jenna. "The cream colored dress, I—uh—picked it for Vere. It's going to make her eyes glow. The sea-green one is yours, Jenna. It should do the same," he added, swallowing the lump in his throat.

He couldn't understand Jenna's reply. She'd dived squealing into one of the department store bags.

He didn't have to look up to know Vere had heard, though. Who cares? He felt like an utter fool.

A fool in love. Hell, that's what I am. A fool in love, with no ride home.

The lump returned to his throat. For the first time in a long time he noticed he'd forgotten to breathe.

Without another word he raised a silent hand to them and stalked out of the salon.

When Dustin finally made it home three hours later, he spent the evening alone in his room cleaning up. He decided to check his phone, but the drawer to his night stand was jammed.

The cardboard hair-color box and his old plane tickets from LAX to DEN were the culprits blocking his entry. He had press to down and tear the box in half to un-wedge the drawer. Staring at the shredded model's face in the bottom of his trash can, he read the words: 'black Italian coffee' to himself as he ran his fingers through his hair.

He hadn't had his own hair colored at the salon because he didn't want Jenna to question why he needed to do that.

Maybe tomorrow, he'd ask Aunt Nan to go get him a new box of this junk. He could color it again himself in the bathroom and be ready to go by Tuesday. Maybe. But more than anything, he simply didn't want to dye his hair anymore.

The only thing left in the drawer was his once beloved cell phone.

He plugged it into the wall and waited for it to get enough juice to power up. He snorted when he noticed his email box and the alerts that told him he now had over 32 new text messages and emails combined. At a glance it looked as though all of them had been sent by Martin over the weekend.

He was not going to read any of his suck-up, fake bullshit. Instead, he did what Martin had asked him not to do.

He called his mother's number directly. It was time.

Her voice mail clicked on without one ring. He hadn't expected her to answer. His mother was a call-screening queen.

Instead of hanging up, he listened like a starving person to the buttery, raspy sound of his mom's polite voice mail message.: 'Hi. You've reached Molly Kennedy. Please leave a message and I'll get back to you right away.'

When the phone beeped he spoke without thinking, "Uh. Mom. It's me. I'm doing all right. Wondering how you are. I—if you have any time—I'd sure like it if you came out here. It would be cool, you know, to see you. Nan would love it and—I miss you. I want to see you. To talk, face-to-face. I want to you know that I'm sorry. Sorry about everything and that I know you are, too."

When he finished, he hung up and unplugged the phone quickly. It was tempting to get into the emails and text messages, but he didn't want to feel worse than he already did. He knew somehow, all that unread crap would add to his angst.

Whatever was in there had come too late. At this point he truly didn't care about anything from his old world besides, fixing things between him and his mom and getting on with his life. On his terms.

Tomorrow he'd delete all of it without opening even one.

He placed the phone back and grabbed up his guitar. He flipped the amp to low volume, and played, making up yet another sad, sweet, song that he didn't write down.

He couldn't.

This one, like all the others, was about Vere and how she looked today, yesterday, and the first time he saw her.

How she made him feel.

The lyrics flowed into him as easily as rain falling from the sky. It was some of the best stuff he'd ever put together. He tried to talk himself out of his feelings, the pain in his heart, and ignore the word *love* altogether.

But as he played and played, letting the somber tones of the guitar fill the room, he sang everything he wasn't brave enough to utter in words. To himself, to his mom and to his soul.

He let his fingers wander the strings, and allowed his heart to soar all the way to loving Vere how he wasn't allowed to love her face to face. It wasn't enough, it would never be enough.

But it was something.

When his room grew dark, he knew he'd failed miserably once again at formulating a plan on how to fix everything. His stomach rumbled so he finally got up and went down to join Aunt Nan for dinner.

He would wait until after they ate to bring up how he thought he wasn't feeling so good. He'd sit with Aunt Nan and watch her favorite home makeover show. He'd mention how he felt sort of sweaty and dizzy.

He'd then go upstairs too early for bed.

He'd have it all set up, so when he didn't go to school tomorrow morning, Aunt Nan would believe him when he told her that he was sick and unable to leave his bed.

It wasn't that he was acting like a sore loser. That wasn't it.

He did feel sick, because his heart had crumpled into a ball hours ago. An event, he was now certain, had caused the thing to stop beating all together.

For real.

It's not going to fade away by morning that's for sure! And it's not going to get better watching Vere go after another guy.

It will take some damn time.

A damn, long time. With me, sick. In bed.

35: party pointers needed

Vere pelted up the stairs. She had ten minutes to brush her teeth and locate one giant ball of courage.

Dustin was coming over in ten—to *hopefully*—help her with her latest guy exposure coaching session. This lesson, if Dustin even agreed to it, was going to be a doozy.

It was the most important one of all.

Thank GOD Mom and Dad are out playing a tennis tournament this afternoon.

She stopped in front of the mirror and gulped as she reached for the toothbrush. Did she really have the courage to do this? She did. It was just Dustin. *Her Dustin McHugh.* She shouldn't be nervous to ask him anything. He'd said exactly that since their friendship started.

"Ask me anything, Vere," he'd said.

And she knew he'd meant it. He'd helped her with everything else along the way, why not this? If only she'd had more time to talk to him about her crazy plan. But she hadn't seen him all week. With the party she'd been invited to (along with Curtis and everyone who was *anyone*) looming in just a few hours she'd hit the *now-or-never* point!

Dustin had missed school Monday, Tuesday, and Wednesday. Early in the week she'd called over to Nan's place. Dustin had told her he was too sick to see her. Ordered her not to come over. She'd tried once, but Nan said he wouldn't even get out of bed.

On Thursday, Dustin was at school, but every time she caught sight of him, he seemed to be wandering off in the opposite direction.

She could swear the guy had grown deaf or something.

The same thing had happened Friday. She figured he was settling back into his classes. Catching up on missed work. Plus he'd started making other friends besides her. A point he'd made when she finally caught up to him Friday afternoon and he'd told her he was going to the movies with *other friends*.

It still stung a little that he hadn't asked her to come along, because almost an entire week had passed since they'd hung out. So much for them being such best friends, after all.

Vere reached for the dental floss. As she worked the floss into each tooth, she admitted that she was partly to blame for some of it. She'd had such a good week. Their make-overs had caused quite a stir. Vere and Jenna both felt as though they'd entered another world.

Dustin had sure known his stuff. They'd been flooded with so much attention that Vere had acted like a kid in a candy store, flirting and openly chatting with so many different guys she never would have spoken to before. It was fun to be so...*noticed*. So awesome to believe in herself and have real confidence!

By the end of the week, especially Friday afternoon, Vere had just wanted to pull on Charlie's old sweatshirt, clamp her hair into a bun, and return to her former invisible life.

Which is exactly what she'd done all last night and this long, Saturday morning.

It had been enough to rejuvenate her, and with the party looming she'd started to panic.

She thought about tonight—and her week with Curtis.

Since Monday, Curtis had gone sort of crazy on her. She'd loved that he liked her new look. There was also no question left in her mind that the guy had feelings only for her. To have *that* solidified felt great. He'd showered her with attention and compliments. He'd also staked his claim by glowering at any guy whom he thought might be flirting with her. Also a dream come true!

Only, the dream was not what she'd imagined it would be. All that cute knee tapping and the circles he made on her legs, and those smoldering strange looks had escalated a bit too much for Vere's liking. To the point it had started to make her feel creepy just thinking about it.

About him.

She assumed it was nerves and anticipation for the next level. How embarrassing that her next level was only kissing. Everyone else must be way past that—so she had no idea why she would even be afraid. It wasn't as if he were trying to grope up her shirt or anything. He'd been a gentleman. An annoying, loud one that made it clear what he wanted, but still. Maybe her nervousness was annoying him right back.

Either way, she couldn't shake a new feeling she had about Curtis. A feeling she couldn't even define. This feeling kept making her heart race every time he was near, but not in a good way. She'd sort of had the urge to actually ditch drama class because of it. Who ditched class because she was about to go to the *next level* with the boy of their dreams?

It was not like her to even consider that. As the week wore on, the urge to ditch drama class had grown. Curtis seemed to have turned into an octopus. He had grown extra hands, and they were always on her.

And while they were in front of everyone!

She would have to talk to him about the PDA thing, soon.

All of his touching and ogling and deflecting those darn hands had played a major part in why she'd felt so exhausted. She figured she would have to get used to those hands on some level if she was going to be his real girlfriend.

And she did want to be that, but only if he could tone it down.

She'd been invited to sit with Curtis at the *popular jocks and girlfriends of jocks* table in the lunchroom. Jenna had been included, too! Vere's blushing and shy attacks seemed to be quickly becoming a bad memory.

She hadn't turned red in days!

To top it all off, Kristen Hodjwick had been so nice them all week that it had kind of started freaking Vere out even more. Kristen had even invited Vere to the Saturday party she'd been planning. At her house.

As in tonight. As in—at Kristen Hodjwick's house! Unbelievable!

Vere hadn't hung out within a five-mile radius of Kristen since the day of the incident. Tonight was going to be so strange, but wonderful.

Because it means everything is in the past! And that I've got a future! Finally.

Curtis and Charlie had agreed to meet them there. Kristen's house was only one cul-de-sac over. Charlie would have the car so he and Curtis could make it back from some late afternoon scrimmage in time, and she and Jenna would walk to the party and drive home together.

Things had been pretty strange between Jenna and Charlie ever since Jenna's *marriage speech* up at the cabin. Today had been the first day Charlie and Jenna had gone from *dead silence* at school to *speaking a little*. Maybe it was all going to blow over and go back to normal between all of them.

She hoped so. She wanted everything to just feel normal, even between herself and Curtis. She had five hours and twenty-two minutes to get herself together.

It was an unspoken rule that going to this football party and meeting Curtis there would make or break their identity as a real, live public couple. Tonight, she expected at least once, to kiss Curtis. To stake her own claim, on her own guy!

How cool would that be?

The fact that he'd be taking her to homecoming the following weekend was not enough to make their relationship solidly noted. The kiss, in front of everyone, would get them both Facebook official.

Which they still were *not*! Because she refused to send him the 'relationship' request first, and so far, he hadn't sent one to her. *UGH Why?* Maybe he was waiting for tonight too. Because of their past, because of the incident, everyone would be watching. Double watching to see if she'd mess up.

Vere swallowed. Her heart raced in panic at the thought.

This is why she'd called Dustin to come over.

She'd decided she needed to have some sort of insurance against her flailing, kissing past so she wouldn't make an idiot out of herself in front of the entire world again.

She had to practice first. Get some exposure.

And she meant to beg Dustin to help her.

Vere giggled nervously at the thought. She giggled again. Who else could she ask or trust enough with this? Hopefully he would agree. He knew everything about her. He would totally understand her request. No one made her feel safer, or put her so at ease with strange, complicated guy issues.

And that's exactly what kissing was.

Strange, and complicated.

With Dustin, this topic would seem simple.

Vere sighed at the madness of it all and walked into her bedroom. She sat on the edge of her bed, listening for the doorbell. She swallowed another nervous giggle as she looked at her hands.

She prayed down to her toes that she would get through one kiss without sending her poor *BGF* to the emergency room.

36: just one peck

Dustin

"Kiss you? You want me to kiss you?" Dustin pulled off his glasses and all but choked on the green apple bite now lodged in the back of his throat. He coughed and paced the entire length of the Roth basement family room, working to dislodge the chunk of apple. When it broke free, he kept his face completely straight and turned to face Vere. "I thought you said this was something important."

He was grateful for the apple's crisp, tart juice because his entire mouth had gone sand-dry. He said nothing further, kept chewing, poker face on overdrive, and waited for her to continue.

Why in the hell did I agree to come over here?
She'd seemed so desperate on the phone.
She'd said please, and I can't resist her when she says that.
And damn, but I wanted to see her. So badly. That's why.

He'd fallen for the, *I just need a little help, it won't take long,* line. He'd sworn to stay away from Vere, but here he was. Undoing all of the hard work he'd done to try and get over her.

Vere's cheeks were bright red. He could tell she knew it was an utterly insane request, but her gaze held his. And was so earnest and hopeful.

Too damn hopeful.
Hell no, little friend. I can't play with you anymore.

"It is important. Kissing is really important. I'm a proven failure at it. I just want to be sure I have it under control before tonight."

Dustin tried to remain calm. He took another giant bite of apple. He had to keep this light. She couldn't be serious.

"I should have known something was up when you shooed Charlie out of here. Don't you feel bad lying to your own brother?"

Vere blinked at him as though startled. "I did not lie. I told him we were going to go over some pointers on how to get through this party. That is true. The part about how I didn't want him staring at me and making me feel all embarrassed is also true. So, I didn't lie. I need pointers, kissing pointers, and party pointers big time. And besides, he needs to get ready for his Saturday scrimmage."

"I've been to a ton of parties, I am happy to give pointers about that, but you've blown a fuse with the kissing request. Let it go. If you want some coaching on the obvious stuff we can do that, but only that, okay?"

"Obvious stuff. Okay." She breathed out, nodding comically. Obviously beyond nervous. "Like what do you mean?"

"First. Don't get drunk. Don't smoke anything."

"Duh. What are you, my dad? That's easy. I don't drink. We aren't even twenty-one. I seriously doubt anyone will be drinking at the Hodjwick house. And who smokes cigarettes any more? So gross."

Dustin shook his head. "You are so backwards. I wasn't talking about cigarettes, and if you truly believe no one will be drinking at a high school party on a Saturday night then you are too much of a baby to even leave your own house."

"Okay. You don't have to be so cranky," she shrugged. "Well, at least I hope there won't be drinking. How's that?"

"Clueless. Naïve, like you," he answered. He'd feel one thousand times better if he could just convince her not to go to this party. It was worth a shot, so he continued, "If you don't want to be drunk, avoid all beverages that taste and look like fruit juice or that are too good to be real. They could be spiked. The fact that you don't even know this stuff makes me recommend, again, that you don't go."

Vere folded her arms across her chest. Her cheeks had switched color a bit and glowed a lighter pink.

Dustin could tell it was from anger this time, not a blush. "Oh I'm going, buster. So, maybe I am naïve. *Fine*. It's my first party. I have to learn somehow. I'd rather you just tell me so I don't make any lame, humiliating mistakes. What else is on your *obvious* list?"

Dustin's mind spun. At least this conversation seemed to make her forget the fact that she'd just requested he kiss her. Worse, she'd asked him to kiss her in the same tone that she would ask to borrow a pen!

Her words rocketed around his skull so loudly he lost his train of thought, playing them over: *I was wondering if you would kiss me. You know? Just one time for practice—before I kiss someone real.*

What in the hell had she meant by that—someone real? Really?

Dustin scoured his thoughts for a few more obvious party rules, and hoped she couldn't detect that he was about to freak out.

"Hmm," he fronted. "You should never leave a drink unattended. Take it with you to the bathroom. If you forget, then pitch what's left, and start a new one. I mean it. Do that every single time. Also, along that same topic, make sure you always get your own drinks. Never, never, accept a drink from someone you don't completely trust, and even then—get your own drinks."

"Wow. Paranoid much? Maybe these rules are just for the big city." Vere scrunched up her nose. She distractedly pulled two hair bands out of her pocket and wound her unbound hair up into her bun.

He hadn't seen the bun all week. Thursday and Friday, when he'd been avoiding her, he'd noticed she'd worn her hair down every second. Probably for Curtis.

Dustin shook his head, amazed that she could still feel so

comfortable around him when he could hardly look at her without his skin wanting to catch fire. "You really should be watching more nightly news. Everything I'm telling you applies more to the suburbs and small towns than to the cities. This stuff is basic. How can you not know it?"

"I don't know. Just tell me all of it, and please don't forget the *why*, part. You know I have to know why."

Her right hand floated up in that unconscious manner he loved as she did a final check of her bun.

God, how I've missed her face. Her voice...The damn, cute bun.

Dustin had thought creating an entire week of distance between them would have curbed some of his feelings for her, but it hadn't. His craving for hanging around Vere seemed to have doubled. He stared at the soft line of her neck and watched as the freshly cut wisps of hair danced around her brow.

He vowed to keep his voice steady and sarcastic. No need for her to know her power over him. "You keep your drink with you because, *infant*, it's pretty easy to slip drugs or anything at all into someone's drink. It happens all the time. The girls get super drunk, catatonic, whatever, depending on the drug of choice, and well...you know the rest."

Vere raised her eyebrows up high. "Okay. Got it. Keep my drink with me. Check. Anything else on that level that I should know?"

He took another bite of his apple, chewing it while he contemplated what to say to her next.

"Never follow a guy upstairs to where the bedrooms are located unless you are fully prepared to test out the beds, or see other people testing the beds."

"As if I would."

"You might. The cajoling guy lines sound like this: *Hey it's so noisy down here, let's go find a room where we can talk.*"

"Really? That's a line? I guess I would be tempted if a guy I liked said that to me."

Dustin laughed. "You especially would fall for that one, Miss Chatty. Guys know girls love to talk. Teenage guys who have had a couple of beers at a party, even the sober ones, don't really ever want to talk. Get it? *Ever.*"

"Jeez. I get it."

"It's not only the upstairs rooms that are dangerous. Stay out of dens, laundry rooms, back porches and parked cars. Okay?"

"Okay. Got it. Stay in the crowd, avoid all quiet rooms, clutch my drink, and don't trust anyone." Vere giggled.

The sound of her sweet laugh made his heart race uncontrollably. He couldn't help but throw her a small smile. He pictured her in a giant sweatshirt and baggy shorts, clutching a can of soda and shooting frightened daggers at everyone in the room. All the while, she'd be wondering *why* half of the football team seemed to be dizzy and acting funny.

When he looked at her, *really looked*, he knew the confident beauty in front of him did not match the Vere he was thinking about one bit. She wore a fresh white blouse open at the neck. The classic style showed off her delicate collarbones, and he couldn't take his eyes off the gentle pulse beating at the base of her throat.

A lace topped cami all but winked at him near where she'd stopped buttoning the blouse near the top. It winked again as though to show off how perfectly it was accenting the curve of her oh so perfect...

Hell! Dude. Stop yourself. She's doing you in, right here. Right now. She's going to have to fight the guys off her tonight. Other guys. THE lucky, bastard, suck-ass, OTHER guy! Shit.

But he couldn't seem to look away until he admired the rest of her. Her short black skirt looked hot—lightly flared every time she moved. Some see-through fabric at the hem showed off her long, slim legs. She'd worn her brand new black flats that matched too. The entire outfit was adorable. Not too dressy, but it said she was definitely going somewhere special.

The look had also been chosen by him.

To help her. He shook his head, trying to clear it.

To help her.

Stick to the task. Be this girl's friend. It's what she wants...

"You look great, Vere," he said, heart finally sincere. "You're simply beautiful," he added before he could catch himself.

She blushed fire red, and he quickly tried to recover with what he hoped was a bored looking shrug, "I mean, you were beautiful before. I guess I'm saying that I love how you put the outfit together. And tonight...all should work out fine. It's going to be what you want. Perfect. I'm sure of it."

"It's all because of you," she said, her cheeks faded to that adorable pink tint that always tightened his chest. "The homecoming dress is over the top, by the way. Don't know how I'm going to wear it next weekend with a straight face."

"What do you mean?" Dustin was slightly offended. "The dress is gorgeous."

"Gorgeous yes, but it's almost too nice, too elegant for me. I don't know how I will ever pull it off."

"Give me a break. There's nothing you can't pull off. Nothing," his voice cracked.

"Thanks," she said, her gaze met his, full of sincerity and love. But he could tell, it was the lame-ass, sucking, *best friend* kind of love.

Damn you, girl. Don't look at me that way!

"Um. You know I couldn't have made it this far without you," she added. "Not even close."

"Mhmm." He covered a heart-heavy sigh by bitting into his apple again. Turning it and munching it as if he were starving, and this apple might be the most important thing in the world to him right now.

He glanced down at his plaid shirt and crap canvas pants, not missing the irony of his own lame outfit and current bad attitude, next to Vere's shining perfection.

He would give anything to go to that party. To try to mess the whole night up. How he hated the thought of Curtis even touching her.

And tonight, it seemed as if Vere was going to let him do way more than that.

Dustin finished off his apple and tossed the core across the room into a corner can. "Basket!" He grinned, but his cheeks killed from the effort. He upped it to the fake-retainer-super-smile. Only, he felt a bit stupid when she didn't giggle like she normally did.

He realized he hadn't put his retainer back in yet.

He fished in his pocket for the damn thing, grabbed his glasses off the side table as he continued, "Anyhow, good luck. I'm late and...stuff," he lied. "Gotta get ready for going...uh... to my own places."

He made his way toward the stairs, shaking his head at his lameness.

"No wait. What about the kissing thing." Vere's voice sounded so desperate. "You said you'd help."

He was not going to look at her face. "You can handle that on your own. Like I said, I'm out."

"That's just it. I can't. I can't handle it and you know it. Just one peck, please. I have to know if I'm going to freak. What if I can't do it? What if when the time comes I mess it all up? I have to know. Please. One kiss."

He should have kept walking.

He should have bolted up those tan, carpeted stairs like his feet were on fire. Instead, he froze and truly considered it.

One kiss. One kiss. One kiss.

If he agreed, he would be an absolute ass.

And an idiot. That much was obvious.

But he'd been an ass before, and an idiot ever since he let himself fall in love with this amazing girl.

Why stop the stupid-train now?

His heart rate sped up. He took off his ball cap and dropped his retainer and glasses into it. His gut twisted with doubt. Worry. Excitement.

She asked me for this. SHE ASKED ME...

Hell, she's begging me. And it's her first kiss.

Considering the situation...is that such a bad thing to want to be a part of? To simply want to BE Vere Roth's first kiss?

And oh, how I want it. Her.

He knew Vere well enough to understand she'd get all sappy about her first kiss. Maybe not today but eventually.

A first kiss was something everyone remembered.

Something priceless.

She'd think about it. Pull out the memory and realize he was connected to her heart for all time.

Even if he didn't deserve this kiss—even if it was a kiss stolen out from under another guy—he didn't care anymore. He knew he'd have this one, special *forever-kiss* between him and Vere. And since he wasn't going to get anything else, it would have to be enough.

A memory for him, as well. One that nothing—no one— could ever take away.

It felt wrong, but so, damn right.

He vowed to make this kiss as good as it gets.

37: messing everything up: a++

VERE

Dustin set his stuff on the small table next to the couch.

Vere blushed furiously when he appeared to be studying her as though he waited for her to change her mind.

Darn. So much for keeping my cool. I am begging an extremely attractive guy to kiss me, after all. A blush or two is not out of order, even if we are best friends. And I'm not changing my mind! He can make any face he wants to try to discourage me.

I need this kiss.

"Wow. Your hair. It's almost blond again," she said. His hair had grown out some, and with the dark brown rapidly fading away it was the exact color of a lion's mane. A stunning effect combined with his laser-beam eyes.

"Yeah. I—haven't had the chance to darken it again." He shot her sort of a pained look and crossed his arms. "Let's don't talk about silly stuff. Let's just do this. How would you like me to set up the kiss?"

"Uh—on the lips is good? You know...just a standard kiss." She shrugged.

Jeez. This is more awkward than I'd imagined.

Is he hiding a smile? If he laughs right now, I will die.

"Duh. I figured that."

"Ugh. What do you mean, then? *See?* I can't do this. I'm a total mess."

He frowned and shook his head. "I mean we'll have to set the stage. How would you like it to be? Sitting, standing, inside, outside? Have you pictured how this is going to go?"

Vere blinked. "Do people think it through? I thought it was just supposed to happen."

"Guys tend to pre-plan a good first kiss. It makes it easier.

Some basic kiss moments are easy to predict. Like, after the date in the car. Or, the classic teen TV show ending: behind the football bleachers. Or, the famous old-school one: kissing the girl at the front door just before the dad turns on the light. You know."

"You've done that? Planned it? Kissed girls on a porch?"

"Well, not me. I've never actually had the need to plan one. Usually, I'm just approached, or attacked. Whatever you want to call it. But I can imagine that if I *were* on the girlfriend track, my first kiss would require serious planning. I'd want it to be completely unforgettable."

"Oh. That's nice. It's nice to know guys are so...*nice.*"

"Don't say that." He glowered, his gaze unreadable and dark.

"Nice. Nice. Nice. It's so fun to taunt you." Vere smiled as he made another face. She just had to laugh, and so did he, finally.

Her blushing had stopped. They'd returned to their normal banter, giving her courage to move forward. "Okay. Well, since you're the guy, and you say guys plan it, then, let's just go through a typical scenario?"

"Yeah. Yeah. I think I've got it, but at least choose the pretend timing of it all—so I can make the rest up."

Vere paced nervously behind the length of the couch facing their basement entertainment center. She was having a difficult time looking up at him, because he seemed really tall all of a sudden. "Okay. I can give you a starting point. Let's just say this will be an 'end of the date' type kiss. I like the idea that it will be dark. You decide from there. In the pretend car, or on the pretend front porch." Her cheeks were burning as she went on, "But, again, always dark. So when I turn a bunch of colors he won't notice so much."

She stalked across the huge open part of the room and flicked the lights to low.

"Why would anyone care? It's so cute when you blush,"

Dustin said, following her around the back side of the couch.

"It is not. I look stupid, and it gives me furnace-face. And you set it off again. This whole thing is too embarrassing." Vere pushed herself up onto the high back of the couch and let her legs dangle as she kicked her feet into it.

She still had not been able to meet his gaze. "Maybe you're right," she muttered, kicking the couch harder. "I shouldn't have asked you to do this. I'm sorry. God. Is your stomach still all messed up? I haven't seen you all week and now I'm acting insane and—"

"Don't talk yourself out of it now," he interrupted. "I'll walk you through it, so it won't be scary." Dustin came and stood in front of her. She stilled her legs so she wouldn't kick him.

He didn't seem so tall now that she was sitting up higher.

His kind, low voice had calmed her. When she darted a glance at his face, he seemed so sincere.

"Okay," she managed. "Well...how do we proceed?"

"First, let's go back to imagining our perfect date. We've had a blast at the party. We danced a little, but mostly hung out on the crowded back patio, sitting off to one side, holding hands and talking. Hours of just you and me, talking about anything and everything until we forgot we were even at a party."

"Oh. Sure. I love that. I really do." She smiled, liking the way his eyes crinkled on the sides when he smiled back.

Dustin picked up her hand and turned it over. He let his fingers slide between hers and held it exactly how he'd held it when they'd been swimming in the lake. The side of his mouth going up in a little grin. "What do you know? We talked so long that your curfew snuck up on us. What time would that be?" His voice had somehow floated over her and into her.

"Eleven." Vere swallowed. She could picture the moment. She closed her eyes for a second and built the scene. He made it all sound so great...being lost in a crowd...holding hands like this. And his hand was so gentle.

"Okay." He met her gaze. "Let's do this. It's 10:52 PM. I've driven you home and I've been hoping all night for the chance to kiss you on your front porch. Good?"

She nodded. "And I'm nervous."

God. Really nervous.

She went on, "Because the date went so well, and I'm expecting this kiss, maybe? Like I'm *hoping* for one. And I want you to ask me out again."

"Yeah. I'm nervous, too, a little." His voice had dropped. "It's our first kiss, after all." He reached over and smoothed a wisp of escaped hair behind her ear.

Her knees bumped into him and she had to grab onto the couch to keep from toppling backwards. "I—uh—won't have the bun at the party." Vere wrinkled her nose, but when she glanced up he was staring at her hair and her heart did a huge freakish flip. "Should I take it out?"

"I love the bun. Leave it. That detail shouldn't matter anyway because at the end of the date, just before I kiss you, I should be looking at your lips."

Oh God. He's staring at my lips.

"Right. I'll watch for that. The lip looking sign. I think I've done that myself once or twice even. But it never led to a kiss. I'll try to practice longing-lip-looks in the mirror a ton before I go."

He laughed low and ran a finger along the top of her mouth. His touch sent shivers of sparkles down the back of her neck. "You have heart shaped lips in a heart shaped face. Has anyone ever told you? This one—this top lip alone—could drive a guy out of his mind?"

"No. Don't be silly." Vere felt the blush tingle down to her toes. "You're breaking my concentration. Should I stare at your lips the whole time, or should I close my eyes, or what?" She was now officially freaking out. Vere gripped the top of the couch even tighter.

"What are you doing with your hands? Why are they there?" he asked, stepping back slightly.

"I'm worried I might deck you. I'm—sort of off balance and screaming inside, if you must know."

He smiled, his bright blue gaze warm and, thankfully, not judging her at all.

"Try this. Put your hands on my shoulders, or around my neck. Then you won't be able to hurt me. Just in case you start to flail around."

How in the world can he appear so relaxed?

Vere pulled in a deep breath. "Good idea. My hands on his shoulders or neck. Got it."

She let go of the couch to reach for him but lost her balance.

He stepped in closer and gently placed his arms around her waist. He stood between her knees, and felt suddenly way too close to her.

"Thanks for not laughing at me again. It helps." The tingle in Vere's cheeks hit double high. She ignored it and grabbed at his shoulders, trying to keep her balance without looking too much like a dork. Dustin's shoulders were too wide for her to find a stable grip so she held onto his upper arms instead. "How's this?" She glanced up.

"Much better. For now."

She took another deep breath and nodded. "This feels right to me. Is it feeling okay for you?"

"Yeah. We've got this part." His voice had turned husky and his smile somehow reached into her soul.

"Stop that smile. You are so always showing off without your retainer."

"And you're so always jealous of my assets. Now, where were we?"

Vere felt so weird just grabbing onto him like this. "I'm hands on arms, staring at lips." She gulped. "You were staring at my lips back. And I was wondering if I should close my eyes."

Vere couldn't help but stare at *his* lips all over again, and her heart did another flip. They were so full, and gorgeous—AND LIPS—and they were going to kiss her—and she was actually looking forward to it.

Pre-kiss embrace: A++ AND ONE HUGE OMG.

"So...should I? Close my eyes, or not?"

Dustin took in a long breath and glanced at the ceiling. "Right. Should you close your eyes? You'll have to decide that as I go along. Some of kissing has to be spontaneous. Are you ready?"

He tightened his arms around her and she was overcome with a strange, terrible shy attack. "Ready," her voice wavered.

When he brought his face close to hers she dropped her chin and stared at her shirt.

The kiss didn't happen.

Worse, she could no longer look up.

At least she hadn't knocked him out. And at least she hadn't completely flipped. For the most part this was a total win because she wasn't turning purple or blabbing like a fool. Nothing like that.

He unhooked one of his hands from around her waist and trailed his finger down her cheek until it stopped at her chin. He tilted her face back up until his gorgeous, light-blue gaze met hers. His face was inches from hers now.

The guy was just too perfectly made.

Why do I feel like I can't breathe? I'm sure that's normal. I'm sure that's normal. Just hold still. Don't hit him. This is all normal...

She remembered that Curtis had done this move on her once, but it hadn't at all felt this gentle. Her heart hadn't felt aching inside either.

But why does my heart hurt so badly all of a sudden? Worse, do my stupid eyes feel like they are going to well up with tears right now?

"Vere." Her name sounded perfect, rolling off his whisper. "Do you have any idea how beautiful you are?"

She shook her head. "Please—don't make me blush. Not now. I'm trying to be really serious."

"You—we—don't have to do this, you know," he said, his voice concerned, while his gaze seemed to sweep her eyes as though he'd caught on she might be starting to cry. "Hell. We probably shouldn't..."

He knew her too well. And he was too, darn nice.

If she couldn't kiss this beautiful, very nice and safe guy, she would never be able to kiss anyone. She doubled her resolve. "No. I want to. It's just—will you kiss me first, like, all the way? I don't know what to do, okay?"

"Sure." He gave his head a slight shake but his smile warmed her down to her toes. "But...I want you to know that I'm not sure what to do anymore either. Not with you."

She could hear his usual self-deprecating tone on the edge of his voice, but was too nervous to wonder what he'd meant.

It felt right to close her eyes then, so she did. She wanted to hide from the intensity of his gaze. She managed to hold her seat on the back of the couch, and she forced herself to not drop her chin or turn away.

She hoped to heaven she didn't look too stupid as she half puckered and waited.

His hands, ever gentle, had moved up silently under her chin, then touched her along both cheeks.

She instinctively leaned forward, and when his mouth kissed only her upper lip first, it surprised her.

But it felt warm, safe, soft and so sweet. Wonderful.

He pressed his lips harder, lower. Taking both of her lips against his with more tentative pressure.

She pressed back, and he deepened the kiss.

Sparkles shot straight out the back of her neck, down to her toes, and right out the top of her head!

OMG. I'm kissing a guy. And he tastes like a fresh Granny Smith apple! And it's...mmm...feels so...wow...

His hands left her cheeks as his arms came fully around her in a real embrace, and her arms went easily around his back. His body pressed into hers and the smell of his awesome fresh-soap smell surrounded her—while their lips moved gently and sweetly together.

It sent her over the top of any preconceived expectations.

This rocks.

Kissing: No grade high enough. Simply fantastic!

Her heart danced. By now it had performed thousands and thousands of floating butterfly flips. Apples became her new favorite food. Her arms were covered in goose bumps and the butterflies moved to a full riot all through her stomach and lungs.

She opened her eyes and risked a glance at his beautifully sculpted face, and then stared at his half smiling lips, wondering how something as simple as lips could make her feel this amazing.

She smiled up at him and met his gaze.

He pulled back slightly and gave her a strange, worried look. "What? Not good?"

She didn't even care if he thought she was a total freak. Her smile turned into a wide grin. She could not have stopped smiling for anything at that moment.

"What? No. It was perfect. Can we do another? Just one more—to get the lip placement thing figured out?"

Not waiting for him to answer, she leaned in all on her own and placed her lips right back onto his. She opened her mouth a little and pushed out her tongue and flicked it against his smile. Apple-flavored smiles!

He gasped and she could feel him grow tense.

God. Maybe that wasn't done.

Maybe she should have asked first.

She pulled her tongue away and tried the regular kissing thing again. She'd *so* seen this a thousand times on the big screen, and now she was doing it. And that apple flavor was beyond anything she'd ever imagined!

Bonus tingles.

No wonder all that flavored lip gloss junk flew off the shelves.

He groaned and finally kissed her back. The movement of his lips was a bit stronger this time.

She opened her mouth slightly under his gentle pressure to do so. His tongue darted between her lips, swirled around her mouth and then back out.

WOAOOH...

That was so weird, but nice!

French kissing on kiss number two!

Not bad. Why had Jenna called it disgusting last year?

So...freakishly awesome.

Feeling courageous, she decided to copy his French kissing move to give it a try on him. She tilted her mouth to the side and let her tongue dash into his mouth. His lips moved so softly against hers and his arms pulled her closer. She had this sensation they were both actually breathing the exact same air at the same time.

It's possible I'm a total kissing natural!

It didn't take long before Vere's head spun in wild circles all over again. She relaxed, letting herself be swept away.

She turned into water, fire, heat. A person she'd never met before. She held onto him as tightly as she could because her spine had melted. Vere couldn't focus on anything specific beyond the absolute perfect feeling of being in these exact arms, locked in this perfect, endless kiss with his warm, gentle hands working their way up her waist, lighting fires wherever they touched.

They kissed and kissed and kissed and kissed until the room spun farther out of focus.

Until he stepped quickly away, turning his back. "God. I'm sorry," he said, as he ran his hand through his hair. He did not turn back. "I totally lost control."

His breathing was as rough as hers.

Vere was glad he wasn't looking at her, because the sudden loss of contact and the absolute explosions going off in her mind made her topple backwards onto the length of the couch.

Classic.

I do not even care.

I'll never care about anything again...I will just lie here forever not caring.

She swung her legs around straight and lay there flat on her back and stared, still disoriented, at the slow turning ceiling fan. She heard his voice as though it was coming from far away.

"Vere. Did I knock you over? Shit. I'm so sorry! Did I scare you or anything?"

"Sorry for what?" she breathed out dreamily, returning to real consciousness. "Kissing is awesome! And of course you didn't scare me. How could you?"

He came around to the front of the couch and dropped onto his knees beside her. His expression seemed tortured. "I've had a lot of kisses but...never one that has felt like that."

"What do you mean? Was I a total pro compared to all the others?" Vere rolled onto her side and looked at him, still feeling as though she had no bones in her entire body.

"No. Of course not." He shook his head, laughing a little. "You were a disaster at first, if you want a real critique. But then, you figured out the tongue thing. So...then, yes. I award you instant pro-status."

She scrunched her mouth. "Hey. You could lie a little if you want. I didn't notice anything wrong at the start. But...well, wow. Sorry if I wasn't so good at it."

"Vere. You were perfect, even when you didn't know what you were doing. Perfectly cute and—*shit*—what I mean is, that kiss, you and me, what happened there was something else. Something special. Didn't you feel it?"

"I don't know. How many times do I have to say I liked it? Are you fishing for more compliments?"

He moved closer and stared into her eyes as though searching for something. His intense gaze had returned, and it was making her nervous. She hardly recognized him suddenly, but his look also made her feel like she should kiss him again.

But that would be totally inappropriate, wouldn't it?

Class is over, Vere, DUH.

"No. I'm serious. I wasn't going to say anything to you, but after that kiss, I have to at least try." Dustin swallowed.

"Say what? Try what?"

"I'm in love with you."

Her heart clenched. "What? Don't joke. Not about that."

"I'm talking head over heels, down on my knees, from the bottom of my heart, *IN* love, with you, Vere. That kiss blew me away. I know you felt something too—something more for me. Don't you?"

Vere sat up. Her head spun in confusion, and her limbs felt suddenly shaky. "How can you say that? There's no way you're in love with me. We just kissed, that's all. It was great, but it can't be love. Jeez."

"I think it is. I've felt this way about you well before we kissed. I wasn't going to tell you because of Curtis, and because I'm leaving soon. I didn't want things in our friendship to get all messed up."

"Well, they're messed up now." Vere rolled her eyes.

He had to be joking.

"You set it all off. You asked me to kiss you!"

"Yeah, well you've just added to it! MAJOR."

"Believe me. I'm totally sincere. I know I might have waited too long to bring it up. But...I won't be able to live with myself if I don't at least try to convince you of my feelings. Not after that kiss. Not after how it's rearranged my whole heart."

"I think you've lost your mind." She shook her head.

"Give me a chance. Don't go after Curtis. He's not right for you. Besides, how can you even think about him now?"

"Easy. Because I was thinking about him *before* that kiss. It's why I called you over to *help me*, remember?"

"Yeah, but what are you thinking now? The kiss didn't change your mind? At least give you some sort of doubt?" His cheeks had started to turn a little pink.

Her brows shot up. Way UP.

The guy is pulling his own blush! He's serious.

Vere didn't know what to feel or to think, so she got angry instead. "But you're Hunter Kennedy! *The* Hunter Kennedy. As if you totally forgot that part. Hello? You sell out entire football stadiums? People scalp your front-row tickets for thousands of dollars? You wouldn't have even looked twice at me three weeks ago. And you've said it to me more than once. Remember? Because I sure do!"

He sighed and shook his head. His gaze wavered but did not once leave her face. "Yeah, but you know me as Dustin McHugh. And I haven't stopped looking at you or wanting to be near you since the moment I first met you. How about that?"

"That was because Mom and Nan *made* us hang out. Then, *yes*, we became friends. That's all. You made that clear." She threw her arms wide. "Dustin McHugh—*he is*—*you are*—my best friend. *Ugh.* I do know that you are one of the best friends I've ever had." She raised her voice in total frustration. "That's why we hang out. That's why I called you and trusted you with THIS. That's why we can talk so easily, about everything. You're nice to me and I'm nice back. We're friends. Friends play nice. It can't be love."

"Don't call me that. And I'm not playing," he shouted back. "I'm in love. With you. Plain and simple. And I know you feel something for me. Otherwise, that kiss would not have gone down like it did."

"Well it's not like I have any comparisons!" Vere stood up, pushed past him, and walked back to pace around the couch. She felt like she needed some distance between them. "How can you say any of this? You know I like Curtis. And since—before—forever. You and I have only shared a few weeks and two kisses."

"It was way more than two kisses. I think you want the wrong guy." He stood and faced her. She could swear his beautiful, low voice had trembled.

Her heart wrenched into a ball. "But I can't want you. I don't even know who you are. If I feel anything for you beyond friendship—or if you feel anything for me—then it can't be real."

He threw up his own hands. "It is real. I know it is. Why would you say it isn't? Can't you just try to play this out?"

Jeez. He totally didn't get it.

"Play it out with *who*?" she asked softly. "I only know bits of Hunter Kennedy. And Dustin McHugh is a guy we made up together. A character. Like from a book. The kissing was great. I'll admit it till I die. But you know you have major skills in that area. So there is no way we both felt something like *love* during that kiss." Her heart twisted again. "No way. Because as much as I don't know who you are, I have no clue what *love* even is!"

"You're lying," he said. "You have to be."

"I'm not." Vere reached up to tighten her bun. It had sprung loose from all the shouting, not to mention her back-dive off the couch.

I'll call his bluff. Then he'll see.

"Fine," she said. "I know for a fact that Hunter Kennedy would never feel anything for a girl like me, ever. It's been said more than once. And if Dustin McHugh says he's in love with me, what does that mean? For me? Dustin McHugh is fictional, and he's made it publicly clear that I'm not his type either. So where does that leave me? Seriously. Think about it."

His expression grew dark. "If you truly believe that. If you have no feelings for me beyond normal *affection*—then kiss me again. Go on. Kiss me again, look me in the eye and tell me you feel nothing. I dare you."

38: for the sake of practice

VERE

Vere tossed her head and shot him her best eye roll. "Fine. For the sake of practice, I'll do it. You'll see I'm right. You just got caught up in the moment, that's all it is." Vere marched over to him.

How hard could this be?

She paused and stared up at his very perfect face and then fixed her eyes on his lips.

Sadly, that's when her mind went into coma.

She fixated on them.

Whoa. Was this their third kiss? Maybe this was their thirteenth kiss.

She'd sort of lost count on that second round. Maybe he was right that they'd already kissed more than twice. How did one divide up a really long kiss—like when did one kiss start and another end?

Vere swallowed and made a face at him. He didn't even smile, or flinch or glare.

His entire face was now totally unreadable.

Feeling ridiculous because he'd been staring down at her this whole time, acting like some cold piece of marble. And she'd been staring up at him for like two hundred minutes, mesmerized by his lips!

Like a weirdo.

Despite what HE said, officially, for the purpose of making a list about this someday in my journal—I count this as my third kiss.

First was...the first. Him kissing me.

And the second, was all me kissing him back.

And now, this 'challenge kiss'. As in US, kissing each other.

For the sake of practice!

♥ 366 ♥

Time for your recovery, Vere.

Say something! Say something or run.

Vere took a deep breath, closed her eyes for a quick second and forced out some words. "First place the hands."

Great. I sound like a robot.

Dustin arched a brow and folded his arms across his chest as though he meant to make this difficult on her.

Play it cool. You can so, do this.

"I said, first the hands." This time her voice sounded a bit more normal. She pointed to his folded arms. "On my shoulders if you please, so you don't hurt me."

Dustin put his hands out and clamped them woodenly onto her shoulders. "Do you want me to close my eyes?"

Now who was the robot?

The guy had one hell of a poker face. She wished for some of that talent.

"Yes," she answered. At least if she blushed, he wouldn't see. "Now lean down a bit, you're too tall."

Obediently he closed his eyes and bent forward.

Vere felt an anxiety attack setting in. Her heart beat so loudly she was sure he could hear it. She felt pure relief that his eyes remained closed. It gave her the time to compose herself and paste on her own poker face.

Or pucker face. UGH. CONCENTRATE.

She'd show him this was just a plain old kiss and nothing more.

The *feelings* part was *so* not for them.

They were friends. He'd realize it soon enough.

Since his arms were already on her shoulders, she gingerly wrapped hers around his waist and pressed her lips deeply into his. She went for it—pressure, lips half open after the initial contact. To stay on track, she told her tongue to search for that apple taste again.

Yep. There it is, though sadly...it's fading.

She thought she might be doing all right when his mouth opened in response and he started kissing her back. Big time.

His grip relaxed on her shoulders, and he pulled her into his embrace.

She couldn't help but move even closer after that, because he had this cool way of half supporting her weight with his arms. She relaxed and allowed her hands to trail into his hair.

His arms felt so wonderful wrapped around her like this. She tried to keep her head straight.

Love. Special feelings. As if.

Her last conscious thoughts were that all guys probably had big, strong arms that would reach just like this around her. And soft lips that felt like they gave as much as she took. That had to be a normal thing too. Of course, *how amazing a guy smelled* had nothing to do with *special feelings.*

Fresh soap was simply a smell. NOT a feeling. Even if it smelled perfect. Absolutely perfect...

Vere was lost in the kiss. She floated all the way to the moon and back this time. She pulled away to take a breath and almost fainted because he was suddenly kissing the side of her ear, and her temple. Then he kissed a soft line down her neck.

Whoa. Neck kissing rocked.

She had to try it too, so she gently kissed the hollow spot where his heart beat between his collarbones. He had incredibly soft skin—just there.

She felt his hands moving all over her back and slowly up her waist. God but she loved how his hands felt on her...

What was happening? She had to make this stop but she didn't want to.

Just one more...one more...so he would see...so he would understand...so she could know for sure...

She stretched up onto her toes and kissed his beautiful mouth again.

Softly.

Her entire core flamed against him while their tongues found each other yet again. This time she sort of knew him. The weird awkwardness had disappeared.

It—he—*everything*—felt completely right.

She had no concept of how long they kissed after that, but possibly forever had passed them both by.

He straightened, looked down into her eyes and let her go.

Vere stepped back. Her heart felt heavy and her gaze riveted on the pulse beating in his neck. She had no air left in her body. Her knees shook, and the butterflies from her stomach had flown to block her vision and flooded her head with noise.

Any clear thoughts were now impossible.

He said, "If you have nothing to say, I'll go."

Confused and shaken, a lump had formed in the back of her throat. Speaking was now impossible, could he not see that?

She needed time to think.

How was she supposed to know how to define any of this when she'd had no other kisses than his?

So, YES, fine. I felt something wonderful. Special.

Did that make it love? Was one kiss reason enough for both of them to lose their minds and try to change everything in their whole lives? Her heart ached at that thought.

No. He's Hunter Kennedy. I don't even know him, and he can't be serious about a girl like me...he even said so...many times.

Vere knew she needed to be practical for both of them. She operated on facts, and facts would get her through this. She struggled to keep her voice from breaking. "I have to stand by what I said before. Dustin McHugh is not real. We both know it's true. I don't know what else to say to you as Hunter Kennedy," she finished with a helpless shrug. "I just don't..."

His eyes looked funny, different. They'd somehow turned a darker blue. Before she could look again he'd put on the glasses and his hat.

"Why did I think you, of all people, wouldn't use me like

everyone else?" His voice sounded tight, horribly cold.

"You offered. I didn't—"

"Didn't you?" He buttoned his retainer in to his shirt pocket. "Whatever. It's for the best."

Vere glanced at the ceiling.

No more words could come out right now. If any fresh air touched the back of her throat, she'd start crying. His comment was only fair—since they were dealing in facts.

I did just use him. I suck.

"You were right about the kisses. I lost my head after such a long, dry spell. I take it all back. There's nothing there, like you said. We're even now. You helped me. I helped you. The friendship thing is over, though. Thanks for the—fun." He pulled his hat down low and glared at her before turning his back. "Good luck with Curtis."

"What the *HELL* is going on in here?" Charlie's voice exploded into the room.

Vere looked up and gasped, surprised at her brother's intrusion. The cold air blasted her throat, making tears fill her eyes. She struggled to hold them back.

Charlie stood at the base of the stairs with his arms crossed. "Dude. Don't think I don't know you just made a move on my sister. I saw you kissing her."

"How long have you been standing there?" Dustin flicked a sneer back at Vere. "Another Roth kid spying on private conversations. Chronic, that," he said, his voice loaded with pure contempt.

Vere's soul crumbled into bits. She locked gazes with Charlie and shook her head in warning. She would not survive another fight between them. Thankfully Charlie didn't punch him.

"Move aside. I didn't do anything Vere didn't beg me for. Ask her. Or, maybe you approved this part of her ridiculous plan."

Dustin shoved Charlie out of the way and took the stairs two at a time, not once looking back.

"What did you see?" she asked, after they both heard the back door slam.

"Only the two of you, full on, making out, *Vere!* What was that all about? I took off to be polite, but when I didn't hear anything I came back in time to witness the end of your little fight. I'm glad you were fighting and not something else, or that guy would be dead right now. What were you thinking? Did you really ask him to kiss you?"

"Yeah. I thought it would be good...exposure. Practice?" Her voice wavered as one tear spilled out.

"Holy crap! You're nuts, you know that?"

She nodded. More tears crept out.

"What about Curtis? What if he finds out you kissed another guy?"

"Curtis and I are still on. Nothing's changed. I sort of did it for him." She winced. "I was being stupid." Vere cried openly now. "Don't tell. Don't tell *anyone.* Please."

"More crying? That guy has turned you into a crazy person. Since when do you cry all the time?" Charlie yelled, but his hug said he loved her. He kept his arms around her as she sniffled into the front of his shirt. He added, "I'll bash the pop-star anyway, if you want me to. Just for making you cry. AGAIN."

"Oh, shut-up. You will not. He didn't make me cry. I'm just crying because—I don't know. Because I like to cry." Vere sobbed again, now gripping on to Charlie for dear life. She let her tears flood.

"Whatever. That guy is officially on my hit list," Charlie muttered, awkwardly patting her back now. "He's not long for this world, that's for damn sure."

Vere wiped the tears from her face and looked up. "Just stay out of it, Charlie. He was helping. I swear. This is all my stupidity—my fault. I think I led him on. Leave it alone. *I'm,*

I'm, I'm, just..." She gasped for breath and started sobbing again. "*Fine!*"

She wished she could explain what Hunter had said to her. Tell Charlie about Hunter's life. How he'd been so depressed and alone. How he'd said he loved her.

But she didn't know where to start. How could she talk about something—*someone*—she didn't understand herself?

Besides, she had a party to go to.

PART FOUR:
THE OWNING UP:

39: people missed, things forgotten

HUNTER

He kicked holes in the Roths' lawn on his way back to his aunt's house. Everything Vere had brought up had hit the mark, dead on.

How in the hell could he expect Vere to want to be with him when he wasn't even a real person? When he had no idea who he was anymore? Was he Hunter Kennedy, the shut-down pop star from Los Angeles?

Hell no. I know I'm not that person anymore.

But am I some geeked-out, normal dude? A guy who just made out with a girl, thinking he had a chance with her and got shot down?

Double hell no.

I'm not that either...but it just happened to you so...shit. What does that mean?

Was he simply just the most messed up person in the world?

Are you Hunter Kennedy, or are you Dustin McHugh?

As he made his way onto the front porch, he turned and sat on the top step, taking in the purple-orange sunset. He rested his elbows on his knees and let his hands support the impossibly heavy weight of his head.

He couldn't believe how much he really had fallen for Vere, not to mention how he'd pinned his heart to his sleeve back there. How badly she'd crushed it, even though she'd been *right*.

He couldn't stand that he'd let himself even be in such a vulnerable position. It was so not like him to leave himself unguarded.

Rejection—real rejection—was way more painful than anything he'd been through so far in his whole life. He shoved away the images in his mind of the unbelievable kisses they'd shared. How Vere had felt so perfect wrapped in his arms.

He owned the desolation he was feeling now.

He'd walked right in and asked for it.

He should never have kissed her. He should never have played at being *Dustin* so deeply...

At least she'd helped him see that he had an even more disturbing thing to ponder now. Before he could even address how badly Vere had broken his heart, he had to deal with the reality of himself.

According to Vere, Dustin McHugh wasn't real.

According him, Hunter Kennedy—the old Hunter Kennedy—wasn't real anymore either.

Hell. The girl had every right to say what she did.

Are you Hunter Kennedy or are you Dustin McHugh?

Hunter sighed, not wanting to admit what scared him the most: He couldn't ditch the nagging thought that he might be no one. No one at all.

The porch light flipped on, and the door behind him opened. But he didn't turn around. Aunt Nan was probably wondering what the heck was going on. Hopefully she was making some sort of awesome dinner.

Whoever he might be—he was definitely always starving.

He stood and straightened quickly, but kept his back to the door, trying to compose himself. He didn't want her to worry or catch him on the edge of bawling like a baby.

"I'll be right in. Give me a second. Okay?"

The door closed and he was glad she hadn't seen his face. He'd have to hide behind his glasses until he got himself together.

"Hunter?"

He tensed and held his breath. Had he imagined that voice? He looked straight ahead and shook his head.

"Hunter. *Hunter Kennedy.* Can I at least have a hug?"

"Mom?!" He turned to see a very different mom standing by the door. She'd cut her hair short, and was wearing jeans.

Mom never wears jeans, does she? Am I dreaming this?

"I'm sorry," she said. "Please know. I'm so sorry." Her eyes looked huge and very blue under the porch lights. The apology in them seemed so real his heart swelled with hope.

Hunter took off his glasses to get a better look as he approached her. Some more of that suspect moisture had come back around his eyes.

Damn. But it can't be helped.

He launched himself at his mom and gave her the biggest hug he'd ever given anyone in his life. "You got my message," he whispered, not caring that he might be clinging to her.

"Yes," she sniffed, possibly clinging right back. "I was packed that night. I had to see you, sorry it took all week for me to get things arranged with Martin and...other stuff." She wrapped her arms around him tightly.

"I missed you so much. God. Mom, did I miss you." He let the tears come, so grateful to know at the very least, he was still someone's son. He'd figure out the rest soon.

"I missed you too, Hunter. I missed you so much."

40: telling the truth

VERE

It took Vere an entire hour to stop crying. Then it took another hour for her stupid, red eyes to un-puff. It took another whole thirty-two minutes after that to stop thinking about all the insane things Dustin—*or Hunter*—had said. And then it took even longer to get her courage up to come to this party at all.

Which is why they'd made it to Kristen's quite a bit late.

But cool people usually came late, and that's who we are now, right? Cool. Super cool. Even though I don't think I want to be here. Even though I have the urge to go back home and cry some more. UGH.

Vere tried to psych herself up. She was here now, and it was all going to be fine. Everything would iron out the moment she saw Curtis. Just the sight of him would set this straight. She knew it.

Thanks to what happened between her and her *x-BGF*, she had bigger plans than ever to kiss Curtis tonight.

I have to know...

I have to know...what?

She lost her train of thought and pictured herself kissing Curtis. She had to know something about how his arms felt around her.

Yeah, that's it. I'll analyze how his arms feel around me. How his lips fit against mine...and compare. Compare his kiss to the best kisses I'll never get to have again? OMG. Never again?

Vere swallowed and put her hand over her racing heart. She felt herself starting to blush.

Jenna tapped her foot nervously against the freshly painted

wood on the Hodjwicks' front porch. "Okay. So...yeah...are we really going to enter this madhouse?" Jenna asked.

Music blasted from the open dining room window. They could hardly hear themselves talk on this porch. The noise inside had to be deafening.

"Of course. We can *so* do this. Come on." Vere rang the doorbell but nobody came.

Jenna rolled her eyes. "We're idiots. I'm sure you just go in, or whatever." She pushed the door and it swung wide.

The place was filled to the brim. Plastic cups and odd shallow puddles of spillage littered the floor in the entryway. Vere's eyes widened. Mr. and Mrs. Hodjwick were out of town (or tied up in the basement) because, *no way,* would they have allowed a party like this.

She darted a glance at a huge mass of people in the front living room. The whole soccer team it seemed (boys and girls) were crammed onto the formal velvet couches, flinging quarters at a coffee table so they would bounce and land in cups.

"Yeah. Pretty intimidating." Jenna's eyes looked like saucers.

The entire football team was spilling out from Mr. Hodjwick's den as they all crowded around the flat screen, watching some game.

Vere's eyes rounded-out more than Jenna's when they spotted Howie Rutherford sitting crossed legged in the center of Mr. Hodjwick's desk, downing a beer.

Jeez. Play it cool, Vere. Pretend you've seen it all before.

Jenna was lost in the crowd right about when Vere located Curtis dancing with what appeared to be a somewhat drunk, Kristen Hodjwick.

Ugh. Ugh. And Ugh.

It took Vere only three seconds to realize she did not want to be with Curtis Wishford. Not at all. Not one bit. She understood with almost painful clarity what she'd already suspected when she'd been on the front porch.

That she'd totally screwed up! That she had just hurt the one guy she truly cared about and was now in front of absolutely the wrong guy for her.

Kristen had moved in to dance way too close with Curtis. She glared at Vere and stomped away when Curtis shoved her unceremoniously to the side as he spotted Vere watching them.

"Yo mamma. My Vere's looking hot-to-nite," Curtis hollered at the top of his lungs. "Let's dance!"

As if. Did he really just call me 'mamma'?

She had to get out of here. NOW.

Vere avoided eye contact with Curtis and turned away. Maybe she could just slip out and make some excuse to him tomorrow. She didn't think she could even talk to him right now, let alone dance with this guy.

Her heart became trapped in her throat. Before she could squeeze back through the crowd, Curtis grabbed her by the hand and pulled her into an awkward, goofy dance. "Hey, did ya not see me? You're late. What happened?"

Vere pasted on a smile. "Sorry. Got hung up."

Making out with another guy.

Making out major with Hunter Kennedy?

Aaaah. A guy I really want to make out with again, I think.

She looked up at Curtis and wondered how in the heck she was going to get out of this. Curtis was still the same, gorgeous, dark-haired, green-eyed guy she'd always known. And he seemed genuinely happy that she was here. With him.

But right now, he kind of reminded her of a big Labrador Retriever. Nice, slobbery, cute enough...but just too slow.

And again, not for me.

"I'm so glad you made it. I really missed you." He grinned.

She nodded, feeling super guilty. "Aww, thanks." She had to figure out a way ditch him without hurting his feelings.

It wasn't Curtis's fault she was such a mess. That she'd

changed her mind. He'd only ever just been himself with her—so she shouldn't blame him for that.

She was the one pulling the flip switch.

Mind racing for a plan that wouldn't come, she danced with him halfheartedly. He didn't seem to notice she wasn't into it, because he had his eyes closed and was singing along with the song at the top of his lungs as he shook around in a bizarre booty dance!

"I love dancing with you," he shouted.

She nodded, and cracked a fake smile. The poor guy had no idea she was about to run on him. He shimmied his bootie dance toward her, inviting her to grind.

Ugh. Ew. EEEW. Never!

Vere side-stepped him and forced his shoulders back to facing her.

He grinned at her again. "I saved you a beer, but you took so long I had to drink it down for you," he hollered, pulling her close. "Mmm. You feel nice. You look nice." He gripped her waist and shoved his face into the hair at her neck and sucked in a monster breath. "And boy do you smell nice."

Double-EW!

"Don't. I've got to tell you something." She worked to peel his meaty hands off her back. If he only knew how far off the nice list she'd recently flown. "And I'm not nice."

Jeez. I just made out with another guy. No one who's NICE does stuff like that. And I'm about to DUMP YOU.

She shook her head to try and clear her thoughts.

Is ditching the hot football player who's totally into you socially LEGAL? It's not on our Facebook pages yet...so...maybe he just wants to be friends. Yeah...I'll try that speech first...

"Ah, but you are so-so nice. Nice to look at, nice to touch." He'd clamped his arms around her waist again. "Nice to dance with and nice to be with. As in, all mine."

Vere worked to hide her frustrated grimace.

So much for plan A.

The music changed into a slow song, and more couples paired up beside them. He pulled her closer and her forehead bumped painfully against his chin.

Vere felt her temper rising. "Curtis. Listen," she tried again, vowing to never say the word *nice* to anyone again. That word did suck, after all!

Be polite, Vere. You'd have paid money for him to talk to you like this yesterday.

She glanced around, gripping his arms to get his attention. "Curtis, it's so noisy in here and I really need to talk to you. In private. Alone."

He grinned down and had that dumb, *I-know-you-love-me-baby* expression. "That's my line. You scooped me. We can go upstairs. Or I have my mom's van out front." He winked.

She bit back a small urge to dry heave.

Aaaah. Aaaaaaaah. No. No. No!

Accidental party come-on. Failed at Party Pointers 101.

"No. That's not what I mean. I really DO want to talk." She met his gaze and held it.

"Oh, so do I. I can't even wait to get you alone. How about we start talking right now, right here, in front of everyone?"

"Uh. Okay?" Maybe she could pull it off in this crowd. She raised her voice. "I want to tell you that I...JEEZ!"

Vere looked up in time to duck her head to the side.

Curtis had tried to plant a kiss on her!

Bait and switch not working.

ABORT talking! ABORT talking!

Vere twisted in his arms and tried to unlock his dance-death-grip. Thank God she would not have to repeat this suck dance with him next week.

Because homecoming is off.

SO OFF. CREEPER.

"Hey. Why so skittish?" He dragged her toward him again.

"Come on. Show me what you've got. Let's make this official."

"No. Seriously? NO. I just want to talk. Please."

"You'll like it. I guarantee. Then we'll talk. You are just so adorable and so hot right now. C'mon."

Vere glanced wildly around. Couples danced in a crush in every direction. Behind them, a sea of endless babbling, drinking, yelling high school kids pressed in on the edges of the room.

Jenna came into view just as Curtis tried to pull her even closer. Vere shot Jenna her most desperate *holy-help* face signal before she lost sight of her.

She still hadn't spotted Charlie. Her brother would help her. Where was he?

"Come on, Vere, don't be so darn shy. You're my girlfriend now," he said, in the lame pouting-baby voice as he bent his head down, straining toward another kiss.

"That's just what I want to talk about." Vere twisted her head out of his reach. She'd worked her arms free and pushed him back.

"So do I. Isn't that why you're here? To make it official?" Curtis frowned.

"Vere. Vere. I'm feeling sick. We have to go." Jenna, her true hero, had worked her way through the crowd and was attempting a brave, and wonderful rescue.

Vere shot her the *BFF-I-love-you* blink.

Jenna winked back just before she clutched at her stomach and bent over with an amazingly realistic, pained howl. "Vere, you've got to help me get outside. I need air. So...DIZZY." Jenna had shouted the second part of her performance at the top of her lungs right when the song ended.

She'd drawn so much attention to herself that Vere didn't even have to pretend to be surprised as she blinked stupidly at her friend.

As if Jenna sensed there was no going back, she kept her

face in check, and groaned even louder. "Does anyone have some water or any ice? Ohh...woah..." She stumbled and half collapsed on to the floor.

Jenna's Drama Grade: A++!

A few kids wandered over to see if they could help and blocked Vere's view. "Curtis. Let me go. I've got to get her outside. She's going to puke. I can just tell. I know her."

Curtis stopped dancing finally, but instead of letting her go, he'd tightened his grip. "Can't your friend find another baby-sitter? She's totally fine. Look. Other people can handle her."

Vere looked. There were three kids kneeling around Jenna.

"I don't think I can move," Jenna moaned. "Vere! Someone find me VERE!"

"I thought you wanted to talk to me," Curtis said.

"Curtis, she's my *friend*. She needs my help. What's wrong with you?" Vere's head was pounding. Why did Curtis sound like such a whiner? She tried again to pull out of his embrace. The guy was just too strong.

Her heart rate sped up. And not in a good way.

"I sure hope this isn't some kind of pattern with you two. I only want to date you. This is not a package deal." He looked into her eyes but made no move to let her go.

"Did you really just say that?" Vere asked, her mind going white-hot mad.

"Yeah, I did. Hello? Earth to Vere. If you're going to have a real boyfriend then you're going to have to give up hanging 24-7 with your dork entourage. I expect you to hang out with me. Only me. A lot."

"Oh, really." Vere closed her eyes in a last ditch effort to stay calm, but it was way too late.

She saw spots. Little burning spots behind her eyelids, and when she opened them, Curtis Wishford was right in the middle of those spots. He was still talking like a jerk, and he was way too close to her face.

She couldn't believe she'd been so stupid. Why had she come to this party? She pulled and twisted against Curtis's embrace.

Please don't let it be too late to apologize.

Please let him forgive me. Please...

"Come on, Vere, don't be all PMS. Now that we're a couple I was hoping to bury some of our seventh grade teasing tonight. I want to kiss you in front of everyone. One kiss for your boyfriend before you go. Be *nice*."

He brought her forward, his expression determined.

Vere fixated on his giant puffy lips as they jutted obscenely from his face in full pucker. And her imagination took over. He looked exactly like a big, stinky fish.

A giant, pawing, labrador-dog-fish!

Vere squirmed in a panic and shouted at the top of her lungs. "I said, no! As in, never. We are not a couple. I'm not your girlfriend, I won't go to homecoming with you. And STOP calling me *nice*. LET. ME. GO."

Vere didn't know how her arms got loose. She simply felt the back of her fist come into direct contact with Curtis's chin.

Surprised, he released her, stumbled backwards, and tripped on his own big feet.

Or were they paws?

Vere felt just like Jack the Giant Slayer as Curtis stumbled again, and crumpled into the middle of Kristen Hodjwick's living room.

"My friends are not dorks," she finished, but no one heard her, especially not Curtis, who'd been swallowed up in a wall of stunned, shouting people.

Jenna, having just staged the world's fastest recovery, ran over just as the living room erupted into laughter. "Oh. God."

Vere grabbed onto her for support. "Which door is closer? Front or back?" Vere whispered.

"Neither. We're trapped in a sea of drunk creeps." Jenna blinked. "My only word for you, and for what just happened is, WHY?!" Jenna whispered low, "I'll say it again. *Why. Why? Whyyyyyy?*"

Vere clutched onto Jenna as though she were a life preserver. How could she make Jenna understand? She opted for the truth: "I have to get home. I think—no—I *know*. I'm in love with Hunter Kennedy. That's why!" Vere smiled.

"What?!!" Jenna moved in face-to-face with Vere. Jenna had gone completely pale and she seemed to be trying to analyze Vere's pupils. "Tell me it's not that. Tell me you've gone bonkers. Tell me you're drunk, even. But don't tell me you punched Curtis Wishford because you're in love with a pop star on TV?" Jenna hissed. "You don't even like *GuardeRobe*."

Vere laughed long and hard then. Her voice had gone high and giggly. "Not true. I LOVE them now. I know every single song they wrote by heart. Don't you see? I am in love with Hunter Kennedy. Head over heels, in love, with Hunter Kennedy! I even made out with him, for a really long time."

"In your dreams, maybe? Stop talking like this. You're scaring me. People might hear you." Jenna's expression had grown so freaked out that Vere couldn't help but break out into another fit of giggles.

"Oh. God. I know. It sounds so bad." Vere put both hands over her face and tried to clear her head, wondering how she could ever explain this. *IF* she could ever explain it. She'd forgotten that this was all supposed to be a secret.

"What in the heck does Hunter Kennedy have to do with your real life?" Jenna placed her hand on Vere's forehead. "Are you sick? I know what this is. It's hallucinating. Did you smoke anything, or take any pills at this party? Maybe someone slipped you something."

"Jenna. No. He's so great. And sweet. And he used to be so sad. And I made out with him, and he said he loved me." She blushed. "And he's a *really, really, really, really* good kisser."

The noise in the room grew impossibly loud, the crowd

around them even tighter. Howie Rutherford was now standing on the desk in the Hodjwick's den. He was whooping and hollering as he strove to get a better glimpse of Curtis, who was still lying flat on the ground.

Vere cringed, looking at Curtis's motionless body. "Oh, no. Did I knock him out? For real?"

Jenna nodded. "Yep. I think so."

"Vere's finally done it. She's killed Curtis," Howie yelled. "I warned him."

Kristen Hodjwick was pouring cold water on Curtis's head.

"Howie, you suck," Jenna yelled in complete frustration her voice loaded with panic. Everyone laughed even more.

Vere laughed, too, which caused Jenna to look twice as stressed on her behalf. At least they (not counting Jenna of course) all found Vere's leap into the black hole of social oblivion amusing.

"Do you think I should call an ambulance for Curtis?"

"No. Look. He's moving." Jenna grabbed onto her arm.

Curtis sat up and rubbed his chin as he glared confused and hurt eye-daggers at Vere.

She felt really guilty. She would apologize to him right now if she could get through the crowd to him. If he hadn't been so lame a few minutes ago.

"We've got to get out of here." Vere bit her lip, trying unsuccessfully to push back another random fit of giggling. "OMG. It is kind of funny, isn't it? That I knocked him out again..."

In front of everyone? HA!

Jenna pushed Vere toward the door. "Don't speak to anyone. You might be drugged. I've read about this. Do you think you are going to have a seizure or something major like that? Are the walls melting? Did you eat any mushroom looking things?"

"No. Of course not. No melting. No mushrooms!" Her heart clenched. "But, Jenna...I am completely in love with Hunter

Kennedy! Did you hear me? All this time. How could I not have known? Admitted it," Vere whispered. "I love him so much."

Jenna turned and shot her another worried look. Her tone was ultra soothing. "Yeah. I hear you. And I'm head over heels with Harry Potter *and* Peeta Mellark. Stay with me. Okay? I'm right here. I feel your love. Now feel mine and start walking."

"You're such a good friend. You won't believe what I said to him. I told Hunter Kennedy that he didn't even exist. Why did I say that? He's the only guy in my whole life who ever has been real. Who has ever liked me, for me!"

The image of her real *BGF's* heartbroken face came into her mind. "I have to talk to him. Oh, I...I..." Vere started to cry. "And he kissed me...Jenna...it was so wonderful. It was."

"Of course it was. You already said that. Don't cry." Jenna was pushing her toward the door.

Vere cried harder as she replayed what he'd said to her. He'd been so honest. He'd bared his entire heart. Every inch of it while sitting next to her and gazing into her eyes. She froze, cringing at the memory, mostly at the memory of how she'd rejected him.

The guy had been down on his knees! Wasn't that supposed to be the most romantic thing a guy could do?

Vere groaned and put her hand to her head, while the room faded into a horrible, black fog. "I suck. I'm the worst. He will never forgive me." She moaned and her tears flowed unchecked down her cheeks. "Oh. Oh, no. What have I done? How will I ever apologize? How will I? Jenna, I want to die."

Jenna slowly pushed her along, misunderstanding Vere's anguish. "I'm pretty sure there's no getting back with Curtis after this one. And he doesn't deserve an apology the way he was pawing you. Now keep moving the feet. One step in front of another. If the floor seems to be melting that's not real... walk through it."

"Have I told you that also I love you?" Vere sobbed openly now, shuffling her feet, little by little, while she gasped for breath. Jenna had every right to think she'd gone bonkers.

If Hunter's feelings were even half as strong as the imploding, desperate, crippling madness she felt squeezing her heart this very second, Vere figured she'd totally crushed him. She hoped he'd let her explain. Vere looked up and realized the room had finally quieted and everyone was staring at her.

Watching her cry her ass off.

Worse, she was still in Kristen Hodjwick's living room.

She felt like she was in a really weird dream. Vere gasped for air and tried to get control of her tears. "What will I do?"

Jenna took her hand. "I've got you."

Kristen Hodjwick marched straight up and blocked their path. "I'm sure you two don't have to be asked to leave? I can't believe you started punching people at my party, Vere." She shot a grimace at Jenna holding Vere's hand. "God. You are both such *FREAKS*."

Jenna jumped in. "Whatever, *cow*. Consider us already gone."

"No way! No way! *Dudes!* Charlie Roth is on TV. Looks like he's standing in his own front yard!" Howie screeched from the den. "Something must have happened. There's cop cars and everything!"

Vere's heart dropped to her stomach. She and Jenna peered into the den at the supersized flat screen on the back wall. Vere could see Charlie squinting and cringing away from twenty microphones as he was being interviewed by their local TV news reporter.

"Why would Charlie be on TV? He's supposed to be at this party," Jenna whispered.

Vere's entire body filled with dread.

She tugged Jenna's hand as hard as she could.

"No, shit!" Howie bellowed. "He's talking about Dustin.

Dustin McHugh is actually Hunter Kennedy! Charlie's been holding out on the team. It's a whole story about the *GuardeRobe* lead singer dude living in disguise in our town. Next door to the Roth family! And going to our high school! *No SHIT! Dustin McHugh is Hunter Kennedy!* Did any of you know about this? HOLY MOTHER OF GOD! We should head over there. Who knew about this?"

It took one second for everyone in the room to swivel their heads to search for Vere and Jenna.

But they were gone. Long gone.

***

"You better talk as fast as we're about to be running, *Vere Roth*. If you think I'm ever going to forgive you for keeping this secret from me, think again!" Jenna hissed at max whisper. They were now creeping as fast as they could, heads low, through the Hodjwicks' yard, heading for the front gate.

Vere couldn't speak all over again. She felt so sick.

Charlie had blown Hunter's cover! Her over-protective, vendetta seeking brother had gone way overboard.

Could this night get any worse?

And it was all her fault.

Jenna continued her tantrum, "The only thing that saves you at all, is that I get to trade you out now. I'm going to be Hunter Kennedy's new best friend. If you made out with him, and he *says* he loves you, then you're his *girlfriend!*"

They hit the front sidewalk and started running.

Jenna went on, "This means he has a vacancy in the best friend department, just like I do! OMG. I'm Hunter Kennedy's NEW BEST FRIEND! OH. MY. GOD. *Aaaahh!*"

41: misunderstandings

HUNTER

Hunter, Nan and his mom had just finished dinner. It had been strange at first to have his mom sitting at the table, but by the end of the meal, he admitted it felt great that she had come. He stood and picked up his dishes to bring to the sink. "Aunt Nan, mind if Mom and I clean up?"

Nan smiled, getting the point. "Not at all. I have some work to do upstairs."

Hunter's mom stood, grabbed her plate and smiled. "Thanks, Nan. Thanks for everything, the dinner, letting Hunter stay here, all of what you've done."

Nan waved her arm from the doorway of the cozy kitchen. "Stop. We're family. No need for thanks. You two have a good talk." They watched her in silence as she made her way down the hall.

"Hunter, you look great. Really great. I'm glad to see you've put on a little weight." Hunter's mom ruffled his hair. "The lighter-brown color suits you. When you're older, I bet this will probably be your real color."

"Yeah. I like it." He smiled. "The glasses and retainer suck, though. What happened to your hair? And for that matter, why are you so Colorado casual?" Hunter downed the last of his water as he leaned on the counter.

"I've been rethinking my wardrobe. Rethinking everything, really. I needed a change." She was busily gathering up the remaining silverware and serving dishes on the table and brought them over.

"Well, I don't know how the urban housewife look goes over in Los Angeles, but you'll sure fit in perfectly in this town with that get-up. You aren't serious about it, are you? It's *so* not you." Hunter opened the dishwasher and started to load as she passed the plates toward him.

"What if I came here hoping not to be going back to Los Angeles for quite some time? I want to stay, for the rest of the year. Here, with you and Nan."

"Oh, no you don't. You and I are so out of here. I am done with this town, this disguise, all of it. It's killing me. I want to go back. Back to work."

"Nan said you had friends. She told me you'd settled in well and liked it." She wrinkled her brow. Her concerned mom expression was something he'd forgotten.

Hunter grabbed a sponge and walked over to wipe the table. His mom could read him as well as he could read her. He didn't want her looking too closely, not tonight.

"It was fun for a while," he started. "As for friends, I'm down to zero. I hoped your arrival meant you had good news for me? Did you drop the charges? Will you let me go back?"

"You mean you haven't spoken to Martin or the guys? I'm surprised." Her eyes were wide. "I assumed you knew everything and that you'd decided my idea wasn't so bad. When you called me and asked me to come—the way you hugged me outside—I thought." She shook her head. "I thought you knew. I thought that you'd finally read the letter."

Hunter paused and turned to face her. "Nope. I told Nan to send it back to you."

"Oh, God. You don't know." She sighed. "I guess you can add this to my list of parenting screw-ups because I really did it this time."

"Know what? How in the hell am I supposed to know anything if you didn't call me once?" Three months of frustration let loose like a storm in his chest. He sat on the table and put his feet up on a chair. "Why didn't you? Call me this whole time? Why didn't you visit me at Falconer?"

"I did it on purpose. I didn't visit you because I wanted you to have some space to figure some stuff out on your own. I didn't call because I thought you wouldn't listen."

"I'm listening now, Mom. You're freaking me. Start talking." Hunter's heart beat uncontrollably against his rib cage but he leaned back and faked his most relaxed expression.

His mom swallowed, and turned back to the dishes. "I— sabotaged Martin. I refused to drop your charges. I set this all up while you were in Falconer. Your therapist and I were convinced that you needed this change. It's quite unconventional and underhanded the way we didn't tell you all the details exactly; but if you understood why..."

"But Martin said—I thought—I was here to hide from the press, to keep my reputation clean. That's what Martin thought, too."

"That's what I wanted you both to think."

"But why Colorado, why the disguise? I don't understand."

"I sent you here so you could hide from yourself."

"What?"

"The Hunter Kennedy fame had turned you into a machine of sorts. Once *GuardeRobe* became popular, I felt like I couldn't find you. It was like you were hiding. And every day you would shut down on me. You were losing yourself."

"That's stupid. I was right there the whole time. We lived in the same house. It was you who hid out, not me."

She scrubbed madly at a pot but still didn't turn around. "You're right. I was. I was scared to make a change. I thought, eventually you and your fame would time out. End. I was waiting for something besides me to make that call. So you and I could go on with more normal lives."

"You wanted me to *time out*? Who says that?" Hunter shook his head.

"Martin told me every child star had sort of a 'shelf date' where the fans would suddenly tire of them and move on. I believed him. But then *GuardeRobe* started up and became so big. And you loved it. You loved the music part of it. I didn't know how to make it slow down. When Barry mentioned you could use a long rest this seemed like a good plan. I thought, if it worked, that I could save you from yourself." She walked over and sat at the kitchen table next to him, looking totally deflated.

"Save me from myself? You have got to be kidding." Confused, Hunter stood to get away from her to pace the room. "You have two minutes to explain why you thought any of this was a good idea before I walk out of here forever."

"Hunter, please. Try to understand. Our communication was closed off. You wouldn't talk to me. You sure wouldn't take advice from me. I thought I was losing you. For real, losing you."

"Oh, you've lost me all right. This whole experience has made me lose my freaking mind. Is that what you wanted, because it's still going on. Right here, right now, two hundred more brain cells just burnt up."

She tapped her fingers on the table. "I figured if you came out here as Hunter Kennedy, the superstar, then you'd get swept up in all the hype that surrounds you. You'd never have the time or the chance to sort out who you really are."

"Your plan has been backfiring since day one. This deal has messed with my head so much I feel like I know less and less of myself every freaking second. I have no idea what is real anymore. Now I have to wonder if I even have a mom, because a real mom wouldn't do something like this to their kid."

That had gotten to her. She shifted uncomfortably and smoothed her hair behind her ears, something his mom always did if she was going to cry.

She squared her shoulders. "A real mom does whatever it takes to keep her kid safe. Intervening and sending you here was my attempt at that. I'm only sorry it took me so long to realize that I needed to fight for you. I should have never let you sign the contract with *GuardeRobe*."

"So you think you can just rip it away from me now? You're way off, lady. You've just admitted to me that you wanted to kill my career. If I truly have to finish the year here because of what you've done, *GuardeRobe* is over. And that will mean I'm finished. Or timed OUT!"

She nodded. "Maybe. Probably. I still hope so."

He flung his arms wide. "How did you ever get Martin to agree to this? Why haven't I heard from him about your bullshit sabotage?" He leapt off the table and headed for the door. "I'm out. I'm going to call him."

She hopped out of her chair and blocked his path. "I tricked him. I made him believe I was doing everything in my power to play along with him. I actually have to credit Martin for part of it, though. He came up with the last piece of the puzzle for me. He invented the disguise idea. Once that was in place, I knew you'd have a chance out here."

When he met her gaze he knew it was true. "Let me get this straight. I didn't really have to come here? You lied to me, played me and Martin for fools, and ruined my career on purpose. Is that all of it?"

"No. Well, yes. If you put it that way. If only you'd read that letter."

The pounding in Hunter's head had started to slow. He worked hard to understand all that she'd said. He tried to walk in her shoes as Aunt Nan had suggested he do, but this was too much to handle. "What was in that letter that would make any damn difference between us now?"

She sighed. "I thought I was going to lose you, like I lost your father. The letter I left you was about him. How he died."

His mom gasped back a breath, holding back tears.

"Keep talking if you can. It's time for both of us to do this."

She nodded, sucking in another breath. "I'm surprised I beat Martin here. I know he's coming. He must be losing it, especially if none of us returned his calls. Aunt Nan told me you'd turned off your cell. That move bought my plan an extra week."

"I hope Martin's losing it. I hope to hell he's on his way right now. I *so*, need a real rescue from you and your insanity!" Hunter shouted now, "Why in the hell didn't he call me, here? He had the number!"

"Martin did call here. A lot. Nan's been hanging up on him," she said. "She kind of hates the guy. Don't blame us too much."

"Aunt Nan...?" Hunter couldn't breathe. His entire body hurt. "I will blame the hell out of anyone I please. Now tell me about Dad. What happened with my real dad?" Hunter's voice cracked.

His mom looked directly at him. "He killed himself. I can't prove it, but I think he did. He got really depressed and he got drunk just like you did." She blinked, holding back tears. "He went out driving and he crashed his car into a tree. I think." She gasped. "When you wrecked your Porsche and then I found you all cut up and drunk..." She choked on a sob. "I flipped. I did what I had to do. I felt like I had to save you."

"Mom...no...I didn't. Fine. *I did. I did.*" Hunter shook his head and looked away, unable to meet her gaze. His mom's words poured over him.

He suddenly got it. Got *her*.

Got why things had become so broken between them.

She went on, "Martin figured the whole thing out last week, right when you called me. When you asked me to come, I thought you'd read the letter. And that you knew. I hoped you'd made your choice, and that you were inviting me out to stay for good. I guess I should have called you first. I'm sorry. I just got a plane ticket and came. I wasn't thinking. I only wanted to see you. To hug you."

Hunter risked a glance deep in to her eyes. She was sincere.

Afraid. And as sad as he'd been all along.

She also had huge, dark circles under her eyes like she hadn't slept much...in months. He understood where she was coming from now, but it still didn't make him feel any less messed up. Didn't make her choice to stick him her a good one.

Or...did it?

She was his mom, after all. A mom, protecting her son the best way she knew how. It's what Aunt Nan had said all along. Aunt Nan was all the family he and his mom had ever had. And if his mom thought she was protecting his life, it made sense that she'd send him here.

His throat tightened and his eyes grew heavy with his own unshed tears. "You should have told me. You should have talked to me about Dad's possible suicide years ago. We should have talked about him. About what happened with me and the intern two years ago."

She nodded. "I never knew how to bring up the topic of your dad. I thought it would hurt you. As for the intern...and that dirt bag I married. I'm sorry, but it wasn't the easiest topic to bring up. Plus you were on tour that whole year." She sighed. "I thought you wouldn't listen."

"I guess I probably wouldn't have. I was so pissed off at everything after they left." Hunter let out a deep breath and sat back at the table. His fury had completely disappeared leaving behind a raw feeling, but he had to acknowledge the it was a *full* feeling instead of the emptiness he usually felt when he talked to his mom.

He leaned his head on a hand and met his mom's gaze. "You have no idea how impossible and freakish my life has been, masquerading as *Dustin McHugh*." Hunter took in a deep breath, trying to set the information his mom had given him into some sort of order inside his mind.

"You have no idea how ugly and terrifying your agent is when he's angry. This whole time I've been only a few steps ahead of him, playing this game from the other side. It's been hell for me too."

"What did you mean when you said you thought I'd *chosen*?"

His mom sighed and sat next to him. She was taking small, short breaths, obviously still trying not to cry. "When Martin shows up, he will most probably have his lawyer in tow or, at the very least, some emancipation papers for you to sign. He's been working on them since the day he figured out my scheme. If you want me to sign them, I won't contest it."

Hunter shook his head. "Mom. He's been working on that since Falconer. He tried to get me to sign something long ago."

"Oh." She paled. "I guess I underestimated him. I should have understood how difficult it would be for you to be an imposter for the long term. I'm happy I got to talk to you before he got here. I can imagine how Martin would have twisted this story and made me look like the bad guy."

Hunter nodded, thinking about that. Martin would have made his mom sound like a psychopath. One who surely drove his real dad to his death. Sadly, Hunter, most probably would have believed Martin over his own mom. But not anymore. Not after today. He owned his part in it.

"Well. At least we're communicating again," he said quietly. "Even if this plan totally sucked."

"You understand why I did it? Why I was so afraid?"

"Yeah. And *shit*, I'm angry about it, but I get why you went this far. I also get how a possible suicide about a dad I can't even remember would be hard to bring up. We've never talked about deep stuff like that. That would have been one crap conversation between us. I was a kid...so yeah."

She nodded, and moved his hair out of his eyes. "But you're not a kid anymore. Are you?" She smiled tremulously. "When did that happen?"

He shot her a small smile back and shook his hair back down. "It's a recent development. Your whacked plan kind of worked. I've got a completely different perspective on life. Even thought it's only been a few weeks, this place has changed me."

"You do? It has?" Her eyes filled with hope. Happiness, and what looked like relief.

Hunter nodded. "Parts of me. Yes. You'd really sign those emancipation papers? Just let me *go* like that?"

"I never want to let you go. Maybe it's time for me to admit that I might not be very good at keeping you, though. After this latest screw up regarding your life, I'm thinking you've earned the right to make your own decisions. At this point, I only want what you want. I will support you. But you'll have to think it over. Choose on your own. You're almost eighteen."

"Why do I feel like I'm fifty right now?" Hunter snorted.

"I suppose our Los Angeles years have been like dog years, huh? They age you fast."

She looked over, still seeming really forlorn.

Hunter just wanted her to smile, that same smile she'd had for him on the porch just an hour ago. "You know, if I'm fifty, then that makes you like 350, right?"

She smiled up at him, but he could see tears filling her eyes. "I know. I know. I feel older than that. God. I'm so sorry. Will you ever forgive me?"

Hell. Total backfire. Again.

I fail at communicating with women.

He let out a long, heavy sigh, unable not to think of Vere, crying the same way when he'd tried to make a joke at the wrong time.

Hunter stood. He could not sit around and watch his mom cry. He also wasn't quite ready to go into the bigger conversations and apologies that needed to come from him. He needed time to think.

A lump formed in his throat. He had to get out of here. Hunter nodded again and looked away. "Guess I better go plug in my cell phone, huh? Read Martin's emails. Hear his side of all this."

His mom nodded. "Yes. Please do that. It's only fair."

***

Hunter walked through the hallway and up to his room to drag out his phone and plug it in. His mind flying again to Vere. Wishing he could talk to her. Hear what she thought about all this. Without thinking, he dashed back down the stairs and put his hand on the doorknob.

The hall clock said 10:30.

Could she be home already? Would she even agree to see me?
Probably making out with Curtis right now, you idiot.
He let his hand drop off the knob.

The party's probably ramping up, not ramping down.
A soft, tentative tapping at the front door startled him. It stopped and started up again. Someone was knocking!

His heart raced. Who else could it be but her? Maybe she'd been thinking the same thing! That she wanted to see him. That they just needed to hash things out a bit more.

The tapping grew more insistent, and then turned into a loud, firm knock.

"Don't answer that, Hunter. It's late. Let me get it." His aunt called down the stairs, sounding agitated. "I'm just getting a robe. Don't you open that!" she shouted.

Hunter shot a startled look up the stairs at her tone.

His aunt was obsessed with home invasions. She was probably getting out her baseball bat to haul down here. It was way past her bedtime. No one ever knocked after eight.

"I've got it. It's probably Vere," he called up to her.

The phone rang then. Hunter had to laugh. More chaos? No one ever called after nine. Not in this town.

Maybe that's Vere too. Calling from her cellphone while on the porch!

♥ 399 ♥

"I'll just get that phone then and be right there. Don't you open that door without me," Nan yelled again from the top of the stairs.

The knocking continued.

It had to be Vere. The girl had no patience.

"I've got it, no worries!" Hunter grinned, thinking of her cute elfin face all scrunched up and annoyed that he was taking so long. He swung open the door.

Blinding flashes of light overtook him. Startled, he threw his hands up in front of his face as though he'd been struck.

Every ounce of air whooshed out of his lungs.

"It's him! He's in here! *Hunter. Hunter Kennedy!* This way, turn this way. Just one shot. Hunter!"

More flashes and someone started up a noisy generator that put a floodlight on the porch.

He was totally unprepared for the sight of his aunt's front lawn with at least fifty reporters on it. News vans filled the street. Not to mention, every person from the entire neighborhood had seemed to have come out to stare at the house.

Hunter realized he wasn't wearing one shred of his disguise. No glasses, no cap, and his retainer was sitting upstairs in the bathroom, resting in a dish of mouthwash. His plaid shirt had been tossed, forgotten onto his bed. He only had on a pair of canvas pants and a short sleeved, black tee-shirt.

Total exposure. Shit.

The questions fired at him like bullets. He felt each and every one hit him in his chest, slamming out more of his breath, as the flashes from the camera and flood lights held him frozen.

"Is it true you're hiding out here disguised as a dork?"

"Are you really attending Palmer Divide High?"

"Let us in on it."

"Why are you here? Have you quit *GuardeRobe?*"

A man rushed up onto the porch and flashed about 20 fast

shutter pictures. "Who's Dustin McHugh?" he hollered as he fought back the mob of paparazzi all pushing in to take the very same shots.

Hunter managed to close his mouth and throw on his best media smile. "Just visiting my aunt. Little family time, that's all. Don't know what all the fuss is about, dudes." Hunter gave a quick wave and tried to shut the door, but was blocked by a big guy who had at least seven cameras slung around his neck. He'd wedged his boot into the doorjamb, snapping shots of him relentlessly.

The man pressed his camera into Hunter's face and Hunter felt like he was suffocating. He had the odd sensation that he actually might faint because he'd truly couldn't breathe normally right now. The burning feeling in his chest hurt so much it threatened to make him black out.

Hell. I'd forgotten...

Hunter realized just then that he hadn't forgotten, he'd never actually thought about all this in a coherent, detached way before. He was thinking about it now, though.

And he hated it—from the bottom of his heart.

He stood still and did something he learned from watching Vere get through her panic attacks. He closed his eyes. After a moment, he no longer had to make himself breathe. He heard the cameras going off all around him. It sounded like a video game battlefield—and he was the sole target.

He opened his eyes and shook his head at the annoying paparazzi ass in front of him.

Game. On.

"People, stand back. I gave you your shots, now back the hell off."

The man pressed closer, snapping shot after shot as the questions continued to fire at him.

"Is it true you've been in trouble with the law?"

"Los Angeles County police records show a report of

vandalism and a wrecked car at your house a number of weeks ago. Was it you?"

"Can you add anything to the rumor that you tried to kill yourself? What do you say about that? Throw me a bone, dude. I haven't sold a good story in weeks." The annoying guy on the porch pushed closer, his gaze hungry, almost wild.

Hunter realized the questions no longer hurt at all. They were just questions. Questions to be answered, and he was going to choose which ones he'd answer, and what the answers would be.

He sucked in another deep breath and looked behind him. His mom, hearing the commotion had made it into the hallway just as Aunt Nan came barreling down the stairs.

And yes, she did have her baseball bat in tow.

It felt great to have his family standing behind him.

Hunter had to hide a smile as he listened to his aunt talking a mile a minute. "Darn television recorder. If I hadn't been watching that vampire show again, I would have seen this on the news. And, if I weren't so damn old, I'd have heard the commotion outside. Step aside, Hunter. Let me get these bastards off our property."

He realized the man with the cameras had taken at least fifty shots of the scars on his wrists. Who knew what photos the others had taken.

The press crowd grew louder. "Hunter! Tell us if it's true. Did you try to kill yourself! We see the scars. Why is that woman holding up a bat?"

Moving in front of Nan to block her from view, Hunter spoke to his aunt through his grin. "Put the bat down, Aunt Nan. I think we should go with one crazy person in the family at a time."

He flicked a glance back at her. She nodded and put the bat behind her.

His mom stepped forward as though she would say

something to the press. "Let me handle this, Mom. I've got it."

She nodded and stepped back too.

Hunter pushed past the obnoxious guy with the too many cameras and stepped out onto the porch. The night air cooled his lungs and he got a better look at the crowd. He couldn't miss Charlie Roth standing front and center with his arms crossed and a smug grin on his face.

Traitor.

Charlie met his gaze and shot Hunter the *chin-in-the-air* jock salute.

Hunter returned it with his best *you-suck-glare.*

Charlie obviously wanted Hunter to know exactly how his cover had been blown.

Hunter grimaced, not wanting to admit how much that knowledge hurt. Charlie had warned him to stay away from Vere, and Hunter had broken his promise. Hunter didn't blame the guy. But he also didn't give a damn what Charlie thought anymore.

His only regrets were that he'd botched his attempt at being honest with Vere and how he lost her in the process.

The girl should never forgive me. I took advantage of the situation—of our friendship, and I didn't play fair. I owe that girl a major apology. But Charlie? Well, he can kiss my ass.

Hunter would not be passing out any apologies for being in love. *Hell.* The guy had actually done him a favor and didn't even know it. More resolved than ever to speak to the press, Hunter held up both hands and made no move to hide his scars. He layered on his very best, photo shoot smile. "You've found me. Not sure how." He tossed a glare at Charlie before adding, "Yes. These are scars on my wrists. I've got nothing to hide. Now that you've seen them, I mean to make a press statement to all of you. Soon."

Everyone on the lawn and in the street and driveway quieted.

Charlie's mouth dropped open, and even from this distance

Hunter watched as the kid visibly paled.

That's right, bastard. Nothing to hide. Not anymore.

Hunter kept his hands up. Again, making sure his scars were well and truly visible under the bright lights. "Until I get my statement organized, or if you need details about my life here in Colorado, I will ask you to direct your questions to one of my *best friends* here, Charlie Roth," Hunter said, using a scathing voice that said the opposite, while he pointed his index finger at Charlie. "I totally *trust him* to speak for me. He thinks he knows me really well, and he's always wanted a bit of the spotlight so I hope you give him a chance."

Charlie twisted his head around as though looking for an escape.

HA. I'd love to see you try and run from this bunch.

If the situation didn't suck so much, Hunter thought this could be more than funny to watch. Hunter tossed Charlie his widest grin and waved. A few paparazzi had already reached the poor sucker.

Good. Let the ambush begin.

Hunter continued, "In the meantime, you are all standing on my aunt's garden. If you could please..."

As if on cue, a long black limo pulled in behind the media circus blocking the street. Hunter swallowed, maintaining his mask.

SHIT. JUST PERFECT. This has to be Martin.

He shook his head and almost had to laugh.

Hunter counted down what would happen next in his head: *5. 4. 3. 2. 1.*

The crowd shifted and some of the teen spectators at the end of the street started to scream as they, too, spied the limo.

His mom had not been making any of it up. Only Martin would orchestrate a spectacle like this in a quiet suburb. The driver opened the door and his agent stepped out, followed by two familiar looking guys.

*No way. He brought Adam and Royce with him to Colorado?
What new, screwed up game was this?*

Hunter scanned to see if anyone else came out of the limo.
Thankfully, there was no sign of the grinning, *fake Hunter
Kennedy.* If Martin brought the band along minus that freak,
then Martin had meant to blow his cover big time with
this limo-stunt. Who wouldn't have noticed that limo and
GuardeRobe in this town?

Martin had probably tweeted the arrival and called some
of the paparazzi here ahead of time, which would explain the
monster crowd already assembled. Charlie was probably only
responsible for the local news van.

It felt great to know he wouldn't have to hide his scars
anymore. His *crazy* was out in the open, and he didn't even
care. The corporate office at *NewtNet* would have to take him
or leave him, as is.

Hunter shook his head resignedly. He had to plan his next
moves. In the meantime, Martin would be the next victim to
frost this parasite-press-cake for him.

"Oh my God, it's the rest of the band! *GuardeRobe* is here!
Right there!" A girl screamed, then another, then another. Half
the high school's student body had flooded into the cul-de-sac.
The crowd and all the paparazzi rushed around the limo.

Hunter nodded to Charlie, who'd been left in the dust by the
press.

*Lucky bastard, got off easy for now. But they'll be back. You'll
see how it is, friend.*

Hunter turned around and shut the door and locked it, but
not before witnessing Martin and the band needing to haul-ass
back into the limo for safety.

Hell, yes. Colorado had some awesome, dedicated fans!

Hunter had the strangest urge to smile at his mom, so he did.
"Wait till Martin hears that I've spilled everything. It'll take
them at least thirty minutes to make it to the front door. I only

wish I could hear the string of flip flopping lies as they pour out of his mouth."

"Maybe we should turn on the TV so we can watch him." Aunt Nan fisted her hands, as though she wanted to battle.

"I'm proud of you, Hunter," his mom added. She hugged him and he returned it. They both smiled at his aunt who had turned to shove the baseball bat into the hall closet. "I'm going to keep this down here in case I need to take a couple of whacks at that Martin fellow," she said, head still in the closet.

"I'm going to keep this down here in case I need to take a couple of whacks at that Martin fellow," she was muttering, head still in the closet.

Hunter made his way to the foot of the stairs. "Mom, I've still got some thinking to do. Could you put a hold on packing your bags for a bit? I need some time before I face Martin and the guys. Please don't let them in. Tell him he can take the guys to a hotel. That should disperse half of this press. Tell him I'll talk to him *tomorrow*. Not one second before."

"I'd love to." She looked happy, really happy.

"I'll be the first to tell that Martin that he's not allowed to enter this house." Aunt Nan reopened the hall closet as quickly as she'd closed it.

"No baseball bats, okay? Martin shouldn't be hated for being the best in the business. I might need him someday."

"Humph. Speak for yourself." Aunt Nan glowered, but she shut the closet and left the bat inside.

"What do you mean by *someday*?" His mom wrinkled her brow.

Hunter took a deep breath and let it out. "Maybe you two can help me come up with the right way to tell Martin and the guys that I'm staying here. I will only be working during summers. Through high school at least and maybe even college."

42: too little too late

"I know. I know. I suck. I totally suck and you have every right to disown me. But you have to know my parents swore me to secrecy. I was not allowed to tell you about Hunter."

Vere and Jenna had stopped to catch their breath at the swings in their neighborhood park just around the corner from Vere's cul-de-sac. After the mad dash from the Hodjwick hell-party, this was the perfect place to debrief and stuff her brain back into her head.

Not to mention make Jenna understand. "But. BUT HE WAS LIVING NEXT DOOR. GOING TO THE CABIN! PLAYING CARDS WITH ME. AAhhh. AHHAHHAHH."

Vere sat on a swing. She also had to gather her thoughts before killing Charlie for calling the press.

Wait till Mom hears that Charlie outed Hunter.

God. Wait till Charlie retaliates and tells Mom that I made out with Hunter! Whatever. I'm not ashamed of the making out. I'm ashamed that I was the world's worst friend.

That I abandoned him. That I refused to listen.

That I was completely, utterly, and absolutely stupid!

Jenna followed suit and sat in the swing next to hers. She'd been babbling and cursing the whole way here and she obviously still needed to sort through some of this.

"Hunter Kennedy? Hunter Kennedy this whole time, and I never even knew?" Jenna gasped, still catching her breath. She let out a low whistle and dragged her feet through the dirt under the swing. "You. Made out. With Hunter Kennedy! Pinch me, please." She giggled. "You. At the party. Saying all that stuff." She giggled again and then laughed out loud.

"Pinch me back." Vere rolled her eyes, pushed off and started swinging. "He wasn't exactly Hunter Kennedy when I kissed him. He was only a great guy. You know, my friend?"

"You KISSED Hunter Kennedy, but you're calling him 'only a GUY'? Can you NOT hear your own words? It's insanity."

"Yeah...but once we started kissing, his name never even came into play."

"YEAH BECAUSE YOU WERE LOCKED ONTO HIS LIPS. Oh. MY. Aaaahhhh-ha!"

Vere slowed her swing to a stop and turned her head to look at her friend who was now sporting a huge, goofy grin. Vere went on, "Uh. Are you going to yell at me for lying to you? If so, get it over with. And get over who I kissed, too. I need my best friend back so you can help me make a plan, *please*."

"Yell at you? Are you nuts? I'm going to hug you! This has to be the single, most positively amazing thing that has ever happened to us. To me, to you, to this whole town. *OH-MY-GOD*. Charlie was on the NEWS! Your house, too!"

Jenna jumped off her swing and twirled around in circles in front of Vere. "We'll have book deals, photo shoots, you and me on the cover of those gossip magazines. Maybe we will get our own reality TV show. This is going to be so cool. We'll be on TV! Get to go to the Video Music Awards! Aaah! *This. Is. Awesome*," she sang out.

"Oh no. We will not do any of that. Let's just vote on that right now. Besides Charlie's already beat us to the scum-bag-friend-low point. Be calm. Try."

Jenna put both hands on her head. "HOLY COW. CHARLIE IS FRIENDS WITH HUNTER KENNEDY. OMG! I'm friends with HUNTER KENNEDY. AndAhhhAaa-ha-ha!" She twirled and twirled. "My heart is beating so fast, Vere. I'm going to be famous. I. Love. *GuardeRobe*. So. Much."

Vere sighed. "Jenna. No weird behavior, no deals with shady newspapers, no hidden digital cameras in your nostrils.

Nothing. Whatever ideas you are launching in that devious little mind, end it right now. We will not sell him out."

"Fine. No sell out. Unless *my best friend*, Hunter, agrees it is appropriate and he wants to do a reality show featuring me."

"You sound crazy, you know?"

Jenna hopped up and down. "How can you even call me crazy after tonight? I thought you'd gone mental back at the party. As in total, psychotic break mental? You were certifiable right in front of the whole school. When you started laughing, I was sure you'd been possessed."

Jenna mimicked Vere: "*I—I—I think I'm in loooove with Hunter Kennedy.*" Her eyes bugged out and she threw her arms wide. "You saying all that, while Curtis lay flat on his back, while I was faking that cramp! Ha..."

They burst out laughing together and both fell on the sand.

"Oh. My tummy hurts. Stop making me think about it. I can't even go there. I'm sorry. I did sort of lose it," Vere gasped out, staring up at the dark sky.

"You've had almost a month to get used to this 'Hunter Kennedy lives next door' idea. I've only just ramped in." Jenna crossed her arms under her head. "I wonder if this means I'll get to kiss one of the other boys in the band. Royce...or Adam? Which one should I pick."

Vere shook her head. "The clock is ticking, freak-fangirl."

"A little patience. Not yet." Jenna grinned. "Can we just talk about how last weekend I went to a lake cabin and played cards with the lead singer of *GuardeRobe?* And then he bought me a haircut, gave me make up tips and picked us both whole new wardrobes, including a homecoming dress for each of us! Please just let me do a real scream, or something. Please!"

Vere smiled at Jenna. She was so funny. "Bad idea to scream like *that* in the park on a Saturday night. I think we've drawn enough attention to ourselves this evening."

"Don't put me into your messed up *WE* equation. I didn't go ape on the star quarterback because I've been making out with the lead singer of *GuardeRobe*." She put her hands over her heart. "Oh, Vere Roth, my soul-sister! You touched tongues with the lead singer of *GuardeRobe*!" She blinked. "How can you not be dying right now?"

"I am." Vere flushed down to her toes.

Did she have to mention the tongue thing?

Her heart did a major flip. She stood up and went back to the swings. "Come on. I need some serious advice. I need to figure out a way to patch things up and I can't do that until you calm down," Vere pleaded. "I need you. Come back to me. So what if he's a rock star? I don't care about any of that. He's just a regular guy to me. *And to you.* Just try not to think about the other stuff and help me figure out a way to apologize."

Jenna sat back on the swing next to Vere's. "You aren't keeping any other secrets from me, are you? Your parents aren't secret agents? If so, kill me now, because our friendship will not be able to take something like this twice."

"Nope. That's it." She eyed Jenna suspiciously. "As long as we're on this topic, what about you? You floored me last weekend with that whole 'I'm marrying Charlie' speech. So don't act all high and mighty. Your secret crush on my brother ranks as high as the Hunter Kennedy thing. So if there is anything else on that front, spill it now."

Jenna sighed. "Honestly. Some of that crush thing has changed. Charlie and I might not be getting married, either."

"Good! Did you finally realize he sucks?" Vere sighed.

"No. I messed up my whole plan. I came over yesterday. And you were out with your mom. And if you must know, I kissed Charlie in your kitchen. Mega-made-out. As in...LONG-TIME, kissed him."

Vere clamped her hands over her ears. "No. No. NO!"

Jenna nodded. "My marriage calendar is blown to bits but

at least Charlie's taking me to homecoming. We were going to surprise you and Curtis with a double date until you ruined everything."

"Jeez. Stop! Ew. Eeew." Vere's chin had dropped all the way to her knees. "Your turn to say you've been drinking, that you made this all up. Go on." Vere grimaced.

"It's true. We're actually dating now. I can't keep my hands off that guy. YUM. ME. Your brother kisses like a—"

"Eeeew. No. This crosses the line!" Vere pushed Jenna's swing away from hers. "Eew. Eew. Eeeeeew."

"Hey. You said no screaming in the park."

"You will not be sharing any further details with me on this topic, ever." Vere shuddered. "Seriously. You, plus Charlie, is the sickest thing I can imagine. I hope you two break up, and soon. In the meantime can we get back to my FIRST nightmare, please? JEEZ."

Jenna shrugged. "You asked. Fine...let's get back to the Hunter Kennedy topic!" Jenna blinked. "Wow. Vere? How can we even talk about him? Him and you. He's HUNTER KENNEDY."

Vere gritted her teeth. "Ugh. Put that aside. Just listen to the darn facts. My ex-brother (who is now your kiss-buddy/ homecoming date and possible fiancé) just blew the cover of the one guy that has ever liked me—for me—and meant it."

"Processing, formulating. Keep going." Jenna blinked.

"This guy happens to be perfect for me in every way except for the part where he's a rock star and I'm...you know...me."

Jenna blinked. "Yeah, but you just said he liked that part."

Vere's heart clenched. "I know. And I blew him off when he said he was in love with me. LOVE. Jenna. He said the word LOVE."

Jenna shook her head, but thankfully held silent.

"I want to say sorry. But after the way I treated him, and after the way Charlie betrayed him, he might be on his way back to Los Angeles. Oh. And he could hate my guts because I called him a—nobody." Vere's heart clenched and her throat closed up.

Jenna wrinkled her nose. "So, you don't care if you make an ass out of yourself when you're trying to get him back?"

"I can't exactly sink any lower on the 'ass' scale after tonight. Who cares how much more foolish I look or act over this? This is real. I love him. I need to apologize. He deserves that I at least try."

"Okay, then I'm going to help you go after him as long as you are aware of what it might cost you, socially speaking. Oh-my-God! You're going to go after Hunter Kennedy!" Jenna squealed and giggled one last time.

Vere sighed, feeling desolate. "If it doesn't work, then I'm going to wither away of a broken heart and you will be left picking up all the pieces."

Jenna sighed and checked the time on her phone. "We have exactly forty minutes before you're grounded for getting home late. We'll use it like a deadline."

Vere nodded. "Adrenaline rushes might just save me if I freeze up and pull a shy attack. What can we do in forty minutes?" Vere asked.

"Thirty-nine. First let's get back to running."

They jumped off the swings and broke into a jog. "We'll march right on over to Nan's house and just knock on the door. Honesty's the fastest. Practice saying, "I'm sorry. I'm sorry. I'm sorry, I love you, too." Can you do that?"

"Yes. Yes I can." Vere blushed big time as she imagined saying that last part to Hunter.

They turned into Vere's cul-de-sac and froze. The whole planet seemed to be having an all-night party right in front of her house. This was way bigger than she'd expected. She knew the local news van and a few others would be around but what they were looking at was insanity.

Cover blowing media frenzy: A++ for Charlie Roth, the
backstabbing jerk.

There were at least ten news media trucks, some even from
Denver. Maybe Charlie hadn't been the only leak? The end of
her street was loaded down with floodlights and police cars,
along with what looked like every single person from their high
school.

All of this filled their oval cul-de-sac to max overflowing. The
highest concentration of people swarmed smack in front of
Nan's house and spilled over into their yard.

A super-long, ultra shiny, black limo backed away from the
crowd and pulled past them while the crowd screamed and
followed its exit. Vere tried to see into the darkened windows
as her heart sank. When it reached the corner where they
stood, it turned right without even breaking at the stop sign.

"Jeez. Jenna. We're too late. I think I'm going to die. If he
was in there, he must have seen us. He's so out of here. So over
me. I guess I deserve it."

Jenna gave her a quick hug. "You don't know that. We're
down to thirty minutes. It is what it is. Let's at least try to get
to his door."

A police car pulled up next to them. "You kids need to go
home. This cul-de-sac is closed."

"But, Officer. I live right there." Vere pointed to her house
that now seemed about two million miles away. She just
wanted to crawl into bed and have a good, long, cry.

"Sure you do. Do you think I was born yesterday?" The
policeman sneered. "Now move along."

"Wait. I'm not lying," Vere insisted.

"Prove it, and I'll drive you as close as I can."

"Oh thank you sir," Jenna gushed, rescuing Vere from
speaking as Vere handed the officer her driver's license.

He sighed and handed it back. He looked as though he
wished he hadn't promised to drive them closer. "Hop in. Do

you two know this *GuardeRobe* band? Things should settle down now that they've driven away. What a nightmare. Those screaming teenagers popped my eardrums."

"*GuardeRobe* rocks!" Jenna said, as they jumped in the back seat. The officer proceeded to flash his lights and clear a pathway through the middle of the crowd.

"He's gone now, huh?" Vere asked halfheartedly, trying not to cry. "I saw that limo. Did he drive away?"

"No, that limo brought the rest of the band to town. The lead singer, he's still here on your street. With his family. The other guys have gone down to a local hotel. I wouldn't expect things to calm down in Monument for awhile."

Vere's heart soared. She grabbed onto Jenna's leg and flashed her a look as she started chewing nervously on her lip.

"I've still got a shot," she whispered.

There were a dozen policemen manning a line of yellow 'Caution' tape that separated the crowd from all the houses in the cul-de-sac. As the police cruiser crept through the throng, Vere caught sight of a very frustrated Charlie, trying to get away from a couple of cameramen and reporters.

"Officer! Please stop. That's my brother. Can he hop in with us? I'm sure our parents are freaking out. I can see them on the front porch. Probably looking for us."

The man sighed and stopped. "I'll have to walk you from here, anyhow. Go get him, and I'll see you through this mess."

Vere hopped out of the car with Jenna right behind her. "Charlie! Charlie! Over here!" Charlie turned at the sound of her voice but the look he gave her was not good. It was some sort of warning glance, as though to tell Vere to run.

Vere vaguely noted that Kristen Hodjwick and friends were each in front of different news cameras. They must have all left the party and driven over here. What in the heck would the news want with Kristen? For that matter, it seemed as if least half of the junior class was standing in front of some camera.

Were they *all* getting interviewed?

Vere tried to ignore the chaos and stared up at Hunter's room. The lights were out, but she could swear she saw TV lights flickering. Had she imagined it, or had his curtain moved as well?

Hunter. See me. Please see me and come out!

Vere waved frantically at the house just in case. Her heart sank when she realized she was now simply one of about two hundred other (way prettier) girls, waving at his window behind the police line.

Ugh. He'll never spot me, because he's not looking for me. After how I treated him, it's up to me to get to him, I think.

Acting like a dork groupie, was not going to help. She dropped her hand, embarrassed, and felt her cheeks tingle. Vere eyed the two policemen talking to each other on Nan's front lawn and then her gaze travelled to the two policemen guarding the front door.

"We'll never get in there," Jenna whispered, echoing her thoughts.

"There they are! *That's Vere and Jenna,*" Kristen screeched just as Charlie reached them. "They must have known all along!"

The officer was getting impatient. "Come on, kids, I don't have all day. Why is everyone pointing at you two?"

"Vere. Vere Roth?" A stranger's voice called her name. "A photo if you don't mind, Miss Roth."

Vere swiveled her head to look behind her. "What?" A flash went off, blinding her.

"Uh-oh," Jenna gripped her arm. A swarm of people, lights, and escalating noise surged toward them.

The officer shouted. "I don't know what is going on, but you three get back into the squad car, right now."

The three of them backed away while the officer held up his hands to stop the reporters. He called for backup into his walkie-talkie.

In seconds, the officer was swallowed up in a sea of flashing cameras and crushing reporters. Jenna, Vere, and Charlie jumped into the back seat of his squad car and ducked down.

"Don't say anything to any of them," Charlie hissed. "Don't either of you answer one question from these crazy people. The entire school has been interviewed and they know you and Jenna were Hunter's only friends. They want your story. Hell, they want to know everything about us."

The reporters were rocking the squad car. Vere didn't think the police officer was coming back.

Vere glared at Charlie. "We aren't the ones who ratted out a friend. You suck, Charlie. You suck. Why did you do it?"

"I didn't understand. He kept making you cry, so I figured he'd broken your heart. I thought this would get rid of him for you." Charlie sounded very apologetic. "I had no clue the deal was reversed. You totally dogged him today, didn't you? That's why he was so pissed." Charlie chuckled. "You broke *his* heart. How was I supposed to predict *that* when I'd been working so hard to make sure he didn't break yours?"

She nodded. "I didn't—I—I was in denial and I lost my head—or I don't know what."

"I heard you knocked out Curtis, too. You are on some kind of guy wrecking rampage," Charlie groaned. "Poor Curtis. Bet he didn't see that coming. He'll never speak to me again."

Vere grimaced, her tone apologetic too. "I punched Curtis because I like Hunter. And Curtis wouldn't listen or take his meaty, pawing hands off me. What else was I supposed to do?" Vere shuddered, remembering. "The guy's an octopus."

Charlie shrugged. "He thought you two were going out. Did you know Kristen Hodjwick has been going nuts talking crap about you?" Charlie shook his head. "So...why were you crying after you kissed him?"

"Because he told me he loved me, and because I was all

freaked out."

"No. He dropped the *L-bomb* and you crushed him?"

"Stop saying that! It's not my fault you overreact to everything, Charlie. I have it all figured out now. And I can't even talk to the guy. AND IT'S YOUR FAULT. If I didn't love you so much, I'd hate you big-time."

Charlie whistled low. "I thought he'd totally taken advantage of you. I'm sorry, but he's a guy and I know how guys are. After I saw you two kissing, I assumed the worst about him. I'm sorry. I blew it. I love you back, by the way."

Vere made a face. "I know you do. I forgive you, but Hunter shouldn't."

"No shit. I saw the huge scars on his wrists. Why didn't you tell me he had all that other stuff going on? Did you know?"

Vere nodded. "Yeah. We talked about it at the lake a bunch. Right before you punched the heck out of him."

"Damn. I SUCK." Charlie flipped off a reporter who was trying to take a shot of them by lying on the police cruiser's hood. He looked over at Jenna. "How you handling all this, beautiful?"

"Awww." Jenna shot Charlie a soft-eyed-puppy look.

Vere shoved at his arm, but had to smile at that. "Oh shut up! EW. Eeeew."

She banged at her door and tried to open it even though she knew the back seat would had some kind of police 'prisoner safety lock' on it. And it did. "We are trapped in this car, does anyone even care?" She banged on the glass again.

Charlie hadn't heard her. He was making goo-goo eyes at Jenna. He'd dosed Jenna with his *manly* wink and eyebrow wiggle, and Jenna was actually gushing at him.

Eew. This is going to take some serious getting used to.

UGH. Jenna has LOST her mind.

Charlie leveled Vere with his most serious stare. "Do you think Hunter will talk to you after what I did? And after what you said to him?"

Vere's heart dropped to the center of the earth. She shook her head. "It's probably too late to salvage anything for either of us, but I do want to tell him I'm sorry. I owe him that, at least. And so do you. We were his friends."

"I was such an ass. He will hate me forever. He got some revenge by setting these dogs on me though," Charlie said with a rueful smile. "Worse, Mom and Dad are going to give me the hellish 'disappointed in you, son' speech." Charlie rolled his eyes. "God, how I hate that speech."

Jenna put her arm around Charlie. "It's not too late. Hunter was your good friend. He was also in love with Vere only a few hours ago. I'm sure he still is both. We just need to get them into the same room, minus any of this." Jenna waved her arm to the mob scene outside the car.

"Any ideas?" Charlie asked.

Vere peered out, but could see nothing but camera lenses pressed into her window. She fished in her pocket, pulled out her trusty rubber bands and deftly shoved her hair into a bun. "I've got a plan, but it could brand me as an idiot forever."

"Hello, as if that's something new?" Charlie teased.

The police officer had made it through the throng and was just about to open their door.

"We have exactly twelve minutes until curfew. Who's in for running?" Jenna piped in.

Charlie leaned forward. "Home sweet home, here we come. You two squeeze in behind me. I'll use a full tackle if anyone gets in our way, not counting the police, of course," he added.

The officer leaned down and knocked on their window as though to warn them to be ready.

"Guys. If we still have twelve minutes, then head for Hunter's house. This is not something I want to sleep on. I mean to talk to him right now."

The door swung wide, and they bolted toward Nan's house.

43: introductions

HUNTER

Hunter had systematically read every email from Martin.

His agent had done a perfect job of painting his mom as a negligent, career-killing parent. If he'd been in his previous state of mind, when he was angry about everything—and pissed at her—he would have bought into Martin's schemes.

He would have driven away with Martin and the guys without once looking back. Not at this town, not at his mom, and possibly not even looking back for Aunt Nan or Vere.

His heart clenched at that thought.

True to her word, his aunt had not let Martin, Royce or Adam enter the house. After much shouting, and Hunter refusing to appear, they'd left in the limo. He'd stood at the window, watching them depart.

He could still call Martin and have him come back. It would be very easy to request a truce between his agent and his mom.

If that is what I want.

But it isn't.

He'd decided he still wanted to stay. Finish out the year. For better or for worse. If Vere didn't want to be part of that, he'd understand. Hell, he deserved it. He never should have challenged her with that last kiss.

He surveyed the madness in the street below from a long crack in the curtain, while listening to the news droning out on the TV in his room.

It wouldn't take long for this circus to get bored with his story. Especially once they realized he was here for the long haul. The town would get used to him, the high school kids would get over him, and then he could just get on with his homework and hanging out like before. *Hopefully.*

And minus the canvas wardrobe, the glasses and the stupid retainer. He wasn't sure how things would turn out with Vere, but he just didn't want to give up on her...on them.

Even if the girl only wants to be friends. It will be enough. It will have to be enough. I'll take what I can get, without stepping over the line ever again. Even if it kills me.

And it will kill me. Oh, hell...it will.

He could not take his mind off their last kiss. It had blown him away. He also couldn't take his mind off their first kiss... or the second...or the way she felt in his arms...or how badly he wanted hundreds more kisses.

Please. Please. Please. Let her be thinking the same thoughts. Let her change her mind.

He'd stood at that window in his room for what seemed like hours, looking for a sign of her and smugly watching Charlie being pestered by the press. The local station had moved to running the story live without breaks as though he were some kind of criminal holed up in his home with hostages.

When he heard Kristen Hodjwick's voice come on the air, he asked his mom, who'd come in to hang out with him, to turn it up. The annoying cheerleader started off with the typical lies, like how Kristen had *known Hunter's secret all along,* and that they were *great friends.* She'd even had the nerve to mention that he'd asked for her phone number once!

Hunter smirked at that, remembering her cold snub on his first day when he'd spit-lisped all over her.

When the reporter asked Kristen questions about Vere, she remarked that, *Vere most probably didn't even like guys 'in that way' and that's why she hadn't noticed Hunter Kennedy was living next door.*

The reporter had loved that one. He laughed and agreed with Kristen, because, "who wouldn't notice a rock star living next door?"

Hunter's surge of protectiveness for Vere had almost made

him crack his teeth. When Kristen had smiled with mean delight into the camera, telling the reporter how *Vere was sort of a freak in their whole town anyhow,* Hunter had wanted to kill her.

But then Kristen said, "Earlier, this very night, Vere Roth punched the school quarterback just because he'd tried to kiss her! So what does that tell you about the girl?"

Hunter's heart soared.

"Did you hear that, Mom?" Hunter asked, his heart racing double time. "Did she say that Vere *punched* the football quarterback?" His lungs flooded with butterflies. "I didn't make it up in my own head, did I? Tell me you heard that, too, please."

"I think that's what she said." His mom swung her legs off the side of the bed and sat up.

Hunter had run from watching the video feed back to his window. He searched the crowd for a new sign of Vere.

"Who is this Vere Roth?"

"She's my friend. Hell, she's my everything."

"I thought you said you didn't have any friends? So she's your girlfriend?" His mom frowned, obviously confused.

"She used to be my friend. I'm hoping that now, she *might* be my girlfriend," Hunter answered, searching desperately through every single face in the crowd as he continued, "She also has every right to hate my guts. So I'm not sure."

"Okay. I won't ask." His mom frowned.

"It's complicated." Hunter had not taken his eyes off the street from that point forward. His mom got tired of waiting for him to give up and went to her room to change for bed. He refused even to turn and say *good night,* just in case.

When he'd finally spotted Vere, waving up at his house, his heart almost exploded. The girl was just so adorable. He saw her look at all the girls next to her, and did not miss her moment of doubt. He could almost read her mind as her face had turned red with obvious embarrassment when she'd realized she was just one of many standing in line to get to him.

He wondered how she could not understand there was no girl in the world that compared to her? Had he not made that clear when he'd bared his soul to her after they'd kissed? He'd tell her again, and again until she believed it...after he'd apologized and kissed her, of course.

The press spotted Vere and Jenna, and created a tornado swarm around them. Charlie tried to fend them off, but it wasn't working. He watched as Jenna, Charlie and Vere dove to safety into an open police car.

He dashed out in to the hall. "Nan! Mom. I see Vere. I'm going out to get her."

"Hunter. No. That's not a good idea," his mom called out.

He'd bolted down the stairs and out the front door without thinking of a proper plan. He'd only made it to the yellow taped line and now stood trapped on the inside of it. The press and ever growing crowd of *GuardeRobe* fans pushed in against him, screaming for photos and autographs.

He worked hard to maintain a straight face.

Why in the hell had I thought I could get through and rescue her from the squad car? So much for my knight-in-shining-armor act.

He couldn't even see Vere or the squad car through the crowd!

"Young man. Mr. Kennedy!" an officer shouted. "You're going to cause a riot. Get back in your house."

"Sorry, sir. I can't do that. Not yet," he shouted back, scanning the faces in the crowd that were lit by the news van lights.

He saw her bun first, and then a burly policeman pushing Vere, Charlie and Jenna through the crowd.

His mom and aunt had run out behind him, both in their bathrobes. He tossed them a grateful smile, checking Nan's hands to make sure the woman had kept her promise and left the baseball bat inside.

"Hunter, what are you doing?" his mom hiss-whispered.

"I don't know. Following my heart I guess. And she's out here. Don't you see? I've got to get to her. Now."

Hunter pushed his way forward, never taking his eye off Vere's magnificent bun, and made it into the center of the throng.

"Hunter. Hunter. Over here! Smile this way," a reporter shouted, right in his face.

"Ooooh. Hunter! Hunter Kennedy's right there. I love you. HUNTER I LOVE YOU SO MUCH!" The sound of screaming girls flooded his ears.

Hunter's head pounded as his fans swarmed even closer around him. This was just too much. Hunter wanted to deck the reporter and squelch the screamers with a fire hose or something, but he had nothing that would stop them.

His first urge was to punch everyone and anything that was keeping him separated from Vere, but he held back. He took a deep breath and calmed his temper.

The media and fans were here from another world.

They operated on other-world rules.

He had to remember that and play by them correctly or he would lose. He smiled when he realized he did have something he could use to stop it all. He had himself. He could use these rules to his benefit, but in order to do it well, he needed to get the press on his side—and fast.

He looked toward Vere and realized she, Jenna and Charlie were surrounded as well. He worried Jenna might overreact to the press's barrage of questions. Or Vere might get really shy and do one of her babble attacks. Even worse, Charlie might pull something even stupider than Vere if he felt his sister was being threatened. And then all would be lost for Hunter, because Charlie would easily throw punches at anyone and get himself arrested.

Jenna looked as if she'd already started up! She seemed to be poking an officer over and over again in his chest as she yelled at him, and the paparazzi standing in the back had started to take some shots of Jenna's obvious tantrum.

This was not good.

His friends had no idea how to play this game. Hell. He'd wanted this meeting with Vere to be much different than this, more private to be sure. But now that he had her in his sights he was not going to let her go again.

Game on. Time to roll the dice.

"Guys. Guys." He spoke quickly and very loudly so the media zombies nearest to him would all focus and quiet down. "You've got to help me. My homecoming date is standing just over there." He pointed toward Vere.

Some of the reporters turned their cameras around. "Where? Which one? Homecoming? Really?"

"The cute girl with the bun. She doesn't know she's my homecoming date because I haven't asked her yet and that's because I can't get over to her. If you let me through, I promise to wait until you have all your equipment and cameras turned back on before I ask her out. What do you say? Help a guy get a date and move some of these fans back for me? If you do, the story is yours."

The paparazzi nodded, jockeying for position. They quickly were able to create a long pathway in the direction of Vere.

Hunter pushed his way through them and glanced up just in time to see one of the officers hauling Jenna and Vere toward Mr. and Mrs. Roth, who'd come out to stand on their lawn. They were obviously waiting to collect their wayward children. A second officer had Charlie in what looked like a painful arm lock and Hunter, for the first time, was finally able to lock gazes with Vere.

When she saw him, she doubled her efforts to get away from

the officer. "Hunter!" She squirmed desperately against the giant arm that held her. He was elated, watching her efforts to make it over to him.

Damn, but the girl does want to see me!

"Wait!" Hunter shouted as the opening widened more. He was able to break free and run forward. "Please! Let them stay." The press closed in behind him and he caught up to Vere and Charlie just as they were being deposited over the police tape that blocked the crowd from the Roth's front lawn. "Please. Let me talk to my friends. If that's what they still are," Hunter finished, tossing each of them a worried look.

Charlie flushed.

"Friends or not, we have to get this neighborhood back in order. Mr. Kennedy, return to your residence," the officer shouted.

"Hunter, we're so sorry about all of this," Mrs. Roth called out. "Officer, can we please talk to him. Just for a moment?"

Vere, Charlie, and Jenna turned around. Hunter darted a grateful smile at Mrs. Roth. "If you'll allow me, officers, I've got a few things to say. I promised these reporters not to shut them out. I kind of want all of you to hear what I have to say, anyway. Once they get this story, they will all head out."

The officer took note of the rolling news cameras and shifted to the side, making sure he was going to be in the shot. Hunter almost had to laugh at that. "You have two minutes, Mr. Kennedy," the man said, straightening his back and preening for the camera.

Hunter nodded his thanks and walked over to Vere and took one of her hands. The small smile she gave him flooded his heart with happiness. "Everybody ready and rolling?" he asked the press, waiting while a few swapped equipment and found a good position.

He was rewarded with a laugh and some smiles from the paparazzi as they got situated.

They were eating out of his hand, thank God.

Dustin was pleased to see his mom and Aunt Nan had made their way to the front of the crowd and would be able to hear what he was about to say.

He nodded once to his mom to show her he was okay, because she looked really worried and freaked out. She returned it with a tremulous smile and a small confused head shake, but did not move to intervene.

"First, to the entire Roth family. I want to publicly say thank you for helping complete my disguise, and show me the ropes around this town and school."

Hunter pointed to each person and the press made sure they were all photographed. "This is Charlie, Vere, and Mr. and Mrs. Roth, and my friend Jenna. They sort of adopted me, and helped me hide out in this town as a kid named Dustin McHugh. I've never felt such love and acceptance from strangers before. This family is over the top. And don't even get me started on the delicious food." He winked at a glowing Mrs. Roth.

Hunter could not believe this was working so well.

The crowd had grown so silent he felt as though he were on a movie set.

He couldn't believe all these people wanted to hear his story so badly that they would sit out here in the middle of the night and listen to this. He looked wildly at all of them and almost panicked but knew he had to go on. If they wanted to listen, he would talk. He shot his aunt a smile.

That's what real men did, right? They talked.

He darted a glance at Vere's giant, luminous eyes for courage, pulled in a deep breath and motioned to Vere, Charlie and Jenna again. "These three are my best friends here, and, if you must know, my only true friends. Anyone else who says differently has been lying."

Hunter glanced to the back of the crowd and noted that

most of the junior class that he could see wouldn't meet his gaze.

Take that, Kristen Hodjwick, wherever you are.

Hunter turned back to the people in front of him. "I'm seriously hoping these three will still be my friends after you all leave town. Don't blow it for me by pestering them so much they hate me, please?"

A few reporters had the good grace to laugh at his comment.

Jenna beamed, and Hunter locked gazes with Vere.

Her eyes had that larger-than-life-sparkle going on. He could sense she wanted to tell him something but she was pulling in breath after breath. Trying not to cry.

He winked and gave her hand a squeeze.

"Courage, beautiful," he whispered, moving closer.

Charlie whispered, "Dude, I'm sorry. So sorry I blew your cover. I didn't understand."

"Please, no apologies. I think, after tonight we're on even ground." In a lower voice he continued, "you did me a favor, dude. Trust me, my agent had already blown my cover way worse. All these people are not here from the phone call you made to the local news. I'll explain it all later."

Charlie's eyes widened with relief as Hunter went on, not wanting the press to get distracted. "I have more to say, if you all don't mind. Mostly about my disguise. And why I was hiding out here using a different name. After that, I have a more serious question for my best friend, Vere." He looked at Mr. and Mrs. Roth and then pointedly at Charlie before adding, "if I have your blessings."

Charlie nodded, Mrs. Roth beamed, and Mr. Roth shot him a short, curt and disapproving grimace.

Damn. I'll work on Mr. Roth later.

Hunter turned and took Vere's other hand.

The cameras went wild.

He could feel her trembling so he leaned in and whispered

so only she could hear. "If you cry right now, I'm going to lose my nerve. You okay?"

She nodded.

"Good." Hunter pulled Vere forward and reintroduced her to the press with his arm around her shoulder. "Everyone, this is Vere. She's possibly the sweetest girl at Palmer Divide High, definitely the most beautiful." His let his voice drop a bit and met her gaze. "Today we had a bit of a fight, but yesterday we were best friends. I'm hoping this press event can record the two of us making up."

Vere blushed and tried to turn away from the cameras in her face. "Come on. I do not need to be fire-engine-red for the entire country," she whispered, pressing her head into his shoulder.

"Planet. UK-Daily is front and center," he teased. He was relieved to see her tears had abated. "She's also humble and very, very shy. Please, go easy with this girl and back up."

The cameras moved back.

Vere shot him a glare. "Why did you have to say that?"

He smiled at her pinched face. "Because you are. And I love that part about you."

She flushed even more.

"I'm sure you see why I'm going to make it no secret that I'm head over heels for this girl. I almost lost her to another guy by not telling her my feelings soon enough. Maybe if I say them in front of you all, we can print it up, she will read it herself and finally believe me."

"Did you almost lose her to the high school quarterback?" someone asked. The crowd erupted into a rash of unintelligible questions and shouts.

Hunter held up his hand and the noise died down. "Yes. I almost lost her. I tried to tell her how I felt this afternoon, but it came out badly because when I finally came clean, we hadn't officially met. I made a mess of it all."

"What do you mean by that, Hunter? You've been here for almost a month. You said you met the Roths on the first day. They were in on the whole disguise," a man contested.

Hunter swallowed. "Yeah, well...I asked her from day one to think of me as *Dustin McHugh*. As just another kid. That's how everyone here knew me and treated me. I did the same in my own head. I was wrong to take my disguise so far."

The video cameras moved closer. So many lights flashed at them that Hunter was temporarily blinded. Vere shut her eyes. Everything faded out and he focused all his energy on her.

She pulled against his hand, and he could tell she just wanted to run for her house. All while her cheeks flamed that adorable, rose pink color.

"You've lost it," she whispered finally. "What are you doing with all these cameras? And me?"

He spoke only to her. "Before we move forward. Before one more minute passes, I'm introducing myself to you. Right here, right now, in front of the whole planet."

"What?" Vere glanced nervously about. And, with a move he'd grown to love more than ever, she reached up and unconsciously checked her bun. "Hunter. You don't need to do this. I *know* who you are. I was so lame. And I'm sorry. I get it now. The feelings are real. You are more than real. I just want to talk to you away from here." Wisps of golden-brown hair framed her face and danced around the back of her neck as she shook her head.

God, but I can't wait to get my hands in those little curls. Kiss that neck again...

Hunter didn't miss the fact that the reporters were riveted on her. They saw what he saw, that even in her messy bun, and a tear stained face, this girl was simply riveting. She had already charmed everyone in front of her with her quiet blushes.

He moved his mouth close into her ear, drawing up the flowery smell of her into his nose as he tried to explain, "I want everyone else to know who I am, too, including me. Help me through this. It's something I need to do. I won't make you stay if you absolutely don't want to, but I have to finish this out. When you're with me, Vere, I feel like there's nothing I can't do. Stay for me? Please?"

"Okay. For you." She half-smiled and tucked herself in closer under his arm. She held onto him for dear life as she arched her brows. "But don't you let me go, or leave me alone in this crowd. And then, we are *so* out of here."

Another rush of pink flamed her cheeks and his eyes riveted on her lips. She was chewing nervously on the top one again.

Damn. That. Adorable. Lip.

"Shit. Now, where was I?" Hunter uttered, realizing he'd truly forgotten everything but her sweet mouth.

"You were introducing yourself to all of us and embarrassing me," she whispered.

He could tell she was trying hard to get back her bravado. He grinned down at her.

Vere tilted her head to the side and scrunched her nose.

His stomach filled with butterflies. It couldn't be helped.

It was Hunter's turn to tremble. He felt his arm shaking against her shoulders. He shook himself and righted his thoughts. But kept his gaze locked with her eyes.

"Vere. I'm Hunter Kennedy. Some of this you know already, some you don't. I'm a guy who was so lost and depressed that I freaked out and tried to hurt myself because I felt so down. I was a complete ass to my mom, and I crashed a Porsche onto my own front porch. I crashed it hard enough to also hurt myself with that deal too. Luckily, I didn't get hurt."

Vere raised her eyebrows and furrowed her brow, but said nothing. She didn't have to.

Tears had pooled inside her eyes.

"Let me start again. I'm Hunter Kennedy. I will most probably spend the rest of my life proving to my mom, my aunt and my friends, and fans that I'm okay—not sad anymore. That I'm truly sorry for not reaching out and asking for help instead of taking matters too far. Going to a place I never wanted to go."

He searched the crowd until his gaze fell on his mom and Aunt Nan. He was pleased to note they were both with him and hearing his apology. Vere put her arm around his waist, drawing his gaze back to her.

Always back to this amazing girl.

"You were sad. None of that was your fault—"

"I know that. But I was also living a really strange, shut down and selfish life."

"You are anything but selfish. Don't say that about yourself."

He shook his head. "I was selfish today when you asked me to kiss you. Instead of walking away like I should have, I couldn't." He swallowed and ran his free hand through his hair before going on, "I wanted to be your first kiss. I knew that even if you never spoke to me again, you'd at least possibly remember me over Curtis. See? Selfish."

The cameras fired, and the crowd went silent as the paparazzi creeped even closer with their digital recorders picking up every word and blink he and Vere put out.

"Wow. Okay. I'll need time to think about that." Vere flushed, her gaze bewildered and pleased all at the same time.

Hunter had to look away from her or he was about to be selfish again and kiss her right there.

He scanned the crowd, feeling suddenly lost and confused, but pressure from Vere's gentle arm brought his gaze back to her and again, he found his center.

He started again, this time speaking to the press face on. "I'm Hunter Kennedy, and the most important thing I want you all to know is that I got really sad back in Los Angeles. I made some terrible choices that almost ended my life."

He smiled at the cameras, hamming it up now with his

trademark grin. "But now, I'm okay. I'm not ashamed of what I did, nor will I hide how I felt because I think it might help others to know what I went through. I'm happy to be alive and so thankful that my suicide attempts failed."

Vere choked back a sob. "God. Hunter. So are we."

He looked down at her and wiped away a tear. "I want to stay and finish high school, here, in Colorado."

"You do!" She beamed. "Really?"

"I hope my agent and band will wait for me, but I'll understand if they can't. But I need to do what's right for me, and staying here," he pulled Vere tighter before continuing, "feels right."

The media erupted into a new round of frenzied chaos. Everyone seemed to be moving and shouting disjointed questions as they pressed in even closer to Hunter and Vere.

"That's good enough. You've said enough," Vere insisted over the noise.

He interrupted her by putting his finger gently, very gently, on her lips.

"I want to be sure we all get it. Including myself. Including my family, and yours."

The crowd quieted again. He looked away from Vere and continued to face the crowd.

"Vere, until I came here, and met you, I didn't understand that I was more than a lead singer of a band. I was so shut down, I couldn't even pick my own socks, remember?"

Camera flashes and whispers ramped up all around again. She nodded.

"You were the first person who made me realize that I needed to start choosing again or I would never be happy. So thank you for that."

She shook her head, but he interrupted before she could speak, "Let me say it one more time. This one's all yours, Vere." He grinned.

She turned bright pink all over again.

"I'm Hunter Kennedy. Real—flesh and blood. Just a normal guy, with a crazy job that's currently on hold. I was pretending to be someone else; but our friendship was—*is*—completely real. I love music, poetry, drama class, hiking, swimming in lakes and spending every free minute I have talking to you."

She gasped and then bit down on her bottom lip. He could tell she was about do that crying thing.

"Don't cry," he pleaded. "I have to finish. For the first time in my life, I love and understand the person I see when I look in a mirror. It's the same person I see reflected back at me in your beautiful eyes. It's simply *me*. And I like me how you like me. As is. Scarred, with a too-low voice, always hungry and everything else in between."

She smiled and he knew she totally got what he meant.

"This is a gift *you* helped me find. I don't think I will ever be able to repay you for showing it to me."

"You—don't need to—ever—and you know—you—just— you—" Vere gasped and shook her head. He could tell her shyness was not allowing her to continue. Her eyes held back a tangle of words he knew she wanted to shout out in his defense.

Damn, but she's so cute like this.

He moved aside, and took up both of her hands in his again. "I know it's too much for you to hear all of this in one night. But I have to say it again. I've fallen completely in love with you, Vere. I'm tired of hiding and pretending. I hope you will at least take a chance and go out with me. Get to know me as Hunter Kennedy? You once told me I could be perfect boyfriend material. I'm hoping it could be easier than I once thought. I'm also realizing the sweet, romantic stuff you believe in might be the way to go for us."

Vere smiled wider, seeming to get some control.

He let go of one her hands and ran the back of his finger

across her burning cheek. "So, what do you say? Even though we've only just met? And even with my crazy life? Would you consider me, your bestie—who wants to be so much more than that—as your homecoming date?"

Vere nodded. "I'd love to go with you. But—no—wait!"

Hunter paused. His heart stopped beating "But what?"

He and the waiting crowd went completely silent.

"What?" You're killing me. *What?*" He tightened his grip on her hands and looked into her big, brown eyes. "Don't change your mind. Please."

She raised her brows and managed her impish challenge-grin. "Well...um. What's your name again? Did you say it was Hunter? *Hunter Kennedy?*"

Everyone laughed, including him.

Hunter swept her into a spinning hug, desperate to have his arms all the way around her as he responded to her question, "Yes, yes, yes and *yes*! Hunter Kennedy. That would be me."

Vere, now grinning madly, surprised him when she planted a quick, soft kiss right on his lips as he set her down.

He couldn't help but kiss her back for a very long time while the crowd cheered.

Best part? Vere didn't seem to care they were kissing in front of everyone.

And everyone's parents.

THE END

Anne Eliot lives in Colorado and writes sweet, bestselling teen romances about high school and/or first loves about teens growing up, falling in love but who are facing some tough issues.

Thanks so much for giving your precious reading time to this book. Reviews are important and help authors be found by other readers. If you liked this book, please recommend it to a friend or review it if you have time.

I also hope you will try my other teen romance:

almost,
a love story...

by anne eliot

Free sample chapters are on Amazon.com!

For silly-fun please follow me on Twitter: @yaromance

I would also be honored if you would 'like' my Facebook page, or want to email/message me directly there or on Goodreads.com!
https://www.facebook.com/anneeliotauthor

www.anneeliot.com
Anne Eliot
'BEST FIRST KISSES'

RESOURCES

A huge thanks to **Cari Rhea** and **Kathy Loew** who shared thier own stories of teen depression with me. Writing this story has made me so aware of how many people feel sad and alone. If you are depressed, or thinking about self harm, or have thoughts of suicide, or cutting, please reach out. Don't hide or be ashamed of anything you feel but please don't hurt yourself.

You are not alone. You are NOT alone.
YOU ARE NOT ALONE.

Tell someone. Talk to someone. Please. Ask for help.
You are important, you are beautiful and you are worth everything.

There are best friends and amazing people you haven't met yet...they are real...and they are waiting for you. Please.

For immediate help and links to suicide hotline phone numbers in your country, get on the internet and search:

teen depression or suicide hotline

This search method is a good starting point to find the places and phone numbers nearest you and in your own country. You can also use these searches if you think a friend might show signs of depression.

Many **national suicide hotline numbers** have people manning the lines 24 hours a day. Your school can also help, but you must be brave and reach out to ask for help. There are many websites with interactive chats, stories you can relate to, and groups who are available on Facebook and Twitter as well. Please search some keywords, tell an adult or someone you need help, or call your national suicide prevention hotline to simply talk things out.

Keywords that might help your Twitter and Facebook searches for support and people to connect with on the topic of depression: teen suicide help # stop suicide # depression # mental health # stop self harm # teen suicide # self harm # sad # cutting # staystrong # warning signs of depression # stay positive # suicide hotline # end bullying now.

The Thank You List:

There are so many people to mention here, but first and always, I have to thank my family. My sweet husband Tom, my beautiful daughter Kika, my wild-child Wilson, plus, all six of my parents: Louise and Louis Nelson, Chuck and Connie Powers, Bob and Jackie MacFarlane. Again, thanks for your love, patience and support.

The Book Makers Crew: Artists Peter Freedman & Katja Kulenkampff. The best editor/ readers/friends in the world: Lana Williams, Michelle Major, & Kika MacFarlane. Jennifer Jakes and Kim Killion of Hot Damn Designs DeAnna Knippling, there are NO words. Tracie Schultz who is so busy and who I miss so much. Laura Hunter, xo. To the crew who found me the right Hunter and Vere: Kika & Kylie. To Saoirse O'Connor, I must credit your constant, cute red cheeks and also Kimmie Stattman, Mackenzie Weller, the YAromance.com girls, Tweet masters and future world rulers. You all looked at page after page. To Becca H., Maddie D., Maddie J., Katie P., Valerie Y., Anahid B., Greta H. who came to Colorado from far away Germany. <3 Also a big shout out to Iver T. and Masha K. who stole our hearts, became part of our family. #LOVE. To sweet Keva O'Connor. Katy Offen, Kylie Nash again and Sammy Loew. I am so lucky to know you all. A special shout out to Jenna and Sydne Shattuck who were the first to know Hunter so many years ago even before *Almost*. You girls all rock. Always. Again. Forever. Lastly, to One Direction and The Wanted, because you work hard.

To the amazing Jeff Bezos, Jon Fine and ALL who work for writers at KDP and KDPS, at Amazon and CreateSpace. Your work, your store, your easy publishing tools, PlugIns, devotion to making this easier for the writers to write and get paid—and the readers to discover the books they want—plus your unmatched customer service is so appreciated. Thanks for being in my dream-come-true. Also thanks for the Kindle Fire and Free Kindle-readers big and small. (And for the sync-thing because it's so awesome)! Also, thanks for creating a store consumers trust so much. THANK YOU. You've changed my small world while ever changing how the planet reads, buys and writes books. #SOgrateful #kindle @amazon

To my awesome agent, Jane Dystel of DGLM. Thank you for signing me, believing in change and making my dreams come true in ways I never thought would happen. I can't ever repay how you've all made me smile. Also, hugs to Lauren Abramo and Rachel Stout. <3 Thanks for knowing what the big words in the smallest of fonts really mean. I'm so over the moon for all of you. #fangirl

To the cheerleaders, the people who love books, and the people who love romance: FIRST, to the awesomeness that are the communities found at Goodreads.com and Shelfari.com. There is no better fun online than hanging, checking out books and meeting readers there. If you are on, drop me a note! #LOVE

A special huge heart and hug goes to the little stack of emails, notes and addresses I've kept next to my computer all these months. Thank you Eva Segerblom, Thessa LaJoice, Laura Wells—tweet-cheering me on for those last edits—THANKS. To: Adriane Boyd, Tasha Winters, Amanda Tuzi, Casey/C.J.- :) Melissa Rodriguez-Wyer, Amanda-writer The inspiring Mrs. B/ Joy. #FF @joyousreads, Diana Ivonne, Jennifer Halligan #FF @bookandlatte for getting me to Romantic Times. SupaGurl Heather, Ashley B., And from Indonesia <3 blogger, Putri Utama! I'm so grateful to have met you all! *Judith Tanini heart of gold, Kayla S., Heather L., Tabby V., Erin & Emily legit twins, Mandy I., Team FRED & Miss Moorhouse, Lila Felix, Jennifer N. Shelly Crane.* How you have you all made my life so fun and full of laughter. #nowords #loveForever

I have to mention Geoff Foley and Deb Walker! xo DOUBLE THX. Illy & Tim Horton's coffee. The sweet people at my neighborhood Chipotle, Noodles, Keva Juice and PeiWei. Without you, my family would starve. Carolyn Thomas my first librarian who shelved me in the YMCA Snow Mountian Ranch Library! Always the Burren in Co. Clare, Katy Perry and The Avett Brothers for brain-dreaming spaces. Joseph Campbell #always. Ever a kiss for my awesome lost-book-club friends, All at Celtic Steps <3 and the Irish Dance moms and sweet dancers who were all around me while I wrote this. #missuguys! Ladies in the neighborhood coffee groups—the Foothills Pool gang, Betsy at OLIVER's DELI (and Justin)! The Colorado College friends and neighbors I don't have room to list. This book was written around the years we've shared our lives. Thanks everyone, so much, for cheering me along this journey. Julie Rothschild. #want2listALL

And always: Sharon, Jenna and Sydne. I miss you so much. Giovanna and Elmer. There are no words for how much I love you. Masha K. daughter and sister who stole our hearts back to Russia, come back The MacFarlanes, Nelsons, Dawkins esp MC <3, All Mercados, The Sfalcins, C.J. <3, McDonalds, Hemphills, Carla P., Grandos/Nespolos/Tiabis, O'Connors, Nashs, Covingtons, Woods, Farquhars, Rheas, Wellers, Litvacks, Loews, Rothschilds, THE Wilsons, Brodys/McKeevers, Stattmans, Offens, Barrs/Austins—Anna n Emily, Gardners, Rileys, Drapers, Beauvais girls <3, Kraemers n Clarks n Hubreds move back. :(And neighbor Clarks! <3 Anna in NYC, The D'Oria family, the Powers Clan. Ella James and Beth Ballmano my first-book launch buddies. All at AACL & AAHS: Mr. Madsen and Mathnasium with extra hugs to Tessa Paul, Teresa Brown, Constance Ricotta, Mr. Taylor, Mr. Jesse, Miss O, Miss Helen, Miss Cooper, and Miss Olson. Without you teachers, this book would not exist. And you know why. His name is Wilson. xo #LOVEuTEACHERS xox to Don my mailman, too!

My writer hearts: Lana Williams, Michelle Major, Cindi Madsen, Jennie Marts, DeAnna Knippling, Marty Banks, Jodi Anderson, Donna Koppleman. I love how you all never give up. #Keep-writing.

Hugs to the Indie Pub Lunch Group and to the Sunday SCBWI SoCO members, the Pikes Peak Library District plus the awesome fellow members of Pikes Peak Writers, and Romance Writers of America (RWA). #whew

gunnison county

Libraries

connect.   discover.   imagine.   learn.

Gunnison Library
307 N. Wisconsin, Gunnison, CO 81230
970.641.3485
www.gunnisoncountylibraries.org

39670850R00265

Made in the USA
Middletown, DE
23 January 2017